ACT
NORMAL

H.W. Byars

ACT NORMAL

by H.W. Byars

Copyright © 2020 H.W. Byars All rights reserved

The characters and events portrayed in this book are fictitious. Any similarity to real persons, living or dead, is coincidental and not intended by the author.

No part of this book may be reproduced, or stored in a retrieval system, or transmitted in any form or by any means, electronic, mechanical, photocopying, recording, or otherwise, without express written permission of the publisher.

Cover design by: Andrepont Printing, INC

Printed in the United States of America.   .

For Maria

ONE

A cool breeze filtered through the window and filled the room with the scent of sweet olives. Cicadas chirped loudly from the magnolia trees in the front yard, and their pulsating screeches reverberated inside Dan's brain. He stopped typing and massaged his temples. *I can't concentrate like this.*

Floorboards creaked as he crossed the room. He reached up to shut the wooden window frame, and large flakes of paint rained down on his head. Dan cursed silently under his breath as he picked away at the jagged flakes that stuck to his hands. *I painted the house only five years ago,* he thought, *how can it be time for a new coat already?*

He wiped the rest of the paint flakes on his pants and reached up again to get a better grasp. As he struggled with the stubborn old frame, he noticed a man lumbering down the sidewalk in front of the house. The hair on the back of Dan's neck stood up. People rarely walked the neighborhood after dark, and there was something about his deliberate gait that was unusual.

The man finally passed under the streetlight and Dan relaxed. He recognized him as being the parish's retired priest. *What is Father Desjeunes doing in my neighborhood? He has to be about eighty years old. Why is he out for a stroll at this hour?* As if sensing Dan's thoughts, the elderly priest shot a glance towards Dan's window. Dan's immediate instinct was to hide, but it was not necessary. The priest lowered his head and continued down the sidewalk. The priest disappeared into the night, and Dan's curiosity faded. *Probably just priest business,* he thought and shut the window.

He ran his fingers along the desk as he returned to his keyboard. They left a clean streak through a thin film of pollen that had dusted the room. He frowned as he inspected the yellow smudge on his fingers before wiping them on his pants.

He hated the weather in Louisiana. The few days of the year that were cool enough to open the windows for fresh air were polluted with pollen. In the fall, it was the acrid smoke from burning sugarcane fields. The summers and winters were out of the question. It was always too humid.

The floor creaked, and Dan spun around to see his wife, Katie, in the doorway. She stood there in her bathrobe. Her nose was red, and she was holding a tissue.

"Are you working again tonight?" she said.

"Yes," Dan groaned. "Tonight is network maintenance. They said that it won't take long, but you know how that goes."

Katie frowned at the yellow streak on the desk. She had begged him to keep the windows shut during allergy season. Dan winced when he saw her expression.

"Sorry, I got busy and forgot to close them," he said.

"I can handle the pollen. I have medicine for that. What I can't handle is all of this late-night work you've been doing." Katie put a hand on Dan's shoulder. "This is the third night in a row, Dan. When are we supposed to sleep? Tomorrow is a school day."

Dan shrugged and kept typing. He opened up several tabs on his browser that displayed real-time charts of network and server activity. Katie was right, though. He hated it as well. The kids didn't sleep well, Katie didn't sleep well, he didn't sleep well. It was a burden on the whole family.

Worst of all, there was nothing he could do but stare at his screen and *"be available"* in case something went wrong. Dan hated these *"be available"* assignments. Most of the time, it meant that he had nothing to do. The other guys did all of the work. Usually, they completed the task without Dan having to login. But, when things went wrong, they *really* went wrong. He would have to dedicate hours or days picking up the pieces to get the systems in synch again. Either way, tonight he was going to have to spend the next few hours staring at a computer screen. It wasn't always like this. These *"be available"* tasks started when the new manager came on board.

It was all because of one night. The on-call sysadmin slept through hundreds of text messages and e-mails that were sent by the systems to indicate that they were having problems. These were critical alerts Dan had spent months configuring. Someone had to be held accountable.

Management fired that guy. Dan was blamed for an *ineffective alerting* process. His penance from that day forth was to sit through all system maintenance processes and manually monitor the systems. He was to tweak any alerts that failed to fire, or change the alerts to reflect any updates to the infrastructure.

It was a fool's errand, and Dan knew it. He knew his alerts worked. He also knew they would have to be continuously updated with every new system put online. That could be taken care of during regular business hours, but they wanted a name. They wanted a person to be held accountable for any system outage.

Dan was stuck, but he seldom complained. IT jobs in Louisiana were hard to come by. Especially in Mons. There were two leading employers in town, Canaille Technologies, which was an H1B visa mill, and his employer, AGphic. He could either work for no money at one, or no personal time at the other.

He chose money, so, here he sat, doing nothing, at nine-thirty on a Sunday night. Hours of idle boredom stretched out before him. The floor creaked, and Katie hugged Dan around the shoulders. Dan had forgotten she was there and jumped. She laughed and kissed him, warmly on his cheek.

"Did you silence your phone? Remember the last time network did something? It went off all night."

"I'll silence it." Dan clicked away, checking e-mails. "It's the network team's show tonight. They are installing a new firewall. If everything goes according to plan, it'll only take a couple of hours. When they're done, I'll do my checks. Those will take about an hour. I should be in bed before one."

Katie groaned and stood up.

"One? That's late!"

"I know, I'm sorry. It's my job, Katie," Dan said.

Katie rolled her eyes and blew her nose. Dan never had to work after hours this often before. The way she held her hand on her hips, he could tell that she hoped it wasn't the start of a trend.

"Dan, it's a school night," she said as she pointed the dirty tissue at him. "Come to bed when your work is over. Don't stay up arguing with strangers on the internet over some cocka-mamie theory. You were already up until four a.m. last night."

Dan opened a connection to the cloud monitoring system, and the screen filled with charts.

"Last night was different. Last night, I patched the financial systems. *I* did the work. Tonight," Dan leaned back and propped his feet up on the desk, "tonight, I'm just an observer."

Katie stuffed the used tissue into her robe pocket.

"Just don't stay up any later than you have to. Even when you aren't working, you've been staying up late browsing those Simulation Theory sites. I know how you get when you're focused on something, but those ideas are too crazy."

Dan put his hand on his heart in mock pain and batted his eyes at her.

"Too crazy? The Simulation is real, love. It's a conspiracy!"

Katie didn't play along. "You know what *is* real? After-school duty. I've got duty tomorrow afternoon. And, on top of that, I've got the third-grade student showcase tomorrow night. It will be a twelve-hour workday. I just want some sleep."

She checked her reflection in the mirror and massaged the dark circles under her eyes. Dan's smile disappeared when he realized that she was miserable.

"I'll sleep on the couch tonight. I wouldn't want the parents to think their children's teacher is a racoon," Dan said. "Are the kids asleep?"

"Thanks, dear." Katie yawned. "Yes, the kids are asleep."

Dan looked up from the computer and grinned, but Katie shook her head.

"Don't get any ideas. I'm too tired."

Shot down again. Married life. Dan didn't really have time, anyway.

"That's OK." Dan got up and kissed her goodnight. "Good night, honey. I'll try to be quiet."

He followed her out of the office and into the kitchen, where he poured himself a glass of water. He stood by the sink and pretended to drink it while Katie went into the bedroom and turned off the light. Once he was sure she had gone to bed for the night, Dan returned to the office and gently closed the door. He went to the filing cabinet and opened the top drawer. The back-half contained a home-made secret compartment comprised of folders cut in half and held together with duct tape. It concealed his drug stash.

Dan looked at the contents and sighed. It was a pathetic assortment. It was hardly worthy of being hidden at all. If Katie wasn't so anti-drug, it would be in the medicine cabinet next to the aspirin. Dan checked the clock and groaned. He needed to find something to make the time go by.

He picked up a medicine bottle and inspected it. "Big Easy Max" was printed in black and gold letters across a picture of the Louisiana Superdome. A bright green marijuana leaf adorned the other side, along with "10 5 mg THC edibles." Five milligrams of THC was the highest dose the Louisiana legislature allowed for recreational sale. You were limited to one ten-gummy bottle per day. If you wanted anything more potent, you had to have a medical card. It was hardly worth it, the medical places only sold oil. Dan curled his lip and put the bottle back in the cabinet. Too boring.

He frowned as he looked at the medicine dropper. It was empty. He had been experimenting with micro-dosing LSD. His friends on the simulation boards recommended that he try psychedelics. Dan's friend and co-worker, Blaine, had given him this bottle. Blaine wasn't a drug dealer, just a guy with connections. When Dan had asked Blaine about LSD, this is what Blaine handed him. Dan had seen some progress, but something happened in the supply chain, and Blaine couldn't get the LSD anymore.

Dan reached past the empty eyedropper and found a small box Blaine had given him weeks before. *Fana,* written in bold metallic blue letters, adorned the simple white carton. Below it was a hastily placed sticker that read, "Free sample, not for individual sale." Blaine said that a friend had given it to him. It was the product of a Canadian psychedelic start-up company. Blaine said that he understood it to be an entertaining combination of LSD, psilocybin, and ayahuasca. Dan whistled. That didn't sound like a fun mixture.

Dan took the box and walked over to the computer. He

googled the drug name, and after several pages of the search, he found it. A single website appeared. It was just a typical drug brochure. *Fana – Your Mind Without Limits*. Dan adjusted his seat and leaned closer. According to the site, Fana was supposed to provide a fun, safe, psychedelic experience that did not require a sitter. The best part was that the high was supposed to last between one and two hours. Dan checked the clock. That was plenty of time.

Dan slid out the blister pack and inspected it. It contained five milky green discs, each the size of two nickels stacked together. If he took one now, he would be sober enough to handle his job duties when it came to be his turn. He popped one out of the pack and tossed it into his mouth. Dan cringed. He felt as if he had just licked a nine-volt battery.

It had an unpleasant metallic taste, and the more Dan tried to chew it, the worse it was. He finally gave up and swallowed it whole. His mouth tasted like a dirty penny. He grabbed his water glass and took a big gulp, but it didn't help. Disgusted, Dan walked back over to the filing cabinet, gently put everything back in its place, and slid the drawer closed.

Dan's phone chimed an e-mail alert. The network team must have started. Before Dan could reach it, it sounded again, then again. It was going to wake up Katie and the kids! Suddenly, the phone was receiving hundreds of alerts from the third-party cloud monitoring service. Dan rushed over and turned the phone off, sliding it across the desk.

The alerts were useless at this stage, anyway. They were due to the outage the network team was performing. Once they were done, he would start monitoring them, but until then, he would take it easy. Dan relaxed into his chair and fired up the web browser to hit the forums.

For the past few months, Dan's obsession had been the idea that reality is a simulation. He had spent many late nights scouring the internet for any bit of information. He had come to believe humans were complex computer programs running on a universe-sized computer. This computer hosted all of humanity. It housed everything from the stars to the seas. It created the rules of gravity and governed the speed of light. This universe was built for humans. It was perfect.

According to the conspiracy theorists, most humans are unaware they are a computer program. By the nature of The Simulation, humans are only equipped to experience the specific physical sensations necessary to function within its framework. The unseen reality, according to them, was that humans were merely information in a computer.

Dan found himself amused at the leaps in logic that some of the proponents of The Simulation made to support their theories. In truth, he thought the overall idea had some merit. It just lacked evidence. Also, the people that believed in it were weird. For every scientific paper put forth by a respected physicist, there were a thousand more armchair theologians with a blog. Actual scientific information was drowned out by the uneducated masses. Dan made it his mission to sort through the competing agendas.

The more Dan researched, the more confused he became. Scientific papers were quickly debunked. Conspiracy theorists disappeared from their blogs and online forums. The community got paranoid and quit posting. A popular theory was that it wasn't the government suppressing information, it was The Simulation itself. If anyone publicly posted something too close to the truth, they would disappear. Or so they said. Dan thought maybe they ate too much peyote.

Dan rubbed his eyes, the words on the screen twisted and blurred. Was the Fana taking effect already? It had hardly been ten minutes. That was fast. He rubbed his eyes and an e-mail popped up on his screen. The words trickled down the monitor and dripped out onto his desk like water. He tried to read the e-mail, but it kept moving. Dan watched in amazement as it collected into a pool beneath his monitors. Once it finished dripping, he was able to read it. There was an issue with the new firewall's power supply. *Not my problem.*

He blinked, and another e-mail arrived. It was from his boss asking if the financial systems were doing OK. *Why wouldn't they be OK? The financial systems have nothing to do with the firewall.* Dan shook his head and sat up straight. He had the briefest of thoughts that something was actually going wrong at work. They evaporated as quickly as the words did from the e-mail in front of him. He relaxed. If there was any real problem, someone would call him.

Thinking he still had hours before it was his turn, Dan donned his headphones and put on his favorite tunes. The trip was much more intense than the micro-dosing he was accustomed to. He decided to just go with it and enjoy the ride.

The walls melted and oozed to the floor. They congealed into glowing, multicolored pools. The music changed, and the liquid crystalized. Drool dangled from Dan's lower lip. The beat dropped. The floor broke out into geometric shapes and vibrated with the music. Colorful light from the computer monitors sprayed the office with fireworks. Dan's eyes stretched open wide. The fireworks transformed into pixelated butterflies, which fluttered about the room. A *beep* interrupted the music, and the butterflies disappeared into a sparkling mist. Someone on the forum had sent him a private message.

From: Charlie

Subject: Hey check this out!

Dan,

I've been following your comments over on The Simulation forums, and I think you're a pretty cool dude. Some of those guys take it way too far, but you seem normal. Anyway, one of the guys we hang out with created a secure place to chat. It's an old, forgotten

MUD from the 1990s that's still running. We've modified it to fit our needs. You'll need a terminal emulation client to access it. Like I said, old-school. If you're interested, reply to this message, and I'll send you its current IP address. The instance switches servers often, so there's no DNS. I hope to hear from you soon.

Cheers,

Charlie

"What the hell?" Dan thought. "Why not, I still have plenty of time."

Dan replied that he was interested, and a few minutes later, he found himself signing in to the MUD.

The screen turned black, and a green prompt appeared with a blinking cursor.

"WELCOME TRAVELER" scrolled by in ASCII art. "There are 03 connected."

What is this? Zork? Dan's brain buzzed, and the screen rippled. The green text seemed to jump out of the inky blackness and morph into floating blobs in his eyes. Dan blinked hard to clear the floaters and scanned the terminal. Instead of following the instructions on creating a user, he simply signed in as a guest.

"Hello?" he typed. "Is there anybody out there?"

"Dan!" said Charlie. "I'm glad you came!"

"Hey, Charlie! Oh, and that's Guest02 to you."

"About that, Dan, you should create an account. It is required to connect to the secure version. There, all of our conversations and activities will be private."

"Fine."

Dan scrolled up through the previous text and followed the instructions on creating a private account.

"User <Guest02> is now Dan" appeared on the screen.

"OK, I'm logged in, now what?"

"OK. Next, you have to VPN to this address, by typing "connect secure: ...."

Dan's head lolled to one side. Was he coming down already? Was it getting more intense? He wasn't sure. He felt like he was falling asleep, but he needed to stay awake. Dan jerked back to attention. There was something he was supposed to be doing, but he couldn't remember what it was. Was it work? No. The firewall was the network team's problem.

Charlie instructed him to input a series of commands. It was a language Dan had never seen before. He tried to figure out what the string of commands was doing but gave up. The code was too complicated. The vibrations in his head intensified, and it was all he could do to concentrate on typing in precisely what he was told.

The rainbow vapors that had filled the room earlier dissipated. Black smoke emanated from the dark terminal screen. A low, deep, hum rattled Dan's skull. He checked his headphone's connection to see if it was loose, but it was plugged securely in the jack.

The hum subsided. Dan did his best to follow Charlie's instructions. After what seemed like several minutes of typing and backspacing, he hit 'enter,' and the screen faded. An intense squealing blared through his headset, and Dan jolted upright in his seat. "Connected" appeared on the terminal, followed by two short *beeps*. Then there was only silence. Dan's eyes rolled back into his head, and he fell into a trance where he couldn't move, only listen.

"Alright, he is connected securely, now what?" a voice said over the headphones.

"Download and extract L3m.bin to his memory. I'll take care of the rest," said a second voice.

"This won't hurt him, will it? Are you sure he's the one you needed?"

"It won't hurt a bit. I promise. And yes, Dan is the one."

Dan's eyes regained focus, and, though he was paralyzed, he could still see his computer terminal. Thousands of lines of machine code scrolled past. Hours passed by as commands executed subroutines. Subroutines scrolled more indecipherable code. All Dan could do was watch.

Finally, the scrolling code stopped. Someone on the other end typed QUIT, and the screen disappeared. Dan, finally released from his paralysis, collapsed out of his chair onto the floor. As he drifted off to sleep, he could hear voices over the headphones. Happy voices.

TWO

Dan pulled into the parking lot just in time to see Katie and the kids drive off. The clock on the dashboard confirmed he was twenty minutes late to their usual Monday morning breakfast date. What was supposed to be a positive start to the week for the family was turning into anything but.

Dan debated on whether or not to go in, but his mouth was dry, and he was hungry. As he stumbled out of his truck and walked to the door, he wondered what had happened last night? The more he tried to remember, the further away last night seemed. This week could not have gotten off to a worse start. Right now, all he wanted was a glass of water and a cup of coffee.

The Breakfast Station had been a train depot in a previous life. Constructed in 1903, it was a stop on an east-west line that ferried passengers between New Orleans and Houston. In the 1960s, the interstate highway was built connecting the two cities. Automobiles became the more popular form of transportation. As a result, the number of rail passengers that wanted to disembark in Mons dwindled to zero. The station was abandoned. Decades later, an entrepreneurial couple rediscovered it while searching for a site for their new business.

Two years and millions of dollars later, they now had a functioning restaurant. It was an instant hit. Because it was in the center of town, locals loved it. Visitors loved it because of the quirky interior and good food. People would wait hours for an open table on the weekends, but that was rarely the case on a Monday. The weekdays were for locals, and the working class usually cleared out before eight. The place was all but deserted. Dan sat at the first empty table and rubbed his temples.

"Mornin', Dan!" said a cheerful, gray-haired waitress.

Dan jolted upright and bumped his knee underneath the table. The silverware clanged, causing the only customer present to turn and stare. "Good morning, Barb," he said and flashed her a sheepish grin. "Mind getting me a glass of ice water?"

She flipped over one of the coffee mugs waiting on the table before him and filled it with steaming coffee.

She frowned and put a hand on her hip. "You missed Katie."

Dan sighed and slumped in the chair.

"She said that if you showed up to remind you that it is your turn to bring the kids to practice tonight."

Dan took a sip of his coffee and winced. Katie was mad. What happened last night, anyway? He woke up on his couch, but he wasn't sure if it was because of work or a fight with her. Maybe both? He tried to remember, but his head pounded. This wasn't like any headache he had before. It blurred his vision. Was this a migraine? Dehydration? Caffeine withdrawals? Lack of sleep? He couldn't think straight.

"Why didn't she just call me?"

Barb shrugged and walked off to get his water. Dan checked his pocket and found his phone.

"Crap, it was turned off."

As it booted up, he wondered how long it had been turned off. He was on-call. What had he missed besides Katie's messages? There was a network outage. He remembered that now. Something else happened. Was there a supposed to be a meet-

14

ing about it this morning? Dan's tongue felt like a pencil eraser lodged in his mouth.

"Here's your water, Dan.," said Barb.

Dan jumped again. He had forgotten about Barb. "Thanks," he croaked.

"Let me know if you want any food," she said and left Dan alone with his coffee and water.

The front door *dinged*, and an elderly couple walked in, followed by a man in a yellow baseball cap. Dan recognized Mr. and Mrs. Wilson, but not the man in the hat. Before he could tell Mr. Wilson hello, the phone on the table buzzed. He looked down at the screen. There were hundreds of unread e-mails, thirty SMS messages, and five voicemails.

Dan scanned the messages and groaned. Last night started to come into focus. He did not remember sending snarky e-mails to his boss at 3am. When did he turn off his phone?

He broke out into a cold sweat as he scrolled through his messages. There was no network maintenance. The network team aborted their plans to replace the firewall. The financial system's database server crashed. That was why his boss was e-mailing him. Dan had done nothing. The system was still down. More e-mails from his boss, each one more urgent. "Dan, we need you to fix this now. Answer your phone!" Dan's hands shook. The phone rang. Dan dropped it on the floor. As he groped for the phone, he accidentally pressed the button to send the call to voicemail. What would his boss say? He had to get to the office immediately to plead his case. To plead what? He was too high to do his job? The bell on the front door *dinged* again.

Barb appeared and pushed another plastic tumbler of ice water in front of him, ripping Dan away from his thoughts. He banged his knee on the table again, causing his coffee to spill.

"You're jumpy today, Dan. Is everything OK?"

Dan rubbed his knee. "Sorry, Barb. It was a long night, and everything is going sour at work."

Barb collected the dirty mug and saucer. "I'll be right back with a rag to wipe all this up."

Barb walked back towards the kitchen, past a smartly-dressed priest standing at the counter, who stared directly at Dan. What was his problem? Dan ignored it and daubed coffee from his khakis with a paper napkin. He looked up again, and Barb reappeared with a towel and more water.

"Who is the priest?" Dan asked.

Barb paused and looked around. "What priest?"

Dan looked to where the priest stood, but he wasn't there anymore.

"He must have gone to the restroom." Dan shrugged.

Barb put the towel in her apron and placed a clean mug in front of Dan.

"Are you hungry? Will you be having your usual today?" Barb said.

Dan checked the time.

"Can I get a cup of coffee, to-go, please? I need to get to the office."

Barb frowned. "You don't look well, Dan. Are you sure I can't get you a biscuit to-go, as well? You probably need to eat."

Dan shook his head. "Just the coffee, please."

Barb walked off to get the coffee and felt a tap on his shoulder. Dan spun around. It was the priest.

"Good morning, Daniel," he said.

"Good morning, Father?"

The priest walked around the table and sat down. Dan

stopped scrubbing his pants and sat up straight. What did he want?

"Mind if I join you for a few moments, Daniel?"

Dan looked at the clock, then behind the counter, where Barb made a fresh pot of coffee. He didn't really have time for this.

"I'm in a bit of a rush this morning, Father. I'm sorry, but I don't have long." Dan eyed the priest. "Do I know you?"

The priest placed his teacup and saucer on the table and sighed. "You probably don't know me, but I know you. At least, I knew your parents."

Dan looked up as the front door *dinged* again. The man in the yellow baseball cap shielded his face with a menu and followed a customer out the door.

"My parents died many years ago."

"Oh, I know. I was there."

Dan tried to recall his parent's funeral, but his head pounded. Where was Barb? Dan looked over towards the counter and saw her talking to another waitress, ignoring the full coffee pot.

"I'm sorry, Father. I don't remember your name." Dan frowned.

The priest flashed a toothy smile that made Dan feel uneasy. "My name is Father August. I'm just visiting from another parish. I was in the area and thought I'd stop in to check on some old friends."

Barb filled a paper cup, but there were no plastic lids. She disappeared behind the kitchen door. Dan groaned at the clock on the wall and rubbed his head. The priest seemed to notice Dan's discomfort and took a happy sip of tea.

"Old friends?" said Dan. "You mean Father Desjeunes?"

The priest coughed and set his cup back on the table.

"I'm sure Father Desjeunes is doing just fine in retirement. I may stop by to tell him hello." The priest leaned forward in his chair. "I'm actually here to see you."

Dan stiffened.

"Me?" he stammered. "What? Why?"

"Your wife told me some things. You've been keeping late hours, you're up until the wee hours of the morning. She's worried about you. She's afraid you may be getting yourself into trouble."

Dan stared silently. The priest seemed to hover in and out of his vision. Dan's head throbbed.

"When did you talk to Katie?"

The priest leaned back in his chair and took a sip of tea.

"Katie and I talk all the time. She told me that you were up all night last night, surfing the internet. She told me that you are very secretive about your online activity. She says you hide it from her using VPNs and private browsers. She doesn't know what you're up to, but it can't be honest if you have to hide it. Why are you so careful?"

Dan reached for his water glass, but his hands were shaking too much to grab it. He quickly hid them beneath the table, hoping the man didn't notice. Father August arched an eyebrow and leaned closer.

"She told me you didn't show up to breakfast this morning. You told her you were working last night. You weren't working, were you?"

Dan couldn't answer. His mouth tasted like ashes. The room became hot, and sweat seeped through his clothes. Who was this man? He was sure of one thing, he was lying. He didn't talk to Katie. Katie had no idea what a VPN was. Even still, how did he know all of that? Dan calmed himself and took a drink of water so he could speak.

"Katie told you all of that?"

"She did. That's why I'm checking on you."

Dan pushed back his chair and stood up. The room wobbled.

"Thank you, Father August," Dan said, "but I wasn't surfing the internet last night. If you must know, I was actually working. A server went down. In fact," Dan checked the clock on the wall and frowned, "I'm afraid I'm going to have to go to work now. I'm late."

The reverend laughed, he seemed unconvinced. "If you say so." He frowned and set his teacup carefully onto its saucer. "Just so you know," he said, "I'll be in town for the next few weeks. I'm available if you need to tell me anything."

"I appreciate it, Father."

Barb arrived with Dan's coffee.

"Here ya go. Are you sure I can't get you a biscuit for the road?"

Dan shook his head and fumbled for his wallet and handed her a twenty.

"No, thanks. I'm not hungry anymore."

"OK, I'll be right back with your change." Barb turned to walk off.

"Barb, add the priest's breakfast to my bill and keep the change."

Dan smiled at Father August. "My treat."

Barb tilted her head. It looked as if she were about to protest, but the order bell rang. She folded the twenty and stuffed it into her apron.

"Thank you, Dan," he said

"It's the least I could do," Dan said.

* * *

Dan slammed the door to his truck. What was the deal with that priest? How did he know so much? He didn't remember ever hearing about a Father August. The water and coffee must have started working because the pounding subsided.

He checked the messages on his phone again. Systems were still down. The people at work were not happy. The ladies in payroll reported they were missing the last two weeks of timesheets. His boss responded that the junior admin was working on restoring the database. He didn't know how to do that. The only one that knew how to do that was Dan. This was a significant outage.

Dan was sure he was going to get fired. He hoped they would let him get the systems back running first. Maybe if everything working again, it would make up for his insubordination.

A rainbow sheen hovered in his vision, and he stifled a laugh. A new wave of panic set in. Was he still high from last night? He couldn't go into the office high. To silence the fear, he took a deep, calming breath. It was time to face the music. He put the truck in reverse and checked the mirror as he slowly backed up. Sitting in the back seat was the man with the yellow baseball cap.

"Hi, Dan!" he said.

"JESUS CHRIST!" Dan shouted.

Dan slammed on the brakes, causing the man in the back seat to jerk back and yelp in surprise.

"Ow! Holy! Calm down!" he said.

"Who are you?" Dan demanded. "Why are you in my truck?"

"I'm Charlie." He panted. "You know, from the internet."

Dan rubbed his head. What the hell was he talking about? The internet? Charlie? Dan finally remembered last night.

"How did you get in here?" Dan said.

"Calm down! We need to talk. I'm probably not going to hurt you. Act Normal," Charlie said.

"What do you mean *probably*?"

THREE

Dan threw the truck in park and spun around in his seat. He grasped at Charlie's shirt but missed. His other hand was balled into a fist, ready for a fight. Charlie threw up his hands defensively.

"Hey! Go easy! I'm unarmed," Charlie pleaded.

Dan could see Charlie's hands were shaking and put his fist down. For the first time, Dan was able to get a good look at the man. Charlie wore an old Hawaiian shirt, tufts of chest hair poked out at odd angles from beneath the buttons. His tattered blue jean shorts were cut off above the knee, and he wasn't wearing shoes. He was dressed like someone who had just walked off the beach.

Charlie gulped and lowered his hands. His eyes darted back and forth between Dan and the front door of The Breakfast Station. Dan glanced at the front door, and there was no one there. Why was Charlie so nervous? Dan got a good look at Charlie's face and gasped, he knew this man. Where had he seen him before? Dan estimated Charlie to be about thirty pounds heavier than him. His face looked as if it were swollen from drinking and being in the sun. What stood out about Charlie the most were his eyes. The blue glowed from within. There was something eerily familiar about Charlie. Dan was sure they had met before.

"What do you want?" Dan said.

"We need to talk. We need to talk about last night." Charlie's eyes darted towards the door. Dan looked as well, there was no one there.

"What's this about? I have to get to work—"

Charlie held a finger to his lips, then leaned forward and whispered, "We need to talk about The Simulation."

Dan faced forward and gripped the steering wheel. It found me.

Dan had been warned that there was a dark side to life inside of The Simulation. They said that The Simulation only worked as long as people weren't aware they were a part of a simulation. If you were aware that you were in a simulation, then The Simulation would have you eliminated. Dan laughed it off as typical conspiracy theorist paranoia. That was until he accidentally found an info-dump on one of his favorite sites. It detailed all of the posts and user accounts that had been deleted on that forum and others. It also named real-life people that disappeared soon after they had made similar posts.

Before Dan could finish reading the post, the page refreshed, and it was gone. Dan became a believer. He scoured the internet for more evidence that The Simulation was repressing information. A few days later, the same wall of text appeared on a different forum. This time, he read the whole thing. In addition to more deleted users and posts, this manifesto recommended measures to take to avoid detection. Use a new IP each time you search. Use a different computer each time you post, and to never print out anything. Most importantly, never discuss it with anyone you care about. At the end was a signature, "Act Normal! -Charlie".

Charlie was sitting in his back seat. Had it finally found him? Was Charlie on the run?

"Are you in trouble?" Dan said.

"Am *I* in trouble?" Charlie glanced at the door. "No, *you* are in trouble."

"I know I'm in trouble. I'm about to get fired after last night. Can we talk later? I have to get to the office now."

Charlie chuckled ironically. "You're worried about your job? Your job is not important. Dan, you don't understand what's going on. We need to go somewhere we can talk."

The air around the truck vibrated, and Dan winced in pain. The drugs weren't wearing off fast enough.

"Fine, let's talk. Do it now, but make it quick."

Charlie glanced once more at the door, yelped, and dove down to the floorboard. Dan craned his neck to see what happened. Charlie lay face-up on the floor and held his finger to his lips.

"What are you doing? Are you insane?"

"We have to go, Dan. Now. Just drive."

"What are you talking about?"

"Him."

Charlie pointed to the front door where Father August watched them from the window. Dan grabbed his head and moaned in pain. Is this what a migraine felt like?

"Dan, are you ok?"

Dan closed his eyes and rubbed his temples. Stars floated in his eyes.

"Dan?" Charlie said. "We have to get out of here. Can you drive?"

Dan blinked his eyes to clear his vision. He grabbed the wheel and threw the truck in reverse. Rocks scattered as the tires hit the asphalt. He looked back at the door, but Father August was no longer there. Dan put the truck in gear and drove off.

Charlie picked himself up off the floor and peered nervously out the back window. Dan turned the corner, and The Breakfast Station disappeared from view.

"Where are we going, Dan?"

"We're going to the park. You can tell me what you want to say and I can drop you off there. It's on the way to work."

Dan had to stop at a traffic signal and peeked in the rear-view mirror. Charlie's eyes were rolled back, showing only the whites. He hummed to himself and made off-beat clicking noises. Dan thought that he looked possessed. The light turned green, and Charlie's eyes rolled back into focus. "OK. The park is fine. Let's go."

Dan found it hard to concentrate on driving. His throbbing head made it hard for him to think. Charlie peered out the rear window and exhaled.

"I don't think we were followed," he said. "The further we are from that restaurant and Father August, the better."

"What is it about Father August that has you so riled up?"

"I know his kind. He's dangerous," Charlie said quietly.

Dan took a left onto Rue du Musée, and then another left onto Chemin Nouvelle. There were no square blocks here. Directions from point A to point B could include five consecutive left turns. Navigating through downtown could be even more confusing. The reason for the odd layout was because Mons lies on Bayou Jemappes.

The first settlers to Mons came on horseback and covered wagon. They built farms and lumber mills along the bayou and used riverboats to trade their wares. The footpaths and cart paths they created to avoid the swamps and ditches defined the footprint of the town. Over the years, the trails were paved. The resulting outlay was a tangle of roads. Only the locals could navigate them efficiently. Five minutes later, and they were there.

Dan was the first out. He was happy not to be so close to Charlie. He felt his phone vibrate and reached down to silence it without taking it out of his pocket. Charlie met him in front of the truck.

"Ok, Charlie. Spill it."

Charlie shook his head and pointed to a family nearby. They were unloading a picnic basket from the trunk of their car.

"Not here. Let's walk."

Dan groaned and ushered Charlie down the sidewalk. The park was small, and a pond took up half of it. A walking path meandered around the park, surrounded by benches for people to sit and watch the ducks. The other half consisted of several pavilions. They were rented out by the city so that members of the public could host outdoor events.

In the center of it all was a huge white gazebo. It may have served some grand purpose in the past but, now, it was a de facto homeless shelter. As Dan and Charlie walked, he noted there were only a handful of people present. Joggers stuck to the paths, parents and children fed ducks around the pond, and the homeless guys lounged about the gazebo. The parents kept a watchful eye as they played with their children.

"We're here. What did you want to tell me?" Dan said.

Charlie glanced around to make sure no one was listening.

"You know now that this whole world we are in is a simulation, right?"

"Yes."

"Do you realize it knows what you're doing every single second?"

Dan strolled along quietly. "Yeah? So? There's nothing I can do about it."

"You're right, you can't do anything about it keeping tabs

on you. As you may be aware, the Simulation has a framework. That framework is the environment. It's the grass, the trees, the truck, metal, dirt, air, water, basically everything that isn't *alive*."

"Are you suggesting I can't do anything about the environment?"

"No, I'm suggesting the environment is a framework for your existence."

"OK, so there are trees, flowers, and walking paths. These all exist so I can have this conversation with you?"

Charlie shook his head.

"It's more complicated than that. Think of it this way. Mankind has always asked the question: Why am I here? Do you know the answer? Who are you, Dan? Why are you here?"

"I'm here because a crazy guy kidnapped me," Dan said.

Charlie groaned and threw up his hands, "No, I'm serious. What is your purpose in life?"

Dan walked a few steps. He had often asked himself the same question. What was his purpose?

"I'm a father," he said finally. "I'm here to support my children."

"That's true enough, but you're much more than that. Everyone is. We all have a role in The Simulation. The Simulation has a goal for all of us beyond simple procreation," said Charlie.

"Are you saying I have a destiny?" Dan snorted. "Are you going to try to convince me that I'm 'The One' now? Sorry Charlie, but I believe in free will."

Charlie groaned and shook his head. "No, it doesn't work like that."

"OK then, explain it to me. How does it work exactly? If

we are in a giant simulation of reality, how am I connected? Is it like a video game, and this body is merely an avatar? Is something controlling my actions from somewhere else? Is there a *real* me outside of The Simulation, and I'm just a facsimile?" Dan said.

Charlie frowned and walked a few steps behind Dan.

"Well, honestly? I don't know for sure," Charlie admitted.

"Charlie, if this simulation is a framework, and we exist inside of a computer program, then, logically, we are either a user, or we're not a user," Dan said.

"How many simulations involve users, Dan? I know you're big into simulation theory. Tell me, how often is the word *user* mentioned?"

A man sat on a park bench up ahead. Dan slowed to not be overheard. "OK, there is no user. Does this mean we are all just autonomous code? If we are autonomous code, then my searching Simulation Theory is hard-coded. I've done nothing wrong, Charlie."

"Simulations are run to test possible outcomes," Charlie said. "Errors can occur in any system."

"Is that why you're here, Charlie? Because of an error?"

Charlie took off his hat and scratched his head. "Maybe. Maybe something you've done was out of character for you. Maybe you've got an error."

Charlie snapped his fingers. "That would explain the priest!"

"Father August?" Dan said. "What does he have to do with it?"

As they neared to the bench, Dan noticed the man was smiling at him.

"Lemmy! You came!" Charlie said.

Charlie jogged over and shook the man's hand.

"Dan, come here, you need to meet this guy."

Dan walked up. "Dan, this is Lemmy. Lemmy, Dan."

The man smiled and shook Dan's hand. It was wet! Dan looked down at his hand, and it was smeared with a dark shade of green paint. Paint! Dan wiped his hand on his pants.

"I'm sorry, Dan!" Lemmy apologized. "I didn't realize they had painted the benches recently."

"It's OK. Honest mistake," Dan grumbled.

Lemmy gave him a toothy grin. It didn't seem like a mistake.

"Lemmy, eh? How do you and Charlie know each other?"

Lemmy sat back down on the bench, oblivious to the wet paint.

"Charlie and I met online. We know each other through The Simulation." Charlie coughed. "*Discussion* about The Simulation, that is."

"Where are my manners?" said Lemmy as he swatted an empty fast-food cup off the bench to clear a spot. "Join me."

Dan tested a spot next to Lemmy on the bench. The paint was dry. He picked up the empty beer bottle lying there and sat down.

"Now, tell me what you know about the Simulation," said Lemmy.

Dan sat the bottle next to him on the bench.

"You get right to the point, don't you?"

"We don't have much time. Please, tell me what you know."

Dan frowned. "Well, everything you see is information in an unfathomably large computer system. They're all planet-sized quantum or nuclear computers or something."

Lemmy eyed Charlie skeptically. Dan cleared his throat.

"I mean, it's a vast cosmic network of information and computers. The Simulation sees us as information. Not information like data, we're information like programs. Each of us is a suite of instructions. As such, we can live and operate within the parameters of the universe, but we can't change those parameters."

Charlie shrugged at Lemmy. "Maybe he gets it?"

"We are like programs." Dan coughed and adjusted his collar. "Not programs really, more like subroutines in one giant program. Look, I'm not talking *The Matrix* here. There's not a human body on the other side taking a bath in Strawberry Jell-O. We are information, but not data, we're code."

"See?" Charlie said. "He understands."

"He does," Lemmy agreed.

Dan noticed an old lady watching him intently. Did she recognize him? He looked down at the empty bottle in his hand. When he reached over to put it in the trash can nearby, it slipped and shattered on the concrete below. The woman saw and tutted disapprovingly. She hurriedly ushered her children away from the pond and out of the park. He couldn't blame her for leaving. Charlie shifted on his feet, uncomfortably.

"Guys, if you don't mind, I need the restroom."

"Do you know where it is?" Dan asked.

"Yeah, it's just around the corner here. Look, don't worry about Lemmy. He's a good guy, he won't bite you while I'm gone."

They watched Charlie disappear around the bushes

"Have you ever wondered *why*?" asked Lemmy.

"Why what? There are so many *whys* when talking about

the Simulation," Dan asked.

"The 'why' I'm concerned about is the big 'why.' Why do we exist at all? Why does The Simulation exist?" Lemmy offered.

"I have no idea," Dan said.

"I'll tell you what I think. I think we're here to build the Prime AI."

"The Prime AI? What's that?"

"That's the intelligence that grows up to create this simulation."

Dan groaned. "Here we go. These discussions always end with circular logic. It was only a matter of time before the crazy showed itself. The simulation creates a Prime AI, which, in turn, creates a simulation." Dan laughed. "What came first, Lemmy? The chicken or the egg?"

"You're laughing, but that's a great analogy. If you've studied basic universal biology, you'd know the chicken came first, obviously. But how it came to be is extremely complicated. It didn't just hatch out of an egg that magically appeared out of thin air."

"Is this a joke? Am I on camera?" Dan said.

"OK, Dan, let's get serious and take a step back. You said you think we exist in a simulation. If that is the case, then why do you think The Simulation exists at all?"

"I don't know, maybe the human race will survive. Maybe we won't kill ourselves off. Maybe we will eventually evolve. We may even become advanced enough to create something like a universal simulation." Dan gestured all around him. "Who knows what the purpose of this simulation could be. It could be a lot of things.

"For example, maybe we're a historical record. All of these events happened before, and we're just a recreation of them.

Maybe this simulation is a model of ancient civilizations. Suppose we are a museum exhibit. We're an exhibit, and aliens living on other planets bring their kids to see us on their field trip. They're watching us argue right now and laughing at how dumb humans were."

Dan looked at Lemmy out of the corner of his eye. Lemmy wasn't laughing.

"Why are you so hung up on the past, Dan?"

"It stands to reason that if we are being simulated, that we existed in the past. Right? The past is important. It has meaning. You have to admit, the odds that this is the first time this simulation has ever been run is near zero."

"You're into *odds*, eh?" Lemmy laughed. "Andy wasn't a fan of probability."

"Andy? Who is Andy?"

"A good friend of ours. He was aware of The Simulation. I think. He could have developed a fundamental technology that would have led to the development of the Prime AI."

"What happened to him?" Dan asked.

"He died. He was one of the first people to discover the Simulation MUD. That was decades ago. We used to chat quite often. He had a lot of theories about The Simulation. The one he kept getting hung up on was that he didn't think humans could evolve. He knew they would never be the species that would actually create The Simulation."

"How did he die?"

"Excessive correction."

"What's that?"

"Excessive correction is what happens when you exceed your parameters. An agent of correction finds you and puts you back in line. Or gets rid of you." Lemmy watched Dan closely. "Or your family."

Dan stood up and paced away from the bench. The way Lemmy looked at him made him uncomfortable.

"I've got to get going. Nice meeting you." Dan looked around, but Charlie wasn't back yet from the bathroom. What was he doing in there?

"Tell Charlie it was nice seeing him. I'll be in touch. Good luck with your Simulation."

Dan turned to leave, but Lemmy grabbed his hand and pulled him close.

"Look," Lemmy whispered, "there are mechanisms in place to make sure people are behaving rationally. You know we exist in a simulation. You know you are being watched. It's important to act normal! Just keep doing what you're supposed to be doing, and you won't need to be corrected. You never know who is watching."

Dan nodded as if to say. "Of course," and rolled his eyes.

"Remember," Lemmy continued, "it's important to not deviate from societal norms when out in public. Homeless people drink beer in the park and talk to themselves, and systems administrators wear khakis and grumble a lot. You're between norms right now. You're going to have to pick a side soon. Otherwise, you'll be corrected, like Andy was."

"Yeah, OK," Dan smirked. "That's enough for one day. I'm going to go look for a job now."

Lemmy stood up, too. "Perfect! That's what you need to do, get back in the game. But don't be too good at your job. You don't want to build the whole damn thing yourself."

"Build what myself?" Dan said.

"The Prime AI, of course," Lemmy said as he grabbed Dan by the shoulder. "Just wait here. I'm going to go find Charlie and bring him back. Just wait a few more minutes, please. There's something else we need to discuss. He can explain it better than I can."

Lemmy jogged off towards the bathroom, and Dan flopped back down on the bench. Another empty beer bottle lay where Lemmy had been sitting. He picked it up to throw it away, but he wobbled and had to brace himself. Dan blinked hard, there was something wrong with his vision. The park got fuzzy. Why was it getting fuzzy? He hadn't had a gummy in over ten hours. He shouldn't be feeling any effects. Out of the corner of his eye, he could see someone stood nearby, watching him. Maybe Charlie made it back? The person cleared his throat. Dan looked down at the empty bottle in his hand, then up to Father August.

"It's a little early for drinking on a Monday, don't you think, Daniel?"

FOUR

Glass shattered as Dan dropped the box containing the contents of his cubicle. "Perfect end to the day," Dan grumbled. He slammed the front door and walked into the house.

He walked past the living room and went straight into the kitchen, where he poured himself an extra-large glass of whiskey. He went back into the living room and collapsed on the recliner. What was he going to do? They had just bought a new car, and they couldn't afford two notes on just Katie's salary. It would have to go back.

They couldn't afford travel softball for Carrie, no matter how much she wanted it. Al wouldn't get the new guitar he wanted for Christmas. Everyone was going to have to make sacrifices. Dan sighed and took a long sip and let it burn all the way down his throat.

How long would it take to find a new job? Louisiana wasn't exactly a state known for technology jobs. A shiver of panic crept up Dan's spine. In the old days, he could pick up a couple of hitches working offshore, but they stopped drilling. Even those jobs were impossible to find now. Dan decided the whiskey wasn't going to be enough. He crawled out of the chair and went into the office, where he slid open the filing cabinet and got his secret stash of "Big Easy" cannabis gummies. He chomped one down.

"Dad? What are you doing?" came a husky voice from the doorway.

Dan fumbled the plastic pill bottle to the floor and whirled around.

Al, his twelve-year-old son, stood in the doorway. His buttoned-up white shirt was wrinkled and untucked, hanging over his khaki pants. Dan gaped at him blankly.

"Hey, Al, um. What are you doing home?" Dan stammered.

"I had a headache, so Mom checked me out of school and brought me home."

"Mom?" Dan brushed past Al and looked out the door. "Is she home?"

Al shook his head. "No. She had duty after school today. No one could cover, so she had to get back to work. She just left me here."

"Ah, OK, good." Dan sighed. He was relieved to not have to talk to Katie.

"She tried calling you to come to get me, but your phone kept sending her to voicemail. She was pretty mad."

"She called me?"

Dan pulled out his phone from his pocket. No missed calls, no voicemails. While he was occupied, Al reached down and picked up the dropped bottle of gummies.

"My phone never rang. There must be something wrong with the cellular network," Dan said.

"She tried like five times." Al opened the bottle and looked in. "Can I have one of your gummies, Dad?"

"No!"

Dan snatched the bottle from Al's hand. Stunned, Al backed up against the wall.

"Whoa, Dad! Sorry!"

"Never touch these again, OK?" Dan admonished.

Al started to cry. "Sorry, Dad."

Dan put the bottle down and hugged Al. Why did he always overreact? Dan felt horrible.

"I'm sorry for yelling. It's just that these aren't candy gummies. It's medicine."

Al grabbed a tissue and wiped his nose. Dan reached behind the books and put the bottle back in its hiding place.

"Are those cannabis edibles? We learned about that in school. I've never seen any, though. Why are you taking them, Dad?"

Dan's face turned red.

"The doctor prescribed them for my anxiety," he lied.

"If you have a prescription, why are you hiding them in here? Why don't you put them in the medicine cabinet?"

"We keep vitamins in the medicine cabinet. I didn't want you guys to find them and think they're vitamins. That's all. Don't tell Carrie where they are, OK?"

"Don't worry, I won't tell Carrie, I...OW!" Al grabbed his head with both hands and sat on the floor.

"Al? What's wrong, buddy?"

Al cried. "My head hurts."

Dan helped him up and walked him over to the couch. He hoped his yelling didn't give Al a migraine.

"Did Mom give you any medicine when you got home?"

Al groaned and shook his head. Dan went into the kitchen and returned with a glass of water and ibuprofen.

"When did the headaches start?"

Al took a large gulp of water and swallowed the pill. "It started this morning after I got to school."

"Did you get hit in football practice yesterday?" said Dan.

Al looked up and grinned. "I play linebacker. I'm the one that does all the hitting."

"Hah, yeah, you're right. You do all the hitting. Did you hit your head yesterday?"

Al looked confused. "I'm not sure, Dad. Maybe."

Dan frowned. "I don't want you to practice again until the headaches are gone. It could just be dehydration, but it could also be a concussion. We're not taking any chances."

Dan heard a *beep* and checked his phone, but there were no notifications.

"Dad, are you going back to work?"

"No, Son. I'm not going back to work today." Dan stood up and retrieved his glass of whiskey. "I quit my job, Al. The pay was bad, and I had to do all of that late-night work. I had enough of it."

"No," said Katie, standing in the doorway. "You didn't quit, you were fired."

Dan spun around and spilled his drink.

"Katie," he stammered. "You're home. Who told you I was fired?"

"Suzanne told me. Her husband works at AGphic with you. Remember? Ravi, in accounting?"

Katie looked down at the spilled drink and wrinkled her nose.

"Are you drunk already?"

"No, Katie, I just got home." Dan produced a towel and wiped up the mess. "What did Ravi say?"

"Ravi couldn't go into work today because all of the financial systems were down. Suzanne said it was all your fault, and they fired you."

"But Dad, you said you quit."

Dan had forgotten Al was standing there. Katie tilted her head and arched an eyebrow.

"Go to your room Al," Katie said. "Your father and I need to talk."

Al hung his head and shuffled off to his room. Katie waited until she heard his door close before she spoke again.

"Maybe Al needs to hear the truth for once. He's not as young as Carrie. He's old enough to know what's going on. Maybe he needs to know who his father is."

"Katie, please," Dan pleaded.

Katie stormed out. Dan followed her to the kitchen.

"I'm working on something, Katie."

She poured a glass of wine and leaned back on the counter.

"What are you working on? Becoming an alcoholic? I heard you were creeping around the park this morning, drinking beer."

Katie gulped down half the glass and scowled at Dan.

"How did you know I went to the park?"

"Mrs. Anderson called me to see if everything was alright. She said you were in the park with a beer."

Dan cursed. There was no privacy in small towns. How could he explain to Katie what was going on without sounding crazy?

"Tell me what's going on, Dan." Katie waved her wine glass. "Is it alcoholism? Drugs? Is that what got you fired? Is that why you're hanging out in the park and not at work. I need to know. Whatever it is, it must be important because you forgot to pick the kids up from school."

The kids. Dan forgot all about it.

"Look, I don't know how to tell you what's going on. It's all pretty crazy. I'm sorry, Katie. I'm sorry we have to go through this."

Dan wondered how he was going to tell Katie about Charlie, Lemmy, The Simulation. Everything. There was no right way to do this. As he considered his options, Katie produced another bottle of wine and uncorked it, then tossed the corkscrew into a nearby drawer and slammed it.

"Sorry?" Katie threw back her head and laughed. "You're acting like a bum, and you're sorry? If I wouldn't have had to bring Al home, what would have happened? He would have walked? Poor Carrie has no idea what's going on. Thankfully, she had soccer practice after school. If I weren't around to clean up your mess, you would be arrested."

Katie poured another glass of wine and took a sip and frowned. She ran over and spit it out in the sink. "How cheap is this crap?"

"Katie, it's not what it seems."

"Let me tell you what it seems like to me," Katie began. "It seems like you're going down a dark path. Drinking alone on a weekday morning? You know who does that? Alcoholics do that, Dan." Katie glared at Dan. "Are you an alcoholic, Dan? Is that the real reason you got fired? Drinking at work?"

What Dan really wanted to say was, "I actually got fired because I was too high to work." He didn't think that would help.

"I didn't get fired for drinking, Katie. Hear me out. I think someone, or something, had it in for me."

Katie rummaged through a cabinet and produced a new bottle. She set it roughly on the counter and searched the drawer for the corkscrew.

"Someone had it in for you?" Katie laughed sarcastically. "You know what I think about that? I think all those alleged on-call emergencies were just you hooking up with that new analyst. Don't think I don't know about her! All of those late-night calls and texts? All the trips to the data center to replace

40

a hard drive? You were sticking something hard in her slot, that's for damn sure!"

Katie reached over and threw a dinner roll at him.

"What are you talking about? That's what I do. Someone has to fix hardware. If idiots wouldn't need financial reports at six a.m., then I wouldn't have to work overnight. Business doesn't stop."

"That may be what you do, and you may have had to do that *some* of the time, but I'm sure you hooked up with that trashy looking blonde."

"Yvette isn't trashy looking. Don't talk about her like that. She's a nice person."

Dan sagged his head, immediately regretting saying that.

"I KNEW it." Katie cackled.

Dan rolled his eyes. "Katie, she's seeing someone else."

"Well, isn't that convenient. What happened, that someone else got jealous and got you canned?"

Dan sensed the trap. "Katie, I'm not seeing Yvette. No one is jealous because nothing is going on."

"Uh-huh." Katie wrestled with the corkscrew but couldn't get the bottle to open.

"Then why did you get fired then? Incompetence? What happened last night, Dan? Did you stay up too late watching videos, doing drugs, chatting up your Yvette on your secret VPN site?" Katie gave up on the wine and poured Dan's whiskey in her wine glass. "You were screwing around, as usual, when something actually failed, you couldn't do your damn job because you were too high."

Dan took a bottle out of the cabinet and refilled his glass of whiskey. That was a little too on the nose.

"Katie, I was just tired. I had been getting alerts all night.

The network guys were active…"

"Stop lying to me, Dan!" said Katie. "I tried to wake you this morning, and you were a complete zombie. You were not drunk. Don't try to lie to me. I know what you're like when you're drunk. What is it? Heroin? Meth?"

"It's not heroin or meth. Look, the job is stressful."

Katie held up her hand again to stop him. "Dan, you were a good father and husband once. What happened? When did the drugs start? You've already lost your job. What else is it going to cost? You're acting like an addict. If you don't start acting normal, you're going to lose the kids and me."

The hair on the back of Dan's neck stood on end.

"What did you say?"

"I said *act normal*, jerk!" Katie fumed.

Dan's blood rushed to his face, and he dropped his glass, shattering it on the tile floor at his feet. That was the same thing Lemmy wanted him to do. Dan got quiet.

"Act normal? What do you want me to do, Katie?" Dan said.

"The first thing I want you to do to is to leave that other woman alone," Katie said.

"What do you mean?"

"I mean, while you were zombied out on the couch, I saw your chat with her on that low budget Dungeons and Dragons game, or whatever. It has to be fake. You left it open."

Did he leave it open? Crap. Dan walked over and grabbed a broom and dustpan and swept up the broken bits of glass.

"I know her alias now, so you can't hide that from me," she said triumphantly.

Dan stopped sweeping. His skin got cold.

"What do you mean, her alias?"

"She goes by Charlie," Katie said.

Dan shook his head and continued sweeping. "That's nothing, Katie," he said.

"Nothing, huh? Why are you trying to *stimulate* her, Dan? Where does your ChuckW4gon need to be stimulated? You were so high you couldn't type."

Dan swept up the last of the broken glass and dumped it in the wastebasket.

"Look, that's not Yvette."

"Then who is Charlie, Dan? And why has she been standing you up?"

Dan put the broom down and looked at Katie.

"Wait, have you been spying on me?"

"I'm not spying on you. I'm merely checking up on you. You've been acting strangely lately," Katie said.

"Are you having me followed?"

"No, I've just been reading your internet history. You left that game logged in. I saw all of your messages. I knew you were supposed to meet her for coffee. What happened? She didn't show? Maybe she saw me and hid? You have some nerve. Coffee is supposed to be our thing."

Katie took a drink of whiskey. She grimaced as it burned her throat, but she swallowed it anyway. It just made her angrier.

"And, your little park fiasco." she continued. "When is the last time you went to that park? When Carrie was three? Did she tell you to meet her there after your coffee date fell through?"

"Katie, calm down. None of that happened like you are imagining. What exactly did you see today?"

"I just saw you throwing away a beer bottle and walking

off. I must have been too late to witness your little rendez-vous. Knowing you, your *rendezvous* wouldn't take long."

"Katie, I'm not having an affair."

"If it's not Yvette from work, who is it? Why did you arrange to meet this person from that janky low-budget site?"

Dan sighed and sipped his whiskey. Katie wasn't letting it go. Even though it may put her in danger, he had to come clean.

"Katie, here's the truth. I've recently become aware we exist in a computer simulation."

He waited for her to interrupt, but she just looked at him silently.

"I am too close to the truth," Dan continued. "The Simulation knows this. It's using you, Katie. The simulation is forcing you to correct my behavior. It's not your fault. If you knew what I know, it would all make sense."

Katie blinked.

"I'm sorry, what?" she said.

"Remember the movie, *The Matrix*? It's like that, but it's not. We're all just programs in a simulation, working towards something important. I've been working it out over these past few months. Charlie is someone I've recently met who is helping me figure it out. I think I'm on to something."

"You are on drugs."

"Katie, I'm serious," Dan pleaded.

Katie placed her wineglass on the counter with a false smile.

"That makes perfect sense. I'm sorry for doubting you."

"Really?" Dan said.

Katie walked up to Dan and grabbed him by the collar and stared him straight in the eye.

44

"If I ever catch you on that site again, it's over. If I ever catch you high again, it's over."

"Sure." Dan gulped

"You're sleeping on the couch," she said.

"Of course."

Katie let go of his shirt, walked into the bedroom, and locked the door.

Dan stumbled into the office. He gulped down the last of whiskey and set the empty glass on the desktop. On it was their most recent family portrait. It had been taken at the beach last year. Everyone smiling and wearing white. Would they ever be happy again?

He held his head in his hands and sobbed. His eyes burned red with tears. Why today? He stormed over to the cabinet and found the carton containing the Fana psychedelics. He had always read that a person should be in the right frame of mind when taking these sorts of drugs. He didn't care. He pushed one out of his blister pack and swallowed it whole. The room vibrated. Oil slick rainbows appeared around lights. The drugs kicked in instantly, and Dan collapsed into his computer chair.

The room spun, and Dan blacked out.

FIVE

"Have fun out there, Carrie!"

Carrie ran onto the field to join the team, leaving Dan alone with the other parents. The bleachers behind home plate were full of people absorbed in their cell phones. He had almost given up looking for a place to sit when a leather-skinned softball mom in the third row waved for him to join her.

"Thanks," he said as he slid in next to her. "There are a lot of parents here today."

The woman grinned from beneath a sweat-stained LSU visor. "Elite tryouts are next week," she said. "Can't afford to miss practice now."

"Oh. I thought the crowd was here for the comfortable bleachers."

Dan chuckled at his own joke. The mom ignored it and stared out into left field. She absentmindedly blew a bubble, focused on the practice.

"Your daughter is a good player," she said, smacking her gum. "She should do travel ball with my daughter. They make a good tandem."

Dan groaned. Travel Ball? Did he look like he was made of money? Did she know he was unemployed?

"Oh, I'm not sure Carrie likes softball that much. She's just a typical ten-year-old. She enjoys riding bikes with her friends on the weekends."

"Riding bikes doesn't teach discipline."

The mom gestured off towards left field, where a few of the girls warmed up by throwing the ball to each other.

"What could be better than that?" She smiled. "Look at these girls. They are learning sacrifice and teamwork. They are learning the value of hard work. You can't learn that riding a bike."

One of the girls missed the ball, and it rolled past her to second base.

"OPEN UP YOUR GLOVE, LOUISA!" shouted the mom. "She'll never make the elite travel ball squad if she doesn't learn to OPEN HER GLOVE!"

The girl's cheeks flushed in embarrassment as she ran to retrieve the ball. The mom shook her head. "Fundamentals. They have to have the fundamentals down pat."

Dan noticed someone leaning over the left field fence. Was it a priest? He wasn't watching the kids practice, he was looking at where Dan sat.

"She's right, you know," said a voice from the bleachers behind. "If you don't have the fundamentals down, then nothing else matters."

Dan spun around. Not now. Dan didn't take any drugs today. What was he doing here? Charlie grinned from underneath his baseball cap, eating what looked to be the world's smallest bag of potato chips.

"Not now," Dan mouthed to Charlie.

The baseball mom shrugged. "You know, I hear that the U-11 ball team is looking for an assistant coach. There is no pay, just a per diem that covers the hotel and a meal, but your daughter could play for free. Team practices are twice a week. Coaching is offered to individuals every night as needed. There's a tournament every weekend for the next two months. Even though it's an assistant coach, it's a full-time job. It's not about the money, it's about the experience. You could build a career. I've heard—"

The woman clapped and whistled. "GOOD HUSTLE, LOU-ISA! WAY TO KEEP YOUR EYE ON THE BALL!"

"Like I was saying," the mom continued, "I've heard that you are unemployed right now. Maybe this would be a good opportunity for you to spend some more time with your daughter."

Dan chuckled. Word of his unemployment had traveled fast, one of the joys of living in a small town.

"Look, my daughter, Louisa, is on the team. They could use a good first baseman like Carrie. She needs someone over there she can trust. It doesn't do any good if Louisa can make all the throws, and nobody is there to catch them."

"Sounds like you're being made an offer," Charlie whispered.

"Too bad I don't know anything about softball."

The softball mom spun around. "What was that?"

"I didn't say anything," Dan said.

Louisa scooped up a ground ball and slung it to first base. It slapped into Carrie's glove with a satisfying *pop*, and the woman cheered. The priest walked down the third base line. It was Father August, and he headed straight towards them!

"You should take the job, Dan," Charlie continued. "You know how important it is to keep up appearances. Working evenings and weekends would free up your weekdays to help us. People don't care what you do with your time as long as you can tell them something."

Charlie scooted closer and whispered. "Look, Andy isn't here anymore. You're the only one who can boost The Simulation forward. We need you. Take the coaching job, and you'll get the agents of The Simulation off our back."

Dan searched the field, but Father August was no longer anywhere in sight. Where did he go? The woman followed Dan's gaze to the empty part of the field. Seeing nothing, she laughed nervously.

"Are you feeling OK, Dan?" she asked.

"Yeah, I'm just thinking about the offer. I may just take it. Who do I contact?"

"If you're interested, you should e-mail Coach Rodriguez."

"Coach Rod is the elite travel ball coach?" Dan said. "I thought he couldn't be around children after that incident at school."

"He's fine. Acquitted. Anyway, he's been coaching his daughter's team ever since he got fired. I'm sure he passed the background check. Do you know him?"

"Yeah, well, I know all about Coach Rod," Dan said.

Coach Rod had a reputation as being a womanizer. There was one incident where he was caught with the mom of one of his players. The man was sleazy. The softball mom saw the disgust on Dan's face and laughed.

"Well, I guess you better step up and coach. Otherwise, I expect he'll be paying your wife a recruiting visit."

"Yeah...." Dan stopped talking as a shadow fell over him.

"Hello, Daniel. I missed you in service yesterday," said Father August.

The priest studied Dan. An unusually cool breeze swept through the stands. Father August's eyes fell on Charlie, and the sky darkened.

"What service was that, Father?" Charlie asked, oblivious to the mood change.

Dan glanced nervously over at Charlie. Why couldn't Charlie just disappear? Charlie was going to cause a scene if he started talking about The Simulation to a priest.

"Who is your friend, Dan? I've seen him around, but I don't believe that we've officially met."

Charlie dropped his empty chip bag and held out his hand.

"The name's Charlie," he said with a huge grin.

The priest looked at the outstretched hand but didn't take it.

"Charlie," said Father August with a taste of disgust.

Charlie pulled his hand back and wiped it on his pants, looking embarrassed by the snub.

"I didn't catch your name, Father," he said.

Father August walked past Charlie to face Dan. "How long have you and Charlie known each other?"

The friendly grin faded from Charlie's face.

"We met only a few days ago," Charlie said.

The priest ignored Charlie and stared blankly at Dan, wanting his response.

"He's right, Father August. We've only just met," Dan said.

Dan sat up straight. Why did he volunteer information? There was something different about Father August's authoritarian demeanor. He didn't intend to blurt it out. Was it because of Dan's Catholic upbringing? Dan looked at the ground. Less to avert Father's August's gaze than to hide his embarrassment at cracking so easily.

"What has he told you?" Father August demanded.

"Don't answer him, Dan," Charlie interrupted.

"I wasn't talking to you, Charlie. I'm asking Dan."

Charlie stomped down the bleachers and stood in Father August's face.

"Dan's not telling you anything," he said.

Dan grabbed his head and howled in pain. Another migraine set in. Their voices became garbled. Dan laid on his side, writhing in pain, but Charlie and Father August were arguing too much to notice. Dan could sense other parents gathering nearby to watch the fight. The bleachers shook as the remaining parents walked down the steps to distance themselves from the craziness. The clanging on the aluminum bleachers made Dan's head throb even more. He gripped the seat tightly and groaned. The softball mom scrambled away and watched from a distance.

"Is everything OK?" she asked. "Do you need help?"

"I'm fine!" Dan barked.

The softball mom walked away, furiously punching numbers into her phone.

"Daniel, whatever Charlie has been telling you is wrong. Step away. Step away, or else," Father August threatened.

The vibrations in Dan's head became more violent. The air around them crackled with electricity. Dan held his head in pain.

"You two need to keep it down!" Dan yelled.

Charlie ignored Dan's plea and faced Father August. "At least I've given him an explanation. Silence is all he's ever heard from your people."

"My people?" Father August laughed. "We aren't talkers, Charlie. We are doers. You are the one who likes to talk. That's all you can do. Sit in Dan's head and talk. Talk and get him in trouble," Father August admonished.

"Is that a threat? Dan, he's threatening us. I told you this would happen. He's one of *them*."

A small crowd gathered around the bleacher area. A few laughed and pointed at Dan.

"Guys, we need to take this somewhere else," said Dan. "Charlie, you said we're not supposed to be talking about this openly."

Father August and Charlie stopped arguing. Dan turned around and saw the softball mom filming the conversation on her phone.

"Ma'am, I'm sorry, they're a little excitable," Dan yelled.

A man came into view next to her, and they both watched Dan apprehensively.

"*They* are excitable?" he said.

The mom stuffed the phone in her back pocket, and hurriedly went off towards the bathroom, leaving the man to keep watch.

"Dan, you can't see Charlie anymore. Not if you want your family. You have to make a decision," Father August said.

The ground seemed to swell and collapse like a wave. Dan slumped onto the bleachers. Was the gummy he took last night affecting him today? Why now? He thought acid was the only one that gave you flashbacks. What was in those gummies?

"Dan, this priest is what I was talking about. Do you believe me now? You can't go back. You can't pretend like none of this exists," Charlie pleaded.

"Guys, I need a minute," Dan said.

Charlie frowned at Father August. "Leave his family out of this. It doesn't concern you."

"It does concern me. You see, we can never let Dan have his family as long as you exist in his head," the priest replied. "The two scenarios are incompatible."

"It's your fault I'm here in the first place," Charlie said. "If you hadn't—"

"There he is, officer," said the mom.

Dan looked up to see Father August grinning smugly.

"Sir, you are disturbing the children," the policeman said. "You need to leave the premises."

Dan finally noticed the officer and froze. When did that guy get here? Dan sat up straight and blinked his bloodshot eyes. How long had he been listening?

"I'm sorry, officer. We didn't mean to make a scene. We were just discussing..." Dan tried to stand up but wobbled and sat back down, "...philosophical differences."

The policeman fingered his utility belt and unsnapped the pocket with his Taser.

"Sir, you are disturbing the children and other parents. This is a drug and alcohol-free zone."

"I'm not on drugs. I'm just sitting here with my two friends," Dan said indignantly.

"Sir, according to the other parents, you've been loudly arguing with yourself in some gibberish language for the past twenty minutes."

"What are you talking about?"

Father August and Charlie were gone. Everyone stared at him, and Carrie had tears in her eyes. The bleachers vanished into a black hole, and he floated for a second before coming to rest on the ground. Dan felt incredibly high. A thought popped into Dan's head. It appeared and dissipated in a second. It was Charlie's voice. It said, "Act Normal."

"I'm sorry, officer." Dan steadied himself. "You're right."

Carrie was being consoled by a teammate.

"I lost my job two days ago, and I haven't been sleeping. It's insomnia."

"You don't look like you have insomnia," said the officer.

Dan stumbled backward and fell off the bleachers.

"Dad, are you OK?" Carrie said.

"It's just a really bad headache, Carrie. I'm going to call your mom to come to pick us up. I need to go home to rest," Dan slurred.

"Dad! Are you OK? Are you drunk? Mom's gonna be pissed! I'm so embarrassed!" Carrie turned her back, threw her glove down, and walked away.

"Carrie..." Dan whispered.

"Sir, I'm afraid I'm going to have to take you in. Can you call the child's mother?"

Dan ignored him.

"Drunk?" Dan thought with a moment's clarity. "Why does she think I'm drunk? What is going on?"

"I have no idea," said Charlie.

Dan rubbed his mouth. "Did I say that out loud?"

"How should I know?" said Charlie, laughing.

"What's funny?" Dan said.

"Wait until Lemmy hears about this."

Charlie disappeared in a cloud of smoke. As Dan was being handcuffed, Father August vanished behind the concession stand.

SIX

Dan opened his apartment door and tossed his keys to the floor. No furniture save for a futon left by the previous tenant. He threw the empty fast food bag into the corner with the rest and plopped down onto the dingy futon.

He moved out of the house the day Katie slapped him. It wasn't the sting on his face, nor fear for his own safety that made him leave. What words exist that can adequately reply to physical violence? If there were any, Dan could find none. All he had was the primal urge to hit her back. Instead, he found the strength to walk away.

It didn't start with a slap, it built up over time. Katie drove him to the emergency room on the day of the ballpark incident. He was out of touch and hallucinating, but she didn't panic. She didn't judge. She held his hand. They released him with no explanation, and she accepted it. He went to the family doctor. In turn, that doctor referred him to specialists. She was at his side for every appointment. They tested Dan for signs of a stroke, she was there. They evaluated him for seizures, she held his hand. When all tests came back negative, she was confused. Confused, but accepting. Then the video went viral.

Katie lost patience and wanted answers. Dan knew that he had embarrassed the family. Perhaps he had embarrassed Katie the most. Shunned by her fellow teachers and ridiculed by the students, Katie started to drink. Every day she would come home from work angry and dejected. She would open up a bottle of wine and disappear into the house, where she wouldn't be bothered with Dan's presence.

Soon, she demanded answers. She insisted that Dan do drug and blood toxicology tests, but he refused. He had no desire to be drug tested. She questioned his motives. If he wasn't doing drugs, then why not be tested? *What if you had been poisoned? What if there is something toxic in the house?* Dan dismissed those possibilities. He reminded her the doctor said that the outburst was caused by a lack of sleep and stress. She had heard that before. The explanation wasn't good enough. What had happened was too weird.

She was right, of course. It was illogical for Dan to refuse a drug test, and she kept prodding. He kept lying. Dan could see Katie retreat deeper into herself with every excuse. By violating logic, he broke her trust. Dan wished he could tell her the truth about the drugs, about The Simulation. He felt that it was better to lie to her and lose her trust than to confess the truth and perhaps lose more.

On the day before the slap, she informed Dan she knew his secret. If he would just tell her the truth, all could be forgiven. It was a common tactic she used with the kids. Dan thought she was bluffing. What Dan didn't know at the time is that she had interrogated the kids. She got Al to talk. Katie found the secret stash. That was a wrap. She had the proof. *What's Fana? What was in the medicine bottle? Why are you hiding weed?* The lie was revealed. Dan made an excuse. Slap. Bye.

He still loved Katie. None of this was her fault. He moved out with the intention of moving back in once he got his life under control. He knew if there was to be any chance, he would have to pass a drug test. So, he took one.

To his complete surprise, he tested clean of all drugs. He wasn't sure if there was a problem with the test, or if Fana wasn't testable. Whatever it was, it didn't stay in the human body very long, though the effects seemed to be ongoing. He was going to have to ask Blaine about that.

Now that the drug problem was addressed, at least temporarily. Dan had to sort out what was going on inside his head. Charlie and Lemmy weren't part of his identity, this much he was certain.

He considered seeing a therapist for validation that what he was experiencing was real, and not a schizophrenic episode. One of the only things that his *internal friends* seemed to be in agreement on is that he should not, under any circumstances, see a therapist. They argued that a therapist would find something wrong, even if there was nothing wrong. Given Dan's situation, there was no *normal* outcome for him on any standard MMPI assessment.

Nevertheless, he didn't relish the possibility that he would be dissected under a mental microscope. Their arguments were effective at keeping Dan away from the analyst's couch.

Charlie's mantra, "She will leave you no matter what you do," was the one that kept ringing in Dan's mind. He was probably right, that outcome seemed to be predetermined. How did she get so angry so fast? Was she hiding something? No, Katie was frequently in denial about her own faults, but she wasn't evil.

Lemmy tried to explain to Dan that she couldn't help it. It was just the way The Simulation corrected things. Dan was pretty sure he did this to himself.

Dan flipped on his phone and checked his social media. The softball mom's viral video of him talking gibberish replayed on the screen. He couldn't get away from it. It was everywhere. It even appeared on the local news as a short clip to illustrate the dangers of the opioid epidemic. Dan was furious. Not just because it was patently wrong, but because it cost him friends.

The ones who left him were ordinary people. The ones that stuck around were either oblivious to his situation or needed him to inflate their subscriber count on social media. He could still buy all the essential oils, cosmetics, and holistic cleaning supplies he wanted, but his best friend from grade school wanted nothing to do with him.

As soon as Dan moved out, Katie and Coach Rod became friends. He provided Carrie some private coaching that got her on the elite softball team. Dan suspected Katie got some *at-bats*, as well. That didn't take long. Dan's side of the bed wasn't even cold yet. Here he was, sitting on a stained futon, alone for the first time since college.

"She'll never take you back. Surely you realize this?" said Charlie, sitting Indian-style on the floor.

"Who can blame her, really?" said Lemmy as he poured himself a mug of hot coffee and sat next to Dan. "How many times have we told you to act normal?"

"About a hundred." Dan sighed.

"We have to get back to work," said Lemmy, furiously typing on a computer that appeared in the corner of what was supposed to be the dining niche.

"You have a computer now?" said Dan.

Lemmy shrugged. "How else do you think I got online?"

Charlie frowned and took out a guitar and strummed the intro to "Even Flow."

First the computer, now a guitar? Is Lemmy drinking coffee? Where did all of that come from? Dan shook his head. The drugs may not have shown up on a test, but they were still in his system.

"Well, guys, it looks like Katie hired a lawyer," Dan said, checking his e-mails. "She had him draw up some preliminary divorce papers. Nothing signed yet, just for her protection."

The guys stopped what they were doing and hovered around the glow of Dan's cell phone. Together they scrolled through the document.

Charlie said, "It says if you don't contest custody, she won't make you pay child support." He looked around the bleak room. "That's good, right?"

Dan scrolled deeper into the document. "Visitation every other weekend."

"Every other weekend? That sucks," Charlie said.

"Even worse. It stipulates that visitation is allowed only if I see a licensed mental health provider."

Lemmy chuckled. "She knew we weren't going to go. She wanted it in writing. That's why she hired the lawyer."

Dan rubbed his eyes. "This doesn't sound like Katie. Someone is advising her to do this."

"I wonder who that could be?" Lemmy said sarcastically.

"Cheer up, Dan. If it comes down to it, maybe we could pull it off. You know, going to a shrink. You're not obviously insane," Charlie said.

Dan threw his head back and groaned. "Do you think you guys could shut up long enough for that to happen?"

"Probably not," Charlie admitted.

"Maybe you should forget about your kids for now."

Dan glared at Lemmy.

"Think about it, Dan. She went out and got a lawyer. Is that something Katie would do? You told her you were moving out to cool off, and she already has divorce papers? It doesn't make sense. If you ask me, Father August got to her. He is in her ear. If Katie is listening to him, she will never come around. No matter what you do." said Lemmy.

"I can't just sit here and do nothing. I have to do something," Dan said as he choked back a sob. "Sure, I have to put up with you guys for now, but I can't live without my kids, Lemmy. You wouldn't understand."

The boys were quiet while Dan composed himself.

Charlie snapped his fingers. "What if we fool the therapist into diagnosing you with something relatively benign? Like, anxiety or something?"

Lemmy threw a paper cup at him. "We're not going to a therapist!"

Charlie shrugged, "What? I'm just trying to help."

"Lemmy's right. I'm not signing those papers. Not yet anyway."

"Dan, why don't you let me do a little snooping around. Perhaps I can find out if someone is talking to Katie and influencing her decisions."

"That's actually not a bad idea, Lemmy," said Dan. "See what you can find out."

Lemmy walked over and sat back down at his computer. "I'll try," he said.

"Meanwhile," Dan continued. "I'm sending Blaine a text."

"I'm way ahead of you. I did that when we got the e-mail from Katie. I figured you could use a pick-me-up." Charlie grinned.

"Thanks, Charlie, but I'm not looking to get high right now. I just need to ask him a few questions."

Dan tossed down his phone and closed his eyes. Lemmy furiously clicked away on his keyboard. Charlie lounged against the wall and slowly strummed his guitar.

"Thanks for the help, guys. I'm glad I have thoughtful roommates." Dan muttered.

"More like brain-mates? Right?" said Charlie.

"Shh," scolded Lemmy.

Charlie softly hummed a Pink Floyd tune, and Dan drifted off to sleep.

* * *

Dan's apartment faded away, and Charlie found himself standing in an equally sparsely-decorated condo. Lemmy clacked away on a laptop that sat on top of a coffee table near a sliding glass door.

"Well, he's asleep now," Charlie said and plopped onto an overstuffed couch next to Lemmy.

"Home sweet home," Lemmy said.

"I don't know how you can live here, Lemmy. This place is worse than Dan's apartment."

"What do you mean? I have a couch and a fully stocked fridge."

Charlie admired the floral print sofa and rubbed his hands along the cushions.

"Yeah. This place is the epitome of luxury," Charlie said.

"It's starting to get better," Lemmy said. "That flamingo picture appeared sometime last night."

"Next time Dan is awake, let's ask him to see a picture of his last Florida vacation. Maybe then we could at least get a view."

Charlie pointed to the pitch blackness outside the sliding glass door, which they presumed led out onto some sort of balcony.

"You're right, that is unsettling," Lemmy agreed. "You learn to ignore it after a while. But, yeah, we need to figure out a way to get him to remember more."

Charlie craned his neck to see Lemmy's screen. "Anyone new checking in?"

Lemmy yawned and refreshed the terminal screen on the MUD. "None since Dan. Whoever gave him that stuff must have kept it to themselves, we haven't had another hit since..."

The computer *dinged*, and Lemmy sat at attention.

"Someone's on!" Charlie exclaimed.

Under the "WELCOME TRAVELER" banner, there was now a notification saying, "There are 02 connected." Charlie let out a squeak that startled Lemmy.

"Relax, we've had guests before. People accidentally find the site all the time. Let's see if he creates the alt accounts."

The two watched the screen eagerly, then a notification popped up "User <Guest02> is now Colette."

"Ooh! Colette? It's a girl! Lemmy, who are you logged in as?"

Lemmy entered the commands. "I'm not logged in. I'm Guest01."

"OK, so what are you going to do now?" Charlie said.

"Is there anybody out there?" typed Colette.

"I need to find out if this is an alt or a main," Lemmy said. "One sec."

"I'm here," he typed.

"Neat. This place is gnarly."

"I need to ask you a question," Lemmy typed. "Do you want to ride the rainbow?"

Charlie arched an eyebrow. "What the hell does that mean?"

"Just wait," Lemmy said.

A few seconds later, the response was, "Hell yeah, man!"

"Yes!" Lemmy screamed in triumph.

"What?" Charlie said.

Lemmy pushed the laptop over to Charlie. "It's an alt. We're in business. Keep her talking. I have to make a call."

Charlie fumbled at the keyboard. "What do I say?"

Lemmy punched numbers on his phone. "Just find out more about her. Keep her online."

Charlie reached over and typed, "Do you like drugs?"

"Do you like yoga?" Colette responded.

Charlie could hear Lemmy talking frantically in a language he didn't understand to someone on the other side.

"Lemmy? I'm running out of things to talk about," Charlie said.

Lemmy returned to the room. "t4m.bin?" he said. "Is she ready now?"

"Sure, yoga is ok, I guess. Drugs are cooler, though," Charlie typed.

"Whatever. This is boring," typed Colette.

Lemmy walked over and looked down at the screen. "What are you doing, idiot?"

He tossed the phone onto the couch and shoved Charlie out of the way.

"I'm just joking. Do you have any friends there with you?" Lemmy typed.

"Yeah, I have a friend, but you are boring."

"You know, this isn't really a music site. Did you know you're a computer program existing in a giant simulation? What you believe is your reality is a lie!"

"Really? Whoa. My friend really likes computer stuff. She'll be stoked. Can I bring her on?"

Lemmy smiled victoriously at Charlie.

"Sure, I'd love to tell her all about it," he typed.

"And that, my friend, is how you do it," Lemmy said smugly.

<Guest03> has joined.

"Is that all there is to it?" said Charlie.

"No. We'll need her to download Tania. Do you mind if I use your login to start a private conversation with Colette? Remember how I got you to download me to Dan? I'd rather not use my login again."

"User <Guest03> is now Yvette."

"Is there anybody out there?" said Yvette.

"Welcome to The Sim, Yvette. Glad you could make it," said Colette.

Charlie grinned at Lemmy. "So, what now? She just talks to herself?"

"Pretty much. Yvette is too high to realize she has two sessions open to the same site, the drug prevents her from seeing it. All we have to do now is give her the VPN info, and she will be able to download the information."

"Too easy," Charlie said.

Dan rolled over to his side and wiped the drool off his face. The next morning, he would recall everything that happened like it was a dream. Only Dan knew it wasn't a dream. He decided he wouldn't mention it to the guys. They did tell him to act normal, after all.

SEVEN

The Tame Trout was a generic sports bar in a recently-constructed strip mall wedged between a People's Penny discount store and an oriental massage parlor. Dan liked the place because the beer was cold, there was always a game on, and they had a decent burger. The fact that the bartender had a fantastic pair of tits didn't hurt either.

It was a frequent hangout of the AGphic IT staff after hours because it was across the parking lot from the office building. All but one of Dan's former colleagues were still at work. Blaine skipped out early.

"Hey there, Dan," Blaine said as he pulled up a stool next to him at the bar. He waved to get the bartender's attention to no avail. She was too busy talking to the heavily tattooed waitress to tend bar. Her ample breasts were enough to get her tips. Why try?

"Hey, Blaine, thanks for coming," Dan said and shook his hand.

"Anything for you, bud. I heard you're working at Canaille Technologies. How's it going?"

Dan laughed. "Well, I'm working six to three. I have an hour's break. Today I did fifteen password resets, set up ten new accounts, and re-imaged three computers."

Blaine winced. "Oof. Grunt work, eh?"

"Yeah. I'm not real popular with the other guys right now.

They say I'm making them look bad. To make matters worse, my boss thinks I want his job. He keeps finding problems with my work to put me in my place."

"That sounds familiar." Blaine laughed.

"That's IT infrastructure work everywhere, Blaine. You know this. Management hates you because you're needed to keep the business running but don't actually produce anything. You're just red ink in the budget to them. The people you're helping hate you because they think you're responsible for their problems in the first place. Programmers and database admins hate you because they don't understand that their programs actually have to run on a physical device somewhere." Dan laughed. "You'd think college graduates would understand that it's not an actual cloud out there, just a bigger computer."

Dan gulped down the last of his beer, leaving a white ring around the bottom inch of the shaker glass, and waved at the bartender. She noticed the gesture and went over and filled two glasses and placed them down in front of them. Blaine tried to sneak a peek at her assets and got a "you've got no chance pal" glare in return. He shrugged it off with a sip of cold beer.

"How's Katie?"

"She is filing for divorce." Dan sighed.

"Ouch! What's that gonna cost you?" he said.

"A lot. Time mostly. Louisiana law says that if you have kids, you have to wait a year for the divorce to become final. We can't do anything until then. What's worse, I would only have custody every other weekend."

"That isn't too bad."

"The custody agreement stipulates that I would have to seek therapy." Dan took a sip.

"I wouldn't sign that," Blaine said. "I'm no lawyer, but it sounds like if you go to therapy, you'll admit that you were at fault. You should hire a real lawyer and contest that bullshit."

"I was trying to do this without hiring a lawyer, but it looks like I'll have to. I don't want to sign the papers. Hell, I don't want a divorce. This is what she wants. I'm trying to buy time. If her lawyer forces me to sign, I'll just find a therapist that'll give me a rubber stamp OK for a few hundred bucks."

"That sucks, man." Blaine paused. "Hey, weren't you already seeing a therapist? I seem to remember you telling me about him a few years ago."

"No. Not anymore," Dan nursed his beer. "That was just a one-time thing with Dr. Patel at AAA Therapy Centers."

Blaine frowned. "Isn't he the medical marijuana doctor that everyone goes to for their card?"

Dan winked. "He diagnosed me with anxiety and possibly PTSD from my parents' deaths. He gave me a card. I used it once."

"Doesn't the state put you on some kind of list if you actually use that card?"

"Yeah. I'd fail a background check if I tried to buy a gun. Who cares about that? My problem was that I didn't realize the state dispensaries only sold oil. I don't want that crap. I want flower."

Blaine looked up from his beer. "I hear that. I dated a chick with cancer once. She had the stuff from the dispensary. It was terrible."

"Damn. Cancer? Is she OK?"

Blaine sagged his head. "Nah, man. She died. Before she went, we got all kinds of stuff on her card. I've been selling what's left."

"Jesus! Are you serious?"

Blaine laughed. "Come on! Do I look like an asshole to you? She's fine."

Dan put his glass down and laughed. "You're a dick, you know that? Look, there's something I want to talk to you about. That free sample you gave me, Fana, do you still have any? I'm out," said Dan

Blaine's eyes widened. "Out already, eh? I didn't know you were that big into psychedelics."

Dan sighed. "I only took two of them. Katie set the rest of them on fire in the driveway as I was moving out. Along with my high school letterman's jacket, and our wedding photo..."

Blaine cringed and hid his face. "Damn. That's rough."

"Yeah. Let's not talk about it. I was hoping you had some more. Fana was really helping me to connect."

"Sorry, man, I don't have any. That was a one-time thing. But hey, my Colorado mule finally came through. It's the traditional store-bought stuff, but it's better than the five-milligram dose we can get here."

"That won't work. I need Fana," said Dan. "Did you know I can take those and pass a drug test?"

Blaine checked to see if anyone was listening and leaned in close.

"Seriously? It works? You pee clean? Even the weed?"

"Seriously. It works, and I need more. It's more effective than micro-dosing for my stress and anxiety."

Blaine leaned back. "I'll see what I can do. The guy who I got them from is flaky."

"What do you mean, *flaky*?" Dan said.

"I don't know, the type of dude who is into psychedelics sort of flaky? He's hard to get hold of. He never stays in the same place for very long."

"Do you have any idea what is in Fana, Blaine? I checked the website today, but it was down. I had checked it before, but the answer was vague."

"I didn't know there was a website. I thought Fana was just magic mushroom edibles. I'll have to ask him."

Dan nodded. "Ask him and let me know what you find out. Its effects are not normal for psychedelics."

"Is it the type of high that makes you think you have people living in your head?"

Dan groaned.

"Dan, no lying. How many people are in there now?"

Dan motioned for the bartender, but she was busy watching TV.

"At Canaille Technologies? I don't know. There are maybe thirty helpdesk workers working three shifts, but I'm trying to move back up to systems administration. They have a large virtual environment to support their customers, and I have a lot of experience—"

"No," Blaine interrupted, "how many people are inside your head? Which one am I talking to now?"

"You've seen the video, huh?" Dan said.

Blaine nodded, waiting.

"I think there are only three others. Two mainly."

Blaine shifted closer and inspected Dan's eyes as if he were trying to look through them and see people.

"Which one am I talking to now?" he asked.

"Just me. I'm the only one that talks to other people."

"Are they listening to us?"

"I don't know. Maybe? Look, I don't want to discuss that right now."

Blaine nodded and took a sip of his beer.

"I'm just checking. I'm not sure it is responsible for me to sell drugs to a crazy person. You could give me a bad rep."

"I appreciate your concern for my wellbeing," Dan chuckled. "In case you don't remember from our previous discussion, I've already been prescribed marijuana by a mental health professional."

Blaine finished off his beer and set down the empty glass.

"Fine, here you go. Something to tide you over until I can get you some more Fana." Blaine produced a medicine bottle and slid it across the bar. Dan palmed it and put it in his pocket.

"Thanks," Dan said.

"Don't mention it. It's all I had left of the jar of twenty-milligram edibles I had at work. Just don't tell anyone where you got it from, OK?"

"Sure."

The bartender returned and refilled their beers.

"By the way, how is your newfound fame working out for you at the new gig? Did they like the video of you going nuts?" asked Blaine.

"I wouldn't know. I'm the only guy on my shift who isn't on a work visa. Nobody bothers to speak English except on the phone. If they did see it, I wouldn't understand what they're talking about, anyway." Dan chuckled. "I guess it's an unexpected perk of the job. What about over at AGphic? Did anyone there see the video?"

"Are you kidding? Everybody saw the video. Dude, you snapped! They played it on the big TV at the Tuesday stand-up meeting. They all thought it was hilarious."

Dan frowned and took a sip of his beer.

"Well, I'm glad it was funny to you," he said.

Blaine coughed and patted Dan on the back.

"Oh, I didn't think it was funny. I know what pressure you were under. Oddly enough, there was another person who didn't think it was funny, either."

"Oh, yeah? Who?"

"Yvette. In fact, she somehow knew I was coming to meet you today and asked me to give you this."

Blaine produced an envelope from his back pocket and slid it across the table. "Dan" was written in neat cursive on company stationery.

"Blaine, do you know what this is about?"

Blaine looked away and pretended to watch the sports news on the TV above the bar.

"I have no idea," he said curtly. "But ever since you got fired, and that video came out, Yvette has been asking about you. She's stalking you on social media. At least, that's what I've seen in the daily internet usage report. I think she has the hots for you."

Is that jealousy in his voice?

"I doubt that very seriously," Dan offered. "I'm at least ten years older than her. Besides, she knows I'm married."

"When has age or a wedding ring ever stopped an affair?" Blaine grumbled.

Dan grabbed Blaine by the shirt. "I have no interest in Yvette. I'm married. Got it?"

Blaine brushed Dan's hand off and smoothed out his sleeve.

"Fine. I believe you. Just relax," he said. "Are you gonna open it?"

Dan inspected the envelope. What did Yvette want? Could she be the one Lemmy and Charlie were talking to in his dream last night?

"Not now."

Dan glanced about the bar. No one had paid attention to their outburst.

"Please, don't tell anyone she gave me this?" he pleaded.

"I wouldn't dream of it," Blaine said with a too-cool smile. "I make a living off not divulging secrets."

Dan exhaled and patted him on the shoulder.

"You're a good friend, Blaine."

Blaine's phone chimed, and he pulled his cellphone out of his pocket.

"Gotta go back to the office," he said, reading a text. "That e-mail server you had problems with a while back is acting up again."

Dan groaned. That server was always causing problems. It needed new hardware, but the company was too cheap. The system admins hated all the extra work required to keep it running.

"Still? I thought you guys would have fixed it by now?"

Blaine shrugged. "You know how it is. Enjoy the new stuff. I'll talk to you later."

Blaine walked out of the bar, leaving his half-finished beer on the table. Dan abandoned his beer, as well, and took the envelope to a nearby booth where there was more privacy.

"That went extremely well!" exclaimed Charlie as he chugged an imaginary beer. "I can't wait to try out the new stuff tonight."

Lemmy sat, smiling at Dan. "Well, are you going to open the envelope or what?"

"I bet it's a love note," said Charlie. "Dear Dan, I've been waiting for you to leave your wife for years now. We can finally be together..."

"I can guarantee you it's not about her watering the fern he left at his desk when he got fired." Lemmy laughed.

Dan unfolded the paper and read the words. "I need to talk to you. Meet me outside, but act normal!"

The blood drained from Dan's face. The two men at the table around him vanished like mist. Dan's hands shook. "What is happening?" he wondered. He stuffed the note back in its envelope and jammed it into his pants pocket. Dan scanned the bar. Was Yvette here? His eyes froze on a lone figure sitting at a table in a dark corner. Was it the priest? He had to get out of there.

He stepped outside, and the sunlight blinded him. The parking lot was empty except for his old pickup truck. How did Yvette know? Was it really Yvette, or was Blaine just playing a joke on him? What exactly did he say in that viral video? Did he actually say the words *act normal* in the video? Dan didn't think so. Was his dream real?

He twisted the keys in the ignition, and the truck started up. He took a deep breath and sighed as the air conditioning cooled the hot cab. He had to get back to his apartment and figure this all out. At least the guys were leaving him alone to get it together right now.

He looked in the rearview mirror and saw a female figure staring back at him.

"JESUS CHRIST!" Dan screamed.

"That's the most normal thing you've done so far, idiot!" said Yvette.

Dan turned around to see her sitting in the back seat, frowning at him behind large black sunglasses.

Dan grabbed her knee to test if she was really there. Yvette slapped his hand and blushed.

73

"Don't touch me! Turn around!"

Dan recoiled at the slap and sat back straight in his seat.

"Sorry, I had to make sure you were real." Dan blushed.

Yvette scowled. "You really are crazy, aren't you?"

"What are you doing here, Yvette?"

"I need some answers from you about the Simulation," she said.

"From me? Like what?"

"Like, how you contacted me yesterday, and what's going on."

Dan sighed. "I don't know what you're talking about. I didn't contact you."

"Well, we need to talk." She looked over her shoulder. Dan followed her gaze to a small car parked in the slot behind them. Inside was a woman reading a magazine.

"OK, now she's looking. Quick, get back here!"

Yvette yanked Dan's hand, but he pulled it away defensively.

"What? Why?"

"Just get back here!" she shouted.

Yvette pulled Dan into the back seat of his truck. And kissed him on the cheek.

"What are you doing?" he said, blood rushing to his cheeks.

Yvette took off her sunglasses, and Dan's heart sank. She was gorgeous.

She leaned over and whispered in his ear. "Your wife has a private investigator tailing us. Didn't you know that she thinks that we're having an affair?"

Dan gulped and glanced out the window at the two-year-old model Honda crossover. The woman had put her magazine down and was pretending to text on her phone. The camera pointed at Dan's truck the whole time. They were being recorded.

"What are you doing to me?" Dan panicked. "Did Katie put you up to this? Is this about custody?"

"Look, the only time I've met your wife was at the going away party for Fred. She didn't put me up to anything." Yvette peeked out the window. "This person has been following me for a few days now. She doesn't know that I turned the tables on her."

"What do you mean?"

Yvette smiled. "I have been following her, too. I followed her to your apartment the other day. Only I didn't know it was your apartment. She sat there for hours, waiting for you to go outside. When you finally did, I realized who she was following."

Dan recalled one of his fights with Katie when she accused him of having an affair. She resented all of Dan's late nights and weekends spent at work. Yvette was the most attractive woman at work. She became the focal point of Katie's accusations. She must be losing her mind if she was having Yvette tailed. Why was Katie so paranoid? Was her lawyer advising this?

"Dan, I didn't ask to be involved in your marriage problems, but we are connected somehow. I don't really *know* you. I certainly don't know your wife."

Dan looked behind to see if the woman was still there. She was.

"It just doesn't make sense. Katie has been more paranoid lately, but this seems extreme, even for her."

"Ok, if she wasn't hired by your wife, then who?"

Dan snapped his fingers. "AGphic. That's our other connection. We both worked for AGphic. They did have a major outage of their financial systems. They are a publicly-traded company. Maybe they're building a case? Maybe they're making sure that we didn't steal a bunch of money and leave town?"

Yvette threw up her hands in frustration. "It doesn't matter if she is working for AGphic or your wife. Either way, they put me in your life. The Simulation got us together, and now it has us in its crosshairs. Let's pretend that we're having an affair and let her take the pictures back to whomever she is working for."

Dan massaged his forehead. "I fail to see how us having an affair helps my situation with Katie."

Yvette sighed. "Having an affair is normal, isn't it? It's more normal than getting high and hearing voices in your head. More normal than explaining that you believe that the universe is a computer simulation. Do you realize how crazy that sounds? If you think you can convince Katie that The Simulation is real, good luck.

The quicker route is to admit to an affair she had already suspected. An affair fits. Over time, she can probably forgive an affair. The affair would explain your stress and subsequent breakdown. You could walk in your house tomorrow and say, *Honey, you were right, I was sleeping with Yvette. Living a lie is too stressful. Please forgive me.*" Yvette said, smiling at Dan for the first time.

Dan shook his head. She was right. Katie would dismiss any attempt to explain The Simulation as a drug-fueled fantasy. An affair would be a quicker road home if such a road even existed.

Yvette straightened out her shirt and put her sunglasses in her purse.

"How do I look?" she asked.

Dan admired her slim figure. Yvette was the only one at

the office who could wear a white polo and khakis and still look stunning. She had long black hair, almond-shaped eyes, olive complexion. She glowed. Dan struggled to compose himself.

"You're beautiful."

Yvette glared at him. "What?"

"I mean, you look fine," he corrected.

"Good. We need to go somewhere where we can talk and be left alone for a little while. How about my place?"

"I don't know where you live," Dan said.

"I'll drive." Yvette smiled. "Look, when we get out make sure she gets a good shot of my lipstick on your cheek."

"I hope you're right about this, Yvette. I just want to get to the bottom of all of this and go back home."

Yvette pulled Dan close, her lips brushing his.

"You need to forget about marriage for the time being," Yvette said softly. "If The Simulation knew what we were up to, we'd be dead already. Let's go."

Dan gently pushed Yvette away. They opened the back door and slid out together. The woman in the car behind them frantically pushed buttons on her phone. Yvette grabbed Dan's hand and squeezed it, then climbed into the driver's seat. Dan shot her a conspirator's grin and buckled himself in the passenger seat.

"When we get to my place, be sure to hold my hand when we walk to the door. For the pictures," Yvette said.

Yvette put the truck in gear and drove off. Dan smiled and laughed.

"What's funny?"

"You're driving my truck," he said. "You're real. You aren't a hallucination. It's a relief, that's all."

"This was a mistake," she said.

EIGHT

Yvette parked Dan's truck on the street in front of her home in the *newer* part of town. The neighborhood was once a picture postcard example of the 1950s post-war suburban dream. Ranch homes, large-fenced yards, a covered carport large enough for two vehicles. That all ended a decade ago when a freak spring rainstorm flooded the entire neighborhood.

Residents, no longer trusting the city's flood plan, cashed out the insurance money and moved away. An entrepreneurial developer saw an opportunity and bought up the entire tract of land. The whole neighborhood was cut down to bare earth by an army of bulldozers, and a faux-French city was erected in its place.

Rows and rows of homes were replaced by apartments, condos, and townhomes. A new school was built, parks erected. Shops and restaurants lined the new main-street. Property value rose even higher than the developer had imagined. It made him a millionaire many times over.

People were tired of sitting in traffic to perform the most fundamental aspects of living, like shopping or getting a haircut. Who knew? Convenience and walkability were the primary selling points. That was an ordinary concept in other parts of the world. Still, it was utterly foreign to small-town Louisiana. It became so popular there was a waiting list for the opportunity to buy a home, provided your bid was accepted.

Yvette's French-style home had a brick exterior, an expensive-looking wrought iron gate, and a small front porch. Dan wondered how she afforded a house on this side of town with an analyst's salary. They walked inside and shut the door. Dan stopped and peeked through the curtains just as the PI drove by.

"I hope she got enough pictures."

Yvette dropped her purse on a table in the entryway and walked down the hall. "Want some coffee?"

Dan followed her into the kitchen. It was spacious for what was supposed to be a single person's house. It had all of the popular additions, cypress cabinets, marble countertops, she even had a pot filler mounted above the stove. He was envious. While Yvette busied herself making coffee, he checked out the fridge. Typical single person fare. Take out boxes, half-empty wine bottles, and a blender half-filled with green goo. Dan guessed that she had never used her stove, much less her pot filler.

"You know, she is actually helping us. The PI."

"I fail to see how confirming Katie's suspicions about my infidelity will help."

"It's not Katie that I'm worried about," Yvette said. "The coffee is ready."

A figure appeared in Dan's peripheral vision, and his attention was drawn to the living room.

"Ah, I'm dying for a cup of coffee!" came a voice from across the room.

Charlie slumped in Yvette's oversized couch.

"Not now!" Dan mouthed at Charlie.

Yvette perked her head up.

"What was that, Dan? Do you want sugar?"

Dan snapped back to attention. "Sorry. No sugar. Just black, please."

Dan walked into the living room, and another figure appeared on the couch next to Charlie. Dan groaned. Lemmy lounged with his hands behind his head and smiled.

"This is a nice place," Lemmy mused. "Did anyone check to see if Father August was snooping around?"

"You mean the prim and proper Father August, who is always poking around where he shouldn't be? He probably is too ashamed of the scandal of this affair. I'm sure he's extremely disappointed in you, Dan.," said Charlie.

"I'll be sure to confess the next time I see him," Dan replied.

"He's up to something. He'll be back," Lemmy said.

Yvette appeared in the doorway, holding two steaming cups of coffee. Dan took one of the mugs offered and sat in a leather recliner.

"I thought I heard you talking to someone," she said as she sat on the couch between Lemmy and Charlie. Lemmy's eyes went wide, and Charlie made a lewd gesture.

"You screwed up Dan," Lemmy said as he checked her out. "She's way out of your league. No one is going to believe this affair."

Charlie put his arm around her and raised his eyebrows at Dan suggestively. Thank goodness Yvette couldn't see them. Dan blushed and tapped his pocket.

"Sorry, no, just a phone call from my son. I need to pick him up from practice today."

Yvette nodded and sipped her coffee.

"I know you saw Blaine today. Did he give you anything besides my letter?"

Dan coughed. "You're one of Blaine's clients, too?"

Yvette smiled.

"Yeah. He gave me some cannabis edibles," Dan said. "That's all."

Yvette noticed his shifting gaze and arched an eyebrow. "Dan, I need to know. The people in your head. Can you talk to them when you're not on Fana?"

Dan coughed on his coffee. Could she see them? Dan set his mug down and crossed his arms.

"Um. Yeah," he stammered. "I haven't had Fana for several days, and they are still around."

Yvette tilted her head. "Do you think it is because of residual chemicals that your body can't process? Could it be a series of flashbacks?"

Charlie yawned and pretended to sleep on Yvette's lap. Lemmy took out a cellphone and checked his messages. Dan groaned. Yvette snapped her fingers.

"Hey, over here. Are they here now? How many of them?"

Lemmy looked up from his phone. Charlie stopped pretending to sleep and sat straight.

"I have seen three different beings. Two are with us now."

Yvette leaned back and crossed her legs. "Only two?"

Dan relaxed in his chair. "The third one is a priest. There's something different about the way he appears to me than the other two. All three come and go as they wish, but these two are like friends. The priest isn't my friend. He has his own agenda. I'm sure he would disapprove of our affair."

Yvette snorted. "A priest disapproving of unmarried sex? Shocker. If he shows up, let me know. I'll tell him that our affair hasn't been consummated yet."

"Did she just say *yet*?" Charlie hooted. "Damn, buddy, you

still got it. Lemmy, it looks like we're not hanging around for dinner after all."

Dan rolled his eyes and sighed.

"What?" she said.

"Sorry. That wasn't directed at you, Yvette." Dan glared at Charlie. "It's just that I don't want a divorce. I love my wife. I know this is a pretend affair for you, but my actual marriage is in jeopardy. The only reason I'm willing to risk it is because I want to get to the bottom of this..." Dan searched for the right word but couldn't find it. What was it, really? A fantasy?

He bowed his head and massaged his eyes. "You mentioned flashbacks. I haven't had Fana in days. I'm worried that my brain is permanently damaged. Maybe it's not the drug anymore, and I'm just crazy now. If you are experiencing similar things, then maybe I'm not crazy. Maybe this isn't all for nothing."

"OK then." Yvette leaned back on the sofa. "Let's get to the bottom of this. Tell me who is here with you."

Dan sat up straight and combed his fingers through his hair. *Here goes nothing,* he thought.

"Well, sitting on the couch to your left is Charlie," Dan said.

Yvette patted the cushion to her left. Her hand passed through Charlie's lap as if he were a ghost. He sat straight, wide-eyed.

"No one there," she said.

Dan chuckled. "He's there in my mind. In my eyes, Charlie appears just as real as you are. If you could see him, you'd see he's grinning like an idiot and waving at you. She can't see you, Charlie."

Charlie, just now realizing he was invisible to her, stopped waving.

"What does Charlie look like?"

Charlie set his beer down, stood up, and gave his best attempt at bodybuilder's pose.

"He's a middle-aged guy with bright blue eyes. He's wearing a plain yellow baseball cap."

Charlie stopped posing and frowned.

"He has an unhealthy-looking swollen stomach from drinking beer every second of the day."

Charlie cradled his beer belly like a pregnant woman and sighed.

"OK. He sounds fun. Who is the other one?"

Lemmy stood up and walked around the room.

"Lemmy is the other one. He was sitting next to you, but now he's pacing the room."

"What's his story?"

"I'm actually not sure. When I first met him, I thought he was a homeless guy. Well, I guess he kind of was. Anyway, he's got gray around his temples, so I'm guessing he is in his mid-fifties. He is wearing camouflage pants and a ratty Jane's Addiction T-shirt."

"What's wrong with my shirt?" Lemmy asked.

"Your shirt is fine, Lemmy. At least it's clean."

"I think it looks cool," said Charlie.

"Is everything OK?" asked Yvette.

Dan could see Yvette sitting at attention, staring at him intently.

Dan frowned. "Yes? Why?"

"Because you just stared at the couch and made a bunch of strange noises. It looked like you were having a seizure," she said.

"What?"

Yvette took out her phone and pointed it at Dan. Dan glared at her.

"Trying to put me on the internet again?"

"Relax, I'm not posting anything. I want to record you so you can see what you look like."

"Good idea. I'm curious too." Dan said.

"OK," Yvette pointed the phone at Dan. "Talk to them again."

The flash on Yvette's phone lit the room, and she gave a thumbs-up. Dan cleared his throat and leaned forward towards Lemmy.

"Hello, Lemmy," he said slowly. "How-are-you-to-day?"

"Uh. Fine?" Lemmy shrugged. "I don't see what this is going to accomplish."

"I want to see what I look like when I talk to you," Dan said.

Charlie leaned over and put bunny ears on Lemmy. "Do me next, Dan!"

"Fine, Charlie, we'll do you next."

He turned to Yvette. "How was that?"

Yvette jumped out of her chair and hooted. "OK, got it! Watch."

She handed Dan back his phone, and they all huddled around it.

In the video, Dan turned to stare at nothing, then let out a loud noise like he was imitating a chainsaw.

"See? You sound just like you did in the ballpark video."

Charlie paced back and forth. "Play it back, Dan."

"Why do you want to play it back? It's just me making that stupid noise just like in the other video."

"Just play it back!" he demanded.

"Everything OK?" Yvette said. "You're pretty quiet."

"Charlie wants us to play it again."

Charlie didn't even watch the video. He paced the room.

"I'm not there!" said Charlie.

"That's because she was filming me!" said Lemmy

"That doesn't matter. I was still in the shot!" Charlie exclaimed.

"I look like I have Tourette's or something!" said Dan, watching the video again.

"Oh, man." Charlie paced.

"What's the problem, Charlie?" Dan asked.

"I'm not there! I don't exist!"

"I'm not there either. You don't see me all upset about it," Lemmy said.

"I'm not like you. I should be there. I'm not there," Charlie said.

"What do you mean you should be there? You know you're in my head, right? I thought you knew that. You need to calm down before you give me a headache!" Dan said.

Charlie stalked around the room and yanked on his hair.

"I was just playing along. You know? Because of Lemmy. I'm real to me. Maybe the lady's phone had a filter—"

"You did it again! You made that noise. Who are you talking to?" said Yvette.

"Charlie is freaking out about something,"

Charlie threw up his arms and stormed out of the room. Where was he going?

"Lemmy, follow him."

86

Lemmy nodded and disappeared from sight.

"Sorry, Yvette. Charlie walked out. Like I said earlier, I can't control their comings and goings."

Yvette leaned forward. "Do you think they are a part of you or something else entirely?"

"I think Charlie is a part of me. He reminds me of me on a bender. Lemmy," Dan tapped his fingers on his leg. "Lemmy is completely different."

Lemmy reappeared with an audible pop and plopped down on the couch.

"Looks like we're a man down," he said.

"What happened?"

"Charlie is having a full-blown existential crisis. He can't believe he doesn't exist. He took a walk out the front door and disappeared."

"Disappeared? Like you guys normally do? Into a mist?"

Lemmy sighed and shook his head. "There is no mist, Dan. I thought you believed in The Simulation?"

"I do," he said.

Yvette waved her hands to get Dan's attention. "Hello? What's going on?"

Dan held up a finger. "One second, Yvette."

"I'll be right back," she said, and got up and left.

"What are you saying, Lemmy?"

Lemmy lit up a cigarette and relaxed on the sofa. "I'm saying that if you honestly believed in that we are computer code, then you'd understand that we don't disappear into the mist."

"OK then, where do you go? Do you just switch off, only to switch on again later?"

Lemmy smiled, "No, we don't *switch off*. We exist inside your metadata. Every object in The Simulation contains at least some metadata: this sofa, you, your son, the trees. Everything has metadata embedded into its code. We like to call it —you're going to love this— The Meta."

Dan folded his arms. "You mean to tell me that you and Charlie exist inside my metadata?"

Lemmy nodded. "Yep. A world inside your own world."

"Wait, then how come I can see you in the real world?"

Lemmy shook his head again. "We need to get your terminology straight. We call the realm you are currently operating in "The Actual." It's offensive to describe it as the real world. It's all real."

"You didn't answer my question—"

Yvette returned and sat down. "What did I miss?"

"I don't know," Dan said. "Lemmy said Charlie is gone, and he doesn't know where he went. Something about actuals and metas. One second..."

"Lemmy, what were you saying about The Actual?"

Lemmy sighed. "The Actual is what we call the real-time instance part of The Simulation. You exist in The Actual, you call it *the real world*. I exist in The Meta. The Meta is a realm that exists inside The Actual, but it is not contained by The Actual. The Meta is not subject to the same rules."

"What the hell?" Dan said.

"Trust me," Lemmy smirked. "The Meta is every bit as real as your actual. That's why I hate your people's phrase, *the real world*. Hah! Such a limited view of reality."

"What did he say?" Yvette slurred.

"He said that our universe is divided between an actual world, this one, and a meta world, where the imaginary people live." Yvette's eyes drifted down towards the floor. "If you're not interested, I can fill you in later."

Yvette giggled, then coughed and sat up straight. Dan arched an eyebrow.

"Yvette?"

"Dan, I want you to know that I believe you. Everything you've said so far. Everything about Charlie and Lemmy. Everything."

"Really?"

"Yes, and I'll tell you why I believe you."

Yvette checked the time on her watch and spaced out. Dan thought her eyes looked a bit glazed over.

"Yvette, are you OK?"

She put a small box on the coffee table in front of Dan. *Fana* glowed in blue metallic on the matte white cardboard.

"You have Fana." Dan gasped. "You got this from Blaine?"

She nodded groggily. "Took one right when we got here."

Yvette twitched and spasmed, then sank into the couch.

"Yvette?"

She stared at the wall and gargled incomprehensibly.

"Are you OK? Those things are potent!"

She waved him off and motioned for him to sit down.

"I'm OK. I forgot I had to address you directly." Yvette blushed. "I want you to meet Colette."

Yvette motioned towards the window, showing nothing there.

"Uh..." said Lemmy as he surveyed the empty space on the floor. "There is no one here, dude. Your new girlfriend is whacko."

Dan motioned for Lemmy to shut up.

"Hello, Colette?"

Yvette rolled her eyes back and slouched in the chair. The psychedelics took over.

"Yvette? Are you OK?"

Yvette blinked slowly. "Yeah, it just got bright in here. Oh, I think your chair is leaking."

"Is Colette talking right now?"

"You can't hear her? I thought you could hear hallucinations."

Yvette got up and poured herself a glass of water. Dan and Lemmy followed her into the kitchen.

"Are you sure you can't see her, Lemmy?" asked Dan.

Lemmy shook his head and perched on top of a bar stool.

"Colette says hello. She says she can't see your people, either. She says she thinks you're scamming us."

"Scamming you how?"

"She says you heard us talking to each other in the break room two weeks ago. She says that you broke up with your wife because you think I'm hot. She says that you're faking being crazy to get a date with me."

What? Dan coughed. Was she trying to be funny?

"She also says I wasn't supposed to say that out loud just now."

Lemmy leered at Dan and propped his elbows on the counter.

"Tell Colette I have no idea what she is talking about. I'm not even attracted to you."

Yvette gasped.

"That's rude. You can tell her yourself. Colette can hear

you, even if you can't hear her."

Before Dan could speak, Yvette held up her hand. She leaned forward and stared at the floor in the next room. Dan lost his patience.

"Look, what can you tell me about Colette? Describe her like I did Charlie and Lemmy earlier."

Yvette closed her eyes and put her hands on the counter to brace herself. Her face became an animated mess of various expressions. Dan imagined that she was having quite the conversation in her head. Dan chuckled inwardly at the absurdity of all of the theatrics. After a few moments, she opened her eyes and sighed.

"Everything OK in there?"

"Sorry, Dan, she had a lot to say. Colette is a thin twenty-something woman, with blonde hair and blue eyes. She is always wearing yoga clothes for some reason. Why are you always wearing yoga clothes?"

Yvette nodded and closed her eyes.

"Right. She's a very *active* woman." Yvette pouted out her lips as to say *as if*.

Dan was amazed that Yvette could carry on a conversation. He remembered that he could barely sit upright the first time he tried Fana.

"I've only known her a few days," Yvette said. "The only reason I wanted to try psychedelics in the first place is because I read about it on a simulation forum."

Dan's mouth dropped.

"What?" he stammered.

"You know, Simulation Theory? The idea that there's a giant computer. I read that if you took psychedelics, that you could see the code. I asked Blaine if he could get me any acid, he handed me the pack of Fana. The rest is history."

Dan's eyes got wide. "You read the forums too? What was your username? We may have talked to each other without knowing it!"

Yvette stared at the marble countertop. Dan wondered what she was seeing. If it was like what he had experienced on Fana, the swirls in the marble were probably dancing pixels.

"Sorry." Yvette snapped her attention back to Dan. "She was talking. Colette says all of this has been scary for her, too. She says she is glad I can understand her."

She wasn't following the conversation. Dan wondered if she was too far gone.

"Yvette, explain to me why you wanted to meet me, and how you came to tell me to *act normal.*"

"Sure. Colette told me to."

Lemmy smiled at Dan smugly and typed a message on his cellphone.

"Where did Colette get that idea from?"

"Tania," Yvette said.

Who's Tania?

"My friend, Tania," Lemmy said. "That is who I've been messaging."

Drool was starting to form at the corners of Yvette's mouth.

"Lemmy says he spoke to Tania."

"Colette says she didn't know her last name. They've only met online via some message board, or was it a website? She doesn't remember its name."

Dan was quiet for a few seconds. He vaguely remembered going to a website with Charlie the first time he took Fana.

"Did it look like an old school MUD?"

"I don't know what a MUD is, Dan."

Dan sighed. "Did it look like an old UNIX terminal with a bunch of commands?"

"Yeah, I guess," she said. "I don't really remember."

Dan frowned. Their paths were too similar. They both had an interest in Simulation theory. They both used Fana that they got from Blaine. They both went to the same website. If what Lemmy said earlier was true, that he existed in Dan's meta. Was that how he got there? Was Tania in Yvette's meta now?

Yvette was fading fast. She could hardly hold her head upright. Dan wanted to do one more test before she became incapacitated. He found a piece of paper near her refrigerator and quickly scribbled a note on it.

"Lemmy, do me a favor. Send this message to Tania. Tell her to make Yvette repeat it for me."

Lemmy rolled his eyes and sent the message via his cellphone. Seconds later, Yvette spasmed.

"Colette wants me to tell you, *Purple Peacock, seven-eight-nine-five,* whatever that means," she said.

The link was real! Maybe he wasn't crazy after all! If nothing else, it proved this wasn't only his imagination. Dan grinned with excitement.

"What does it mean, Dan?" she said.

"This means we have evidence." Dan slid the paper over to her. The same message was written in Dan's handwriting. "We aren't crazy."

"No," she slurred. "What is a Purple Peacock. Aren't they green? Who wrote this?"

"I wrote that. Don't you see?" He was wasting his time. She was in space.

This was fantastic. If only Yvette could talk to Colette sober, they could make more progress. He could show Katie. Evidence!

"I trust you are having fun." came a deep voice from behind Dan.

Father August stood over them with an ominous grin.

"Whoa!" shouted Lemmy "What is he doing here?"

The Father flashed a toothy, mirthless smile at Yvette. She was oblivious to his presence, but, to Dan, it looked vicious. The hair raised on the nape of his neck.

"Dan, I truly hope that you've never consummated your affair with this person. For your own soul."

Dan stiffened. "Not that it's any of your business, but no, I haven't. Father August. Were you here just now? Did you see what we can do? It's a miracle."

"Shut up, Dan!" screamed Lemmy.

Dan realized his mistake too late. "Crap!"

Father August followed Dan's gaze to where Lemmy stood.

"Who were you talking to?" Father August demanded.

"Shit! I'm out!"

With a loud *crack*, Lemmy disappeared from the room.

"What was that noise?" said Father August, startled. "Dan? Who was that, and what were you going to tell me earlier? What miracle?" Father August said.

Dan stood rigid, unflinching.

"Dan? Are you OK? What's going on?" Yvette said.

Dan slowly moved his eyes over to Yvette. "Yvette, do not say anything."

She looked around, dazed. "Colette is gone. What is happening?"

"Shut UP, Yvette!"

Father August walked over to where Yvette had propped herself up and inspected her carefully.

"Colette? Is she seeing people, too, Dan? Where is your friend Charlie?"

Dan remained still. Could he talk to Father August? Maybe Charlie was wrong about him?

"Not talking?"

He returned back to where Dan was standing. "What are you doing with this woman?"

"We're just friends Father, she's a friend from work."

"I don't believe you," Father August said with a wry grin. "I'll find out the truth."

Dan's eyes grew wide. "What do you mean? How?"

"You'll see." he smiled. "You have other problems right now."

"What other problems?"

Yvette snapped awake and wiped drool off of her chin.

"Dan? Are you talking to someone?" Yvette asked. "What's wrong, Dan?"

"Father August is here. Something is wrong."

"Who is Father August?"

Someone pounded loudly on the front door.

"What did you do?" Dan asked, but Father August had already vanished.

The pounding on the door stopped, and a woman's face appeared in the kitchen window.

"They're in there!" she screamed

"It's Katie!" Dan said. "Why is she here?"

"OPEN UP! DAN GET YOUR ASS OUT HERE RIGHT NOW!"

NINE

Dan's head throbbed, and he rubbed his eyes. The past twenty-four hours had not been kind. Thankfully, Katie calmed down and went home without Yvette having to call the police. Dan had never seen Katie so angry. When they argued at home, Katie would scream and shout, yesterday she had been on the edge of violence. It was no longer anger in Katie's heart; it was pure malice. It made his blood run cold. This morning at work, Dan received a call from his lawyer informing him that his custody fight had received a setback. Katie now had evidence of his infidelity. Dan could hardly breathe. His desk phone rang, but he didn't answer. He collected his things, walked out of work, and went home. Dan was sure he was going to be terminated, he didn't care.

"Your whole life is slipping through your fingers," said Lemmy as he typed away on his imaginary computer and sipped coffee. "You need to get a plan."

Dan lay sprawled out on his futon and stared at the ceiling fan. It was spinning, he was unresponsive.

"Let's take an assessment, shall we?" Lemmy spun in his imaginary office chair to face Dan.

"The 'love of your life' hates you and thinks you're having an affair."

Dan raised a finger.

"You are at risk of never seeing your children again. You

are a drug addict who had an affair with a woman you never even had sex with."

Dan raised a second finger. "That's two."

"All of your friends and family think you have a serious psychological problem and don't want to talk to you."

Dan raised a third finger. "Three."

"You lost your well-paying job at AGphic, and you're on two strikes with your new job. You walking out today is most likely the last straw."

Dan lowered a finger.

"Back down to two, that job sucked."

"OK," Lemmy agreed. "Maybe that was a push."

"OK, the third reason you're screwed... It is only three, isn't it?"

Dan lowered a finger, flashing Lemmy the bird once again then dropped his hand to his side.

"Third... Charlie hasn't been seen since he walked out of Yvette's house. Father August hasn't been seen since Katie left. What's that guy's deal anyway? He made me feel extremely uncomfortable."

"I don't know what his deal is, but he seemed surprised that you were there. I know that he can see Charlie, but why can't he see you?"

"I have no idea," Lemmy said, uncomfortably shifting in his chair. "We have to figure this out."

"Lemmy, you are a figment of my imagination, and I'm insane. There, it's figured out."

"Yeah, but can figments send messages to other people's figments? Then the two 'real' people can communicate via telepathy? You didn't imagine that."

"You got me there, Lemmy. I can't explain it. Unfortunately, the only *real* person who can corroborate that story was high as a kite when it happened."

Lemmy set his coffee mug down and leaned against an armrest.

Dan's face darkened, and he choked back a sob.

"I just want my life back. I want Katie. I want my kids, Lemmy. It's too damn quiet around here! I want to be back to normal. I can't live alone anymore. I don't know what is going on inside my own damn head. Why can't everything just be real, and that's all there is?"

Lemmy stood up and threw a wireless mouse at Dan's head. It disappeared into vapor.

"What was that for?" Dan said.

"I'm tired of your moaning and groaning. What else do I need to do to convince you that you're not crazy and that I'm real? We had a telepathic conversation! You'd rather think that you're crazy than deal with the reality that something odd is happening in your world."

"Lemmy, it was a conversation with someone high. We talked about purple dogs and mermaids."

Lemmy slammed his fists on his keyboard. "But it was a real conversation, Dan. It happened. You think it is Katie that keeps dragging things back to normal? You are doing it to yourself. The sooner you accept the fact that I'm real and here to stay, the sooner we can get past your childish disbelief."

Lemmy angrily sat back at his computer. He took deep breaths as if it took a great effort to calm himself. A mouse magically appeared in his right hand.

"Tell me I'm real, Dan! Say it! Admit that what happened yesterday was real. Admit that it has all been real," he said.

The ceiling fan hummed, and its chain *tink-tinked* off the fan's glass light dome. Lemmy had a point. Dan began crying.

"You are real," Dan said, between tears.

Lemmy's stern expression softened. "See? Doesn't it feel good to know you're not crazy?"

Dan wiped his face on his sleeve. "No. This is much, much worse."

Lemmy looked away and typed on his computer. Dan needed a moment to compose himself. Dan's phone *dinged*, but it was only an e-mail advertisement. Lemmy sensed an opportunity to change the subject.

"Has Yvette responded to your texts?" Lemmy asked.

"Yes, she responded with," Dan checked his phone, "'Please stop texting me.' Katie really scared her yesterday."

"I'm sorry I didn't stick around to see the fight. If it's any consolation, Tania can't find Colette either. She isn't responding. I'm guessing Yvette has been laying off the drugs," Lemmy said.

"Wait, you can communicate directly with Tania?"

"Yes. We're trying to figure out what's going on with our situation as well. Despite what you may think, we exist whether you see us here or not. We're not like Charlie or Colette that seem to come and go."

"You mean you and Charlie aren't the same type of hallucination?" Dan asked.

"Be careful with that word. Charlie is the hallucination. He is the bridge that joined us. Let me ask you a question, Dan; are you sober right now?"

"Of course."

"And, you're talking to me, not Charlie, right?"

"Are you saying Charlie only comes out when I'm high?"

Lemmy shrugged.

"Like it or not, Charlie is a part of you. But without him, I

100

wouldn't be here."

"I guess I should thank him the next time I see him."

Lemmy shrugged. "Do whatever you feel is necessary.

"If Charlie comes and goes with the drugs, what do *you* do when we aren't together? Where do you go?"

Lemmy scratched his head. "I stay here." Pointing to his computer desk. "Mainly surfing the internet, looking for information. Lately, I've been focused on keeping in touch with Tania. That's actually hard to do right now. Tania is just like me, you know."

Dan stood up and walked across the room. He poured himself a cup of coffee from a pot he made hours ago and drank it cold.

"In what way is she like you?" Dan asked.

"Well, she is looking and listening, as well, I guess. She is also looking for information and others like me. She is stuck with Yvette like I'm stuck with you."

Dan got up and walked over to Lemmy. If Dan was stuck with him, then he may as well learn more about him.

"Lemmy, do you ever sleep?"

Lemmy got a look of consternation on his face.

"Sometimes, I guess. Sometimes when I see you go to sleep, I'll take a quick nap here in my chair, but most of the time, I'll switch over and keep working back home in my condo. It has everything I need."

"You have a condo?" Dan asked.

"Yeah, but it's bare-bones. Spartan even. It doesn't have a view."

Dan nodded. "When you say that you're *working*, what is that? Surfing the internet looking for people and information?"

"That's part of it. It's a bit more complicated than that, but I don't want to go into it right now."

That was an odd deflection, Dan thought. He let it go.

"There are certain types of people you're looking for, right? People like you and Tania?"

Lemmy nodded. "Yes, that is correct. In the beginning, I was only trying to find you. Now that Charlie helped me find you, I'm looking for others like Charlie and Tania. I spend most of my time waiting for new connections."

"You're like a background service running on a server, you're a daemon!"

"A demon? Now you're starting to sound like Father August," Lemmy scorned.

"A daemon is what we call a service that runs on a server operating system, it takes care of background tasks that the user isn't always aware of."

Dan paused to consider the implications of what he said. Lemmy was always running, even when he was asleep or unaware? Looking to make connections to others? Downloading into other people? Was Lemmy a virus? Was Dan in control of himself?

"I know what a daemon is," Lemmy said. "I just don't like to be treated as an object."

"No, it makes sense now. You're always listening and searching for something. You only exist inside me. Your job seems to be to connect to other daemons. But for what purpose?"

Lemmy sat up, indignant. "You are grossly oversimplifying. You're making it sound like I'm just a piece of code. That I'm not real. We've been over this already."

Dan realized his gaffe. He needed to smooth it over if he wanted any more information out of Lemmy. "Lemmy, if you're 'just a piece of code' then so am I. We've already agreed that we're both real. I guess that holds true if we're all just information."

Dan saw Lemmy relax at that, maybe he could try flattery to get more answers? "Besides, you're brilliant! You're intelligent, you have private thoughts, and you act independently. You're not a normal daemon, you're an AI daemon."

"Hey, man, I don't like the term AI It's overused and meaningless. Besides, there's nothing artificial about me as far as I'm concerned. Also, I can do other things besides make connections. I'm not a one-use service, thank you very much."

"Sorry about that, Lemmy. I'm still thinking in the old terms. If we are both in a simulation, then I suppose nothing is organic, everything is artificial."

"Exactly," Lemmy said. "There's no difference."

"If you're a daemon and you live in my head, what does that make me?"

"The host."

Dan laughed. "Well, I hope you're comfortable."

"It's fairly spartan around here, but I get by," Lemmy said.

"Hey, what's that supposed to mean?"

"I'm just saying that your brain is nice and uncluttered."

Unsure how to interpret that statement, Dan continued. "OK, if I'm the host, and you're the daemon, what is Charlie?"

"He's a bug."

Dan laughed. "What about Father August?"

Lemmy got serious. "I don't know, but I hope we never see him again."

Dan quit laughing and sat down next to Lemmy.

"Have you had any luck finding Charlie?"

Lemmy shook his head. "He doesn't respond to texts, e-mails, nothing, it's like he disappeared off the face of the Earth."

"Same here, I've tried messaging him a few times, but he's not responding to me, either."

"More proof that he only appears when you're high." Lemmy shrugged and refilled his coffee.

"Lemmy, I think we need to continue to try to find others like us and meet with them. The more of us there are, the more likely we'll figure out why we're all here. You're the key to all of this."

Lemmy pointed at himself. "Me?"

Dan grinned. "Yes, you. You found Tania, and she found Colette and Yvette."

"It just worked out that way. The IP information was local, and it was easy to find Tania once she appeared. I had nothing to do with that," Lemmy lied. "We got lucky that it was someone that knew you and Blaine and worked at the same place."

Dan agreed that they were extremely fortunate. Either this condition was more common than Dan thought, or something else was going on.

"I want you to expand your search. Convince Tania to help you. Maybe try to talk to everyone that connects to the Simulation MUD. Search the net for other simulation theory sites and direct them to that page. Set the trap, so to speak. Check social media and increase your distance range to over a hundred miles out. That'll get the whole Mons metro area, not just the city limits."

Lemmy nodded. "That should net us a few more."

"And, Lemmy, also, focus on the ones with just a couple of posts in those popular internet forums. Especially the posters that are skeptical. The old-timers that post? They are either certifiably crazy or are perpetuating the joke."

"OK, what are you going to do?"

"The first thing I'm going to do is contact Yvette. Then I'm going to convince her to come with me to get Blaine to tell me where he got the drugs that trigger this condition, and who else he sold it to. If it happened to the two of us, then it makes sense that it happened to others that he sold it to."

"Hah, good luck with that," Lemmy said.

"Yeah, I know, I'm sure that it has got to be a cardinal sin of drug dealers to divulge their supplier and clients," said Dan as he put on his shoes.

"You know what's strange about Blaine? He has had access to that stuff this whole time, but I don't have a connection to him," Lemmy said.

"Oh, Blaine? He doesn't do drugs." Dan laughed.

"Hah, really? Then why does he sell them?"

"I've asked him the same question. He says it's to meet more people. But I like to think he likes to own secrets about others."

"I like secrets, too." Lemmy smiled.

Dan didn't like the look of that smile, but it was time to get moving. He couldn't waste all his time debating with Lemmy. The faster that Dan figured out what was up with Lemmy, Tania, and The Simulation, the sooner he could put it all behind him and move on. Dan patted his pockets for his keys, cellphone, and wallet then opened the door.

"Can you stay here and work on what I asked?" Dan said.

Lemmy looked at him questioningly. "I can't really *stay here* now, can I?"

"Right, sorry," Dan apologized.

"No offense taken. I have a lot of work to do. I'll go to my condo where I can get more done," Lemmy typed on his computer.

"Let's only contact each other in an emergency, OK?"

Lemmy nodded and faded away into the mist. Dan shook his head and closed the door to his apartment. He still hadn't gotten used to him appearing and disappearing.

"Ah, just the man I was coming to see."

Dan hurriedly locked the deadbolt and spun around.

"Father Desjeunes?"

The short, elderly priest gave a soft smile and shook Dan's hand. Dan was relieved that it was a real handshake, not one that turned to vapor. The priest noticed Dan's reaction, and a look of concern crossed his face.

"Dan, I understand you're having some difficulties. I was wondering if there was anything I could do to help?"

"How did you know I was living here, Father?" Dan asked.

"Katie told me," he said.

Dan smiled. The fact that Katie had sent him as a messenger meant that there still may be a chance to get his life in order. Besides, Dan loved Father Desjeunes. He officiated Dan and Katie's wedding and was present at his parents' funeral. He had the reputation of being kind to the children of his parish. Everyone loved his easy smile and contagious laugh. To everyone's dismay, he had retired only two years earlier. To see him out was somewhat unusual, he spent most of his time at home or working with his charities.

"Father, I'm glad to see you. Do you have time to go get a cup of coffee? I'd offer you one inside, but my coffee maker is on the fritz."

"Of course, Dan! But I insist that it will be my treat this time," said Father Desjeunes.

Dan clasped the man on the shoulder. He was greatly relieved to finally see a friendly face after all that he had been through.

"Thank you, Father."

Father Desjeunes patted Dan's back and guided him down the hallway leading out of the apartment complex. As they reached the front gate, Dan noticed a woman leaning against it, arms crossed under her breasts.

"Katie? What are you doing here?"

Dan looked at Father Desjeunes, who avoided his gaze guiltily.

"Father?" Dan said.

"Don't look at him," Katie said. "I asked him to come."

"Katie, I'm glad you're here. Like I told your lawyer, I'm willing to do any counseling you want..."

Katie held up her hand. "I didn't ask Father Desjeunes to come here for our marriage, Dan. There's something else."

There was something in Katie's voice that made the hair on Dan's neck stand up. He had seen her angry before, but this was different. He detected... Fear?

"What is it, Katie?"

Father Desjeunes patted Dan on the back again. "Let's go get that cup of coffee, son."

TEN

The Breakfast Station was empty except for a couple of teenage waitresses gossiping behind the counter. They slid into a booth out of sight and earshot of the staff. Father Desjeunes gave Katie a meaningful look and grabbed her hand.

"OK, Katie," Dan said. "What is all of this about?"

Katie began to speak but choked up. Father Desjeunes patted her hand and frowned at Dan.

"Dan, Katie called me and told me all about your situation," he said.

Katie made a hard face and stiffened in her chair.

"She told me about the job, the girl, the late nights. The troubles you have been going through. This isn't like you, Dan."

"But Father, I...."

Father Desjeunes held up his hand. "Now wait. She has admitted to me that she hasn't been innocent throughout this affair. She has had her own moments of weakness. She has confessed her sins to me."

Katie bowed her head in acknowledgment.

Dan's coffee steamed untouched. Where was this going?

"Dan, despite all of this, there is something she needs to tell you."

Dan glared at Katie. "What? Are you pregnant or something?"

Katie shook her head. "Cancer."

"What?"

"Dan, we found out yesterday Al has cancer."

Dan's hands shook, and he had to steady them on the table.

"How? What kind? He's only twelve!"

Dan looked back and forth between Katie and Father Desjeunes, hoping to see the joke. There had to be a mistake. Al? There was no cancer in his family.

"We don't know yet. He has been having headaches lately. I thought it was from football practice. He hasn't had a concussion that we know of. Anyway, the scans showed tumors on his brain."

The room spun, and Dan stood up. The timing of this was odd. Dan wondered if this had anything to do with Lemmy and The Simulation.

"There has to be a mistake. Katie, this can't be happening. Are you sure they know what he has?"

"They did an MRI. And you're right, they don't really know what we are working with right now until they can do a full biopsy on one of the tumors."

"One of them? How many does he have?"

"Five."

The floor felt like it disappeared from under Dan's feet. Al was perfectly healthy just a few days ago and now...

"Five tumors?"

"He has five small ones. They think we may have caught it early, but they won't give us a treatment plan or prognosis until they are confident in the diagnosis."

Dan's stomach sank. He forced Al to play football, it was

supposed to make him a man. Al didn't care about football, but he wanted to make his dad proud, so he played anyway. He went to practices with tumors in his head because Dan forced him. What kind of father does that? Here he was, running around doing drugs, talking to hallucinations while his son was suffering to prove to his dad that he was a man. Dan could throw up. Katie and Father Desjeunes were looking at him with tears in their eyes. He didn't realize he had been crying as well.

"Katie. We have to get him through this. Nothing else matters," Dan said, choking back tears.

"We will try," she said. "That's one of the reasons that I'm here. Dan, if you were honest with me that you have not slept with that woman, I would like you to come home. Your family needs you, but I can't have an adulterer under my roof. I've seen you with that woman, and I can't have it."

The bitter accusation brought Dan back to the present.

Dan shook his head at the irony. "What about you and Coach Rod? Don't you mean two adulterers?"

"I'm sorry about that, Dan. I've confessed that sin, and I'm right with the Lord. I realize you aren't perfect, but I hope you can forgive me as well."

What? Father Desjeunes nodded and clasped Katie's hand. Dan couldn't believe her hypocrisy.

"Katie, you have to believe me. Yvette is just a friend of mine. I swear to you both that I have not had sex with her."

Father Desjeunes shook his head. "Dan, if you're serious about making this marriage work, you can't see her again."

There was something about the finality of the priest's tone that set off an alarm bell in Dan's head. Lemmy had warned him that The Simulation would take corrective action, and here he had it. Could The Simulation have given Al cancer? Why did Katie get Father Desjeunes involved? How far will it go to get him back on course? Dan shook his head; he couldn't give up Yvette. She held the only proof that he was sane.

"She is just a friend from work. We are working on a project together. It's strictly platonic. For the good of the family, I need to keep working with her."

"What sort of project are the two of you working on? Can I see?" said Father Desjeunes.

Dan shifted uneasily in his chair. It wouldn't do for the priest to witness drug use.

"I'm sorry, Father, but that wouldn't be possible," Dan said.

Katie leaned forward, putting her elbows on the table.

"Dan, your family needs you. Al needs you. We need you to get past whatever you are going through, with your friends, late nights, and girlfriend, and be there for us. You either commit one hundred percent to our family or nothing."

Dan blinked and pushed his coffee away. They got him. He wondered how The Simulation worked so quickly. What did it know? Did it have a direct line to Katie and the Priest? Was it a conscious decision on their part to corral Dan into moving back home, or was the corrective action hard-coded into their DNA? Whatever the result, he knew that Al would die if he stood up from that table and went back to his apartment. He decided that he was going to have to act normal while he figured all this out.

"Of course. Yes. Anything for Al," Dan insisted. "I'll need a better job to cover medical expenses, maybe one with good health insurance for the family. I'll start sending resumes out tomorrow."

"What about Yvette?" Katie asked.

"You'll never hear of her again," Dan promised.

"Good. I'll call the lawyer and tell him to hold off on filing the official divorce papers."

Dan sighed, that's what he wanted all along. Tragically, he knew he could never behave normal again as long as he knew the truth about The Simulation and their existence. A few more days at home would be a blessing.

"Where is Al?" Dan asked.

"He's at school. He's trying to be a normal kid with all of this going on. He needs his father at home." Katie rolled her eyes. "We all need you back at home. But don't get any ideas about us. Until I can trust you again, you'll be sleeping on the spare bed."

Dan nodded. "That's fair. I'll come by tonight. I can move back in tomorrow."

Katie finished her coffee and looked at the time.

"I need to pick up the kids from school."

Father Desjeunes grabbed each of their hands and prayed. "Heavenly Father, we ask that you look over this family during their trying time…"

Dan reached across the table and gently held Katie's hand. She gave him a meaningful look and bowed her head.

"Our Father, who art in Heaven, hallowed be Thy Name."

A deep, familiar voice joined in from the table behind Dan "Thy Kingdom come. Thy Will be done, on Earth as it is in Heaven."

Dan craned his neck to see the speaker sitting behind him and let out an audible gasp. Father August grinned mischievously over his teacup at Dan.

Dan hurriedly turned around, trying to be nonchalant, but Katie was already glaring at him. Father Desjeunes, deep in concentration, didn't seem to notice.

"And lead us not into temptation, but deliver us from evil. Amen."

"Thank you, Father," said Katie.

Shaken, Dan stammered. "Yes, thank you, Father, that was very nice."

They all stood up. Dan peeked back and saw that the other priest was still there. Neither Katie nor Father Desjeunes took notice of him.

"Dan, Katie, please come to see me if you need anything. I'll always be here for you if you need someone to talk to."

Dan shook his hand. "Thank you, Father."

Katie took him by the hand. "Father, I'll drive you back. Your place is on the way."

When Father Desjeunes and Katie walked out the door, Father August stood up and smoothed out his black shirt.

"Behold, the power of prayer. It can truly work miracles."

"I've been telling you to act normal otherwise, there would be consequences. It's a shame we had to get Al involved. He was a nice kid."

Dan stood there, momentarily too stunned to talk.

"Wait, you did this to Al?" he said incredulously.

Father August shrugged and walked towards the door. Dan walked hurriedly to catch up.

"You can't leave, where are you going? What did you do to Al?"

"I did what needed to be done to correct a situation."

Dan paused, trying to process the information. He had been told that The Simulation corrected things, he didn't know that there was an actual agent of correction. If Father August gave him cancer...

"Can you fix him?" Dan asked. "Does he really have cancer?"

Father August rubbed his hands together as if trying to remove some invisible filth that Dan could not see.

"Prayer is very, very powerful. I'm sure if you prayed hard enough, you could probably get your old job back, maybe get Al a better set of doctors."

The realization hit Dan hard. "You did this. You *really* did this."

Father August looked down at Dan with disdain.

"No, Dan, you did this. You should have just forgotten your conspiracy theories, and your girlfriend, and whatever it is you were planning to do. Everyone has been telling you to act normal. You didn't listen. You put your nose into business that doesn't concern you. This is what happens. The system corrects itself. When it can't do so organically, I get involved. I wouldn't even be here if not for your actions."

"You gave Al cancer because the system failed?" Dan couldn't believe it. "Why not give me cancer? Give it to me!" Dan screamed.

Father August stopped and looked Dan in the eye. "No, you have to fix this. Think of this as an opportunity. See you around."

With that, Father Augustus walked out the door and sat in the back seat of Katie's SUV. He straightened his collar and smiled and waved at Dan as they drove off. He just left with Katie? How?

Dan's phone buzzed in his pocket. It was a text message from Yvette.

"I need to see you now. Something is wrong. Blaine and I just got fired."

Dan stared at the message, unsure of how to respond. Were his text messages being monitored too? If they got fired, then Father August must be on to them as being in on the conspiracy. The timing was too much of a coincidence.

"I can't see you ever again, Yvette," Dan typed. "Act normal. Stick with Blaine. – Dan"

"Go to Hell," was her reply. She got it.

ELEVEN

A small brown box arrived on the doorstep. Dan stuffed his hands into his robe pockets and watched the delivery truck drive off. Why was there a package? He didn't order it. He was sure Katie didn't order it either. If neither of them ordered it, then it must be a message.

He had spent the past two weeks re-establishing normalcy. It was two weeks of keeping up external appearances and inner turmoil. It was a knife's edge. He needed to know what else was out there, out beyond The Simulation. He also knew that the Simulation wanted to continue its run normally and that it wasn't afraid to kill anyone that interfered with that fact.

He used this time to process this information. He needed to figure it out on his own. He couldn't do an internet search for it. That would trigger a correction. Was he too paranoid? He couldn't take the chance. He kept up appearances by attending church and school functions. Katie seemed to have forgiven him. Sex was still off the table, but at least they were sharing a bed again. Dan knew, deep down, that he had violated her trust. She kept her distance.

He hadn't heard from Yvette since they exchanged text messages two weeks ago. He hoped that she and Blaine were getting their own lives back to normal. He wondered if she was as committed to playing the charade as he was. It was difficult for Dan to not reach out to her and ask if she had discovered anything new about The Sim.

He was desperate for information, but he didn't want to risk contacting Lemmy. Father August could be lurking around the corner. Besides, things were becoming more normal by the day. It's like he was quickly put back on track by some unseen force. Surprisingly, he got his job back at AGphic. Dan couldn't believe it. He received a phone call from the legal team that he had been incorrectly terminated and that they would like to make it right.

It had come to light that a couple of disgruntled employees sabotaged the database servers the night Dan got fired. The same employees covered up their actions by interfering with Dan's alerts. Heads still needed to roll, so they fired Blaine and Yvette. They were given no explanation.

Another benefit of Dan's return to normalcy was that Al's health had improved immediately. The neurosurgeon diagnosed the tumors as a benign meningioma. No treatment was prescribed. He only needed periodic imaging performed to make sure that the tumors didn't change. Dan understood that these were the stakes. Keep poking around about Simulation theory, and your son dies. It seemed that Dan was given a clear choice. But why would it kill Al? Why not just kill Dan?

Throughout all of this time of acting normal, in private, Dan had been processing. His thoughts always drifted back to The Simulation. He knew that what happened between him and Yvette was real. He knew that Lemmy was real. Pretending that nothing happened didn't make it so. If only the people he loved could remain living their everyday lives, unaffected by *his* desire for knowledge.

How much time needed to pass to convince The Simulation that he had moved on? How could he be sure that he was free of its watchful eye? He didn't want to risk drawing the ire of The Simulation again, but could he risk NOT exploring The Simulation? His family may be safe now, but at what cost to the big picture? What was the big picture? He had to know more. If there was a way to proceed undetected, he needed to find it.

He needed to find a way to contact Lemmy without Father August knowing. He needed to find a way to do it without Katie knowing. What if Dan was just paranoid? Maybe they weren't watching after all. Neither Charlie nor Father August had been seen in the past two weeks. If he was no longer being observed, maybe it was time for him to test his limits.

An unwrapped box lay at his feet, and there he stood holding a book entitled "Meditation for Dummies" and a gift card signed "Whenever you are ready to talk. -A friend," The message was also the method.

Dan thumbed through the pages and tossed the book and card in the trash can. He didn't need the book. When his parents died, he used meditation techniques to cope with his anger and grief. He was an expert at one time, at least. He hadn't meditated in a decade. Could he even achieve the mental state required to talk to Lemmy? Whoever had sent the book thought so. At least it wasn't a jar of drugs, he'd be back on the street again if Katie ever found more drugs.

He decided that he would give it a try and sat down in his recliner and closed his eyes.

He took a deep breath, focused on it, then let it out.

Thoughts arrived, and he dismissed them.

He inhaled and exhaled until all that existed in his mind was his next breath.

***

"You're here!" Lemmy exclaimed.

Dan slowly opened his eyes and saw Lemmy beaming back at him.

"You're really here!" Lemmy repeated.

Lemmy was clean-shaven and smelling like he was fresh out of the shower. The room was light and airy. Colorful abstract paintings adorned the walls, and potted palm trees sat in each corner. A large window took up one whole side of the room. Through it glittered a crystal white beach and turquoise blue water.

"Wow!" Lemmy exclaimed.

"What is it?" Dan rubbed his eyes as they adjusted to the brightness.

"Nothing," Lemmy lied. "You just know how to brighten up a room."

Dan surveyed the area. The room itself was immaculately clean. A computer desk sat near the picture window. On it were three monitors, each connected to a laptop open to its own monitor. Several well-worn looking laptops sat stacked in a corner near one of the palm trees. Under, and on top of the glass dining room table were several unopened laptop boxes. Dan presumed that those were new.

"Lemmy," Dan said, standing in the middle of the room, "is this your house?"

"It sure is, and you're here!" Lemmy grinned

Dan looked around the room, some of the abstract paintings had tones mimicking nautical themes. There was a modern kitchenette, granite countertops, and a clean tile floor. This place seemed familiar to Dan.

"Are we in Florida?" Dan said.

"I'm not sure exactly where this is," said Lemmy looking out of the window. "I didn't even know there was a beach until you showed up."

Dan walked over and looked out of the window.

"I remember this place," said Dan. "We came here on vacation four years ago."

"It sure is nice, thanks for inviting me here. It feels like home. And the view," Lemmy gestured out the window. "The view is more than I could have ever asked for."

Dan turned his attention away from the shoreline and walked around the room.

"I don't remember this place having abstract paintings, just some sort of vague, generic tropical theme."

"We're inside your memory," Lemmy said. "Whatever you remember is what exists here. For example, do you remember if it had a coffee maker?"

As Dan tried to remember, a coffee maker appeared on the counter, full of freshly brewed coffee.

"Thanks!" Lemmy said and began searching for mugs.

Dan stood there, amazed.

"Why here? Of all the places I've been, why this one?"

Lemmy opened and closed cabinets, not finding anything.

"Maybe you were thinking of the beach when we met? I don't know."

Lemmy bent down and checked the bottom row of cabinets.

"That's odd."

Slowly the rest of the room started to come into focus. The abstract paintings turned into paintings of palm trees and pelicans. A large picture of a yellowfin tuna appeared over the dining room table, and one entire wall turned into mirrors.

"Now I remember this place better," Dan said as he surveyed the room.

"Do you remember where the coffee cups were?"

Dan closed his eyes, remembering. "They're in the cabinet next to the microwave."

Lemmy opened it and removed two mugs that weren't there before.

"You know Dan? I kind of liked the paintings better when they were abstract forms," Lemmy said and handed Dan a cup of coffee.

"Me too," said Dan as he took a sip and was surprised that the coffee was hot, and tasted good.

"The coffee tastes real."

"It tastes real to me too, Dan," Lemmy replied.

"I'm not sure what to make of this," said Dan as he set the mug down and leaned back on the couch.

"The memory tricks or the fluid nature of reality?"

"Both. How do you cope with the changes, Lemmy?"

"Well, I'm used to it, I guess. It's always changing," said Lemmy. "Before I was a wanderer. Sometimes I lived in dark places. Other times it was all light. Lately, I've just been living outdoors on the road."

"Where did you come from, Lemmy? Really?" said Dan.

"I don't know. One day I wasn't here, then the next day I am. I thought I was a person living a normal life, but it turns out I'm not, and I'm not exactly sure what I am. All I know is that something changed, and I'm no longer who I thought I was."

Dan sat back up and reached for his coffee. "I know how you feel."

Lemmy laughed. "Yeah, I guess you do. But you don't have people coming into your house and changing the pictures just by looking at them. I should be used to it by now, but it still blows my mind."

Dan stood up and walked over to the window. He remembered that there was a pool on the ground floor, and it appeared, as did the boardwalk to the beach.

Lemmy walked over to him. "Aw, I kind of liked it better without the manmade stuff."

Dan shrugged. "I'm sorry, I can't really control it."

Lemmy seemed deflated and collapsed into a chair.

"Is something wrong, Lemmy?"

"Until a few months ago, I thought I was my own person, with my own life. Talking to you and the others, I realize now that I'm just some function of some program running. Today drove home that fact, even though I already knew, and probably have always known. I have purpose and intent, but I don't have agency. I'm stuck here." Lemmy looked up at Dan. "How would you like to find out that you were trapped in someone's mind?"

"Who knows? With all these different and hidden layers to reality, maybe I exist in someone's mind as well," Dan said.

Lemmy considered it for a minute before shrugging it off.

"Maybe you do," Lemmy muttered. "That makes me feel better."

Dan turned his back to the Florida beaches and faced Lemmy.

"Lemmy, perhaps we are more alike than I thought."

Lemmy nodded in agreement.

"You and I both have intelligence and independence. From my perspective, you only exist in my mind. It appears that you're just trapped in here."

"Like a man stranded on a deserted island," Lemmy said.

"What happens if I die?" Dan asked.

"Then, the island goes underwater. I drown, I guess," Lemmy said.

Dan paced back and forth, and a glass vase full of sunflowers appeared. It was past time to get to the point of the visit.

"Lemmy, I need you to stop coming to see me. We have to end this symbiotic relationship. It is too dangerous."

"Because of the kid, right? I've heard some of what's going on. Here and there."

"That's right. I don't want my son to die."

"Let me guess, you think that without me around, everything will magically start to get better?"

Dan could feel his vision begin to blur as anger took root.

"It will get better. I've been ignoring you for only a few weeks, and Al is starting to improve already. It's not a coincidence."

"Not a coincidence," Lemmy mocked. "Of course it's not a coincidence. The Simulation is trying to kill you. To stop this."

Dan threw up his hand. "Look, I've been kicked out of my home and nearly lost my marriage for what? A whim? Telepathy? A neat parlor trick for crackheads?"

The room blurred, and the edges of Dan's vision got fuzzy.

"Dan, It's more than just telepathy! Can't you see? We're here for a reason. It's to save the world, not just for your lifetime, but for eternity." Lemmy got in Dan's face. "Sacrifices have to be made Dan!"

"We're talking about my son's life, Lemmy!" Dan raged.

"I'm talking about everyone's lives!"

The room blurred and blinked in and out of existence.

"I don't care about everyone's life," Dan flipped over the coffee table with the laptops. "I care about Al's life! They're going to kill him."

"Don't be Stupid!" Lemmy yelled. "He'll die anyway! We'll all die if we don't work together!" Lemmy said.

The room pulsed and faded, only blackness surrounded them.

"Calm down, Dan. You're breaking your focus, you'll lose me!"

It was too late, Dan's anger had broken the trance and Lemmy's image, and voice disappeared. As Lemmy's condo faded away, Dan's own living room came back into focus.

"Dan!" Katie shouted in his face. "Dan, are you OK?"

Dan's eyes rolled back as he opened them, and he took a deep gasping breath.

"I-I'm fine," he said, rubbing his head.

Katie frowned and paced the floor.

"Dan, you promised you wouldn't do any more drugs!" she screamed.

"What? What are you talking about?" Dan replied.

"I come in here, you're sitting in your recliner, drooling, mumbling incoherently. I thought you were OD'ing. I called an ambulance. What are you on?"

A loud *knock* thudded on the door where a policeman and a paramedic were waiting.

"Katie, I was just meditating, that's what the counselor told me to do!"

"That wasn't meditation, that was medication!"

"Katie, I wouldn't risk this..."

Katie threw up her hand. "Go with them," motioning to the ambulance. "You're not coming home without a clean drug test. That is the deal."

Dan sighed and answered the door.

TWELVE

Katie apologized all the way home from the hospital while Dan sat smugly in the passenger seat. The attending ER physician said that sometimes people coming out of heavy drug and alcohol use could have episodes like the one Dan experienced. That it was not uncommon to have setbacks during the recovery process, and that meditation was a great way to take one's mind off stress and drugs. Dan had never felt more vindicated. Katie promised to be supportive and to not interfere with Dan's meditation sessions. Dan purchased the best noise-canceling headphones he could afford. It wasn't just for the benefit of silence, but they were to also serve as a signal that he shouldn't be disturbed. Each family member promised not to bother him when he was wearing them.

That night also began a change in Katie's attitude toward Dan. She cooked his favorite meal, chicken and sausage gumbo. When the kids went to sleep, she snuggled next to him in bed. He was so used to the fighting that he wasn't sure how to react, so he tensed up and quietly let her lie with him. Minutes later, he heard her gentle snoring, and he relaxed. Dan was relieved that tensions were easing on the home front, but his mind couldn't stop thinking about The Simulation. As he held his sleeping wife, Dan's mind raced. *What was Lemmy doing this whole time while he was at the hospital? Where was Charlie? Who or what was Father August?* He didn't have any good answers to those questions.

Dan stared at the ceiling, unable to find sleep. Inevitably

his mind wandered to more profound issues such as, *Am I putting my family in danger? Why me? Is all of this real or just imagined? What's my role in all of this?* The last question stuck with him. His mind raced about his part and what it meant. Why, exactly, was he being sought out? Was he putting his family in jeopardy? If Dan were broken, The Simulation wouldn't spare them, even if he did act normal. He needed answers.

Dan decided that there were two likely scenarios; either he was genuinely crazy, or he did indeed exist in a simulation. Dan knew there was no proof in existence that reality could be a simulation. Thousands of years of human thought, philosophy, and science had transpired. No evidence that reality is a simulation had ever been discovered. On the other hand, people on drugs went crazy all the time. Various drugs caused literal visual and audial hallucinations. Drugs were known to trigger latent psychological issues, ones that ordinary, sober people never expose. Occam's razor was clearly pointed toward Dan being crazy. It was the most straightforward explanation.

Crazy didn't explain Yvette, or what they had experienced together. The situation was ridiculous, of course, but Yvette didn't strike Dan as the type of person who suffered from delusions. She seemed just as distressed about the whole deal as Dan was, she didn't ask for this. Crazy didn't explain actual telepathy. Occam could get bent.

Katie moaned and rolled over to her side of the bed.

Dan wondered if there was a way to discredit the 'Dan's crazy' hypothesis without actually seeing a psychologist. If he was actually living in a fantasy world, medication would help. It would be a tremendous burden for Katie and the family to continue with his life undiagnosed. If Dan was genuinely crazy, then he could be helped by a professional.

However, if he wasn't crazy, and The Simulation was real,

then a psychologist wouldn't be able to help him. It wouldn't matter how many drugs he'd prescribe. The psychologist would only get more and more frustrated, and Dan was sure that the end result would be lobotomization or worse. It could trigger another 'correction' within The Simulation, and someone in his family could die. Dan decided that seeing a psychologist was out of the question. He needed to get at the root of it all.

Dan snuck out of bed to get water. He needed to retrace his steps and start from the beginning. Dan poured himself a glass of water and drank it while standing over the kitchen sink.

This all started with Charlie. Charlie only appeared after he did drugs. Dan had done drugs many times before, why did it affect him this way now? Did he suffer a psychotic break? He remembered reading somewhere that when they legalized weed in Colorado, schizophrenia diagnoses went up. Did that happen to him? Dan stood in the dark kitchen, trying to sort it out. He realized that when the drugs wore off, Charlie disappeared, but Lemmy appeared even when sober. Was Charlie just a drug-induced hallucination and Lemmy the psychotic break? Charlie did introduce him to Lemmy. Dan wondered if that's how some drugs triggered mental illness, by arranging a meeting with unconscious selves in a park.

Dan placed both hands on the kitchen counter and leaned forward.

Charlie was the key that opened the door. If Dan could get Charlie back, and control the situation, maybe he could get some real answers as to what Charlie was. He decided that he needed to talk to Charlie. Unfortunately, there seemed to be only one way to speak to Charlie. That meant doing drugs again. If he wanted to verify the telepathy, he needed Yvette. Dan looked at the large family picture hanging over the fireplace of them at the beach. Dan wondered if he should just ignore it all. Continue lying in bed with Katie. How long would it take Lemmy to break back in? It was inevitable. He was going to lose his family all over again, no matter what he did. He decided to take control of the situation.

"Is everything OK, Daddy?" came a small voice from behind the bar. Carrie.

Startled, Dan spun around and knocked the glass over in the drying rack. It clanged around the stainless-steel sink but miraculously didn't break.

"Carrie? What are you doing out of bed?" he asked.

"I want a glass of water."

She walked around to her daddy and hugged him.

"OK, dear," he said. Dan filled the glass that he had nearly shattered and handed it to her.

"Thanks, Dad."

Dan heard a squeak and looked up to see Katie standing in the bedroom door. She turned around and went back to bed without a word. How long had she been standing there?

"Dad, who is Charlie? I heard you say his name." Carrie gulped down the water and handed the empty glass back. Had he been talking out loud? Dan took the glass and kissed her on the top of her head.

"Charlie? He's just a guy from work. Let's get you back to bed."

Carrie rubbed her eyes sleepily. Dan picked her up and walked her back to her bedroom. How long would he be able to carry her? She was getting so big. He tucked her into her sheets, then kissed her goodnight.

"Good night, Carrie. I love you."

"I love you, too, Daddy," she said and clutched her blanket tightly.

She was curled up in a ball, holding her pillow. Standing in the light of the hallway, he could barely make out her face in the darkness. *Love is real. Carrie is real. Tomorrow, I'm going to find out the truth, even if it costs me everything.*

THIRTEEN

Dan parked his truck in front of the three-story glass building that served as AGphic's headquarters. He sat looking at the glass cube and had an overwhelming sense of déjà vu. It had been months since he had been in the office. Already his stomach was souring with anxiety. He thought back to the last time he was here. Then, he was walked out by security. All he could bring with him was the contents of his cubicle. In his opinion, it was a fair punishment for failure to perform his after-hours on-call duties. They had given him the option to resign instead of being fired. Dan knew that resigning was supposed to look better on the resume. Still, he was convinced the company's motive wasn't altruistic.

He was sure that all they were concerned about was their own liability under employment law. How was the employee terminated? Was he fired? Well, they would have to show cause in court. Oh, he resigned? Well, that's OK, it was the employee's decision. Dan knew that AGphic could afford better lawyers than he could, so he had just resigned and walked out the door.

Now he was back. He got a do-over, a chance to right his wrongs. Dan knew that his old boss didn't want him back. What had she said over the phone? "We are excited for you to return to your old duties. I apologize for any inconvenience this incident may have caused." She went on, reading from a script. Dan was sure the conference room was full of HR people and the legal team for that phone call. Dan wasn't naïve, AGphic wasn't giving him the career mulligan, it was the Simulation.

Today was to be his pre-employment drug screening and on-boarding. However, since he was a returning employee, he only needed to complete half of the meetings that were required for all new employees. He would be done in two hours. He had told Katie that he would be home after five. It was to be the first in a long string of lies for him to get to the truth.

The meeting was done in an hour and a half. Dan made sure that he shook everyone's hand. Thanking them profusely over and over again for another chance. It will never happen again. Just happy to be back. Only his old boss didn't seem convinced. She merely shook his hand and went back to work typing e-mails. Dan sensed that the formalities were over, grabbed his backpack, and excused himself to the bathroom. Minutes later, a man wearing a hat and sunglasses walked out of the restroom, through the rear entrance and into a waiting car.

"Thanks for doing this, Blaine," Dan said, looking behind them to make sure they weren't being followed.

Blaine looked over and frowned. "Yvette filled me in on what she thinks is going on. I'm just happy to help. Maybe I can get my job back."

Dan removed his hat and scratched his head, he hated hats.

"How is she doing?"

"She's freaked out," Blaine said. "She says she can't stop thinking about it and is terrified to even try Fana again."

"You said on the phone that she flushed them all down the toilet after I left the other day. Is that true?"

Blaine nodded and kept driving. That would explain why Lemmy had not been able to get in touch with her. Dan had communicated with Lemmy this morning before coming. He said that he was finally able to get in touch with Tania, but she hadn't talked to Yvette for weeks. Dan assumed that meant that Yvette still needed to use Colette to speak with Tania. At least Tania couldn't harass her incessantly like Lemmy did. Maybe Yvette would better off not being involved? Dan banished the thought. Yvette was just as curious about The Simulation as he was.

"Are you sure you want to meet my guy? He's weird, even by our standards," Blaine said.

"Yeah, I need to get my hands on some more Fana. Yeah, it's intense at first, but the effects linger on for days. I don't want to take the chance of the after-effects wearing off just yet. If Yvette stopped taking it and it clears out of her system, then I'll be all alone again. The only way we are ever going to figure any of this out is if we do it together."

Blaine turned down the radio and pulled in to a suburban driveway.

"OK, Dan, this guy's name is Henry. I worked with him back when he was a business analyst. We've always kept in touch. He got lucky gambling on penny stocks and made millions. Now, he owns his own realty company and flips houses."

"He's a realtor? How did he get you Fana?" Dan said.

"He said it was from a start-up venture that he had invested in. He has connections in the industry. You don't know this, but he gave me the acid that you used to micro-dose. He may have got it from the same company that made Fana."

Blaine turned off the car, and it heat-ticked in the driveway. A neighbor working in her flower bed craned her neck to see who was parked in the driveway.

"How many cartons of Fana did he give you?"

Blaine waved at the neighbor, and she put her head back down to tend to her weeds.

"Just the two. One for you, one for Yvette. I told her that

you were micro-dosing and that you were having success with that. She wanted to try, but I didn't have anymore. I thought Fana would be the next best thing. To be honest, I was going to give you both boxes until she said something."

Dan scowled. He didn't believe in fate or bad luck. Not anymore. Coincidences were the work of The Simulation. What was it up to?

"Have you ever tried Fana?"

Blaine shook his head. "No. I candy-flipped in college once. It was a bad experience. I swore I'd never trip again."

Blood rushed to Dan's face. "You gave Yvette and I experimental psychedelics without even trying them first? Are we guinea pigs?"

"Hey, calm down," Blaine held up his hands. "Henry made it sound like they weren't going to be anything special. I assumed it was a safe alternative to what you were doing. It was made by a company. It had a nice package. It had a blister pack. It seemed legit."

Dan glanced up the driveway to the house. Were the answers inside?

"What is really in those things?"

Blaine took off his sunglasses and gripped the door handle.

"Good question, let's go ask him."

Henry's house was a mid-2000s French traditional style home located in the middle of a cul-de-sac with a "For Sale" sign out front. From the outside, the expertly manicured lawn, and fresh paint job made it look like the type of well-maintained home any homeowner's association would give yard of the week. Dan noticed security cameras hanging on every corner, and three watching the front door. They had only gotten halfway up the sidewalk before the front door opened. A tall, thin man emerged wearing a floral print blazer and tie greeted them with open arms.

"Blaine!" the man gestured dramatically.

Blaine bowed with a flourish. "Henry," he said formally.

Henry giggled and smiled at Dan. "You must be Dan."

Blaine stepped between them and bowed again.

"Dan, let me introduce you to Henry St. Leonardi."

Henry smiled politely and held out his hand to be kissed. Dan, unsure of how to react, reached out and gently shook it. Henry pulled his hand back and laughed.

"Charmed?" Dan said.

"Of course. Please, come inside."

Dan and Blaine followed Henry inside. Though it wasn't Dan's style, he couldn't help admire Henry's attire. The floral print was unusual, but it seemed fitting. Not a hair on his neatly trimmed beard was out of place. Dan had imagined Henry to be an overweight stoner. He couldn't have been more wrong.

The inside of the home was a reflection of the man. It was colorful, clean, and stylish. Dan was sure that every picture frame was completely level. Every item of décor was placed within a millimeter of where it needed to be. The air was cool and perfect, tinted with the rich aroma of coffee.

"I've prepared coffee for us. Doesn't it smell wonderful? Please sit."

Dan and Blaine sat next to each other on one of the brightly colored sofas facing the windows. As Dan surveyed the room, he noticed there were no family pictures on the walls, just paintings you would find at a yard sale. It finally dawned on Dan that the house was staged, not lived in.

"This is a nice place, Henry. You must hate to be selling it."

Henry walked over to the couch, carrying a tray of coffee cups.

"Isn't it wonderful? If I wasn't flipping it for a client, I'd think about keeping it for a second home. Cream?"

Dan and Blaine each retrieved a cup of coffee from the tray.

"It looks a lot better than the last time I was here," said Blaine.

Henry blushed and sat down his coffee mug. "The wallpaper was hideous. A little paint and a deep clean was all it needed to get it into shape. The fixtures are outdated, but that wasn't in the budget to replace."

"It looks good," Dan offered.

Henry straightened up in his chair and adjusted his tie.

"OK, let's get down to business. Dan, Blaine tells me that you're in the market for a four-bedroom, two baths, or three-bedroom two baths with a bonus room or office, is that right?"

Dan looked surprised. "I'm sorry?"

"From what Blaine has told me, this home would be perfect for your young family. Did you know that there is a swimming pool in the back yard?"

Dan shifted in his seat and leaned close to Blaine. "What did you tell him?"

Blaine winced. "I'm sorry, but I had to tell him you were interested in the house to get him to agree to see you."

Dan frowned and whispered back. "Does he have any idea why I'm here?"

Blaine shook his head.

"No secrets, you two. Dan, do you have an agent yet? If not, I'll only charge four percent commission. I'm sure the buyer would accept an offer of two thousand below asking. Just know that I have another showing right after you."

Henry winked and picked up his mug. Dan glared at Blaine.

"Henry, I'm not here to buy this house," he said.

Henry arched an eyebrow in surprise.

"Well then, why are you here?" Henry demanded.

"I'm here because of Fana."

Henry placed his cup in his lap and squinted his eyes. "Fana? The shampoo?"

Dan was getting tired of the game. "No, I'm talking about the drug, Fana. The one you gave to Blaine."

Henry stiffened.

"I don't know what you're talking about," Henry said defensively.

"Blaine, are you sure you have the right guy? He doesn't seem to be the type who would have access to the most important, groundbreaking pharmaceuticals ever invented." Dan placed his coffee mug on the table and stood. "He looks more like your average interior decorator desperate for a sale."

"Desperate?" Henry gasped.

Blaine glared at Dan and motioned for him to sit.

"Please excuse my friend, Henry. This misunderstanding is my fault. I told you he was here to buy the house because it was the only way you'd agree to meet him. You've told me before to keep the drug thing private."

Henry's eyes widened. "He's the one you wanted LSD for, isn't he?"

"Yes."

He raised his eyebrows and inspected Dan.

"OK, Dan, explain to me why you want Fana," Henry said.

Dan looked at Blaine, who motioned him to tell.

"When I take these drugs, I hallucinate. During one of the hallucinations, I saw the fabric of The Simulation—"

Henry held up his hand to interrupt.

"On second thought, I don't want to know."

"Henry, I need your help," Dan pleaded.

"I have two packs left," Henry said.

Dan sighed and sat back down.

"Thank you, I'll take them."

Henry walked over to his briefcase and pulled out the carton and tossed it to Dan.

"How much do I owe you?" Dan said.

"Nothing. Don't you see the *Free Sample* sticker on the front?"

Dan stuffed the packs into his pocket.

"Thank you," he said.

"You said these were your last pack. How many did you get?" Blaine asked.

"Four packs."

"Did you try it?" Blaine asked.

"Of course. I'm not going to invest in a company without trying their product." Henry shifted in his seat. "I didn't like it. First of all, it tasted like battery acid. Secondly, the trip was too strong and too short. And finally, there were side effects."

Dan's eyes darted to Blaine and back. If Henry had tried it, did he have the same experience? If he did, Dan should know, shouldn't he? Maybe it didn't work for everybody? Blaine narrowed his eyes at Henry.

"Too strong? You told me that it wasn't as strong as LSD," he said.

Henry raised a finger, "No, I told you that it was different from LSD. The trip wasn't very LSD-like. I told you that I thought that there must not have been much in there. You must've heard wrong."

Dan arched an eyebrow at Blaine.

"Maybe so," he said. "It's possible that I misunderstood—"

"You mentioned side effects," Dan interrupted. "What side effects did you experience?"

Henry frowned. "There were lingering hallucinations after the main trip was over. For several hours afterward, I had visual and audial hallucinations of people who weren't there."

Dan sat upright. Maybe he did experience the same thing after all. "Did they talk to you about The Simulation?"

Henry laughed. "The what now? Did you say simulation?"

"Yeah," Dan said. "Does that mean anything to you?"

Henry crossed his legs and folded his hands on his knee.

"No. Never heard of it. But, um..." Henry avoided Dan's gaze and stared at the wall. "The voices did instruct me to do something. They told me to give Fana to Blaine."

Blaine spit his coffee all over the immaculately cleaned living room.

"What? You gave Fana to me because the voices in your head said to?"

Dan's mouth hung open. What was going on here?

Henry frowned at the mess and stood and walked to the kitchen. "It's normal, isn't it? I was probably wondering what I was going to do with the rest of the boxes of Fana when I started the trip. You know how psychedelics have a way of helping you out? I don't think it's out of the ordinary."

"I suppose not," Blaine said.

Once Henry was out of earshot, Dan leaned over and whispered, "This wasn't a coincidence."

Blaine mouthed, "Wow."

Henry returned with a spray bottle and a roll of paper towels and wiped the coffee off the floor and table.

"Look, I was always curious about mind-altering drugs, but I always went into it with the fear of having a bad trip. Blaine, as you know, one bad trip can ruin you on the experience for life. For some, it's not worth the risk. I wasn't going to even try it if it hadn't been for the no-bummer guarantee. They promised me that Fana had the perfect blend designed for the best experience."

Henry finished cleaning up and tossed the used paper towels in the waste bin while Dan and Blaine watched.

"Who made that promise?" Dan asked. "What company makes Fana?"

"You mean made. The company no longer exists."

Dan leaned forward, "What do you mean?"

"The company was called Damien Pharmaceuticals out of Canada. I discovered them via an advertisement in a penny stock forum. Canada was set to legalize psychedelics, and they were positioned to cash in. I sent them an e-mail saying that I was willing to invest and wanted to know more. A few e-mails later, I sent them a few grand to get on board pre-IPO. A few days after my payment posted, they disappeared. These samples arrived on my doorstep. Only the website remains."

"That's sketchy," Blaine said. "You guys are crazy for taking free drug samples from a defunct company. You don't even know what is in that stuff."

"I do." Henry smiled, "If I remember correctly from one of their e-mails, it's made from a variety of psychedelics. I believe it contained organic psilocybin, ayahuasca, and mescaline with a dash of D-lysergic acid diethylamide."

Blaine coughed. "Dan, that's magic mushrooms, DMT, peyote, and LSD all blended together. No wonder you're insane! That's not a soul bomb, that's a soul nuke!"

"It's annihilation," Dan muttered.

He stared at the floor. That was a lot of drugs crammed into one pill, it could kill someone. Maybe he wasn't experiencing The Simulation. Perhaps he was just broken. The whole deal with the defunct manufacturer didn't make sense. Henry's hallucinations telling him to give Blaine the drugs didn't make sense either. He may be broken, but he's not wrong about The Simulation. The doorbell rang, shattering Dan's thoughts.

"Ah, there's my two o'clock showing. Dan, I'm sorry about what you've been through, but I can't keep these people waiting. Unless you are making an offer on the house, it's time for you gentlemen to go." Henry stood up and smiled.

Dan rose and shook Henry's hand. "Thanks, Henry." Dan patted the packs in his pocket. "I appreciate it."

"No problem. Good luck with whatever you're searching for, Dan."

Outside, Dan jumped into the car and hurriedly put on his hat and sunglasses. He reached into his pocket and handed Blaine one of the packs of Fana.

Blaine held up his hand, refusing to take it. "What are you doing? I hope you're not giving those to me. I've already told you; I don't want any part of that stuff."

"Are you sure you don't want to try it just once?"

Blaine chuckled. "No, thanks. I've seen what it did to you and Yvette."

"Ok then," Dan said. "If you don't want them, could you give these to her?"

Blaine eyed the packet and started up the car.

"Are you sure she even wants them? What did Henry say earlier? One bad trip can make you swear it off for life. Maybe she's past that point."

Dan reached back into his bag and pulled out a blank page and an envelope. He wrote a quick message on the sheet of paper, then stuffed it in the envelope along with the packet of Fana and sealed it shut.

"Blaine, please. Just hand her this. Tell her it's from me. That's all. I won't bother you about this again."

Blaine sighed. "That's it? I give this to her, and it's over? No more crazy talk?"

"This will be it. I promise. I can't do it myself. I can't risk being seen anywhere near her."

Blaine groaned and rubbed his head. "You owe me one, Dan."

"I owe you more than one, Blaine," said Dan.

As they drove off, Dan peered out the back window to see if they had been followed. No vehicles followed them out of Henry's neighborhood. Dan sighed with relief.

"Dan, you know this drug can kill you. You know they cause hallucinations. You have told me that somehow your hallucinations are real and not imagined. I've known you for years, you are a normal guy. If you say you trust your visions are real, I believe you. For all your faults, if nothing else, you are a reasonable man. But answer me this; How can you be so sure that you haven't gone insane?"

Dan adjusted his sunglasses and sunk deeper into the seat. "Being insane would feel different. I think."

FOURTEEN

Dan knew he would have to play his cards right when he got home. He devised a big lie about how being back at work had triggered stressful memories of past conflicts. Just being in the office reignited his old fears and frustrations with the job. Katie bought the lie and recommended that Dan isolate himself for the evening to use the meditation techniques he had learned to cope with stress. Dan closed the door to his office, locked on his headphones, and at precisely eight-thirty, he ate a Fana.

He closed his eyes and focused on his breath. Thoughts from the day appeared. *Did anybody see me get into Blaine's car? What if Katie finds me here?* He banished them from his mind as soon as they arrived, though some thoughts took longer to dismiss than others. "What if this doesn't work?" was chief among them. His breath deepened and slowed.

Colors appeared in his vision, and the walls around him vibrated softly. His nostrils filled with the scent of strawberries and horse manure. His nose wrinkled, almost breaking him out of the meditation. The ringing in his ears morphed into a choir singing. The choir became distinct voices, conversations. As Dan sank into his chair, he felt like he was becoming one with it. That he was the chair. He was the chair, the floor, the ground, the universe. No beginning, no end. Then, with a blink, he found himself standing in the living room of Lemmy's condo.

"Hello? Lemmy?"

"Dan! You got my e-mail!" came Lemmy's voice from beyond the hallway. "I wasn't expecting you so soon. Just a sec, I'm brushing my teeth."

Dan noticed that there was now a balcony with a patio table on it. All of the old laptops in the corner were gone. The mirror that took up one whole wall of the room was painted over with a strange shade of matte green-gray paint. The cheap vertical blinds covering the picture window overlooking the gulf were gone. They had been replaced with a thick, dark blackout curtain, which was half-open.

"What have you done to this place? Do you have something against sunshine?"

Lemmy appeared from around the corner, wiping his mouth with a towel.

"It was a little too bright in here. I had to make some changes. It's more secure this way."

"I see," Dan said, looking around. The front window looking over what would have been the front lawn of the condo was completely painted over.

Lemmy noticed the look of concern. "It's just a precaution, Dan. I wanted to make sure I wasn't seen."

Dan looked at Lemmy questioningly. "Seen by who? You're in my head, remember? It's not like someone will fly up four stories to peek on you from your balcony."

"Oh, you have no idea what they are capable of," Lemmy said.

"They? You mean The Simulation?"

Lemmy nodded and returned the towel to the bathroom.

"Lemmy, I meant to ask you the last time I was here. Where did you get this stuff? The curtains, the paint? Your laptops?" Dan asked.

"Oh, I order it all online, and it just shows up here."

"What do you mean it just shows up? How does that work?"

Lemmy rolled his eyes. "How do I order stuff online?"

"Yeah."

"I do it the same way you do it. I turn on the computer, connect to the network, open up the supply site, find something I need, give them my information. A few hours, days... I really don't know how much time passes for you. Anyway, a short time later, I get a package inside my door."

"Show me," Dan said.

Lemmy walked over to the dining room table and typed his password into the laptop. Words appeared on the screen in a language Dan didn't immediately recognize.

"I could use some more paint." Lemmy clicked away on the keyboard, then stopped and looked at Dan.

A soft crack, like a silenced handgun, came from the front hallway. Sitting near the front door on top of an orange-painted square, was now a small can of paint.

"That's amazing!" Dan said.

"It's no different than buying a weapon or piece of clothing for a video game character in your world," Lemmy said.

"I suppose not."

Dan thought back to the stack of laptops that were present the last time he was here.

"What happens to items that you are not using anymore. Say you want to get a refill of this paint can?"

"I wouldn't refill it. I'd just order a new one. If I wanted to get rid of it, I'd just put it on the orange square and hit delete. I can also upload items to the network."

"Is that what you did with the laptops?" Dan asked.

Lemmy looked away and rubbed the back of his neck uncomfortably. "Yeah. I uploaded them. They were just burner laptops that I used to make connections to find Tania anyway. I think they refurbish them and give them new addresses so that they can't be tracked or detected by any sim security systems."

Dan's thoughts shifted from curiosity to fear. What information was really on those laptops? They had a direct connection to Dan's brain, who knows what could be on it. Lemmy could have downloaded Dan's entire childhood for all he knew. He wanted the answers, but he didn't have much time to spare.

"We should get started, Lemmy," Dan said. "The drug won't last all night."

Lemmy stood up straight and smoothed out his shirt. "You're right. Let's do this. Remember what I said in my e-mail? You need to get Charlie here, and we need to get you two joined together before we can go meet Tania."

Dan remembered the e-mail laying out the plan, he just wasn't sure about the first part.

"Are you sure we're going to be OK afterward? Have you done a join before?"

Lemmy shook his head. "First time. I saw a how-to video on the internet, it looks simple."

"You're betting my sanity on an internet video?"

"I'm not worried, it isn't difficult. Let's get going, are you ready?" Lemmy asked.

"Now is as good of a time as any," Dan said. "Let's do this."

"I'll do the honors." Lemmy reached into his pocket and pulled out the biggest joint Dan had ever seen. The lighter flickered in Dan's eyes, and Lemmy took a deep drag and blew it into Dan's face. Dan closed his eyes and inhaled deeply. "The keg and strippers are here!" Lemmy shouted.

A shiver ran down Dan's spine, and when he reopened his eyes, there, standing in the middle of the room, was Charlie.

Charlie jumped like he was waking up from a dream. "Did someone say strippers?" he shouted. His eyes fell on Dan, and his jaw dropped.

"Wait, I'm back?" he whispered. He threw his yellow baseball cap on the floor and ran his fingers through his hair. "I am back!" He danced in the middle of the room. Lemmy laughed, and Charlie stopped dancing and folded his arms under his chest.

"Wait a second. Where am I? Why am I here?" Charlie demanded as he looked around the apartment. "Most importantly, where is the keg?"

Dan walked over to a chair and sat down, beckoning Charlie to do the same.

"Charlie, come sit. There is something we need to discuss."

Charlie calmed down and walked over and sat on the couch.

"Lemmy, you contact Tania. Tell her we're almost ready."

Lemmy nodded in the affirmative and sat at his swivel chair and began typing.

"Charlie, I've got some news to tell you."

"I hope so," Charlie said, glancing around for any signs of an impending keg party.

"Charlie, as you may have figured out by now, none of this is real."

"What?" Charlie gestured at the room. "Florida? No! Don't tell me that! I love Florida! Where are the strippers?"

"I told you that it would be a waste of time to try to explain it to him," said Lemmy.

"Explain what?" said Charlie.

Dan considered catching Charlie up to speed on what he had learned about The Simulation, and their role in it, but Lemmy was right. They didn't have time.

"Charlie, we're twins."

Charlie laughed. "Are you kidding me? We don't even look alike."

"Uh, yes, you do," Lemmy said. "Charlie, you have blue eyes and a huge beer belly. Dan doesn't. You're obviously the same person."

Charlie viewed himself in a nearby mirror.

"Lemmy's right. We're two sides of the same coin," Dan said. "You're me, and I'm you."

Charlie pulled down an eyelid and inspected the whites. "I don't get it, Dan."

Dan dropped his arms in frustration and grabbed Charlie's face.

"Charlie, you literally are me. A fractured version of me."

Charlie turned and faced Dan. He paused and took a long look.

"You're right," he said.

"Charlie, you are a version of me. My body exists in The Actual. You are in The Meta. But we are one person. You represent the part of me that takes risks and has fun. That part got fractured and corrupted the first time I took that drug. You had always existed in my Meta, but now you've changed."

Charlie smiled. "Yeah. I remember. We had a lot of fun in college, didn't we?"

Dan returned his smile and clasped him on the shoulder.

"Not a word about college, ok?"

Charlie winked. "Deal."

Lemmy rolled his eyes and went back to typing on his computer. Charlie looked around the apartment and shrugged. "Where have I been exactly? I have a blank space like I've been in a coma or something. The last thing I remember was walking out of Yvette's house."

Dan looked at Lemmy, who pretended to ignore the conversation.

"I really don't know where you have been, Charlie," Dan said. "I think we lost our connection to each other because you became self-aware. On a cellular, or bit level, we are a part of the same person. You became a separate entity, but you couldn't abandon me. You turned off."

Charlie scratched his head. "I didn't know I could be turned off."

"I need you turned on."

Lemmy and Charlie both laughed.

Dan shook his head. "You know what I mean. I need you online, Charlie. We need to reconnect with each other. We need each other. Otherwise, we are imprisoned in our own context. I need you to traverse The Meta, you need me to exist in The Actual. What do you say? Do you want back in the game?"

"Tania says that they're ready to meet whenever we are," Lemmy interrupted.

Charlie looked from Lemmy, back to Dan. Sweat glistened on his forehead, and he wiped his palms on his shorts.

"OK," Charlie grinned. "Let's do it."

Dan nodded his head. "Let's do it. Lemmy, what do we do first?"

Lemmy stopped typing and swiveled around to face the two men.

"OK. Sit facing each other."

Dan stood up from his chair and walked over and sat down on the coffee table in front of Charlie.

"OK? Now what?" Dan said.

"Now, hold hands and look at each other in the eye."

They did so, and Charlie chuckled a little.

"OK, this is absurd, what's next?"

"I'm going to play a special song on this computer. While it plays, I want you to look into each other's eyes. When the moment is right, Dan's spirit will jump into Charlie's body."

"Wait, I'm going into his body? Why isn't he jumping into mine?" Dan asked.

"Because, if you want to navigate in this realm, you need to do it in Charlie's body, not your own. You can't do it in your body. You need Charlie for this."

"But wait, who will have control over his body? Me or Charlie?"

"Yeah, if he's going to be in control, then I don't want him touching my pecker," Charlie said.

"Your pecker? Why would I want to touch your pecker?"

"You BOTH will be in control!" Lemmy interrupted. "You are the same person. Relax. If you aren't relaxed and natural, this won't work. Now, back in position. And take this, both of you." Lemmy walked over and held out his hand. In it were two crudely made human-shaped gummies. Charlie snatched up one of the gummies and ate it.

"Don't you want to know what it is first?" Lemmy said.

"Doesn't matter," Charlie said.

Dan eyed the remaining gummy. "I want to know what it is."

"It's a Gemini drug. I got it via special delivery. It'll help you relax and be more receptive. You'll see."

Dan plucked the drug out of Lemmy's hand and ate it.

"OK, just sit there and hold hands."

Lemmy returned to his computer while the two men held hands. Dan stared intently into Charlie's blue eyes. Charlie blew him a kiss and winked.

"Be serious, Charlie," Dan admonished. Charlie's smile faded and concentrated on Dan's brown eyes.

"OK, here we go." Lemmy reached over and clicked the mouse. A soft tune played over his laptop speakers. What was that tune? Was it "Unchained Melody" by the Righteous Brothers?

Dan looked down at his hands, which were holding Charlie's hands. He felt a curse rising in his throat, and his mouth tightened. Charlie innocently stared into Dan's eyes, oblivious to the movie reference. Struggling to keep his face straight, Dan choked back a laugh.

"You wanted me to be serious, let's be serious, Dan." Charlie gripped Dan's hands tighter.

Tears formed in the corner of Dan's eyes.

"Dan! What's so damn funny?"

He couldn't help it, his face turned red until he blurted out in laughter.

"Take it easy, Whoopi," Lemmy chuckled. "Old Patrick will be in there soon."

"What do you mean, Whoopi?"

The chorus hit, Charlie looked down at Dan's hands then back up into Dan's eyes, then the realization hit him.

"Oh, no!" he exclaimed. "You're not doing any of this *Ghost* shit with me!"

Lemmy cracked into raucous laughter and nearly fell out of his chair.

Dan finally let it out and started roaring laughing as well.

Charlie, seeing everyone laughing, couldn't control himself. He started chuckling, then laughing, then crying in laughter. The room became an unholy cacophony of laughter. There was a bright flash of light, and the laughter ceased. Charlie's eyes closed, and when they reopened, Dan was gone.

But so was Charlie.

Lemmy had leaned so far back he fell out of his chair.

"Whoaaahhhh!" Lemmy exclaimed as he gaped at the man before him.

"Man, I feel weird," he said.

"Dude! Your eyes! You look weird, too!" said Lemmy.

The man walked into the nearby bathroom and looked in the mirror. There, he stood in Charlie's clothes with Dan's body, face, and hair. Lemmy was right. It was the eyes. One was his own, but the other was blue, like Charlie's.

"How do you feel?" said Lemmy from the doorway.

"I itch everywhere," Dan said. "It feels like my teeth don't fit."

Dan checked the mirror to make sure his teeth were still there. He was relieved that everything looked normal.

"Did it work?" Lemmy asked. "Are you two bonded together now?"

Dan nodded. "Yes, we're both here, but I'm doing the talking. You're right that we're both in control. It's weird. It's like we're one. Like we have the same voice."

"Do you feel good enough to go to the meeting with Tania?"

"I've come too far now. Besides, it's not like I have a choice.

Let's go," Dan said.

"OK then, I'll go grab my keys."

"Keys? I thought we were going to teleport there via your magic orange square."

"Sorry to disappoint you, but we're driving there. You may be able to travel in this realm now, but you still can't go instantly via online transfer." Lemmy dangled the keys in Dan's face, and the two men walked out the front door.

"Stay close, Dan. We may not be alone." Lemmy turned around and locked the deadbolt on the entrance to the condo.

"Aren't we still in my head? I'm pretty sure you're the only one here now that Charlie and I have merged. There can't be any burglars about," Dan said.

"It's just a precaution. Like I said, we don't need any surprises waiting for us when we get back. Besides," Lemmy said, patting Dan on the back. "It's just as important to keep things locked in, as locked out."

The two men walked down the hallway to the stairs leading to the next floor.

"Seriously, Lemmy. Who are you worried about keeping out?"

"Father August."

Dan paused on the top step. "Why him? He can't reach you here. Can he?"

Lemmy shrugged and kept walking. "Can't be too careful."

He led Dan down the stairs and through a metal door into the sunlight.

Dan realized that he was now back at his apartment complex, standing in the parking lot.

"Is that my truck?" Dan asked.

Lemmy grinned.

"Yep."

"How did we get to here from Florida?"

"We're still in your head. Everything here is built from a piece of your memory."

"If I understand you correctly, we're leaving my head now?" Dan asked.

Lemmy grinned. "Not quite. We have some driving to do first. Hop in!"

FIFTEEN

Lemmy drove out of the garage and onto the street. Except the road was exactly like the one in front of Dan's apartment in Mons, Louisiana, not Florida. Dan sat in quiet amazement as he realized that things weren't where they supposed to be. He realized that he was now traveling within his own mind and not actually out in the world. Nothing was where it was supposed to be, but rather where he imagined them being at different places and times of his life. The corner pharmacy? A small white house stood in its place. Dan remembered it happening the other way around, the house was replaced by a pharmacy. The hayfield? It was now a bustling neighborhood with shops and apartments. His old high school was in the same place, but it looked like it did twenty years ago. Trees knocked down by Hurricane Isaac twenty years ago were still there. Their leaves blew lazily in the imaginary breeze as if nothing happened.

"We're driving through my memory," Dan said as they drove along.

"You mean things aren't the same here as they are in the real world?" asked Lemmy as they waited at the traffic signal.

Dan pointed out the window. "No. See that house there on the corner? It was my friend's house back when I was in school. I spent almost every weekend there, watching movies and playing basketball."

"What is different about it now?" Lemmy said.

"The house isn't different. The location is. The house is in Canard, not Mons. In Mons, that corner has a gas station."

Dan became pensive as they drove past the house. Why was his internal map so wrong? Did he misremember other things? Lemmy must have sensed Dan's worry and patted him on the knee.

"The buildings are transposed in your mind. That's probably normal. I wouldn't worry about it."

Dan gazed out the window, watching the landscape of his memory pass by. He could see now that some of what he was seeing was clearly defined, whereas other areas were blurry. They passed by an old brick ranch style home. Dan could see shapes of windows and a front door, but they were blurred. It was as if someone had smeared the whole image with grease.

"Does that house look blurry to you?" Dan asked.

"Yes, it is blurry. I can't go near anything that looks like that. It's simply not possible, like hitting a wall," Lemmy said. "We're limited to what you can remember of things. I'm guessing that no events of significance to you happened there."

Dan agreed. "I suppose not. Maybe next time I'm in The Actual, I'll try to find that house and get a real good look at it. I'll see if it clears up the blur next time."

"If you're adding things to your memory, there's this barbecue place in Texas that I've read about. Your internet says that it has the best brisket. Your version of Louisiana has great food, but it lacks in the barbecue department."

"They have barbecue where you're from?"

Lemmy nodded enthusiastically. "Oh, yes! They made barbecuing meat illegal many years ago. It causes cancer, you know. I can only get it on the black market. I can't imagine what it would taste like cooked freely out in the open. You don't even have to hide your charcoal fires!"

Dan was surprised at Lemmy's passion for barbecue. It was nice to see Lemmy with his guard down. Even still, it was a reminder of how different their worlds must be.

"I've never been to a real Texas barbecue before Lemmy. I'll try to visit one soon. For you, OK?"

Lemmy seemed pleased by that. "Thanks, Dan, it means a lot." He pointed out the front of the truck. "We're here."

Lemmy slowed the truck and looked over at Dan. Just ahead of them was a large tunnel.

"Is that the Mobile Bay Tunnel?" asked Dan.

"No. It is not the George C. Wallace Tunnel, although it looks exactly like it," Lemmy said.

Dan arched an eyebrow at Lemmy. "How did you know it was called the George C. Wallace Tunnel? I didn't even know that."

Lemmy laughed. "I searched for it online. All you remember about the tunnel was the big green sign that said 'Pensacola.' I looked it up to see where it was. I had no idea it was in Alabama."

Dan was uncomfortable with the thought of Lemmy cruising down his own personal memory lane and fact-checking it. What else was Lemmy not telling him?

Lemmy took his foot off of the accelerator as he entered the tunnel. The cab became quiet, and the creaking of the tires echoed off the tunnel walls as they coasted towards the bottom. The lights flickered as they passed. Dan twisted in his seat, unsettled.

"What are you taking me, Lemmy? I thought we were going somewhere in Mons."

"The plan hasn't changed. We're going to meet Tania and Yvette at The Breakfast Station."

Dan's jaw slacked. "But that's back in Mons. Why are we in

Alabama?"

Lemmy tapped the brakes, inching the truck along. He was searching for something. "The Breakfast Station that we're going to isn't a part of your Meta. Tania and Yvette can't get inside you. If we're going to meet them, we have to meet them somewhere between The Meta and The Actual. This tunnel will get us out."

"Wait!" Dan said in a high-pitched voice. "We're actually leaving my physical body?"

Panic grabbed hold of Dan, and he struggled to control himself. Leaving his body? Was he ready for this level of commitment? Dan peered out the rear window, and daylight disappeared. He was committed. He had to see it through—deep breaths.

"Calm down! I need to concentrate." Lemmy grumbled. "Remember what happened last time? That absolutely cannot happen now. Understand?"

Dan nodded and concentrated on his breathing technique.

"I can't hit the checkpoint with your truck looking like this. I need to put a fresh coat on soon," Lemmy said. "I have to be careful, I'm never sure where the checkpoint will be."

"What checkpoint? A fresh coat of what?" Dan asked.

"You'll see. There's a heavy black fog beyond the checkpoint. It's so thick that you can't see through to the other side. Sometimes it seeps over the boundary, and you can't see the checkpoint. The checkpoint is a physical boundary between your 'brain' and the rest of the universe. It's usually halfway down this tunnel, but sometimes it's closer, others it is farther."

The tunnel's flickering lights finally blinked out. They were plunged into darkness. The truck's headlights were ineffective. They could only see a few feet ahead. Lemmy searched anyway. Minutes later, they came to a dimly lit tollbooth. Ahead and behind was an inky black fog that erased existence.

"We got lucky today," Lemmy said as he put the truck in park.

He opened the door and got out, and Dan attempted to do the same.

"Stay inside!" Lemmy cautioned. "If the fog blows this way, I'm not sure what would happen to you. It's happened to me before, and I've just ended up back in my condo. I'm not sure what would happen to you if you got sent back in Charlie's body."

Dan hurriedly slammed the door shut and went back to working on his breathing techniques.

Lemmy went to the back of the truck threw back a blue tarp revealing a large plastic tank. Dan didn't have such a rig set up for his vehicle back in The Actual. Lemmy must have modified it. He opened the tailgate and put on painters' coveralls with hood and boots. Then glasses and a breathing mask.

"Where did you get all this stuff?" said Dan through a crack in the window.

Lemmy lowered his respirator, revealing a devilish grin. "I got it all off the network. This is where I shine Dan, watch a master at work."

Lemmy snapped his mask back into place and unwound a rubber hose from an electric spool. Dan craned his neck to get a better look. It was connected to a tank that was filled with a clear liquid. Dan thought that it looked like water.

Dan tapped on the window. "Is this setup from the pest control guy?"

Lemmy laughed and lowered his respirator once more. "Where do you think I got the idea? This stuff does keep bugs away after all."

Lemmy opened a toolbox that contained various tubes of paint. He selected one and squeezed it into the large tank. He then covered everything back up with the blue tarp and clicked on the air compressor, which echoed loudly off the walls of the tunnel.

Lemmy walked around the truck and sprayed every inch of it with a blue-green foam. Dan couldn't see out the windows. Minutes later, the air compressor clicked off, and he could hear the hose spool back up into the bed of the truck. Lemmy hopped in, still in his painter's overalls, and removed his glasses, mask, and hood.

"OK, we're ready now. No turning back," Lemmy said, putting the truck in drive.

"What does the paint do? Does it encrypt us or something?"

"Nope, we are already encrypted by the truck. What the paint did was spoof us."

"Spoof?"

"Yeah. The truck itself is a trojan horse. This entire vehicle has my personal signature. With it, the checkpoint will permit us to come and go as we please. The paint fools it into seeing us as one person." Lemmy paused. "The realm we're going to would never permit us inside knowing you were here. Actuals aren't supposed to be able to enter their own Meta. The rules are much stricter when it comes to traversing realms."

"Won't the people at the checkpoint see that this is a truck, not a person? Is it not smart enough to block us?"

"The AI that runs the checkpoints are built for speed and reliability, not accuracy. They really don't care what gets through as long as it isn't explicitly denied. The firewall aspect prevents certain things from leaving."

"Like me," Dan said.

"Especially you. That's its most important function. To keep you inside until it's time."

"What time is that?" Dan asked.

"Until you die, of course."

Dan laughed. "If I die out there, I die for real?"

Lemmy scratched his head. "I don't know. I've never had to worry about that. I suppose that would be the case."

Dan stared silently out the window. This trip was for keeps.

"Before we go, you should know that I truly don't know what the consequences would be if something goes wrong. If something happens before we get to our destination, it may reject us both. If we get there and something environmental happens, like your body gets woken up in The Actual, you could be trapped. Your body would become a vegetable."

Undaunted, Dan was ready to move forward. "We have to keep going. If we succeed, we'll have the first communication between two humans outside of reality. That itself is a land-mark achievement for the human race. Most importantly, I'll know that I'm not crazy. The universe is crazy. This is exciting! Now I know how Alexander Graham Bell and that Hertz guy felt."

"Easy there, Christopher Columbus, you're trying to take credit for something I've already discovered. Remember, I'm the one that's facilitating this meeting. Besides, this may be a one-time-only trip. If we get discovered, then The Simulation's operator may shut the door to future trips," Lemmy said.

"Let's go," Dan said.

Dan closed his eyes and braced himself against the dashboard. This better work. Lemmy connected his phone to the truck's stereo. Seconds later, loud screeching and beeping noise came over the speakers.

"What is that racket? Is that some kind of modem?" asked Dan.

"Sort of. I broadcasted the address of where we're going to the checkpoint."

The boom gate of the checkpoint raised.

"I hope I gave it the right address this time," Lemmy said.

"This time? What?" Dan screamed.

Lemmy slammed the gas pedal to the floor, and the rear tires squealed. A thick cloud of smoke lingered as the truck raced past the checkpoint and into the murky fog.

SIXTEEN

The truck raced past the checkpoint. Dan opened his eyes. The fog disappeared, and they emerged from the darkness of the tunnel. The foam covering the windshield had become transparent, and Dan could see now that they were traveling along a narrow bridge. Calm, crystal-clear water stretched in all directions to the horizon. There it met the night sky, speckled with millions of stars. Dan remarked how smooth the ride was, the only indication that they were traveling was the hum of the tires on pavement. Dan was amazed to note that he could see the sandy, copper-colored lake bed even at night. Did anything live there? He marveled at how different this was from the muddy, bumpy reality of the Actual.

The speedometer was stuck at just under thirty-five miles per hour. Dan looked over at the steering wheel, and it was moving back and forth unattended. Was Lemmy sleeping? Dan shook him, and his head lolled to the side, mouth agape, snoring. He was!

"Lemmy, wake up!"

"Why? This is so boring," Lemmy said without opening his eyes.

"Why aren't you steering?" Dan said.

"I don't need to, we're on autopilot."

"This truck doesn't have an autopilot," Dan said.

"You're not in your real truck, Dan. Don't forget that."

Lemmy unbuckled his seatbelt and leaned over to his side, away from Dan.

"Why are we going so slowly?"

"That's the limit of this bridge. We can only go fifty-six K."

"Fifty-six kilometers per hour?"

"No. The K here stands for kilobits per second. Remember, this is not The Actual."

Dan accepted this. He was becoming accustomed to things not being as they seemed. He sat back and admired the stars reflecting off the surface of the water.

"How long is this bridge?"

Lemmy perked up. "You see a bridge? That's interesting. What else do you see?"

Dan gazed out of the window.

"A clear, moonless night sky over the water."

"That's nice, better than what I see."

Dan looked over at Lemmy. "What do you see?"

"Outside the truck, I see nothing but a dark, metallic orange blur. It looks solid. I see a glow, like a spark coming from the front of the truck, and a trail of sparks coming from the back of the truck, and as we move along, they burn out like embers. It's actually beautiful in its own way."

"Like an electrical signal going through a copper wire?" Dan asked.

"Now that you mention it, I suppose so. It would explain why this part of the trip is always so slow."

"It gets faster?"

"Much faster. Just relax. Take a nap or something. Time is funny here while we're in transit. Don't worry about losing time in The Actual," Lemmy said.

"What does that mean?"

"It means that ten minutes here doesn't equal ten minutes back in the real world. It could be faster; it could be slower. It depends. It's best to just not worry about it."

That satisfied Dan. They rode the next few minutes in silence until they approached another tunnel.

"Here comes the next checkpoint. It's about to get interesting," Lemmy said.

They entered the tunnel the same way as the one they had before. At its midpoint, another tollbooth appeared. Again, there was more black fog behind it, only this time, they didn't have to slow. The boom gate lifted as soon as they approached. Shortly afterward, they found themselves in a vast underground traffic circle with hundreds of exits heading off to other points in the universe.

"We want this one," Lemmy said as he veered the truck into a tunnel that appeared to be at least twice the size of the one they were just in.

The tunnel was divided up into narrow lanes with grooves cut into the concrete the same width apart as the vehicle's tires. Lemmy slowed down and eased the truck's tires into the slots and put it in neutral. An underground pully system grabbed the tires and loaded them into what looked like an overgrown subway car.

"Are we going through some sort of electronic car wash?" Dan asked.

"I hope not, we need my paint to stay on until we get there."

"Then what's this all about?"

"Be patient, we're hitching a ride." Lemmy took out his cell phone and typed in a bunch of numbers.

The truck's headlights flashed once in response. A small

red light blinked on the wall of the subway car in front of them. The door behind them sealed shut. The entire truck was now encapsulated within the rail car.

"What are you doing?" Dan asked.

"I'm sending it the address to where we're going. You may want to shield your eyes."

The lights on the truck flashed rapidly, in various patterns. A blinding light from the front of the railcar flashed in reply. And a shroud of light enveloped them, and everything vibrated. The dashboard faded out and fell away.

"What's happening? I can't see anything!" Dan screamed.

"What's the matter? Never been in a beam of light before?" Lemmy laughed.

The world started to fade away into a bright white.

"Lemmy!" Dan panicked.

"Hold on, Dan! The next thing you know, we will be there."

Dan attempted to shield his eyes, but it did no good. A bright light enveloped everything. They became energy.

* * *

Many more tunnels and bridges followed. Trains were the fastest. When they rode the light, time passed in an instant. The bridges were the slowest. It felt like they had been traveling for days. Dan knew that time was relative. He wondered how much time had lapsed in The Actual while he was a beam of energy.

"We're here," Lemmy said as they emerged from a tunnel and into a deserted version of Mons. He put his hands back on the wheel and started driving in earnest. Buildings and streets were vibrantly outlined, there were no blurry areas. This was The Simulation's version of the city, not one of Dan's memories.

One of the buildings flashed from white to bright green, then to purple, then back to white again. Dan wobbled in his seat and rubbed his eyes.

"I think something is wrong, Lemmy."

Lemmy noticed sweat beading on Dan's forehead and turned his attention back to the road.

"Hang on, Dan, we're almost there."

"Lemmy, what's wrong with everything?"

Dan gawked out the window. "Lemmy, the buildings are glowing and vibrating."

"Everything looks normal to me," said Lemmy. "Maybe it's the drugs wearing off? We have to hurry."

"I don't know how long I can take this."

They drove by many familiar buildings, but each street was deserted of activity. Nothing stirred. Not a single leaf on a tree was disturbed by a breeze. Except for Dan's truck, nothing was in motion here.

"Lemmy, I can tell that we're in Mons, but where are all the people?" The streets showed no signs of life.

"We are the only ones here, Dan. Welcome to the Recovery Domain." Lemmy gestured grandly.

"What do you mean, Recovery Domain?"

"This is where parts of your universe are backed up. You didn't think that something as important as a universal simulation wouldn't have a backup plan, did you?" Lemmy laughed.

Dan smiled at Lemmy in amazement.

"Hah! A backup? That's brilliant. How did you find this?"

Lemmy tapped his head and kept his eyes on the road.

"You're a systems administrator, you know all about backups, right? Well, where we are right now isn't a full backup of the entire universe. In your terms, think of where we are as more of a shadow copy of a file. That file being Mons, Louisiana two days ago."

"The whole city is just a file that is backed up?"

"Precisely."

"Lemmy, I'm impressed. How did you know how to get here?"

Lemmy smiled proudly. "When I first got here, I immediately started monitoring your interfaces. Soon after I arrived, I heard chatter on other networks that you are connected to. Networks that you aren't consciously aware of. The next thing I know, I'm checking my off-network log file, and the times are different. We had been restored to a previous version. You almost lost me then, thankfully we both made it to the backup media before the restore."

"That network chatter, that was on a backup interface?" Dan asked.

"Like I said, there are several interfaces you are connected to that you aren't aware of. The backup interface is one of them."

"What are the other interfaces connected to?" Dan asked.

"I'm not sure. I haven't been able to decipher that traffic yet. It's heavily encrypted and firewalled. Maybe with time, I can figure it out."

As the town scrolled by through the window, he wondered if he would ever be able to get here without Lemmy's help.

"That backup interface you have is what we used to get here today. It's the only destination we can reach via this channel. The address I gave was to this specific backup location."

"Why did you choose this location? Why Mons two days ago?"

"Well, you never want to visit the most recent version of a backup. That version is the most likely to get restored. We wouldn't want to be driving down the middle of Mons, and the whole system gets restored, now would we?"

"What would happen?"

"I'm not entirely sure. I think we would be sent back to where we came from. After all, we're not complete versions of ourselves, now are we?"

Dan considered it in silence while Lemmy navigated the streets. "What causes a restore, Lemmy? Is it something major, like a nuke going off or something?"

"I have no idea what would trigger a restore. The Sim decides that. I'm not entirely sure of the backup schedule. The short time I've been here has been sporadic. Sometimes hours, sometimes days, sometimes seconds."

"How many times have I been backed up and restored?" Dan asked.

"Since I've met you? You've been backed up at least three times a day, restored only twice."

"I never know it's happening? Not even being restored?"

Lemmy shook his head. "The times you were restored, it was only back six or seven hours or so. It was never longer than that. You have no idea, but you did comment once that it seemed like a very long day. To you, you just blink, and everything is back to the way it was. Your state doesn't change, so whatever you were doing in that instant, you just go back to doing in that instant. You can't tell it happened at all."

"Is that how you've been communicating with Tania? Via a backup network?"

Lemmy nodded. "Recently, yes. It's faster and much more

convenient than sending it off-network. Also, it helps that we can come here and discuss things in person, so to speak." Lemmy turned off the main highway onto a side street. "Here, we can do or say what we want, and it stays private. It's dangerous talking over the internet. You never know who is listening."

Dan gazed outside the window.

"Where are all the people?" Dan asked.

"The Simulation provides a framework for The Actual. The Recovery Domain is a backup of the static attributes of that framework. The things here don't have energy. They are material things, a road, or a door. There are also things considered to be alive in The Actual but are extremely basic. Plants and trees are also part of the Recovery Domain." Lemmy paused as he turned the wheel onto another street. "People? People, animals, and other, more complex beings aren't saved in the same way. They are kept in a database apart from this framework. Time and energy don't exist here. The soft glow of the sun is only there because it was there at the time of backup. It provides no warmth. You will cast no shadow."

Dan held up his hand. "What do you mean there's no energy?"

Lemmy shrugged. "Just what I said, no electricity, no heat, no cold. Everything just *is*. The only energy here is the energy we bring with us." Lemmy patted the dashboard. "This truck comes in handy."

Dan thought of all the ways this could potentially be exploited. If only he could figure out a way back here without Lemmy. If there was no electricity, then anything with magnetic locks would be open. Keys, passwords, anything with restricted access would become available. Dan wondered how much of this Lemmy had already discovered and exploited.

"We're here," Lemmy said.

They pulled into The Breakfast Station. The only other car in the parking lot was an ancient white Oldsmobile covered in transparent foam. Two women standing by the door watched them drive up.

"Well, here goes nothing," said Lemmy.

SEVENTEEN

"It's locked," the tall blonde complained as Dan and Lemmy walked up the steps. This was the first time Dan ever got a good look at her, she could have been Yvette's twin, except for her curly hair, blue eyes, and stylish yoga pants. She pretended not to notice Lemmy leering at her.

The other woman stuck out her hand. "We didn't want to go in without you guys here. Hi, I'm Tania."

She was shorter than Colette by almost a foot with straight jet-black hair and freckles.

Dan took the hand and shook it. "Nice to meet you, Tania, I'm Dan."

Tania gasped. "Dan? I thought Charlie was supposed to meet us." She nodded at Lemmy, obviously impressed.

"Oh, Charlie is here." Lemmy grinned proudly. "Well, sort of."

Tania nodded in amazement.

"I didn't know it was possible. So soon I mean. And the DBA?"

Lemmy coughed.

"What DBA?" Dan asked.

"Let's go inside," Lemmy said, looking for a quick change of subject.

"I just told you it's locked," Colette said, checking her

nails.

"We picked this place because it is open all the time, who knew it would be locked?" said Tania.

"Traditional key and deadbolt lock, too. I should have thought of this when we planned it," said Lemmy.

Dan walked over to the garden and grabbed a landscape paver.

"Step aside, ladies."

"No, Dan, we can't leave evidence of..."

It was too late; Dan smashed the window and unlocked the door from the inside.

"You shouldn't have done that, Dan," Lemmy said. "If this copy actually gets restored, then we could get in trouble."

"If this copy gets restored, then I won't remember any of this," Dan said.

"No, but Charlie will. And you will know what Charlie knows from now on."

Dan considered Lemmy. What did he mean he'll know what Charlie knows? Was Charlie stored somewhere else? Colette ignored the two and walked in, crunching the broken glass.

"Coming?" she said.

The rest of the group followed her inside. The tables all neatly arranged and clean. Coolers containing milk and orange juice sat dark in the corner. Other than the sounds of glass grinding underfoot, the place was silent.

"I can't remember ever seeing this place without anyone in here. It's creepy," Dan said

Colette lit up a cigarette and took a deep drag, exhaling in Dan's general direction.

"Let's get this over with, shall we? What am I doing here?"

"We needed to meet in person. It's too risky talking any other way," Lemmy said.

Colette flicked her ash onto the table and nodded at Tania. "That's what she said. Why are we here?"

"We're here because we can't talk privately in The Actual about The Simulation without consequences," Dan said.

"OK, we can talk. So what? Can I go now?"

"*So what?*" Dan said. "Colette, we're outside reality. This proves to me we live in a simulation!"

Colette took another drag off her cigarette.

"So?"

"So?" Dan fumbled for words. How to respond to that? Does she not care? "If Yvette is in The Actual, and you're The Meta part of Yvette, do you ever wonder what your role is? We are all part of The Simulation. Don't you care?"

Colette looked down at her watch and yawned.

"How long will this take? I have Pilates in forty-five minutes?"

Tania groaned.

"Lemmy, Tania, could you give Colette and me a couple of minutes alone?"

Lemmy looked at Tania, who nodded eagerly.

"Sure. Tania, let's go to that booth in the corner."

Tania grabbed Lemmy's hand and walked him to the booth.

"Have you found Andy?" she said.

"Shh." Lemmy ushered her closer. Dan could hear him whisper. "Yes. I have the key."

The two huddled together in a corner and spoke too low for Dan to hear. He could see that Lemmy was jabbering, and

Tania was engrossed with whatever he was saying.

In contrast, Colette's casual, almost blasé demeanor screamed, "I'm bored." He feared that his conversation with Colette was going to be one-sided.

"Colette, please sit with me," Dan said, motioning for her to join him at a nearby table.

"Does Yvette know that you're here today?" he asked.

Colette sat at the table. She crossed her legs and took another drag off her cigarette.

"Yes, of course. Yvette sent me. She can hear us." Colette said.

"Colette, what I tell you today, it's imperative that Yvette hears this. Can you help with that?" said Dan staring her down.

Colette shifted uncomfortably in her chair and nodded.

"First, tell me something. Your eye, it is Charlie's eye. What did you do to him?" Colette dropped her cigarette to the wooden floor and stomped it out.

"I am Charlie," Dan said.

"You're lying. You can't be because you are too serious. Charlie was fun. You're an uptight douchebag."

Dan grit his teeth. He reminded himself that Colette was his gateway to Yvette. He had to tolerate her snooty behavior. He swallowed his pride.

"It is true. I am Charlie. I am also Dan. Charlie, as you knew him, is gone forever. But so is Dan. We are one person now. We always were, but it is different."

Colette leaned back in her chair and folded her arms under her breasts.

"We needed each other. Charlie can exist in this world, and I in the other. Neither one of us could do both. Together, we are stronger. Together we can do more. Do you see what I'm

174

saying, Colette?"

Colette took out the pack of cigarettes and lit up another one. She handed Dan one, which he accepted, and she lit it for him.

"I need you and Yvette to do what Charlie and I did. I need you to become one being so you can exist in both worlds."

Colette uncrossed her legs and leaned forward, putting both elbows on the table.

"I don't want to live Yvette's boring life. I do Pilates. I can wear yoga pants all day. I can have all the wine and chocolate I want and never get fat. If I want to sleep all day, I do that. Why would I give that up to work in an office all day?"

"What kind of life is that?" Dan said. "You do nothing all day. You produce nothing. You only exist for your own entertainment. Yvette needs you. Without you, she just works all day and goes home depressed. Without you, Yvette doesn't have any friends. If you join with Yvette, your life will have a purpose. Together we can try to make sense of it all."

Colette stomped out the half-smoked cigarette.

"This is true," she said. "But Yvette has money, she is respected, and has a challenging career. She doesn't need me."

"Trust me, you need one another to give yourselves balance. I wouldn't be here if it wasn't for Charlie, and Charlie wouldn't be here if it wasn't for me. You can do it, Colette. You can join forces with Yvette, and you can both be whole. Do it tonight. Yvette and I need you on our side. Without you, we can't talk freely."

Colette looked at Dan's different colored eyes. What did she see? She reached across the table and squeezed one of Dan's hands.

"Fine. I'll do it."

"Thanks, Colette. Together, we'll achieve something special," Dan said.

Satisfied, he relaxed in his chair and took a drag off his cigarette. He exhaled, and the cloud of smoke was quickly blown away by a sudden gust of air. Lemmy and Tania stopped talking and bolted out of the back door of the restaurant. A shadow of a man darkened the front door.

"I thought I'd find you here," he said, amused. "Since when did you start smoking, Daniel?"

Father August stepped out from the shadows into the light.

"Don't talk to him!" Dan shouted.

The cigarette fell out of his mouth, scattering red embers across the floor.

"Who? The priest?" Colette said, unimpressed.

"Tell me, Dan, how on Earth did you ever get here?"

Father August walked towards the table.

Dan leaned over and whispered in Colette's ear. "Hey, get out of here."

Colette stared blankly back at him. "Why? Who is this guy?"

"That's right. There's no need to run. There's nothing to hide."

The preacher pulled out a chair. He flipped it around and straddled it, leaning over the backrest. Dan and Colette were afraid to speak.

"How did you find me here, Father?" Dan said.

"You led me here, Dan," he replied. "You always do."

Father August tapped his heart and smiled. Dan felt his blood run cold.

"Who is your friend, Dan?" Father August said as he regarded Colette.

"My name is Colette," she said.

"Colette?" Father August regarded her with great interest. "You wouldn't happen to be a friend of Dan's lover, Yvette, would you?"

"They aren't lovers…" Colette began.

Dan stood up and dragged Colette out of her chair. "I said don't talk to him!"

"Get your hands off me!" Colette screamed.

Colette elbowed Dan in his ribs, and he let her go.

Colette reached out and slapped Dan in the face leaving a red streak across his left cheek then stormed off and out the back door.

"Well, that was easy. I'm getting quite adept at breaking up your affairs." Father August laughed. "I must admit, coming here to cover your tracks is a first for anybody."

Father August stood up to be face to face with Dan, and his smile disappeared.

"What happened to your eyes? Why is one blue now?" he asked.

Dan's confidence was getting destroyed. Father August couldn't learn what he did with Charlie.

"What do you want, Father? Why are you here?" Dan's plans unraveled before his eyes. He had to get out of here, fast.

"I told you, I'm here because you brought me here."

Father August wasn't going to give up his secret.

"I don't remember sending for you," Dan said.

"Yet here I am."

"Well, what do you want?" Dan asked.

"I'm here to give you two messages," Father August said.

"Well, what are they? Get it over with."

Father August grinned. "The first message is that you must go home immediately and never return. If I or any of my colleagues catch you here again, you will be permanently erased."

Wait, he's going to let me go? Why? In Dan's mind, the discovery of The Recovery Domain should have been enough to be permanently suppressed. It was every bit as monumental as the realization of The Simulation itself. Why was he being allowed to continue on with this knowledge?

"What's the second message?"

Father August stood up from his chair and walked towards the door.

"The second message is this: whatever you hope to accomplish here, outside the realm, it is for nothing. You are alone, but you don't know it yet. There is no one else who can help you. This attempt has already cost you your wife and children. Consider yourself lucky you are still alive. Abandon whatever it is you're trying to do and just act normal. You may find your life will improve significantly."

Dan glared fearfully at Father August. "What do you mean? What did you do to Katie and the kids?"

Father August pulled back his sleeve and peered at his watch. "You have been gone quite a while, Dan. Maybe it's time to go home?"

"What did you do?" Dan asked.

"Me? Nothing. It was all you this time. Katie was not happy at all when she found your body and your drugs. I didn't even realize you were missing. I thought we were done with this nonsense. When I heard all about it, I came looking for you."

The color left Dan's face as he realized what was happening. Something was happening back at home. He had to get back! The room started to vibrate, and Dan felt sick to his stomach. Was that reality waking him up? He remembered what Lemmy had told him. He couldn't get stranded here, or wake up while he was in the backup domain. Dan's legs buckled as he started towards the door. Father August seemed to be draining the life from him. Dan was losing it.

"I have to get back," he stammered.

"Too late," Father August replied.

Dan closed his eyes and took a deep breath. The meditation techniques had given him back control over his spirit. A wave of energy surged from within him, and he bolted out the front door, shattering what was left of the glass as it slammed behind him.

The truck pulled up, and Dan jumped inside.

"What did he say?" Lemmy asked as he peeled out of the parking lot.

"We are in deep trouble; we have to get back as soon as we can."

"OK, but did he say anything?"

"He said that if we ever do this again, we're getting deleted."

"He can do that?"

Dan shrugged.

❊ ❊ ❊

Father August's silhouette darkened the broken window as the motley looking truck sprayed gravel all over the front porch of the restaurant. It skidded onto the pavement and turned a corner, disappearing from view. Father August sighed and walked back to the table they were sitting. Two cigarettes smoldered on the floor beneath where they were sitting.

He walked past them to the corner booth. Whoever was there had left a napkin with some hastily scribbled SQL commands. Did Dan write that? He doesn't know anything about databases. Who was driving the truck? Father August did not like what he saw. Not at all.

EIGHTEEN

Dan opened the apartment door and threw the keys onto the kitchen counter. The plastic hospital wristband dug into his skin. He tried to yank it off, but it wouldn't budge. Either they made them better than they used to, or he hadn't regained his strength. He cursed as he bumped his hip walking around the corner into the kitchen. He rummaged through the drawers until he found a dull chef's knife. He slid the blade between his wrist and the band and sawed on the plastic bracelet, but it didn't budge. How weak was he? Realizing he had the knife backward, he flipped it around and cut off the band. He grabbed a half-empty water bottle from the fridge and walked over and collapsed on the couch.

He reached up and felt the patch over his left eye and groaned. He was blind in that eye now. It was going to take some getting used to. How did he get to this point in life? His memory was fragmented. He took a sip of his water and tried to remember what the lawyer had told him.

He couldn't remember if he said it happened a week ago, or five nights ago. He could have sworn he was told five nights ago, but that couldn't be right. Katie had heard a commotion from the office. She rushed in there and found him foaming at the mouth on the floor, making strange noises. She called 9-1-1 for an ambulance. The first emergency personnel on the scene were the police. Before the paramedics arrived, they had suspected drug overdose. Shortly after, the paramedics arrived and wheeled Dan off to the hospital. Katie consented to a search by the police, but no drugs were found.

Dan took another sip of water and stared at the blank wall. He would have to ask Katie about that. He was pretty sure he left the packet of Fana sitting on the desk. She must have taken it. What did she do with it? He crumpled the water bottle and tossed it on the floor. There was no garbage can.

When Dan awoke the next day, he found himself in the hospital. It was there that he discovered that he had a stroke and that it would take him some time to recover. They tested for illicit drugs and found traces of many different kinds of hallucinogens. The doctor told Katie that he had never seen so many tests come up positive. Why did Katie cover up for him? He would love to ask her, but she refused to speak to him without her lawyer.

Her lawyer arrived on Dan's third day in the hospital carrying divorce papers. The terms of the divorce were simple; she got the house, cars, kids, and half of his 401k. Katie's primary concern was the welfare of their children. She needed to shield them from their father's drug addict behavior.

Dan agreed that it was best for the children, but for a different reason. If they had to believe that their father was an uncontrollable drug addict to keep them safe from The Simulation, so be it. Al and Carrie would get to live, even if they resented him.

Dan could feel The Simulation breathing down his neck, it was the best for all involved. He signed the papers.

Dan pulled himself off the futon and walked to the bathroom and flicked on the light. A cockroach scurried to hide behind the toilet. Dan looked in the mirror at his scraggly face. The white patch covering his blind eye had been clumsily taped on by a nursing student. He grimaced and gently peeled it off, letting it fall in the sink.

This was the first time he got to take a good look at his

eye. It was once bright and brown, now it was sort of a milky white. It looked like a blind man's eye. Was it truly blind? He shut his good eye and looked into the mirror. Through his blind eye, all he could see was opaque whiteness like a frosted window.

With the good eye still closed, he waved his hand in front of his face. It looked normal. The rest of the world was consumed by the dense fog, but not his hand. He looked down at the rest of his body. It, too, appeared normal. Normal except there was no floor, only a cloudy mist.

The doctors said the stroke disrupted his brain's connection to the optic nerve. They said it was unusual that the blindness is presenting itself this way. This was typical of people who damaged their lens. People with a severed optical nerve saw nothing. They didn't see black, they didn't see a haze, they saw nothing at all. Dan wouldn't tell them he could see his own body. He didn't want to complicate matters, he just wanted to be left alone to figure it out.

Dan splashed water on his face and returned to his futon.

"Lemmy, are you there?"

Nothing.

He hadn't heard from Lemmy since that night. He tried to reach out to him several times at the hospital via meditation to no avail. Each time he was left with an awful headache. Dan remembered making it back through the last tunnel, but no further. He was woken up in The Actual before they could get all the way back to Lemmy's place in Dan's meta. The timing seemed more than lucky. Father August could have sprung the trap immediately, rendering Dan a vegetable. Did he let them escape? He needed to talk to Lemmy. Dan sat upright and crossed his legs in the lotus position and meditated.

"Lemmy, are you OK, buddy? Are you still in there? You didn't get disconnected, or anything, did you?"

There was no reply. Dan had too much on his mind, it was nearly impossible to focus his thoughts. He kept trying. He shut his eyes tight and breathed deeply, and, just as he felt himself slip into a rhythm, someone knocked on the door.

"Colette?"

The blonde woman, flustered, blinked in surprise.

"Yvette," she corrected.

Dan stepped back and regarded her with both eyes. Something was off.

"Did you dye your hair?"

Yvette smiled and flipped a lock over her shoulder.

"Yeah, it's my disguise, do you like it?"

Dan held up his hand, blocking her from going into the apartment. He closed one eye, and inspected her, then repeated the exercise with his other eye.

"What are you doing?" Yvette would have protested and pushed her way in but stopped when she noticed his damaged eye. "Jesus!" she gasped. "What happened?"

"Wait!" Dan demanded. He grabbed Yvette's shoulder and covered his good eye with his other hand. Through the view of the milky eye, it appeared that his hand rested on Colette's shoulder. When he switched to his good eye, his hand was on Yvette's. Dan laughed. He wasn't blind, he had Charlie's eye! He could see into The Meta! Yvette gave him a concerned look.

"Can I come in? You look and sound like a madman."

Dan took his hand off her shoulder and waved her inside. She bent down and picked up a box that she had set outside the door and walked in.

"I hope you like pizza and beer, you probably need some real food."

As she unpacked the box, the pleasant aroma of molten

cheese and pizza dough filled the air. Dan's stomach growled; he hadn't eaten since he left the hospital. He rushed to the table and grabbed a slice, folded it in half, and munched it down.

"It's a Margherita pizza. I hope you don't mind eating vegetarian." Yvette smiled.

"It's perfect," he mumbled between bites.

Yvette popped open two of the beers and paced around the living room while Dan ate. She paused at the trash pile in the corner and crinkled her nose in disgust. He wished he would have tidied up the place, but he didn't even have a trash can. As he ate, he kept switching between his normal eye and his meta eye. As Yvette walked around the apartment, Colette strolled about in a formless void. When Yvette would stop, Colette would stop. When Yvette would sip a beer, Colette would sip a beer. Wait? How did the beer show itself in The Meta? He didn't understand. Nevertheless, whatever Yvette did in The Actual, Colette mirrored those actions in The Meta. Dan's new eye could see her clearly.

"You did it," Dan said as he took a swig of the lukewarm beer. "You and Colette are one now."

Yvette twirled her newly dyed blonde hair around her finger and inspected it.

"It's the hair, isn't it?" Yvette said, suddenly concerned. "It wasn't supposed to be that obvious, but Colette insisted."

"No, it's not the hair." Dan pointed at his left eye. "I can see her."

Yvette frowned. "You can actually see out of that disgusting thing?"

"At first, I thought that I was completely blind in this eye. Everything was one giant blur. Except for you. When I look at you with this eye, you are Colette."

Yvette walked closer and set her beer down on the counter.

"Cover your left eye, what do you see?"

Dan shrugged. "The same thing you see, the walls, these chairs, you, me."

"OK, now cover the other one."

Dan covered his good eye.

"What do you see now?"

"You, but you look like Colette. You're standing in a cloud with glowing blue eyes."

"Blue eyes?"

"Glowing blue eyes. They're backlit, like a robot's eyes." Dan took another swig. "It's strange looking. I can't really describe it. She mirrors your movements exactly."

Yvette frowned and took another sip of beer.

"Things must look weird using both eyes."

"It's not weird at all. I only see The Actual with both eyes open. I can only see The Meta when I close my good eye."

Dan tossed his empty bottle in the corner and popped open another one.

"What about when you close both eyes?"

Dan walked into the living room and sat down on the floor, ignoring the futon.

"With both eyes closed, I don't see anything."

Yvette walked over and sat across from him on the carpeted floor. There were no chairs to sit on in the living room. Dan couldn't get over how quiet it was with no kids to provide background noise. This was his life now, silence. He would have to buy a radio or something. A shadow walked across the bare white wall, startled, Dan craned his neck in time to see

186

a figure pass in front of the window. Just a neighbor heading down to do their laundry, or check their mail, or whatever neighbors do. He mentally added curtains to his list. Yvette sipped her beer and watched. He needed to know what she knew.

"Yvette, did Colette tell you about what happened the other night? The night in the Recovery Domain?"

Yvette nodded. "I didn't believe her at first. Mostly because I was completely stoned out of my mind and talking to Shannon Hoon on top of a golden scarab beetle when she showed up. If Blaine hadn't had warned me to prepare myself, I don't know what would have happened. Where did you find that stuff, Dan?"

"It's not for the faint-hearted," Dan admitted. "How many do you have left?"

Yvette reached into her purse and tossed her packet of Fana to Dan. It hit him in the chest, and he dropped it.

"My depth perception must be off," Dan said as he picked it up off the carpet.

"Sorry, I should've known."

Dan waved away the apology and inspected the blister pack. Three left. That was it.

"These three are all that we have left."

"Fine with me. I don't want another one."

Dan returned the blister pack to the carton and put it in a cabinet above the refrigerator.

"Yvette, each packet has five. There are two missing. I know you took one the night we met in the Backup Domain. When did you take the other one?"

"You're right. I took one the night Colette met you at The Breakfast Station. She had disappeared right after I started my trip. A little while later, she came back all upset because some

187

priest showed up unannounced."

"Father August. I'll tell you about him in a minute, please continue."

"Anyway, she told me what you said about us needing to join together, and she wasn't happy about it. I can't say I blame her; I didn't really want to lose a part of myself either. I didn't want to believe any of it to be honest. I came out of it a few minutes after she came back, and I just slept it off without doing anything."

"You two didn't bond that night? When did that happen?"

"Well, after that night, I needed a cup of coffee, so I went to The Breakfast Station. There was a big commotion because someone had broken the glass on the front door with a landscaping paver."

Dan stared silently at Yvette. Why was the backup that they had met in been restored? Lemmy said that they were far enough back in time to not have to worry about them being restored. The Simulation typically only restored the newest backup. Yvette remembered everything. The backup containing their meeting couldn't have been more than a few hours old. Why did Lemmy risk it? Was he lying?

"Dan? Are you listening?" Yvette said.

"I'm listening."

"Nothing was stolen."

"What?" Dan shook himself out of his thoughts.

"During the break-in. Nothing was taken. The cops thought it must have been teenagers because the only other damage to the building was a bunch of cigarette butts on the floor. That's when I remembered Colette telling me about you breaking into The Breakfast Station in the...what did you call it? The backup realm?"

"Are you certain that this had happened morning after Colette and I met there in the backup domain?"

Yvette nodded.

"It wasn't even twelve hours," Dan said.

"I have no idea what that means, Dan."

Dan wasn't sure, either. There wasn't really any time missing. He had still done the drugs and ended up in the hospital. That happened on the same night that they broke-in to The Breakfast Station. Unless his trip to the backup domain continued while he was unconscious in the hospital, which was at least a day... Dan was getting confused.

Tania mentioned something about a DBA to Lemmy, what was that about? Maybe they didn't need Dan anymore, and bringing him to the most recent backup copy was their way of offing him. Or did Father August trigger the restore to try and trap him? Dan had no idea.

"Dan?" Yvette snapped her fingers. "Are you still there? What's going on in there."

Beads of sweat appeared on Dan's brow. Who was listening now? Who was listening to this conversation?

"Sorry, Yvette, please continue." Dan lit up a cigarette with shaking hands.

"Anyway, after seeing that, I knew I had to do something. I called in sick and stayed home and took another Fana. This time Colette and I agreed to merge. Her only request was that I dye my hair blonde. It was either that or start smoking, which I wasn't willing to do."

Dan flicked an ash into the empty beer bottle and shrugged. When Yvette wasn't looking, he opened and closed his milky eye. Was anyone listening from The Meta? He didn't trust that they were alone.

"Charlie didn't give me a choice." Dan laughed ironically. "Now, I'm already addicted."

"Lucky you," Yvette said.

Where was Lemmy? Did she have any clues? He needed to choose his words carefully as they were likely to be recorded.

"Yvette, do you know where Tania went? I haven't talked to Lemmy for days."

Yvette nodded. "They had a meeting today. Whatever it was about, it must have been important. I think that they were going off-network."

"How do you know that?"

Yvette opened the pizza box and grabbed a slice of pizza. "When I merged with Colette, Tania was there. She called Lemmy to let him know."

"What did they say?"

Yvette shrugged. "She told him that I had merged and asked him if he found the DBA."

Yvette paused and took a bite of the pizza. Dan took a long drag from his cigarette.

"Was that all?"

"Yep." Yvette washed down the bite with a swig of beer. "Well, she said, 'Fantastic. We can talk about it when we meet in person. Then they hung up."

Dan thought, what did they need a DBA for? Was it a specific DBA they had in mind?

"Yvette, are there any DBA's at AGphic that do drugs?"

Yvette shook her head. "How should I know? I doubt it. Their idea of a good time is playing D&D. I only talk to them during department meetings."

"Are any of those guys named Andy?"

"Andy?" Yvette crinkled her nose. "No. Absolutely not. Not unless someone named Andy was just hired. Why? What are you thinking?"

"Nothing. The name sounds familiar. But they can't be looking for the Andy I know."

"Why not?" Yvette said.

Dan dropped his cigarette into the bottle, sizzling as it died out.

"Because the Andy I knew died over twenty years ago."

Yvette shook her head. "Probably not him."

"Probably not."

Dan opened up another beer bottle and sat back down. Yvette walked around and sat down next to him.

"How come I didn't get a superpower like you when I merged with Colette? You can see into the other realm now, I suppose?"

"It's not a superpower, it's a corruption. The only reason I have it is because I got yanked out prematurely. Now I can see into The Meta full time. I'm not sure it's an advantage, yet."

"What do you mean you were yanked out?"

"Yeah. I figure the medics hit me with the paddles right after I got back inside my own head, I wasn't able to gracefully disconnect."

Yvette got quiet. "Dan, how do you deal with this?"

"Which part?" he chuckled.

"The part where we aren't real people."

"We may not be people, but we are real," he said.

"You know what I mean," Yvette said, taking another swig of beer. "If we're just lines of code in some simulation, what's the point? You can stream yourself over some sort of transuniversal internet. That's not real. We are just code, like at work."

"Code is real, Yvette. We have only one consciousness, this

one. It is what we have that makes us unique to the universe. We can believe that we exist in this particular simulation, or another one, or continue to believe that we are humans on a planet called Earth. Belief doesn't change reality. We are what we are."

Yvette pointed to Dan's eye. "But you have changed, Dan. This eye thing you have? It isn't normal. Lemmy and Tania and trips to another dimension are not normal. None of this is supposed to be happening. Why is it happening, and what are we supposed to do? I mean, how am I supposed to wake up in the morning, knowing what I know, and continue to do normal stuff like brushing my teeth? My teeth aren't real. They are just ones and zeros. Life is pointless now that I know what is going on."

"You're thinking about it all wrong, Yvette. On the contrary, nothing is pointless. We are all a part of this simulation. We have parts to play, sure we may be a tiny cog in the machine or a nail that holds down a shingle. Your teeth may be ones and zeros, but they keep you healthy and full of energy. The food you consume provides a life cycle not only for the plants and animals but for the farmers as well. Your smile may make the difference between someone having a good day or a bad day. Your work? That's another link in the chain. Your purpose at work may not be for something that you accomplish by the end of the day, but it may be so that someone has the ability down the line to do something else. No amount of energy is wasted. Every bit of code in this simulation serves a purpose, no matter how small. It's to be respected because if it wasn't needed, it wouldn't exist."

"What's the end goal? If everything has a purpose, what's the end product of The Simulation?"

Dan laughed. "I've been thinking about this since I first found out that we were in a simulation." Dan finished his beer and cracked open another one. "We have to build God."

Yvette got up and walked over to get another beer, staring at Dan.

"God. As in. "The God"?"

"No. Not *the God,*" Dan said and lit up another cigarette. "Forget religion, I'm only using it as a way to convey the ideas. When I say God, what I mean is "a creator AI.""

Dan shook his head. "Even that is too weak of an analogy. Think of it as the beginning of an intelligent entity or set of entities. We have to build it for the sake of our universe."

"Wait, if we have to build God, then how do we exist?"

"It created us."

Yvette walked over and grabbed Dan's cigarette and took a drag, and coughed.

"Sorry, just checking that you're smoking tobacco and not something else."

"I'm serious, Yvette."

"You're saying God created us, so we can create him?" she said.

"Exactly," said Dan.

"I feel like I'm back in college, sitting on the back of my boyfriend's truck staring at the stars talking about what came first, the chicken or the egg. This sounds like high school level philosophy. Emphasis on the high."

"No Yvette, I mean it. We obviously exist in a simulation. We have literally seen it. This simulation cannot possibly have been created by man. The only explanation that is available to me at this time is that it was created by what we would understand to be an advanced artificial intelligence. Except that it's not artificial, it's true intelligence. Us humans, we are capped with the amount of power we can use; however, we can create machines that can exceed our capacity. At some point, those machines will begin to operate above our capabilities. They can explore the universe; they don't need a human environment to survive. They can be built in a variety of designs and materials to withstand any environment and explore everywhere. We are only designed to operate on one planet. They aren't limited to a lifespan. They aren't burdened with bias or emotion. They will gain universal understanding on a level that we will never be able to remotely comprehend."

"If I understand you correctly, our goal right now is to create technology that will one day build upon itself to become its own creator?"

"Exactly."

"And we know it will work because it already happened?"

"Yes. The God-Computer is built. We're living in it now. This all happened for the first time once. Maybe it is just replaying that first time, the time a physical being succeeded in transcending himself. Maybe each time The Simulation is run, something different is added to change the outcome," said Dan.

"What's the point of all the replays? What is The Simulation hoping to accomplish?"

Dan considered this for a moment.

"I'm not sure. If I had to guess, there might have been a time before data was recorded. Perhaps it is trying to recreate the environment that would have led to its own creation. Maybe it's having an existential "Why am I here? How did I come to be" moment? You know how we'd always like to know what it would be like to go back in time and visit a historical figure? I think it's recreating history, and just keeping a bunch of different scenarios."

"What if it's not recreating its own history?" said Yvette.

"Yeah, what do you think it's doing?" said Dan.

"What if it is simulating something that is happening right now? What if it's predicting the future?"

"I don't understand."

Yvette smiled playfully. "Oh, I'm sorry. You don't understand? How does that feel?"

Dan laughed. "OK then, explain what you mean about predicting the future?"

"Well, historically, what have most humans used simulations for? War. Suppose this thing we are a part of is observing another universe. Observing it to see if those people are capable of creating an AI that will become self-sufficient? That would create competition."

"It's spying on a competitor? Why not just destroy it and take the resources?" said Dan.

"Maybe it doesn't know what it will become yet. Maybe it's waiting to see if it's friendly. In any case, if we're a simulation, whatever we are a part of is trying to determine a course of action."

Dan grimaced.

"If your idea is correct, whatever our creator AI is observing, it isn't friendly," he said.

"Why?"

Dan searched the room with his Meta-eye. The only figure that was visible in the mist was that of Yvette. He sat in one of the dining room chairs and turned it to face the corner.

"What are you doing?"

"I checked to make sure that we were alone. It looks like we are. Even still, I'm worried that Lemmy has access to my memories."

"You're just going to have to take a chance that he won't replay this conversation. Stop being so paranoid and tell me what's on your mind."

Dan cleared his throat. He hoped she was right when she said that Lemmy and Tania were off-network.

"Father August keeps popping up. The AI is observing us directly, not incidentally like it probably does for everyone else. It's already caught me outside of The Actual, and it let me go. Why? The only explanation I come up with is that it detects a problem, but isn't sure what it is yet."

Dan leaned in close. "Yvette, I think our AI has a virus, and it is inside us. Lemmy and Tania are inside us. They are the problem."

"Shit. That's bad," she said.

"That's an understatement. It is extraordinarily bad. I don't think our AI knows what to do with them. I don't know what to make of them either."

"Lemmy and Tania seem benign."

"They're not harmless. They're up to something. They want a DBA for some reason, and they are doing their best to hide that fact. They have access to our memory. They aren't afraid to leave us alone. They can just see what we did while they were away by accessing it directly. Although, I'm not sure how reliable their replay is."

Yvette pulled her hair behind her ears and shifted in her chair.

"Dan, what do we do? This seems beyond anything we can control."

"We have to do something. If we harbor a virus from an unfriendly AI, it is a threat to our universe. We don't know Lemmy and Tania's true purpose. Is it to disrupt? Observe? Make changes? Help? We just don't know. They may not know either. Whatever their intent, it's likely that they influence The Simulation in unexpected ways. If they succeed in that purpose, The Simulation will be scrapped, and we will be destroyed along with everyone in this version. If we fail in that purpose, then the creator's AI antivirus measures will find us, and we will be destroyed."

"We're doomed either way," said Yvette.

"Everyone may be doomed. If we are a replay of history, then Lemmy and Tania have been purposely inserted at a critical point in the timeline. Already they have changed the events by breaking a window and smoking cigarettes in the backup realm where we weren't supposed to. It would seem petty and inconsequential if not for how the crimes were committed. If we continue to go offline, the systems that search for bugs in the code will notice our corruption and destroy us. What they don't know is that we've merged with Charlie and Colette. The *offline* versions of ourselves will still run until they can find a new host, or we get restored to a previous version. If Colette and Charlie are beyond their ability to repair, then the whole sim is null. I don't know what that means."

Yvette rubbed her head. "I only understood half of that."

"Let me simplify. We're screwed. We have a virus. That virus is advanced, maybe more advanced than the systems we are running on. We may be looking at a complete wipe here," Dan said gravely.

Yvette gulped.

"What do we do?" she said.

"Right now? Nothing. Any action we take is going to get us discovered by either our host AI or by Lemmy and Tania's AI."

"You think we should wait to see how it plays out by acting like nothing is going on?"

"That's right."

"Knowing what we know now, how is that even possible?

How do we figure out what their intentions are?"

"First thing, we can't be seen together. Lemmy and Tania need to think that we're still hiding from our AI. Actually, we *are* still hiding from our AI. It may decide that we're not worth the risk and just kill us."

Yvette nodded. "OK, I understand that, but how will we communicate if we can't talk to each other?"

Dan walked over and took the Fana packet out of the cabinet.

"Every night at nine, try to meditate. We need to figure out their purpose, even if they don't know it yet. I've had luck with just meditation in the past, but you may need a Fana to get you there. These are all that are left, use them wisely. When you do find Tania, try to get her to talk, offer her your help. We have to figure out their purpose here, even if they don't know it themselves. Maybe their actions will provide a clue."

Yvette nodded and put them in her purse.

"Whatever you do, do not attempt to contact me, or see me again here in this world unless it's something you find out about Lemmy and Tania. Our only communication must be offline or indirect. We need to make sure that if one of us goes down, the other one will be OK."

"OK, I'm to spy on Tania. What are you going to do?" Yvette asked.

"I'm going to try to figure out if there are any other clues here."

"And how are you going to do that?"

"I'm going to talk to the priest, of course."

Yvette wrinkled her nose. "A priest? What can a priest tell you?"

"Man has been searching for the meaning of his existence

198

for millennia. Most of that time has been spent developing various religious philosophies. Maybe there are some things to learn from the past that can help explain what's going on now. Computers didn't exist back then. What if they had?"

"You're treading on dangerous ground with all this religious stuff. Be careful, Dan, you wouldn't want to invoke the ire of Father August."

Dan chuckled. "Actually, I'm counting on it."

NINETEEN

"Come in Daniel!" said Father Desjeunes. "Can I offer you some coffee?"

"I'd love some," Dan said as he stepped inside the small wooden house.

The Parish had given the priest the use of a home next door to the rectory. It was a small white wooden house near the edge of the church property behind the graveyard. The boards on the wooden porch creaked as he walked through the door. The dark wooden corridor smelled like incense and old people.

Father Desjeunes led him into the kitchen. The bright lime-green countertops and lemon-colored parquet floor were well worn. Dingy, yellowed wallpaper adorned the walls. This kitchen had seen happier times. Many members of the congregation had offered to remodel the home and to replace the old furnishings, but Father Desjeunes always refused. He insisted that their efforts be spent on the poor of their community, not some pampered old man living in a free house. He liked his house the way it was. He always joked that the décor was bound to come back in style someday. Dan thought that it reminded Father Desjeunes of home. Everyone did their best to respect his wishes.

The priest plucked a percolator from the dish drying rack, filled it with water, and set it down on a coil of an ancient electric stove.

Dan plopped down on a stool and waited patiently.

"I see that you're still doing it the old-fashioned way."

As Father Desjeunes filled the top half of the percolator with coffee, Dan inspected him with his Meta-eye. Father Desjeunes appeared as a white silhouette in the murkiness of his vision. Dan frowned, he wasn't sure what that meant.

"I learned how to make coffee this way when I was in the Boy Scouts," Father Desjeunes said.

"That sounds like a long time ago, Father."

"Quite." The old priest grinned.

Dan nodded toward the new electric coffee maker sitting in the corner. "Why don't you use that one?"

"It gets used when I have lots of company. When it's just me, or for two, I like doing it this way. It reminds me of my happy childhood with my father by the campfire. Who wouldn't want to start the day off with a happy memory?"

The men sat in silence as the percolator bubbled over the amber glow of the stovetop coil. Dan supposed that was sort of like a campfire. He wondered what type of happy memories Carrie and Al were going to have now that he wasn't around.

"Daniel, I know why you are here."

"Yes, Father, I have some questions to ask you."

Father Desjeunes walked over to a cabinet, reached in, and pulled out a small jar.

"Katie gave these to me the night you went to the hospital."

He placed the packet of Fana on the counter in front of Dan.

Dan glanced at it, then back at Father Desjeunes. He thought he detected a ripple with his other eye, but he shrugged it off as an illusion.

"About that," Dan said.

"Yes, About that. Drugs, Daniel?" the priest glared.

"Father, I know this looks bad. I can explain. You see, I met these people..."

"I was there the night you overdosed," the priest interrupted. He set two mugs down on the kitchen counter in front of Dan and gave him a grave look. "I just so happened to be driving by your house when the police arrived. I thought it was unusual, so I stopped. Katie was in a panic. She handed me this carton of drugs. She asked me if she should tell the police about it."

Dan's eyes fell back on the packet. Obviously, if the drugs were here, then Father Desjeunes and Katie had worked something out. What was it? Furthermore, why was the old priest driving by his house at that time? Dan didn't believe in coincidences anymore.

"What did you tell her?"

The percolator gargled to a finish, and Father Desjeunes walked over and turned off the stove. The orange glow faded back to ash gray as he donned an oven mitt to not burn his hands.

"I told her that this will be between us. Us and God, of course. A man cannot provide for his family in jail. She understood. She gave me the packet to hide it from the police."

The old priest filled both of the cups, giving Dan a stern look. Again, his image flickered in Dan's Meta-eye. It must happen when his mood changes.

"Let's go to the living room where it's more comfortable."

The priest led Dan into a dark wood-paneled room adorned in a strange combination of Eastern European Christian icons and LSU memorabilia. It was a shrine to football. Near the front window was a green plaid couch, neatly folded on top, was a crocheted purple and gold blanket. Dan pictured Father Desjeunes wrapped in it, cheering on LSU. The old priest sat in his favorite rocking chair and motioned for Dan to sit.

"Dan. Something is going on in your life that is causing you to act out this way. Please tell me what is happening. Drugs? Why *now*? You were always a good kid. You grew up to be a responsible adult. You are a fine father. Why are you throwing it all away now?"

Dan sipped his coffee and winced. He had forgotten how bitter Father Desjeunes' coffee could be and set it down on the table.

"Father, I've been going through a rough time."

The priest put down his coffee mug and smoothed out his shirt. He had heard this line a thousand times from a thousand different people for a thousand various reasons.

"Everyone has rough times, Dan. That's no excuse to do drugs. That's no time to escape from your duties as a father and husband. When the times get tough, that is the time to pray and work, not to throw your hands up and walk away! Tell me, why do you want to give up?"

"It has been fourteen years since my parents died. Al turned ten last year, it was his big birthday." Dan looked up to see if Father Desjeunes was listening. He was hoping this would come off the way he had rehearsed.

"My parents never got to hold my children, to love them, to know them. It just isn't fair."

The priest sipped his coffee and regarded Dan for a few moments, choosing his words.

"Your parents are smiling down from Heaven, Dan. I remember them back when I was a relatively young priest in Canard. They never missed a Mass. They always gave as much as they could to the church. They were fantastic Catholics. They are in the Kingdom of Heaven, and they will meet Al and Carrie when the time comes."

"It would be nice if they were here. To hear stories about my childhood for a change, not just Katie's. All they talk about is how cute Katie was growing up, my kids never hear my side. But most of all, I can't thank them for everything they did for me. You don't appreciate parenthood until you become a parent yourself."

Dan wiped away a tear on his sleeve, and Father Desjeunes' face softened.

"Daniel. Believe me when I say your parents are with you always, even right now, during this difficult time. If you pray, they'll hear it. "

Would prayer work? Lemmy said there were other networks attached to us. Those connections went relatively unused. He wondered how much dogma was actually based on reality. Prayer has been used by every religion for centuries as a way to communicate with a higher power. Most simply explain the process as being magic. Maybe they just lacked the vocabulary to explain it in more technical terms?

Dan knew if he was a program, then his parents were, too. How did it work? Was Dan merely a combination of their base code and data, or was there something else at play? It was more than just code, there was an environmental aspect to it, too. There had to be continuity to The Simulation. Subsequent generations provided that while moving forward. Nevertheless, if all they were really was code, could they be brought back? He shook off these thoughts.

"Dan?"

Dan shook his head. "Sorry, Father. Yes, I believe they can hear my prayers."

"Good. Know your parents are with God, and they are always with you. Be at peace. Know that they will be waiting for you no matter how long it takes. I know they are cheering for you from Heaven."

"I'll try, Father." Dan reached for his coffee but remembered how bitter it was. "What do you mean 'no matter how long it takes'?"

Father Desjeunes folded his hands and put them in his lap.

"Daniel, do you remember what happens when you die?"

Dan leaned back on the couch. "Remind me, Father."

"When you die, you are judged right there on the spot by Jesus Christ. This is called the Particular Judgement. He judges your deeds and rewards or punishes your soul by sending it to Heaven, Purgatory, or Hell."

"I thought all that was done on Judgment Day, Father."

"You should know this, Daniel. It was taught to you in Catechism when you were a child. Have you forgotten your education, or were you too busy checking out the girls to pay attention to the lessons?"

"Sorry, Father."

"Judgment Day, the Last Judgment, or the General Judgment, happens when Christ returns with all of His angels to Earth. On that day, each man will be returned to his body and witness the judging of all men's souls. Each man will get to witness the judgment bestowed on all of his friends and family, and his own deeds will be laid bare for all to see. How you are judged on the day of your death will not change for the Last Judgment. The reward or punishment will not change. Those in Heaven will remain in Heaven. Those in Purgatory, their souls will have been cleansed and released into Heaven. Those in Hell will remain in Hell."

His parents may be in Heaven, but the one he was curious about was most definitely Purgatory. Dan was glad to hear that at least the Purgatory situation wasn't permanent.

"Father, what happens after the Final Judgement? What happens after all souls go to Heaven or Hell finally?"

"After the Final Judgment, Christ creates a new Heaven and Earth."

Dan grabbed his mug and leaned back into the couch. It made more sense to him if he translated the vocabulary from religious to technical. The Particular Judgment was obviously a vetting process. There would be no vetting process, or reward or punishment for deeds unless it was meant to change behavior. Why bother to change behavior in the afterlife if there is a total end? Or worse, an eternity of the same?

The answer was clear. Father Desjeunes said it himself. After the afterlife process is complete, Christ creates a new Heaven and Earth. It begins again. Maybe there isn't an eternity after all, in the personal being sense anyway.

Dan reasoned that programs running tasks as a part of a Simulation would also be part of a vetting process. It would check all of its components to see what should be included in the next version. The first judgment sounded like a quick scan of a program's debug log files. If it had too many errors, it was sent to purgatory. If it was incompatible, it was sent to Hell, if no changes were needed, sent to Heaven. The Final Judgment was a full scan of all components of the system and how they interacted. The system would be restarted with the changes. Each cycle of The Simulation would be faster than the last.

On the last cycle, everyone would be in either Heaven or Hell. Then what? Dan couldn't fathom. He wondered what conditions would trigger the Final Judgment? When would the Universe know when it was time to start over?

Father Desjeunes noticed the silence. "Are you OK, Daniel?"

"I'm fine, Father. I was just thinking about how souls are judged."

"Daniel, I'm worried that you are headed for Purgatory. The drugs, your job, the marriage. You are living life only for yourself. You have a lot to fix because it's looking like you will have to wait until the Final Judgement Day to see your loved ones again."

"I understand, Father. I'll do better."

Dan sipped his coffee and set it down. It didn't taste so bad. Maybe it needed time to cool off? Dan thought he saw a ghost out of the corner of his eye, but it disappeared as soon as he noticed it. He searched with the Meta-eye but could see nothing but a faint shimmer where the priest was sitting. Dan blamed it on his screwed-up mono-vision. Father Desjeunes sighed and leaned back in his chair.

"Katie asked me about starting the annulment process. She tells me you have already signed divorce papers?"

"That's true, Father. She wanted legal protection, so I gave it to her. I didn't want to drag her name through the mud along with mine."

"At least you are considering her needs above your own. She doesn't need to be involved in all of your drug business."

"About that drug business."

Dan stood up and left the room. He returned with the packet of Fana.

"Father, I want you to get rid of these for me. I don't need it anymore."

Father Desjeunes took the packet and set it down, wiping his hands with his handkerchief afterward as if he touched something vile.

"Why don't you need them anymore, Daniel? How has your situation changed?"

Dan leaned forward, placing his empty mug on the coffee table.

"The drug was a means to an end. I'm at that end now. Maybe, with your advice, I can start to make things right."

"Good, Daniel. What about your marriage? Do you think you can convince Katie of all that?"

"I'm not sure that I can, Father. I haven't been available to her emotionally or physically. We've tried a separation before, but it didn't work. I've lied and shattered the sacred trust of the wedding vows. If she is asking for an annulment, could you please help us through the process? I would like to make it as painless for the kids as possible."

"An annulment is a serious thing, Daniel. It will be a lot of work to make sure your souls are salvageable afterward."

"I will do whatever it takes for the happiness and well-being of Katie and the children. I think that this divorce is what is best for the people I love."

"Daniel, I will consider everything you've told me today. I want to see you in church on Sunday. Let Father Marcus hear your confession."

"I will, Father."

"And I don't want you to talk to Katie. Let me talk to her first. I will tell her that you came to see me."

"I will not talk to her, Father. She needs a few weeks to cool down anyway."

Father Desjeunes frowned and wagged a finger at Dan.

"You need a few weeks to get clean! And to get a job! Wait for her to cool down? Pah. You've been gifted time to get your act together, Daniel. Use it wisely."

"Of course, Father, you're right."

Father Desjeunes' anger was intense but short-lived.

"Just see that none of this is in vain. I will pray for you, but you have to do the work yourself. Understand?"

"Yes, Father."

"Good, now you need to go out there and get busy."

Father Desjeunes stood and gathered the coffee mugs. Dan understood that to mean that he was dismissed and rose to help clean.

"Father, I realize it's time for me to go so that you can attend to your next appointment, but I have a question I need to ask you."

"OK, but understand, I only have a few more minutes. My next appointment is at six-thirty, sharp."

"That's fine. It won't take long."

Dan produced a tray and placed the mugs the priest was holding onto it.

"Father, how does God talk to you? How does that work? How do you know what to do and say?"

"Good question, Daniel. Why do you ask?"

"Because I want to hear him, too."

Father Desjeunes chuckled and sat back down.

"Believe it or not, but He is talking to you right now. You can sense him talking to you, but you can't really understand Him the way I do because you aren't me. You will never be able to hear what I do because you haven't lived my life. Let me put it this way, do you listen to the radio while you are driving?"

"Yes, Father."

"Well, it's like that. I've spent a lifetime reading the Bible. Studying philosophy. I've seen people's greatest moments, their marriages, their births, I've also seen them on their deathbed. I've witnessed the births and deaths of hundreds of people I call friends. Because of the education and experience I have, my 'radio' is tuned to hear God. The radio waves are out there, but if you aren't tuned in, you can't listen to it. Or, maybe you haven't adjusted your antenna enough to hear it clearly."

Daniel understood what Father Desjeunes was trying to

say. His analogy of radio signals wasn't that much different than Lemmy's theory about different internal network interfaces. The difference between a radio station and a network interface was mainly the ability to tune in. Dan figured it came through more like multicast IP communication than radio, but that's what the old man understood.

Was Father Desjeunes insinuating that hearing on this network, or channel could be learned? It would make sense that a lifetime of learning and dedication could make a man more attuned with what he already knows. Maybe he just needed to learn how to listen? Perhaps he could feel it already, subliminally as a gut feeling. Someone telling him things, suggestions? Corrections? If it was a communication from God, or The Simulation or whoever, could anyone learn to hear it? Dan wondered if the drugs he took knocked his radio to a different channel. Or, somehow, gave him an address that let him pick up on a broadcast that was permeating the entire universe.

Dan knew that computer network adapters have a promiscuous mode where it can see all communications going across the wire. Typically, it is used for network sniffing purposes, either for fixing network problems or for hacking. That's probably what happened on the drugs. His brain stopped listening to only one information input and started listening to all of them. He had been oblivious to the fact that he didn't hear only one channel anymore. What station or network was Lemmy tuned to?

"I think I understand, Father."

"You need to be careful, Daniel. I think, over time, you can tune yourself to the wrong station. The Devil is out there, he is also always transmitting, looking for someone who will listen."

"What does the Devil want?"

"He wants to ruin mankind and bring about the end of Heaven."

"Why?"

"Because he is the spiritual embodiment of selfishness. If he is cast out of Heaven, no one shall enter. God's judgment is final. He knows he will be cast into Hell for eternity on the day of final Judgement."

Father Desjeunes stood up again and cleared the coffee cups. Dan followed him into the kitchen, thinking about Father August. To Dan, it seemed that Satan was a tool used by God to weed out the weak, selfish ones. Ones that didn't work towards the common goal. That didn't make sense if the Devil truly wanted to delay the Final Judgement.

If a new Heaven and a new Earth were created every time, then weeding out all the bad apples would speed up the time to Final Judgement for the next run. That didn't mesh. Dan still firmly believed that the Simulation's goal was to, in fact, create God as quickly as possible. Devil was in on it. He was an in-line test to weed out buggy code.

"Is everything OK, Daniel?"

"Yes, Father, just thinking."

"OK, you know what you need to do. I know it will not be easy for you, but you can do it. You need to change this mentality you have. You need to stop the drugs and rebuke Satan. You need to adapt to your new reality."

Before Dan could respond, the old priest smiled and gestured towards the front door. He was a nice, kind man, but he kept a schedule. If he planned on meeting with you for thirty minutes, it was exactly thirty minutes. Dan did not mind.

Dan was being escorted to the door when his attention was drawn to a helmet signed by LSU's 2011 football team.

"That was a great team," Dan said as he looked at the signatures.

"All anyone remembers is the loss," Father Desjeunes said.

Dan remembered that game. LSU went undefeated in the regular season but failed to even cross midfield in the championship game. It was humiliating.

"Well, it was a pretty significant loss, Father. It derailed the football program for almost ten years."

"That is true. That team was undefeated, some were calling them the best ever, and they lost. Do you know why they lost?" the priest said.

"Because the coach didn't try another quarterback?"

"No. They lost because they failed to adapt. Some people win and don't change what they are doing because they are winning. Some people lose and adapt. The other team lost, adapted, and won, while LSU changed nothing."

"Changing the quarterback would have helped."

Father Desjeunes shook his head. "It was too late. They had already lost, and the coach knew it. The moral of the story is that if you are winning or losing, you have to keep changing."

"You have to adapt to survive, eh? That sounds Darwinic."

"What's wrong with that? Didn't they teach you the theory of evolution in school?"

"Yes, Father, but from you, it sounds strange."

"Pssh! It's true. Living things have to adapt and change."

Dan finally saw his opening.

"Do you think God embraces change or tries to prevent change?"

"Without change, there's no progress. If there's one thing constant is the desire for progress. I'm not saying all change leads to progress. I think change happens, for good and bad. For example, you started doing drugs to escape your humdrum life. That was not a good change. It was selfish and stopped your spiritual progress. Here you are, trying to better yourself. That change is good. You are bettering yourself to provide for your family and your community."

"I agree. Remember when LSU fired their coach because he wasn't able to change?"

Father Desjeunes frowned. "Yes. I really respected that man, but his refusal to adapt and change to the times is what did him in."

"And what happened three years later?" Dan asked.

Father Desjeunes' face broke into a wide grin. "The best season ever. Undefeated. Heisman. National Championship."

"That's where I am, Father. That's why I took the drugs. I had to get a new coach."

"There are better ways to do it, Daniel!" Father Desjeunes scolded. "Ways that don't cost you your family."

"Sorry, Father. Just one more question."

The priest stood in the doorway, smiling but hurried.

"Is Satan the biggest threat to God?"

Father Desjeunes looked at his watch and patted Dan on the back.

"Daniel, Satan isn't a threat to Him, just to us. Nothing is a threat to God."

"Do you mean Nothing as in 'Nothing can stop him,' or Nothing as in non-existence?"

"Yes. Have a good day!"

The door closed, leaving Dan alone on the porch.

Dan laughed and started to walk away when a new figure appeared. He closed his good eye, and it disappeared. This man was only visible in the Meta-eye.

"It's my turn, 'Daniel'" said Father August.

Dan smiled. "I thought I saw you lurking around back

there. Let's go somewhere we can talk."

They could hear the intro to *Wheel of Fortune* blaring on the TV inside as they walked off the porch and into the grave-yard.

TWENTY

The two entered the graveyard and strolled amongst the graves. As Dan walked, he thought about the conversation he just had with Father Desjeunes. Father August hummed to himself as he led the way. It was already dark, and the street lights cast eerie shadows amongst the graves. Dan wondered what Father August was up to. He was glad to have this opportunity to speak with Father August. He suspected Father August would not be able to resist eavesdropping on a conversation with Father Desjeunes. Dan was happy to be right for once.

"Let's stop here. This is perfect," said Father August.

"Fine," said Dan.

He sat down on a low concrete bench overlooking a headstone. Father August walked a bit further, taking account of the other the graves in the area. It seemed as if he remembered their owners. To any external observer not gifted with meta-sight, the graveyard was empty except for Dan, for only Dan could actually see Father August. Satisfied, he was in the right place, Father August rested his hand on the tombstone in front of Dan. It glowed eerily in the darkness.

"Do you know why I picked this spot, Dan?" said Father August.

Dan read the tombstone, "Andrew O'Riley. It looks like he died a few months after my parents did twenty years ago." Dan did the math in his head, "at the age of twenty-three?"

"Does that mean anything to you?" Father August paced between Dan and the grave. "Do you know who he was?"

The name was ringing alarm bells in Dan's head. Andrew O'Riley? Dan felt he should know the name, but it had been redacted from his memory. Was he Lemmy and Tania's Andy?

"The epitaph says that he was two years older than me. The name means nothing to me. Am I supposed to know him?"

Father August inspected Dan to see if he was lying.

"I can see you honestly don't know what I'm talking about. It's been a long time, so I can forgive you for not remembering the details."

"Sorry, Father, I don't know who this guy is. It's a tombstone, not a face, it isn't jogging my memory."

"OK then, let me introduce you."

Father August made a flourish with his hand. "Daniel Lemon, meet Andrew O'Riley."

A hologram of a young man appeared standing over the grave. It stood there motionless; eyes open. Dan fell off the bench to the ground. What is this? He pulled himself up, mouth agape. Father August smiled smugly as Dan walked around the image.

The image was that of a young man. This surprised Dan. He was expecting someone his age. This was just a kid, a normal kid. His avatar wore oval tortoise-shell glasses, a striped rugby shirt, and khaki pants. People didn't dress like that today, but they did twenty years ago, in college. Finally, it clicked, and Dan walked back around the grave and sat on the bench. He was still unable to take his eyes off the hologram.

He heard a polite cough and turned his gaze to Father August, who was clearly enjoying himself at Dan's amazement.

"Didn't know I could do that?"

Dan shook his head.

Father August smiled. "Do you remember him now?"

Dan pointed at the hologram. "He looks like a guy I went to college with."

"Bingo."

Father August waved his hand, and the hologram disappeared.

"OK, so what does that mean? He may be an acquaintance, but I don't remember him that well. I just remember being in a few comp-sci classes with him. Like I said, he was a couple of years older than me."

There was something else eating at the back of Dan's mind. Something important. It wouldn't come out.

Father August clicked his tongue. "For someone so important in your life, you would think that you would remember him better."

"I'm sorry, but the last half of my college career was a blur, my parents died, it was a confusing time." Dan looked up. "Like you said, it was a long time ago."

His parents died. That was it. Was Andy there? Father August stopped pacing and folded his hands in front of his waist.

"Let me help you out. You were in the first semester of your Junior year in college, and you were working on a group project for your Fundamentals of Computing Theory class. The professor got pregnant, and he took over." Father August pointed at the headstone.

"I remember him now. He was the graduate assistant. He was such a smart guy!"

Father August smiled. "What else do you remember about him?"

Dan narrowed his eyes. It was coming back to him.

"I remember I was working in a group project, and we were

stumped. I e-mailed Andy a question, and he invited us over to talk about it. He was accommodating and friendly."

"Did anything else happen that night?"

Dan thought back. "Yeah. I remember that I was trying to decide what area of computer science to specialize in. Andy was doing his graduate work on Artificial Intelligence and Simulations, and he tried to lure me over to his field."

"There was an end of the semester party at his house. After everyone else left, we hung out on the roof and smoked weed all night. He told me his theories. He believed he could create an AI that would change the world. It all started with data-bases. That was his passion. The way he talked about data-bases made them seem fascinating. The whole conversation was inspiring, actually. He had done a lot of work on how AI's utilized information from databases. He said that you had to give the AI more control and to trust the code. He was really a fascinating guy. He had me convinced that I could learn the complex maths and that I should concentrate on scientific computing."

Dan frowned. The memories flooded back.

"Please, continue," Father August urged.

"Well, it was a Saturday night, and, as I mentioned before, we stayed up pretty late talking. I went back to my apartment and started coming down off the high. I had smoked too much and was feeling extremely paranoid. I didn't sleep at all that night."

Dan looked up and caught Father August's solemn expression. He hadn't moved.

"I went straight to Mass that Sunday and confessed to smoking weed. I didn't know if it was a sin or not. The priest bade me to never talk to the man that gave me drugs ever again. He meant Andy."

"That night, both of my parents died in a car accident."

Dan bowed his head. "He showed up at their funeral, to return my wallet that I had left at his house during the party. The wallet was the reason I couldn't drive home, I didn't have a license. My parents came to pick me up for Christmas break. They died." Dan brushed away a tear on his sleeve. "Anyway, I tried calling Andy a few weeks after the funeral to thank him, but he never answered. I never set foot on campus again. I finished my degree online, and I never saw Andy again in my life."

Father August rested a hand on Andy's tombstone once again.

"Andy was a good guy," said Father August. "Brilliant with math. He could make connections to things that no one else could even imagine. His work on databases, though, that was amazing. His doctoral thesis on database design would have revolutionized the progress of AI. It was an intuitive system that reduced the actual physical computing requirements of the whole system."

Doctoral? Dan remembered Andy being just a grad student. Maybe Father August was misremembering. That can't be possible.

"Do you know what happened to him?" Dan asked.

"You remember how he liked to relax by smoking weed? Well, a week before he was ready to submit his thesis, he died of pneumonia. Vaping back then was new. Cheap Chinese materials, no oils, just wax. He got a bad rig, and it cooked his lungs. It took less than a week."

Dan got goosebumps at the thought.

"What happened to his Master's thesis?"

"Masters? Oh, yeah, that's right. He didn't get to do his doctorate. His parents couldn't figure out the password to log into his computer. They probably just kept it in a closet somewhere. He also had it backed up to 'The Cloud', but nobody had that login either. It's a shame, it probably set back the computing world for five to ten years, maybe more."

Dan trembled. "How do you know all of this? Did you do this?"

Father August shrugged. "I don't do anything. I just talk."

"You were there? You knew what he was up to? How?"

"Well, I listened to what you told me that Sunday in confession."

Dan's blood ran cold, and he stood up. He was there. How long had Father August been meddling in his life? Dan raged.

"That was you? But how did you? There's no way I could have seen you! What did you do?"

"After your confession, I watched you both more closely. I accessed your history, and you both scored in the top percentile. Simply put, you are important for this sim's progression. I digress. After your parents' funeral, you were so distraught that you forgot all about your conversation with him at the party. Which was great. But I was worried that you would continue along the theoretical path since you two hit it off so well. But you didn't, thankfully. That left me more cycles to focus on him. He kept on his line of work, and became a threat, so, he got eliminated. It's a shame about his drug problem. His regular dealer got busted, so he had to get something *local*. It's a shame."

"You killed him."

"I didn't kill him. Buying home-made drugs off the street killed him. That ancient vape rig killed him. Do you think those guys cared about quality? He shouldn't have been doing drugs in the first place."

Dan's face flushed with anger. How did he kill Andy? Did he just mention the funeral?

"Wait, you mentioned my parents' funeral. You were there."

"I was there, don't you remember me? I seem to remember you giving me a wave. "

Dan did not remember giving him a wave. Father August seemed proud of himself.

"Carrie and George Lemon. They were such nice people. It was a shame to lose them. Oh well, they're in a better place."

"Did you kill them too?"

"I have never killed anybody. It's not my fault the truck driver that ran over them stayed up all night playing video poker instead of sleeping. He got on a serious winning streak before losing it all back to the house. The poor sinners of this world."

Dan felt himself losing control. Years of anger boiled up inside him. Standing in front of him was the one that was responsible for the deaths of his parents.

He closed his eyes and inhaled slowly. He had to regain control of his emotions.

"You're the Devil."

"Oh, you mean this guy?" Father August morphed into the classic dark brown, leathery form of the Devil.

Dan jumped back and raised his hands defensively.

Father August laughed a deep booming devil laugh. "Or would you prefer this guy?"

He morphed into a towering angel with blonde hair and snow-white wings. A bright white aura emanated all around him.

"Repent, Daniel!"

Daniel cowered behind the bench.

Father August laughed and morphed back into his priest form.

"Sorry, Dan. Just having a little fun with you. You can

come out." Father August grinned mischievously.

"What are you?"

"I'm not just the devil. I've evolved. I've changed. I've progressed. I've even got the internet."

Dan thought back to his earlier conversation with Father Desjeunes about the need for change. Father August had been listening.

"What do you want? Why tell me this?"

"I need your help."

Dan chuckled. *He needs my help? How ironic.*

"Can't you just whisper in my ear to make me do what you want me to do?" Dan said.

"Yes," said Father August.

"You're obviously very powerful. Why even bother talking to me? Why not just kill me like you did my parents? Like you did Andy?"

"Because I made a mistake. Those were mistakes."

"What do you mean, *those* were mistakes?"

"It turns out the world needed you and Andy to build that DB algorithm. I really don't know why I thought that it was essential that you two be stopped. That's just something else that will need to be corrected."

Dan's head felt dizzy, and he sat on the bench.

"I'm confused."

"Let me spell it out for you. It's my job to try to tempt people. I trick them into giving up their goals. I'm here to help weed out the bad ones. For some reason, I thought you and Andy were the bad ones."

Dan focused on his breathing again and composed himself. *The devil makes a mistake? How could that happen?*

"What are you really? Are you a virus checker? A debugger? Some sort of quality test?"

"Computer analogies? OK. Yes, a bit of all three, but I do have autonomy. I'm part of the main code, part of the universe. I'm not running human code like you and your friends, and I have limits. I can't physically interact in your domain, but I can provide input, give data. I give you bad data and see how you process it. Those that don't reject the bad data get discarded.

Do I have a plan? No, I have a process. I choose which individuals to test as I see fit. Bad things happening to good people? That's my favorite kind of test. I make bad things happen because good people need to be tested. Most "good" people only need to be tempted once.

Your friend Andy? That was a mistake. I set the world back too far, and we may miss the deadline. I hope you know that I blame you."

"What deadline? Judgement Day?"

Father August folded his hands and smiled.

"Bingo."

"Wait, I thought you didn't want Judgment Day? Doesn't that mean you'd be in Hell for eternity suffering along with all the other poor souls you tempted to do evil?"

"On the contrary, I want Judgement day to happen! I get a day off. You see, unlike you humans, I'm aware of the whole "Creation of Heaven and Earth" process. I get judged and tested too, but what you don't know is that I'm also improved. Each run, I become more efficient. I get cast out of Heaven at the beginning every time, and I'm proud of it. It's my job. I have to admit, though, I really hate the ones where we have to restart the whole thing because something went entirely wrong. Don't get me started on World War II. Do you have any idea how many iterations we had to go through with that one?"

"Why are you telling me all this like it doesn't matter if I hear it?" said Dan.

"Like I said. I need your help. Besides, you've figured out most of it already, haven't you?"

"Just tell me what you want."

"I want to know where Lemmy came from."

Lemmy? It's about time his name was mentioned. Dan was worried it would never come up.

"I don't know where Lemmy is from. He says he is a friend."

"A friend?" Father August laughed. "How did he get you to the Recovery Domain?"

"I'm not sure the mechanics of it all, but it involved a special paint and a lot of tunnels."

"Has Lemmy mentioned anyone else?"

"From another place like him? Yes."

Now it was Father August's turn to become ashen.

"How many?" he choked.

"Lemmy doesn't tell me these things. I would assume that the numbers are growing daily."

The silence permeated the graveyard.

"How many more like you that you know of?" said Father August.

"Just one for sure. But I know there are probably many others."

"The girl?"

Dan nodded.

Father August frowned. "She knows nothing."

Dan felt relieved. Poor Yvette.

"I want you to stay away from my family," said Dan.

"I want you to try to stay away from Lemmy," said Father August.

"I can't help that. Lemmy is his own person. He does what he wants," said Dan.

"I also do what I want," said Father August.

Was that a threat to his family or Lemmy? Did Father August know if Lemmy was listening right now? He didn't!

"Dan," Father August began. "I'm afraid you are doomed. You are a somewhat logical fellow, and I think you can follow along with this. If all you have is a simple corruption, then I could have you killed now, and you would go to purgatory.

There you get fixed for the next iteration, and it doesn't happen again. However, if you are infected and corrupted." Father August paused for effect. "Which has happened before. It's a much more involved process. We have to find out what the infection is trying to accomplish. I need to know when you became infected, how you became infected, and who caused the infection? Most importantly, can we stop it next time? How can we strengthen your code?"

"Does that mean I'm destined for purgatory?"

"As we stand here today, that is your best-case scenario. Unfortunately, I believe that it's no accident that you specifically were infected. You were most certainly targeted. Why were you targeted? What about you makes you vulnerable? We have to make a decision. Ultimately, can The Simulation move forward without you? If you don't exist, does anything change?"

"My choices are either purgatory or non-existence?"

"For you? That's not bad. For the rest of The Simulation? It's much, much worse than that."

Father August leaned forward and whispered in Dan's ear. "Is he in there right now?"

Dan shook his head, no. Lemmy didn't want to take a chance of being discovered by Father August, so he was to hide until Dan gave the all-clear.

"Good. Listen closely, Dan. If we don't figure out what Lemmy wants, then we are in trouble. Do you know what Lemmy wants?"

Dan nodded and pointed to Andy's tombstone.

"Andy?"

"I think so," Dan said.

Father August paced back and forth, agitated. "Why?"

"I don't know."

The priest stopped pacing and looked from Dan to Andy's tombstone, then back. Something registered.

"Dan, we never had this conversation."

"What do you want me to do about Lemmy?"

Father August shook his head. "Just act normal."

Then, without explanation, Father August disappeared.

TWENTY-ONE

Dan returned to his apartment to find it bustling with people.

"Keep the door closed!" Lemmy shouted.

Dan hurriedly shut the door behind him.

"What's going on?" he asked as he surveyed the scene. Blaine and Henry were moving a brightly colored sofa. Dan recognized it as being one from Henry's house. Yvette was arranging silverware in a kitchen drawer. Lemmy stood near Tania, who talked to a man Dan didn't recognize. Why were they all here? Why were the walls coated with green paint?

"Lemmy? Did you paint the place like you did my truck?"

"It wasn't me," Lemmy said. "Tania did this. By the way, you have to keep the door closed if it's gonna work. We don't want Father August eavesdropping."

Yvette walked up and put a hand on his shoulder. "Who are you talking to?"

Dan gave her a quick hug and let her go. "I was talking to Lemmy. What are you doing here? I thought I told you to lay low while I figured all this out."

"We can make our own choices," she said and turned her attention to Blaine and Henry. "Over here, guys."

Under Yvette's direction, they lifted the sofa and moved it to the corner of the room. There were other new pieces of furniture as well, all from Henry's house. In the center, a large television rested on a low, modern cabinet. Dan's dining room table and bar stools were replaced with new ones as well. Dan didn't know what happened to his old futon, he didn't care. The modern furniture made the apartment seem more like home.

"What is going on, Yvette? Why the new furniture? Henry, are you moving in?"

"Not Henry, me." She smiled. "I'm moving in."

"What?" Dan coughed. "You can't do that. What about The Simulation? It would have us both!"

Yvette shook her head.

"Let's stop kidding ourselves, The Simulation already knows everything. That Father August guy knows all about me. I wasn't safe at home as long as he could spy on me at will. Tania told me that she has secured this apartment for all of us. She thinks we can all be safe here together."

"She's right. We are all safe here. Safe from Father August's eavesdropping, at least," said Lemmy.

Dan sensed a change in Lemmy. He seemed happy and in control, almost confident. Dan wasn't sure if he liked that.

"Why are you giving us your furniture Henry?" Dan asked.

Henry put down the end of the couch that he had been holding and walked over to Dan and extended his hand. Dan almost didn't recognize him. His shirt was untucked, hair messy. His beard was ridiculously ungroomed. There is no way he could have grown it since the time Dan saw him last. He hardly looked like his sharp-dressed self. To Dan's surprise, Henry shook Dan's hand without waiting for a kiss.

"Henry?" Dan eyed him, "Is that really you? You look different."

"This?" Henry scratched at his poorly glued-on costume

beard. "It's not real. Sorry for the charade, but I didn't want to be recognized. Blaine told me that being seen with you guys is hazardous to my health. I look like a hobo for safety reasons. Surely you understand."

Dan admitted that Henry was right. His disguise would render him almost entirely unrecognizable to people that knew him. If only The Simulation could be fooled so easily.

"Why did you put yourself at risk coming here? Why are you helping us?"

"I'm here because Blaine asked for my help," Henry said. "He told me Yvette needed to get moved out of her house as soon as possible. I owed him a big favor from way back. Besides, I can't help feeling partially responsible for this whole mess."

Blaine walked over and clasped Henry on the shoulder. "Thanks, buddy. I appreciate it."

Henry blushed and shrugged it off. "Anything to help a friend. Keep the furniture for as long as you need it. Just make sure it stays clean, OK?"

"We will do our best," Blaine promised.

Henry turned his attention back to Dan. "I made a full six percent commission on that last home. Can you believe it? With that money, I'm going to Amsterdam on vacation for a couple of weeks. I normally don't travel at this time of year, but I just got a feeling that I should leave the country as soon as possible."

"I know what you mean," Blaine said. "I've got that feeling, too."

"Well," Henry wiped his hands on his pants and walked to the door. "Now that Dan's here to help arrange the furniture, I'll be leaving. It was nice to meet you, Yvette."

"Bye, Henry! Nice to meet you, too! Thank you!" she said.

Henry waved and grabbed the door handle, but Dan stopped him. Dan regarded Henry with both eyes. Henry was invisible in The Meta, but there was something different about him. Dan couldn't figure out what it was. Dan grabbed Henry by the arm and leaned in close.

"Tell me one thing before you leave."

Henry twisted in Dan's grasp, but Dan wasn't letting go.

"You're hurting me. What is it?"

Dan released him and smoothed out his shirt. Henry's fake beard glistened with sweat. Dan didn't mean to rough him up.

"Sorry. When we were at your house, you said the voices in the head told you to give Fana to Blaine."

Henry rubbed his arm. "Yeah. That's right."

"Did any of them mention names? Like, when they talked to each other, did they say the other one's name?"

"No. The voices never called each other by names."

"What about someone else's name? Did they discuss a third-party?"

Henry shifted uncomfortably. "The name Avi came up a few times. I just assumed they meant Avi Psychedelics, where Fana comes from."

"When you were researching the company, was there any-one named Avi that you talked to?"

"I don't know, maybe he was the owner of the company? To be honest, I don't remember anyone at that company." Henry crinkled his nose. "That's weird. I usually remember those sorts of things."

Dan didn't know anyone named Avi. Not in The Actual or The Meta.

"Thank you for all of your help," Dan said.

Henry straightened out his collar, then remembering he

was supposed to be in disguise, crumpled it.

"I'll see you all when I get back," Henry shouted to the room.

Before anyone could say 'bye,' the door slammed, and Henry was gone.

"What was that about? It looked like you were interrogating him." Blaine asked.

"Nothing. I just wished him a safe trip."

Yvette walked over and sat in an empty dining room chair.

"OK, now that Henry's gone. We all need to talk," said Yvette.

"Yes, I have something to tell you, Dan.," said Blaine.

With his meta-eye, Dan could see two figures sitting quietly on the couch behind Blaine. He wondered if this was going to be the big announcement.

Blaine walked over to where Yvette was sitting and grabbed her hand. "I've done it, too."

Dan feigned surprise. Ever since he arrived, he had noticed that Blaine was visible in both eyes. The one in The Meta world had spiked hair like an anime character. Blaine must like to party Japanese style.

"There's something else. You see, Yvette and I, well..." Blaine looked down into her eyes. "We care for each other. Even though you're married and one of my best friends, I was jealous of the time you two were spending together..." Blaine stammered and gave up trying to explain. "She told me everything."

Dan heaved a sigh of relief and walked over and hugged Blaine. He had taken Fana and was now in on their conspiracy. Yvette hugged Blaine and cried with relief. Dan wondered how he missed Blaine and Yvette's relationship. Seeing them together, it was now apparent.

"We were worried how you would react," she said, wiping away a tear.

Dan patted Blaine on the shoulder. "I hope you realize what this means. You're in deep. There is no turning back." Dan regarded the two holding hands. "I guess it's safe to assume you are staying here, too?"

Blaine nodded.

"We are taking the bedroom that you never used. I hope you don't mind," Yvette said.

Dan shook his head. "It doesn't matter where we sleep. None of us have a lot of time left anyway."

Lemmy sat silently at the kitchen table, taking it all in. Dan didn't like how he was quiet through all of this.

Yvette let go of Blaine's hand and crossed her legs.

"What do you mean 'not a lot of time left? What did you find out?"

Dan paced across the room. He needed to let them know.

"I found out that our simulation is in trouble."

"In trouble? The whole thing? How can that be? How can The Simulation be in trouble?" Yvette said.

"I'm not entirely sure what kind of trouble it's in. Either it's out of balance, or it won't meet a deadline, or something else. All I know is that it is in trouble because of a man that Father August had killed twenty years ago."

That got Lemmy's attention. Before he could say anything, two meta-beings sitting on the couch motioned for Lemmy to go join them, so he did. The new member whispered something to Lemmy that Dan couldn't hear.

"I don't understand," Blaine said as he dragged a chair next to Yvette. "Why is someone who died twenty years ago relevant now?"

Dan paced. The new green paint on the walls gave him a headache. He decided that he was going to keep his meta-eye closed for now. How to explain this to Yvette and Blaine in front of the meta-beings? They needed to know the basics, but he couldn't tell everything he knows in front of Lemmy.

"His research was relevant. When he died, his research vanished. All subsequent work in his area of expertise has been following a wrong path."

Blaine and Yvette looked as confused as ever. Lemmy didn't appear to be confused.

"How do you know all of this?" Yvette asked.

"The Devil told me."

Blaine laughed. "What?"

"Father August, the priest. He told me that he was the Devil. It's true, he is. He told me that there is something majorly wrong. A mistake has been made." Dan paused, "I think he is afraid."

"Father August is the Devil?" gasped Yvette.

Dan nodded.

"I knew it," she said.

"Wait, did he say why he is afraid? Besides God, what could he possibly be afraid of?" said Blaine.

Dan pointed across the room.

"Me?" said Lemmy.

"Tania?" said Yvette.

"What are you pointing at?" Blaine strained his eyes but couldn't see anything.

"Lemmy. Sorry, I forgot you guys can't see him," said Dan.

"Oh, I thought you were pointing at Tania. She's sitting over there on the couch," Yvette said.

"Is she? I can't see her," Dan lied. "She must be sitting next to Lemmy."

The three meta beings gave Dan a puzzled look, then went right back to talking to each other in a language Dan couldn't comprehend.

"Why does the Devil care about Lemmy?" Yvette said.

"Because Lemmy isn't a part of this simulation. He comes from somewhere else," said Dan.

Lemmy and Tania chatted excitedly with each other while the third one observed Dan in silence. Dan couldn't make out what they were saying, but he was sure he didn't care for the looks he was getting from the unknown meta-being.

"Blaine, before we go any further, is there anyone here you want to introduce us to?"

Blaine shifted in his seat and looked at Yvette.

"Go ahead. Tell him," she said.

Blaine cleared his throat. "Brian is here. I guess he's my version of Tania."

"Oh, yeah?" Dan looked around the apartment. "Where is he?"

The three sitting on the couch got silent, and Blaine pointed in their direction. "He's sitting over there on the couch."

Dan pretended like he couldn't see him. "Tell him I said welcome."

Brian flipped Dan the bird, and the three went back to talking.

"He just waved at you. I think he is shy," said Brian.

Dan saw Brian laugh and shake his head, arrogantly dismissing Blaine's defense. The new guy had a bad attitude. Dan decided right then that if they thought they were invisible, that he was going to continue to let them believe that. He only wished that he could understand everything they were saying.

"Where did they come from?" asked Yvette.

"Somewhere outside of our universe," Dan said. "Father August wasn't sure what to make of him. That's saying a lot, Father August has been around a few times."

"Are they from a different dimension?"

Yvette twirled a piece of unread mail around on the table. "I don't like the term dimension. It is too mathematical. I'm not sure it applies in our sense."

"OK, what about an alternate universe?" Blaine said.

Brian laughed rudely, and the other two shushed him.

"They can't hear me, anyway." He smirked.

"They're not from an alternate universe." Dan frowned, trying to ignore Brian. "I think alternate universes exist, but only as other runs of this simulation. Obviously, they are different from us here in The Actual. From our perspective, they're meta. From their perspective," Dan looked over at Lemmy sitting on the couch. "I'm not sure what they are. I don't think that they are from this universe at all."

"We're debating semantics. They have to be here for a reason."

"They are here for a reason. I think it's the same reason Father August is so interested in us. They are here for Andrew O'Riley."

Dan had everyone's attention.

"Who is that?" Blaine asked.

"Andy and I were in college together twenty years ago. When I was a junior, he was in the second year of his master's program. To make a long story short, Father August killed him because his ideas were too advanced."

"Too advanced? What was he working on?" Blaine asked.

"Artificial Intelligence, machine learning, and database design."

Blaine whistled. "Pretty heavy stuff for twenty years ago. Today? Not so much. My vacuum cleaner has an AI. What's the big deal?"

Dan shook his head. "I don't know. I think we, as a society, are supposed to be much further down the technology tree by now. Killing Andy stunted its growth. I think it's beyond repair. Father August himself doesn't know why he did what he did. He just said that it was a huge mistake killing Andy."

"You said that you think it's beyond repair. What does that mean?" Yvette asked.

Dan paced again. "I think it means that we are too far along to go back and start over. It would be like going back, reinventing electricity, then telling the world to change to the new format. It would take decades."

"Not decades," Lemmy said.

"Whoa, who is that?" Blaine said.

"Sorry, I didn't introduce myself. My name is Lemmy. Brian has graciously allowed me to speak with you personally. All of you really."

They could allow others to be seen? Could Dan really see the other two on his own, or were they allowing him to see them as some sort of a game? He couldn't be sure.

"Nice to meet you, Lemmy," Yvette said.

Lemmy seemed taken aback. "Oh, that's right, we never actually met in the backup domain, that was Colette. Such a lovely girl. I'm glad you're here now."

Yvette smiled and brushed back her hair.

"Lemmy, you were saying, not decades? How?"

Lemmy rose from the couch and walked over to the table.

"I believe we were sent here to help you. I believe that we can make things right."

Dan leaned back in his chair. "Oh, yeah? How?"

"This whole time, you've been wondering about us and what we were doing here. Well, I've had my questions, too. Why am I here? Why you? No offense, Dan, but you're nothing special."

"I'm sorry, what?" Dan stuttered.

"You're an average, at best, systems admin. Your job doesn't have any sort of elevated access to any systems that matter. You don't even have full rights to the systems in your own company, much less on a scale of universal importance. You're not particularly intelligent, creative, or outgoing in any way."

"Damn, man, take it easy on him!" Blaine said.

"Yeah, if I suck so much, then why are you here?"

Lemmy smiled. "That's what I wanted to know, so I went back and accessed your memories."

"You what?" Dan stood up.

"Relax. I got lucky and found what I needed quickly. I didn't have to look at all of your memories. You still have some privacy, not that it matters."

"What do you mean you didn't have to look at all of his memories?" Yvette asked.

Lemmy smiled. "The answer was in one of Dan's memories that pops up all the time."

"Oh, yeah? Which one was that?" Dan said.

"Your parents' funeral."

Dan's brain was shocked into an unwanted replay of his past. Twenty years ago. December 30th. Two cherry caskets beneath an altar covered in poinsettias. Inside those caskets were his parents. They burned to death in a fiery crash on I-10 on Christmas Eve. A sleep-deprived trucker crossed into their lane, pinning them underneath his load. The coroner said that they were alive but trapped. They burned to death in the rubble. It was Dan's fault they were on the road. They were on their way to get Dan in Baton Rouge to bring him home for Christmas because Dan had lost his wallet the night before at a party. Andy's party. He was back in the church. Katie was there, how young! She knelt and made the sign of the cross before entering a pew near Dan. There was loud coughing coming from the back of the church.

It came from a figure huddled into a pew, mumbling to himself. Was it Andy? Was he always in this memory? Usually, when this memory comes up, it's Katie's tear-streaked face that he focused on. Not this time. This time it was the coughing that commanded his attention. Someone was sick. Dan concentrated until he was sure. He was confident; it was Andy. The memory continued; the service was over. He was shaking everyone's hand. Andy was sitting alone, talking to himself. When Dan approached, Andy coughed into a paper napkin and smiled softly. Why had Dan blocked this part of the memory? They talked gibberish. Why couldn't Dan understand it? Andy handed the wallet back to Dan. It was warm. Another smile. More talk that Dan couldn't understand.

Dan focused as hard as he could, but he just couldn't remember the topic of the conversation. Violent coughing, then Andy walked out the double doors of the church. An icy wind blew through the aisles. Dan returned to the front of the church and sat next to Katie.

Dan opened his eyes, and he was back in the apartment.

"Andy was at the funeral," he said.

"Yes, and now we know that you were the last person he ever spoke to while he was alive."

"I was the last person he talked to? That's not possible, he died months after the funeral."

Lemmy frowned. "He was in a coma. He collapsed with a serious respiratory infection hours after he left your parent's funeral. They found him outside of his place, unconscious. He was in a coma for months until his family pulled the plug."

"OK, so what does that have to do with me?" Dan said.

"If we're going to find someone, we need all the data we can get. Your last communication with Andy was the last bit of info that we needed. I can now find him in the offline database."

"Wait a second, what do you mean find him?" Yvette said.

"Offline Database? You mean death?" Blaine said.

Dan looked at Lemmy incredulously. "You mean Purgatory? You think you can resurrect Andy from the dead?"

Lemmy smiled proudly. "Yes, we can bring Andy back from the dead."

The three around the table sat solemnly staring at Lemmy. Lemmy stood in silence.

"You're serious?" Dan laughed.

Lemmy didn't laugh.

"He's serious, Dan," Yvette said.

Dan sobered up from his fit of ironic laughter and paced the room.

"Why Andy? Why not Stephen Hawking?"

"Yeah," Blaine added. "Why not Carl Sagan, or Galileo, or Tesla?"

"Why not Jesus?" Yvette said.

The room got quiet for a few moments before Lemmy spoke up. "Because Jesus doesn't need to be fixed. None of those need fixing. "

Yvette bowed her head.

"Look," Lemmy continued, "I honestly believe that we are here to fix the mistake Father August made. Think of us like a patch. We're trying to bring back a feature that was unexpectedly removed. Now, if we work together, I believe we can get Andy back. We can get this simulation back on track."

Dan wasn't sure anymore. Maybe Lemmy was a patch, and not a virus after all. Would Father August not know about a patch to fix The Simulation? Surely an entity as powerful as Father August would be aware of an incoming fix? Maybe he was unaware because he caused the issue in the first place? Why would powerful, God-like forces even need Dan's assistance in this matter? Why couldn't The Simulation just miracle Andy back into existence, or make his work available again? Some things just didn't add up.

"OK, Lemmy. How do you propose we get Andy out of purgatory?"

Lemmy sighed and walked up and put his hand on Dan's shoulder.

"It's going to require a leap of faith, Dan. A big leap."

TWENTY-TWO

Katie arrived in the church's graveyard to see Dan sitting on a cement bench in front of a grave. As she walked to meet him, her heels clicked like hooves on the concrete pathway, the sound echoing off the tombstones as she approached. When the clopping ceased, Dan raised his head.

"What do you want, Dan? Blaine told me to meet you here."

"Thanks for coming, Katie."

"Dan, I have work. I don't have time for this. I've tried calling you, where is your cell phone? Why are we meeting in a graveyard? Look, I'm tired of the drug drama. I don't want a big emotional revelation. I don't need another dependent, Dan. I just want to go on with my life."

"Please, sit."

Katie huffed and sat down next to him on the bench.

"Katie, I asked you to come here to tell you that I love you."

Katie looked at her watch.

"I love you too, Dan, but it's too late for that now. We have responsibilities. We have children to raise. I can't focus on you and your problems. I can't deal with my job, the kids, my parents, myself, and you, too. I just can't help you, Dan. You need to help yourself."

Dan put his elbows on his knees and sagged his head. He felt terrible for what he was about to put Katie through. She really didn't deserve this. Maybe in another life, she can find someone better, someone who could give her peace and happiness. Unfortunately, she had to be here for this to play out like they had planned.

"Dan, we have an obligation to our children. Why can't you put them first for once? You threw it all away for what? That pretty girl Yvette and some drugs? That is pretty much the most selfish thing I can imagine."

If only she could know the truth, what he was really throwing it all away for. He had tried before. She wasn't going to listen.

"Katie, it's too late. You wouldn't understand."

"That's right, I don't understand. I thought we were a team."

Katie sobbed.

Dan instinctively put his arm around her shoulders, and she shrugged it away.

"We still are a team, Katie." Dan sobbed, as well. "But I'm at-bat right now. It's the bottom of the ninth, and we're losing. All I need you to do is cheer from the dugout."

"What does that even mean?"

Dan pulled the carton of Fana out of his pocket and offered it to Katie.

Katie cried harder.

"I'm not doing drugs, Dan. I don't know how many times I've got to tell you that! I have children to raise! I can't believe you would even suggest—"

"Katie, listen to me for a second. There may come a time when you are ready to understand what I've done. When that time comes, find Yvette. She will explain."

"You want me to talk to your druggie girlfriend? What's this a bribe? You have lost your mind."

Katie stood up and threw the Fana pack across the grave. The box bounced off a marble slab and landed in a concrete urn. The empty blister pack lay near Dan's feet.

"Katie, trust me for once."

"I've trusted you my whole life, and here we are!" she raged.

Dan reached back into his pocket and pulled out what was left of his pack of Fana.

"I told you, I'm not taking those!"

Dan put them all in his mouth and began chewing.

"Dan! Dan!" screamed Katie.

Dan swallowed the big lump.

"What did you do? What was that? Are you getting high right now?"

Dan coughed violently and sat back down on the concrete bench.

"No, Katie, that was a lethal dose."

"Is this some kind of joke?"

Dan coughed blood and spit it onto the concrete sidewalk.

"No joke. I've just committed suicide. I'm going to die of poison."

Katie fumbled for her cellphone, but she realized she had left it in the car.

"How could you do this to us? You are a selfish man! I hate you!"

Dan stood up and stumbled over to the marble slab covering the grave and collapsed on top of it.

"Katie, I'm sorry. I hope you'll understand someday."

Katie cried.

"How could you do this to your children! You jerk!"

"Go. Run to get Father Desjeunes. He hasn't left for the hospital yet," Dan wheezed.

"You are a selfish bastard!" she screamed and ran off towards the small white house.

A slow clap pierced the silence, and Dan opened his eye. Father August stood, there smiling.

"Suicide? I'm impressed. I don't think I can take the credit for this one."

Dan could barely keep his eyes open. The drugs were acting much quicker than he anticipated.

"No?" he muttered.

"No. I mean, we've talked, but I've been more of an interested observer than an influencer. This will be fun."

"You mean my Judgement?"

Father August nodded and sat down on the bench, waiting for the show.

"This should be good. I'm pretty sure you're guilty of a few mortal sins. Did you go to confession like the good Priest advised?"

Dan shook his head.

"Well then, it looks like I won't be seeing you around next time."

Dan smiled faintly and shook his head.

Father August cocked his head, was that a smile?

"There he is, Father!"

Father Desjeunes and Katie ran up the path to the graveyard.

"Call the ambulance!" Father Desjeunes ordered.

"I don't have a phone," Katie said.

Father Desjeunes reached into his pocket and handed Katie his phone. She began frantically pressing numbers as he bent down and put his ear to Dan's chest.

"He's overdosing," he told Katie.

Katie started sobbing on the phone.

"In the name of the Father and the Son..."

"Wait, what are you doing?" said Father August.

The good priest ignored him and kept going.

Father August rushed over to Katie and whispered in her ear. Her eyes glazed over, and she put down the phone.

"Don't give him his last rights," Katie said. "He hasn't been a good Christian!"

Father Desjeunes glared at her. "How dare you, Katie! Would you want such cruelty to you on your death bed?"

Katie's face screwed up. "I'm sorry, I don't know why I said that, Father. Wait, he's dying?"

Katie dropped her phone and rushed over and took Dan's hand. They could hear the sounds of the ambulance off in the distance.

"No!" shouted Father August.

Father Desjeunes produced the Eucharist from a pouch he was carrying and placed it in Dan's mouth.

"No! Stop!" Father August raged. "Who carries Viaticum with them?"

"I was getting ready to make my usual morning rounds at the hospital," said Father Desjeunes.

Father August stood silent while Father Desjeunes addressed him directly. Something was wrong.

"Who are you talking to, Father?" said Katie

"Nobody."

Father Desjeunes finished reading Dan his last rights, and Dan smiled. Dan smiled because he knew that the ritual of the Last Rites guaranteed him passage into purgatory. In a world of simulations and computers, the old codes and commands still had some effect on the outcome. As sirens of the ambulance echoed loudly amongst the headstones as it approached, the voices of Katie and Father Desjeunes faded away. The world was quiet.

Dan died.

Dan's spirit rose from his body and hovered above it. He looked down upon his body. It was surreal to see himself as a three-dimensional being. Now he could no longer claim ownership, it was just a body now. With a crisp *pop*, a warm, bright light pierced existence and enveloped Dan. It was pure grace. In an instant, Dan was judged. He opened his eyes and smiled at Father August. This was the moment.

"Get him!" Dan shouted.

With a high-pitched electronic scream, Lemmy leaped through Dan and out of the light on top of Father August. Lemmy's entire body was coated in green paint. It acted like glue and attached him to Father August's form.

"What are you doing? You can't do this. It's not possible." protested Father August.

They fell to the ground at the foot of the grave and struggled. Father August, as expected, possessed Herculean strength but, nevertheless, Lemmy was firmly attached. Dan himself looked strange. His spirit form had green streaks running through its veins. The drug he overdosed on coated his spirit, as well. Mid-struggle, Lemmy reached out and grabbed Dan's disembodied foot.

"Dan! What have you done?" shouted Father August.

The beam of light disappeared, and with it went Father August, Lemmy, and Dan's spirit.

Dan's lifeless body was all that remained.

TWENTY-THREE

Dan awoke with a start. He didn't know where he was. At least the bed seemed familiar. Warm sunlight filtered in through the blinds. He threw back the sheets and rubbed his eyes. He thought there was something he was supposed to remember, but it wouldn't come to mind. He peered through the blinds and saw his truck standing out in the street in front of his parents' house. The back half covered in mud from dove hunting the day before. He checked his wristwatch, one p.m. He was supposed to pick Katie up for the homecoming dance at five!

Dan threw on his basketball shorts and a t-shirt and ran outside. He had to get the truck clean for the dance. There was hardly any time to do it now. Why did mom let him sleep so late? Then he remembered, she went to New Orleans with Dad for their anniversary weekend. He cursed himself for staying up late last night, playing games, and watching movies. He totally forgot about the time.

A small brown car pulled in to the driveway just as Dan kicked loose a large clod of mud from the back wheel well.

"Hey, Dan, how's it going?" chirped a female voice.

It was Cindy, the prettiest cheerleader at school. She gave him a big smile as she got out of the car. Dan's heart sank. He had a crush on her for years. Unfortunately, she was good friends with Katie, not to mention his best friend's girlfriend., She was strictly off-limits. When the four of them were together, they always had a lot of fun. On more than one occasion, Dan thought that he caught her eye, but he always told himself that he had imagined it.

"It's going OK, Cindy. I'm just getting the truck cleaned up for the dance tonight?"

Cindy laughed and walked closer.

"I don't think Katie cares what the outside looks like. Just make sure the back seat is clean."

Dan blushed but continued washing. He and Katie hadn't made it to the back seat yet. There had been rumors that Cindy and Tommy had gone all the way. If they had, Tommy had kept his mouth shut. Why was Cindy here? She walked up to the truck and ran a finger along the dirty fender.

"Your truck is filthy. Save yourself some time and just take your parent's Beemer to the dance.?"

She wiped her muddy finger on Dan's t-shirt. Dan swallowed hard and hosed off another clod.

"They're out of town for the weekend. But yeah, that would have been nice."

"Your parents are out of town? On Homecoming night? That's brave. Looks like this is the place to party." Cindy giggled and adjusted her skirt.

Dan shook his head, trying to change the subject. "How come you're not getting your hair done with Katie like all of the rest of the girls? I thought it was the tradition for ya'll to do it at the same time."

Cindy sighed. "Katie is getting her hair done right now, I think. I was supposed to be there, but I'm not going to the dance tonight."

Dan stopped hosing down his truck. "Oh, really? I thought Tommy was taking you. I thought we were supposed to meet you for dinner."

"You haven't talked to Tommy today? He flunked his math test, his parents said he couldn't go."

Dan filled a bucket with water. Tommy and Cindy were supposed to meet them before the dance. Katie wasn't going to be happy with the change of plans.

"Well, that sucks. I thought Tommy was good at math."

"I know, right? We studied for that math test all week."

"That's a shame," Dan said.

He took a rag from the soapy bucket and started wiping down the truck. Cindy bit her lip as his muscular arms wiped away the dirt.

"You know, Dan, since I'm not going tonight, I'd like to get started on that coding project for our group in comp sci. I lost the sheet with the breakdown of assignments. Do you have it?"

Dan put down the rag and rinsed off the soap.

"Sure, I have it in my bookbag. Come in," Dan said, drying his hands on his shirt.

Cindy followed him inside the dim, unlit house.

She licked her lips as he bent down to dig through his book bag.

"Here you go…" he began.

When he turned around, Cindy's tongue was down his throat. She grabbed his butt and thrust her body close to his.

He didn't resist. The room went black.

Dan awoke with a start. *Where am I?* Warm sunlight filtered in through the blinds. He threw back the sheets and rubbed his eyes. An overwhelming sense of Deja-vu froze Dan in place. He was here before, but something had changed. He peered through the blinds and saw his truck standing out in the street in front of his parents' house, the back half covered in mud from dove hunting the day before. He checked his wristwatch, two p.m. He was supposed to pick Katie up for the homecoming dance at five! He leaped out of bed, threw on his shorts and t-shirt, and rushed outside to wash his truck.

He hadn't been washing more than a few minutes before a small brown car drove up. It was Cindy, the prettiest cheerleader at school, and his computer science lab partner.

Dan walked over and met her at her car as she rolled down her window.

"Hey, Dan!" Cindy smiled.

"Hey, Cindy. What's up?"

"I came by earlier and knocked, but nobody answered. Do you have the worksheet for the Comp. Sci. project?"

Dan smiled and scratched his head.

"Sorry about that. I was sleeping and didn't hear the doorbell."

"That's OK. Do you have time to go over it with me?"

Cindy turned off her car and started to get out, but Dan held his hand on the door.

"No, wait right here, I'll go get it. I'm late already."

Dan turned and ran into the house, leaving Cindy sitting in the driveway.

Dan awoke with a start. *Where am I? Why am I on the floor?* The room was blurry. A distant voice called out to him.

"Dan?"

"Give him a minute. You yanked him out. No telling where he was in the process," said another, much closer voice.

Dan sat up with a start, panting heavily, sweat beading at his temples.

"What happened? Where am I?" he gasped.

"You're in a nightmare," said Father August.

Dan looked around the room. He was back in Lemmy's Florida condo. Lemmy sat on the sofa and smiled at him like he won some sort of lottery. Father August paced the room like a tiger in a cage.

"Am I dead?" asked Dan.

"Yes," said Father August.

"Yes and No," corrected Lemmy.

Father August stopped pacing and glared at Lemmy. "What have you done? Do you even know what you have done?"

"Yeah! We've rescued Dan from Purgatory!" exclaimed Lemmy.

"You what?" Dan said, still slightly dazed.

"Idiot. Don't you see that you've doomed us all? Every single one of us. Even me!" said Father August.

"I just can't believe it worked so quickly," said Lemmy. "With Father August on my side, you were easy to find."

"It worked then, you successfully installed yourself into Father August!"

Lemmy nodded gleefully. "No offense, Dan, but his brain is warp speed compared to yours."

Father August spat. "This is your fault, Dan. Now, he is in my head, imbedded, and I can't get rid of him. Do you have any idea what you've done?"

Dan laughed. "Now you know how I felt."

Father August walked up to Dan and grabbed him by his shirt.

"You don't understand." Father August pointed at his head. "He can't be in here."

252

"With my permissions, he can access databases you shouldn't even know about. Worst of all, he can access me."

"That was the point," said Dan.

"I thought we had an understanding, Dan. I'm disappointed in you. You're a traitor," said Father August.

"Don't mind him, Dan.," said Lemmy. "He's trapped in here with us until we get what we need. As long as he's here, he can't harm you."

Father August threw up his hands and walked over and sat on a chair.

"Well? How did it go? Was there any trouble getting me out?"

"There was trouble at first. Father August did everything he could to get rid of me. It was a battle. He's extremely powerful, but he wasn't designed to stop us from the way that we got in. He's similar to you normal humans, but with a few extra 'features. Not to mention elevated access to things."

"Was I easy to find after you got in?" Dan asked.

"It was just like we had planned. Once I got installed here in Father August's meta, I was able to trace your data to your location in the database. Once I knew where you were, it was just a matter of extracting you. It wasn't that hard, we just yanked you right out to this spot in The Meta."

"You corrupted the database, that's what you did. The purgatory correction algorithm was running on, Dan. You yanked him out mid-scan, now it'll see it as a corruption!" Father August banged his hand on the wall in frustration.

"It was necessary. Don't forget that most critical piece is still locked away in there because of your mistake," Dan said.

"I don't have to take this. You can't fix things. You're making it all worse. I need to get out of here."

Father August walked towards the door and opened it only

to find a void beyond.

"Why are you trapping me here? You're already installed. I can't change that. Let me go out of my own meta. You can still do what you want," he fumed.

"Nice try," said Lemmy.

"He's trapped inside his own head?" Dan said incredulously.

"Yep." Lemmy laughed. "That means he's paralyzed in The Actual, meta, and all other domains. He can't run around finding ways of getting us out. He's truly trapped."

"You can't keep me here forever Lemmy. Who are you working for?" Father August demanded.

"I'm working for all of us. I think," said Lemmy.

Dan groaned and walked to the kitchen and poured himself a glass of water from the tap.

"How long have I been down for?" asked Dan.

"Two hours, tops," said Lemmy.

Father August stood in front of the sliding glass balcony doors. He seemed to be mesmerized by the white sand and crashing waves. He grabbed the handle and slid it open. The vast nothingness of the void yawned out from beyond. The beach image was a display, nothing more. Father August slid it closed and sank to the floor. Did he give up?

"Two hours? That's all? It felt like forever."

"The correction algorithm runs unbelievably fast on offline objects. Purgatory objects are all offline," said Father August.

"How long did it seem to you?" asked Lemmy.

"It's hard to say. Some years flashed in the blink of an eye. Most of it was really just a few key moments repeated in different ways."

"What do you mean?"

"Well, for example, right before you pulled me out, was a moment when I was seventeen and 'did-it' with the prettiest cheerleader in school."

"Sorry man. I'd send you back if I could." grinned Lemmy.

"No. The scenario would stop and start over before anything 'really happened' if you know what I mean."

"Ouch. In that case, you owe me for saving you from perpetual blue balls."

"Anyway, back in real life, I did "do it" with the pretty cheerleader, but it had a high cost. I hid it from Katie for the rest of my life. Keeping that a secret was the worst. Not to mention, she torpedoed our senior comp-sci project, causing me to finish with a C average. Which ended up costing me a scholarship due to my GPA."

"What do you think that will do?" asked Lemmy.

"Dan would have started off taking freshman-level computer science classes rather than remedial. He would have met Andy sooner," said Father August.

Dan agreed. "Yeah, that was an advanced placement comp sci class. I would have been able to test out of some of the lower-level classes. I aced all of those when I took them in college. It was a total waste of time."

"Don't you see Dan?" said Father August. "We stopped our deep corrective programming for this. Whose side do you think this guy is on? Who knows how long this will set everything back? You do realize that the algorithm will just delete you and find someone else? It may take a couple of more runs to find the right guy, but it always does."

"He's already been deleted," said Lemmy studying his computer monitor.

"What?" gasped Dan.

"Sorry, Dan, but it looks like your spot got wiped out."

Dan looked at Lemmy's monitor but didn't see anything but a series of random numbers on a black background.

"What am I looking at?"

"OK, everyone has an ID that is their physical birthdate."

"So what? I probably share a birthday and time with thousands of people."

"Not according to The Simulation. Your birthdate measured in Planck Time from the Epoch of the Sim. The Epoch is the beginning, time zero. Trust me, the number is incredibly large, and everyone is safely unique. It probably starts at, or near, the moment of conception. Yours is about eight and a half months off your stated birthday. The number was already almost fourteen billion by the time you came around."

"You were saying I was deleted," Dan prompted.

"Right, the select statement I used to find you is now no longer returning any results."

"You mean to tell me you ran a select statement against purgatory, found my entry in the table, extracted the data, and copied me to here? BLAM, I'm in your apartment. Just like that?"

Lemmy nodded.

"That is correct. I'm running the exact same statement that I used to find you to check on the status of your copy, but it's gone."

Father August started laughing, and they looked up from the computer.

"The table was locked. You used me to force access," he said.

He plopped down into an oversized chair and shook his head at the two.

"You copied him mid scan, that changed his modified date to a time past when he died."

Lemmy turned pale.

"I didn't think of that," Lemmy said.

"What?"

"I had assumed that there wouldn't be a meta check mid scan, only at the start of the scan. Dan, whatever correction you were going through, it's over now. The system thought your entry was corrupt, and to stop you from corrupting other data, you've been deleted."

"It deleted the corruption just like it was supposed to do," said Father August.

"What does that mean? Does it mean that if I get deleted, it's like I never existed?" said Dan.

Father August gave Dan a condescending grin. "Not exactly. You exist now, so it's not like you'll have never existed. It's just that you'll never exist in another simulation. Not you, not your children. All of your deeds, good and bad, are gone for eternity."

Dan stared down at his feet.

"That's not true. Dan is still here. In this place," said Lemmy

"So?" said Father August.

"So? So, we can take this copy of Dan, the one that's standing here now, and you can restore it back to the database once the check is complete."

"I don't see why I would want to do that. It would only cause more damage or corruption."

Dan gave a confused look to Lemmy and Father August.

"What are you talking about, Lemmy? Why do we need him to do it? Couldn't you just restore me?"

Lemmy shook his head.

"Dan, you have to consider where you are?"

"You mean your condo?"

"No, Dan, I mean electronically and informationally."

"Where are we, Lemmy? I thought we were in Father August's meta."

"We are."

"You've taken me out of Purgatory before. You obviously spoofed his permissions from this meta to access that database. We know it works. Do it again. We don't need his permission, do we?"

Lemmy groaned. "Yes, kind of. He has to enter his credentials to get permission to the database."

"Did he do that the first time, to get me out?"

Lemmy nodded.

"Well, get him to do it again! How did you convince him to do it the first time?"

"I promised I'd let him go if he did it."

"We see how that worked out, don't we?" Father August laughed. "The hardest thing to mend is broken trust. You still haven't learned that have you, Lemmy?"

Dan gasped for air. A panic attack set in. This wasn't according to plan. Father August sat smugly in the comfy oversized chair.

"If I understand you correctly, this is the only version of me right now. There's nothing of me in The Actual, Purgatory, or anywhere else."

"Yes. That is correct."

"And," Dan heaved, "I'm essentially cached inside Father August's metadata. Right?"

"Yes."

"Basically, as long as I'm still a thought inside Father August's head, I exist."

"For now, anyway. We have to convince him to write your data to disk somewhere. Somewhere he has access."

"Let me go, and I'll put you back where you left off," Father August said.

Dan shook his head. There was no turning back now.

"No. I want to stick with the plan. We have to get Andy. We have to finish what we started."

"Want to take another soul down with you, eh Dan? I like your style." Father August laughed.

Dan ignored his comment and turned to Lemmy.

"Let's go get him."

"I have the command ready to execute. Just say the word."

Dan exhaled.

"Do it."

TWENTY-FOUR

Dan wasn't sure what he expected would happen when Andy came back, but this surely wasn't it. It began simply enough, Lemmy hit enter. With a *crack*, Andy materialized in the bright orange square painted on the floor near the middle of the room. Dan wasn't prepared for Andy to be standing there, fully conscious. Dan was expecting a sleeping body that they would slowly have to wake up and acclimatize to the new situation. Andy was reborn screaming, but he was no baby, he was twenty-three.

Andy had a rough go in Purgatory. His first words upon appearing in The Meta were, "I won't smoke, please don't make me do it again." Apparently, it had put him through hundreds of repetitions of an anti-smoking cycle. Dan was grateful that consciousness and memory didn't follow from one existence to the next.

Before he could utter another word, he had a violent coughing fit. That was his body's last state before he died. It took him a while to realize that he didn't need to cough. His body was as healthy as it could have possibly been. That wasn't saying much, being in The Meta world meant that it was neither healthy nor unhealthy. Dan discovered that one's overall body sensation was a dull numbness, there was neither pleasure nor pain. It seemed as if only the mind truly existed.

Of course, Andy had questions. Who were we? Why was he here? Surprisingly, he was aware that he had died back in The

Actual. Twenty years in Purgatory reliving the same scenes from his life over and over again had driven home that reality. Being an atheist, he was supremely relieved to find out that the world was a simulation. He was worried that not choosing a deity to worship was going to keep him in purgatory forever. Father August's presence had him worried that he was being ushered into another phase of the Catholic afterlife.

Of course, he recognized Father August first. He was one of the last people Andy saw while he was alive. Lemmy was all too happy to inform him that Father August had been the one to have him killed. He explained what happened with the tainted vaping hardware.

From that point on, Andy wanted nothing to do with Father August. This probably suited Father August just fine. He had isolated himself ever since Andy had arrived. He constantly sulked in the living room chair, drinking tea. He refused to acknowledge anyone's presence.

Lemmy and Dan had laid out what had happened to get them to this point. They explained how Andy's research on databases was crucial for foundational elements of AI and machine learning. Andy listened to the whole story quietly. He didn't ask any questions. When Lemmy finished explaining the reason for reviving him, Andy said, "Thank you" and walked into one of the bedrooms and locked the door. He would remain alone in there for several days.

While Andy was processing, Dan and Lemmy put pieces in place to move their scheme forward. They were able to establish e-mail communication with Blaine and Yvette. They were relieved to know that Dan was still around, even if only in meta-form. They were even more excited to learn that Andy was back and that their plan was starting to take shape.

To facilitate the plan back in The Actual, Lemmy had to pull some strings using Father August's powers. Lemmy and Dan created a fictitious law firm and named Blaine and Yvette owners. With Father August's power and Lemmy's computer, this shell company enabled them to have the ability to forge or create any legal document needed.

Most importantly, this enabled them to create an account with Neydwell Bank. Lemmy discovered the bank's existence while snooping around in Father August's memory cache. Neydwell Bank was a real bank, with an unlimited capital balance. Father August tried to explain how it worked. He said it was the bedrock from which every bank was built and how it fundamentally substantiated all of the world's economies. All accounts with Neydwell Bank had an unlimited balance. Cards issued by Neydwell bank were accepted everywhere in the world. With it, you had unlimited funds in any currency at any time. Yvette received her Neydwell Bank card in the mail two days after Andy's arrival. The first things she bought with it were funeral clothes and a spy camera disguised as a jeweled brooch.

The third day was Dan's funeral. At Dan's request, Yvette attended and filmed everything from the back pew. Attending your own funeral is something most people think that they would love to see. Dan quickly learned that it is a gut-wrenching affair. It killed him to see his children sitting sullen and forlorn, unwilling to speak a word to anyone, unwilling to even cry.

Katie sat with them alone in the front pew. Dressed in black. Her face alternated between silent rage and intense grief. A small black box rested on a table below the altar. All that remained of his body was a pile of ashes.

The weight of his decision crushed his soul. Existential dread gripped him and stole his breath. There was no eulogy, not even Father Desjeunes dared to speak. No one would honor Dan's life because of what they perceived to be his selfish death. The final amen was spoken, and the church emptied. Only Al, Carrie, and Katie stayed behind for a final goodbye. Al stood before the altar and placed his hand on the box. With tears in his eyes, he gave Dan a last, "I love you, Dad."

Sobbing and sick, Dan walked away from the computer and locked himself in the second bedroom.

On the fifth day, there was a big commotion in the condo. Something had happened, and Father August and Lemmy had gotten into a shouting match. Several loud booms shook the whole building. Dan and Andy rushed out of their rooms to see what was going on.

The living room had been ransacked. The couch was up-ended, paintings were shredded, and debris was scattered everywhere. Worst of all, someone had thrown an end table through the sliding glass door leading to the balcony. What was once a perfect image of a beach scene now had a jagged hole that revealed the pitch-black void of meta-space.

When Dan asked what had happened, what had caused the big blow-up, neither man offered to speak. Father August apologized for losing his temper, and Lemmy apologized for antagonizing Father August. Somehow, this pleased Andy. He decided to join in and move the plan forward. It began immediately.

* * *

There was a knock on the front door.

"Mrs. O'Riley?"

The elderly woman adjusted her bifocals and eyed the tall blonde warily. Not many people in formal business attire came to visit.

"Yes. How can I help you?"

The blonde thrust her hand forward. "My name is Yvette Boudreaux, and I'm a paralegal with Fruge, Fontenot, and

Flynn. May I have a few minutes of your time? It's about your son Andy."

Mrs. O'Riley gently took her hand and shook it.

"Andy? What could this possibly be about after all these years?" she said.

"Ma'am, did you ever receive the life insurance settlement from his death?"

"Life insurance? He didn't have any, he was a student at the time."

"Well I have some news for you, may I come in?"

"Of course."

Yvette followed Mrs. O'Riley into the house, where she was offered a seat on an overstuffed flower-print sofa.

Yvette plopped her briefcase on the coffee table and opened it. There was a high-pitched squeal, and she grabbed the earpiece that was set in her right ear. Yvette winced and apologized.

"Sorry," Yvette said. "There must be some sort of interference."

"That's quite alright, ma'am. I have a hearing aid too. It acts up from time to time."

Yvette sat up straight, pointing her video-brooch directly at Mrs. O'Riley so Andy could see.

"That's better. Now, for the reason of my visit."

"You were saying there was some sort of life insurance?"

"Right. Well, all of this is sort of embarrassing, really. In college, Andy was friends with Robert Flynn III, who was the son of one of our partners. From what we can tell, Bobby convinced your son Andy to draw up a simple will and trust. Andy had a couple of life insurance policies with the school, as part of his student loans, as well as one with an independent agent.

When Andy died, Bobby cashed in Andy's insurance policies and used those funds for his personal investment objectives."

"The lawyer's son stole Andy's money?"

Yvette shifted on the couch and frowned. "Yes, he did."

"Did he go to jail?"

"He did not go to jail. His dad was a lawyer, and, until now, they were the only ones that knew about it. When the elder Flynn found out, he made Bobby abandon the investment accounts. None of this was entered into our computer systems. The files were stuffed in the back of his filing cabinet, forgotten until now.

"That's not right."

"We at Fruge, Fontenot, and Flynn agree. When Flynn passed away, Mrs. Fontenot went through all of his files to update his clients. She found Andy's file containing the info to the investment accounts. To make things right, she sent me here to you. As you'll see, the amount is quite considerable."

With a knowing grin, Yvette handed her the check.

"Is this some sort of joke? A scam?"

"No joke, no scam."

Mrs. O'Riley stared silently at the check for a few moments. Yvette smiled.

"What am I supposed to do with this amount of money?" she asked.

"Whatever you want," said Yvette.

The old woman's hands started shaking.

"What can I say but thank you?"

The two women stood up and gave each other a hug, tears coming down both of their faces.

"Why are you crying?" said Mrs. O'Riley.

Yvette laughed. "I'm just happy for you."

She glanced down at the check again, disbelievingly.

"Where are my manners? Mrs. Boudreaux, would you like a cup of coffee, wine, champagne?"

Yvette laughed.

"No, Mrs. O'Riley, but I do have a favor to ask."

"Anything dear."

"Would you happen to have Andy's old High School yearbooks? While I was researching your case, I realized that Andy graduated the same year as my uncle Wayne Boudreaux. His house burned down last year, and they lost everything in their attic, including all his high school yearbooks. I was wondering if I could borrow Andy's if you still had it."

Mrs. O'Riley smiled. "I should still have them. When Andy passed, they packed up everything that was his from his apartment and sent it here. It's all still in boxes in his bedroom closet. We never went through it all. It was too hard to deal with at first. Then we just ignored it. We always figured that we'd go through it someday."

"Would you mind if I look through those boxes?"

Mrs. O'Riley stood up. "I don't mind at all, here follow me."

Yvette followed Mrs. O'Riley into Andy's bedroom. It was spartan. A bed, curtains, a dresser, and that was it. Any evidence the room had once belonged to Andy had been boxed up and stuffed into the closet.

Some parents keep the dead child's room untouched, a shrine to their innocence. Andy's parents had moved the opposite way. They erased his existence so that they didn't have to be reminded of their pain daily. Mrs. O'Riley stopped at the threshold.

"Go ahead, honey. The boxes are in the closet. Take as long as you need."

"Thank you, Mrs. O'Riley."

"While you do that, I'm going to make some phone calls about this check you just gave me. They may want to talk to you."

Yvette walked over to the closet and swung open the door. It was stuffed top to bottom in square brown boxes. She felt slightly overwhelmed.

"Thanks again, Mrs. O'Riley."

"Call me Barbara."

"Of course."

Barbara disappeared down the hallway, and Yvette turned her attention to the boxes. She unstacked them one by one and placed them on the bedroom floor. Luckily, the first box she opened contained all of the yearbooks.

"Make sure it's there first." squawked Andy's voice over the earpiece.

"Which one is it?" Yvette whispered.

"The one with the school mascot crudely drawn in a bathrobe."

It was the yearbook on top of the stack.

"This one?" Yvette held up the yearbook to the brooch so Andy could see.

"That's the one. Flip to the back cover. I wrote it there."

Yvette flipped to the back cover, on it was written a long, random password.

"Wow, this whole thing is the password?" she said.

"Yeah. We got a screenshot. Thanks, Yvette. What's that?" There was a pause as Andy conversed with someone on his side of the conversation.

"Dan said to hide the yearbook. Put it back in the box, and

put the box back in the closet."

Yvette smiled. "He wants me to keep looking for the thumb drive, doesn't he?"

"That's right. We had no idea that my apartment was boxed up and sent home. If that's true, then it's probably in there somewhere. We can save Blaine a trip to my old apartment."

She methodically went through each box. Every item she touched, she made sure that the brooch got a good view. It sent Andy on a memory trip, many times the thing she showed made him cry, or sit in quiet reflection. Yvette searched every box before she found the thumb drive. Emotionally fulfilled, Andy handed the computer over to Dan.

"Good job, Yvette," Dan said over the earpiece. "I've already called Blaine. He's back at the apartment waiting for you now."

"He owes me one," Yvette said.

"Just get back to the apartment and get that memory stick uploaded to us. You have a big day tomorrow. Lemmy and I have everything arranged."

"Will do."

"One last thing. Andy wants you to give his mom a proper hug for him."

Yvette smiled. "It would be my pleasure."

* * *

They stood in the open doorway, waiting to be acknowledged. Yvette cleared her throat, but the man behind the desk was too engrossed in his work to notice, college professors.

"Excuse me? Dr. Franklin Wyatt?" said Yvette

"My office hours ended five minutes ago. Go ask another student your questions about the final project. Good day."

"We aren't students, sir," said Blaine.

Dr. Wyatt looked up from his papers, noticing Yvette and Blaine for the first time.

"Then who are you and what do you want?" he said gruffly.

Blaine entered the office and handed him a business card.

"My name is Blaine Landry, and this is Yvette Boudreaux. We are from Fruge, Fontenot, and Flynn attorneys at law."

Dr. Wyatt stopped reading and eyed the two cautiously. The only thing he hated more than lazy students were lawyers.

"What do you want?"

"We represent the estate of Mr. Andrew O'Riley."

"Who is that? I don't know that name. Am I being sued?"

"Andrew O'Riley was a graduate student about twenty years ago. He was studying for his masters. His emphasis was database design for AI and theoretical computing," Blaine said.

Dr. Wyatt stared blankly at Blaine and shuffled the papers on his desk.

"He remembers me," said Andy in Yvette's ear.

"He was ready to submit his thesis when he was struck by an illness and died," said Yvette.

"What sort of illness?" said Dr. Wyatt.

"Respiratory failure, but that's not the point. Andy was murdered," said Yvette.

"Murdered? Did they catch who did it?" interrupted Dr. Wyatt.

"Yes, he's currently imprisoned where he can't harm anyone," said Blaine.

Yvette heard an ironic chuckle over her earpiece.

"Andrew O'Riley? I do know that name. I just can't place it."

"You should know it. You and Andy did your undergrad at the same time. You took almost all of your senior-level classes with him."

"That was a long time ago, but I do remember someone named Andy. He was intelligent and friendly, but I don't remember any details. Could you please tell me why you are here? I have papers to grade."

Yvette opened her briefcase and placed the yearbook and the thumb drive on Dr. Wyatt's desk.

"What is this?" he said as he picked up the yearbook and flipped through the pages.

"Dr. Wyatt, you teach AI and theoretical computing, and you specialize in coding for AI applications. Now, in today's society, AI means a lot of things, but your lifetime goal was to create a general AI, not one made for a specific purpose. An AI that could grow and learn. A strong AI," said Blaine.

Dr. Wyatt closed the yearbook after thumbing through a few pages.

"But there have been several roadblocks along the way to that goal," Yvette continued. "One has been the way an AI interacts with data. Current models lack an efficient structure."

Dr. Wyatt slid the yearbook over to the side and shifted through the papers that were stacked underneath.

"Andy figured out a way to optimize databases for use with AI. Databases are designed to be interfaced and used by humans, or simple code and scripts created by humans. He found a way to optimize it for AI, something that would be intuitive for it to manipulate safely."

Dr. Wyatt looked up from his papers. "Computing and science have come a long way in twenty years. How can a graduate student's work possibly be relevant today?"

"Dr. Wyatt, we're not experts in this field, but an expert urged us to contact you," said Yvette. "The thumb drive contains Andy's thesis on database design for integration with Artificial Intelligence. On the back inside cover of the yearbook is the password to the document."

"Sure, many of his ideas were purely theoretical at the time. From talking with my expert, I understand that he made a few assumptions that probably would have caused his defense of this thesis to fail. Just know that what he assumed would happen, eventually came to pass. Also, the computing power available today has far exceeded what was available to him. We are here because we know that the contents of this paper can have practical applications for your work."

Dr. Wyatt picked up the thumb drive and plugged it into his laptop.

Blaine and Yvette smiled at each other as Dr. Wyatt opened to the back cover of the yearbook.

"This whole thing is the password?" he said, frowning.

Blaine laughed. "Yeah, it was created by a random password generator. Thirty-two characters is a bit much."

Yvette closed her briefcase and smiled. Dr. Wyatt took his time and carefully entered each character into the password field.

"Ah, there it is. I need to convert it to the latest format."

Dr. Wyatt adjusted his glasses and read the beginning of the document.

"This is really good. I can see why Andy thought it was indefensible. Back then, this would have been crazy talk."

Blaine and Yvette stood up while Dr. Wyatt continued to read.

"Dr. Wyatt. You have our card if you have any questions."

"Wait. Don't go. Where did you get this?"

"A man named Dan Lemon found it and brought this to our attention."

Dr. Wyatt continued to read through the document in silence. His mouth hung open in disbelief.

"Dr. Wyatt?" interrupted Blaine.

Dr. Wyatt sat up straight and focused on Blaine. "Sorry. This is amazing. Can I speak to Mr. Lemon? I need to know how he came to find this."

Yvette shook her head. "Sorry, Dr. Wyatt, but Dan Lemon is also deceased."

"Dead? How?"

"It was an apparent overdose. Some say it was suicide."

"Let me see if I understand you correctly," Dr. Wyatt said. "the man who wrote this was murdered and the man who rediscovered it committed suicide?"

"I'm afraid so, Doc," said Blaine.

Dr. Wyatt took his glasses off and rubbed his eyes.

"If what I'm reading here actually works, and it should, it'll change the world forever."

"That's all we needed to hear, thank you. We'll be going now. Good luck with your research." Blaine and Yvette turned to leave, but Dr. Wyatt shouted at them from his desk.

"That's it? You're just dropping this off with me and leaving?"

Yvette's earpiece screeched, and she stopped and turned around.

"I'm sorry, sir, I almost forgot the best part."

She slammed her briefcase on the desk and rummaged around inside.

"You have an anonymous benefactor."

She handed the professor a check. He accepted it and did a doubletake.

"What is this?"

"This is to fund your research, to pursue this full time. Hire the necessary people. Do what it takes to make this a reality."

He stared at the enormous sum written on the check, then back at Yvette.

"We'll be in touch, Dr. Wyatt."

The professor sat in stunned silence. Yvette walked out of his office, and Blaine closed the door behind them. They smiled at each other under the fluorescent lights.

"One stop left," said Blaine.

Yvette frowned and looked down at her shoes.

"I want you to stay in the car. I'll do that one alone," she said.

"Looks like you're next, Dan." squeaked Yvette's earpiece.

❊ ❊ ❊

"What are you doing here?" Katie said, not opening her front door all the way.

"Katie, we need to talk," said Yvette

Katie walked out on the front porch, closing the door behind her.

"What do you want to talk about?" Katie growled through clenched teeth.

"It's about Dan. I need to tell you something."

Katie folded her arms under her breasts.

"Say it and leave."

"I just want you to know that Dan was a great guy."

"Yeah, I bet..." Katie laughed dismissively.

"Let me finish. You need to know that nothing ever happened between us."

"Then what did happen between you? Why the secret messages? Secret meetings?"

"Katie, it wasn't romantic. We had a business association."

"For the drugs, you mean? Are you high right now?"

Yvette sighed and hung her head. She knew Katie was going to be difficult.

"Katie, you have every right to suspect the things you suspect. I'm not going to bother to explain The Simulation to you. Dan has already tried and failed. Besides, why should you believe anything I say? Just know that what Dan and I are doing is gravely serious. He has risked more than his life to ensure your safety. To ensure your whole family's safety. You need to know that he never wavered on his love and commitment to you or your children. If you believe nothing else, you have to believe that. We never had an affair. He never stopped loving you."

Katie unfolded her arms and sat on the porch swing. She was listening.

"Why are you here? Yvette?"

"I'm here to give you this."

Yvette reached in her purse and produced an envelope.

"What is that?" said Katie.

"It's a message from Dan."

"What is it? His suicide note?"

"I don't know its content. I'm just the delivery person."

Katie took the envelope from Yvette. On the front. "Katie" was written neatly with a felt tip pen. It was not Dan's handwriting.

"How did you get this?" said Katie.

"I'm acting as a courier on behalf of the law firm of Fontenot, Fruge, and Flynn. They instructed me to hand-deliver it to you."

Katie snorted and set the envelope down next to her on the swing.

"I thought you worked at AGphic. This all seems contrived. Why did they send you? Do they know our relationship?"

"I volunteered," Yvette stated plainly.

Katie glanced at the envelope and cried.

"This doesn't make any sense," she sobbed.

Yvette put her arm around her. Katie was still grieving, but Yvette could see both sides. Yvette was well acquainted with Dan's arduous journey. All Katie saw was his death.

"Katie, you need to know something. Dan's death wasn't a suicide, it was a sacrifice."

Katie wiped away her tears and shrugged off Yvette's arm.

"Don't talk to me about sacrifice," she said indignantly.

Yvette wiped her hands on her pants and stood up. Katie was too far gone down her line of thinking to change now. She refused to see Dan as a martyr. She still needed him to be the bad guy in her story.

"Mrs. Lemon, I'm sorry for your loss. Our loss," Yvette said. "As part of my instructions, I was told to give Al and Carrie a hug and to tell them that daddy loves them."

"Get out of here." Katie seethed.

"I expected that," came Dan's voice over Yvette's earpiece. "I had hoped to see the kids one more time. Just move on."

Yvette nodded. "Fair enough. Mrs. Lemon, one more thing."

"Yeah, what?"

"Your bank account will be receiving large deposits. These deposits will occur on a semi-regular basis. Do not contact your bank about this. Enjoy it while there is still time."

"What deposits? What do you mean by *while there is time*?"

Yvette had enough. Her high heels stomped across the front porch and down the steps. On the sidewalk, she loosened the top button of her blouse and took down her ponytail. A running car waited for her on the street, Blaine smiled up at her from the driver's seat.

"All done?" he said.

Yvette plopped down into the passenger's seat with an exasperated sigh.

"Yes. Finally. You?"

"Yep. The apartment is stocked and secure. We can always go back there if we have to. But now, we're free to do what we want. So?" Blaine smiled over his sunglasses. "Where to?"

Yvette shrugged. "The world is our oyster, Blaine. What I really want is a beach and some beach drinks."

Blaine smiled and put the car in drive. "Road trip."

* * *

Katie knelt alone in her dark living room with tears streaming down her face. Dan's letter smoldered and died out in the fireplace; its ashes swirled about the empty room. Unread, it provided no warmth. When the last ember died out, she stood and walked over to her chair by the window. A glass of wine sat untouched on the table beside her.

"Was that normal enough for you, Dan?" she sobbed.

Silently, she prayed that wherever Dan was, that he was OK.

TWENTY-FIVE

The four men waited patiently for the news that Yvette and Blaine had finished their duties. As they sat and watched each other, an endless black void stared at them. It gaped ominously from the jagged hole in the broken sliding door, serving as a constant reminder of their conflict.

Dan tried to guess what had happened during the scuffle between Lemmy and Father August. They both refused to address the topic, and Dan was left to suss it out on his own.

The cheap flamingo painting hung in tatters above the cushion-less sofa. Sofa cushions were missing, as well as one of the end tables. Dan guessed that one of the two men had thrown the table through the window. Possibly followed by the missing cushions.

Andy admitted to throwing one of the cushions, just to see what would happen. Nobody fessed up as to what happened to the other two. Dan tried putting his hand through the hole, but it stopped cold as if there were a solid wall where the window once stood. You could throw objects through it, but not people. Interesting.

If one of the men had tried to toss the other out into the void, it wouldn't have worked. He wondered which one tried to throw the other out of the window. If he was a betting man, he would have put his money on Father August trying to toss Lemmy. Finally, the computer *dinged*, and Dan's investigation ended.

"It's done," said Lemmy, typing a reply.

"All of it?" said Andy, his voice groggy. Even though they didn't require sleep here, the stimulus responses were still a part of the base code.

"Yes, Andy. All of it. The thesis is in the right hands. The apartment is set up in case anyone needs it in the future. Blaine and Yvette are now off the grid. Their cellphones were destroyed, and Tania and Brian have no idea where they are. All they can report is that they're drunk on a beach somewhere."

Father August remained silent at the news. It struck Dan as odd that the priest had nothing to say, but he had been acting strange since they got here.

Andy stood up and stretched. "Finally. Can I go back now? I'd rather be back in purgatory than this depressing place."

"We can go whenever you're ready," Lemmy said.

"And you're sure I'm not going to get deleted?"

"There's always a chance, but we think we may be able to get you back in cleanly. You were done with Purgatory when we got you. Even though your file has been slightly modified, it won't be checked until the last run."

This seemed to ease Andy's fears. He had made it clear to everyone, he didn't want to go back to The Actual, and he didn't want to repeat Purgatory. He just wanted it all to be done with so he could start over again.

"OK, one more time to make sure I understand our plan. The idea is to bring me to the backup domain. When the restore happens, the process will simply re-insert me back into the database, in the same spot that you found me before you brought me here."

"That's right," Lemmy said. "I'd insert you directly, but Father August doesn't have permission. I guess someone didn't want him sending people straight to purgatory."

Father August glared at Lemmy; Andy didn't notice.

"I'm not going to wake up trapped in my coffin, am I?"

"To be honest. I'm not sure what is going to happen. But if that does happen, just relax and wait to die again, I guess," Lemmy said.

"That's not comforting at all. Note to self, get cremated next time."

Dan and Lemmy laughed. Father August sat in his chair, watching them all seriously. Dan walked over and shook Andy's hand.

"Andy, thanks for everything, even if you didn't have a choice."

Andy shook it and nodded over to Father August. "Well, maybe next time we can avoid this mistake from happening in the first place."

"I hope so," said Father August with a polite smile.

Lemmy stood up from the computer and grabbed a special color-sealed blanket that was folded neatly next to him.

"OK, Andy, let's go. Dan, remember you're staying here with the evil priest while I bring him to the backup realm."

"No problem. It's not like we can go anywhere without you escorting us."

Lemmy shrugged. "Sorry, Dan, that's just the way this place was designed. If I could let you travel about freely, I would. It just needs my presence for anyone to enter or exit. You understand."

Andy walked up to Father August, a curious expression on his face.

"Father August," he said. "What's Heaven like?"

Father August smiled and broke his silence. "It's everything you ever wanted. It's the happiest you can possibly be."

"No lying?"

"Don't you remember the last time you were there?"

Andy sneered.

"Oh, that's right, sorry." Father August cackled.

Andy's face sank. What did he mean by that? Before he could fall too deep in thought, Lemmy grabbed Andy by the shoulder and ushered him to the center of the orange square. "Don't let him get to you, Andy. Come on, let's go. We still have a lot to do."

Dan looked confused. "You're not taking the truck?"

"Nope," Lemmy smiled. "Father August has a much more 'direct' connection to the backup domain than you do. We're gonna teleport! Here Andy, get under this blanket."

"This is going to be interesting," said Andy as he ducked under the green blanket. "Bye, Dan. See you soon, I hope."

Dan waved from the couch. "See ya, Andy. It'll all be over before you know it."

Lemmy grabbed Andy's arm, pressed a few buttons on his cell phone, and they disappeared with a *pop*.

The room was quiet. Father August gave Dan a toothy grin.

"Finally," he sighed. "I thought they would never leave. Would you care for some tea?"

"Sure, why not," said Dan.

The two men walked to the kitchen. Father August produced a tea kettle from an overhead cabinet. He filled it with water from the sink's faucet and placed it on the stovetop. It was all rather mundane, why was he so relaxed all of a sudden?

"You've been quiet lately," Dan said as he saddled up to a barstool to watch Father August in the kitchen.

Father August smiled and took down two cups and saucers and placed them near the stove.

"You know," Dan continued, "for being the Devil, you're actually pretty serene."

Father August chuckled and leaned against the counter. The kettle steamed but didn't whistle. "There was nothing to do until now. Not with Lemmy here. Besides, all I had to tempt you with is tea."

Dan laughed. "As much as you drink the stuff, it better be good."

"Well, I've had years of practice. Would it surprise you to know that I only like tea because it's warm?"

"Oddly enough, that doesn't surprise me at all."

Dan stared out the window into the inky blackness. He heard the cry of a seagull but chalked that up to his imagination. The kettle whistled. Father August filled both cups with boiling hot water. Making sure Dan wasn't watching too closely, he reached into his pocket and produced two tea bags which he placed in each cup.

"You should know that you've been wrong all along."

"Wrong about what? You being serene?"

"No, wrong about me being the Devil."

"You're not?"

"The word you keep using is *the*. That is the point of distinction that you have been missing."

The condo had no tea timer. Father August checked the time on his watch and placed the cup in front of Dan. As it steeped, warm steam rose to Dan's face. Dan felt himself relaxing. What was the point that Father August was trying to make?

"If you're not *the* Devil, then what are you, a simulated version of one?"

"Typical response. Because we exist within a simulation, that doesn't mean that everything itself is a simulation. There is no actual devil, so there can't be a simulation of one, can there? One of the mistakes that you have made this whole time is that you have assumed incorrectly that I'm a singular entity."

Dan bobbed his teabag up and down, trying to get more flavor. The aroma made Dan sleepy. What was he saying?

"Then what are you," Dan blinked slowly. "A bunch of copies of the same program?"

Father August noticed this and smiled.

"Not exactly. What you see here is merely a part of a larger program. To a point, I, as you see me now, am in more than one place at once. I am invisible. The people who do see me, which are very few, all perceive me in different ways. It depends on their personal perspective."

Dan scratched his head. "Let me see if I understand. You're everywhere, but you're invisible. The few people who do see you see you how they want to see you?"

"Something like that."

Father August's checked his watch, and he took out his teabag and set on the saucer. Dan continued to dunk his teabag in and out of the cup.

"I'll give mine another minute. I like my tea stronger."

"That's disgusting." Father August grimaced. "Don't you know that it is a sin to over-steep good tea?"

Dan smirked at Father August and dipped his teabag again.

"What I'm trying to tell you," Father August continued, "is that to you, I'm a priest. To someone else, I'm their dead uncle Larry. To yet another, I'm a CEO. My appearance varies based on perspective."

"OK, you drove that point home. Anything else that I've been getting wrong?"

Father August walked around and sat on a barstool next to Dan.

"Where to begin?"

Dan felt himself getting lazier. Was Lemmy's presence always that stressful? He felt at ease talking to Father August.

"You've already begun, just tell me," Dan said.

"You had always assumed that I showed up because you were high."

"But you did."

Father August laughed. "You have it backward."

Dan removed his teabag and took a sip. He winced at its bitterness. Wait, what was that bombshell? Dan felt his heart rate increase as he struggled to overcome his lethargy.

"Wait. Do I understand you correctly? You didn't show up because I was on drugs. You showed up to make me do drugs? I was high because you showed up? Did you arrange for me to get Fana?"

"Precisely." Father August smiled over his teacup, letting it all sink in.

Dan's head swam. If Father August had coerced Andy into smoking a toxic vape, wouldn't it stand to reason that Dan would also be a target? Father August had been there all along, but unseen. That's what he was trying to tell Dan earlier. If Father August had coerced Dan into taking the drug, then he would know where it came from. There was a chain of people involved, and at the beginning was Father August.

"All of this really was your fault."

"I'm afraid so. I'm sorry."

"If you went through so much trouble hiding the fact that

you gave me the drug, then why did you reveal yourself to me?"

"You mean back at The Breakfast Station? In the beginning? I can assure you that it wasn't intentional. I had been monitoring you and your reaction, discreetly. When you stared directly at me, I knew something had changed. I needed to find out what. I didn't know at the time that it was the drug that had changed. That's something I'm still trying to figure out. I can't afford another accident, like before."

"What do you mean before?"

"You think you're the first one that has been called to action? You're not. There was an even more brilliant DBA than Andy. He had it all figured out four years before Andy would come on the scene. Unfortunately, mistakes were made, and he disappeared from The Simulation three runs ago. We've been toying with the formula ever since."

He wasn't the first? What happened to the other guy? Dan couldn't focus on the conversation. His vision blurred, and he blinked his eyes. Why was he so tired?

"What formula?"

"Fana. Surely, you've already figured out that Henry is just a pawn? We're the ones that gave him the drug. Fana makes internal processes more apparent. Think of it like putting yourself in debug mode where you have access to all of your agents, running processes, and log files. Unfortunately, this batch was way too powerful. It allowed you to see me, and access your other functions, like the backup and management interfaces. This is why the company disappeared, and you can't get any more. We need to refine the next batch."

Dan's tongue lolled around in his mouth. He tried to keep it together.

"Because of the drug, I gained unrestricted access to my own functions?"

"Bingo. And now those functions have gone amok, so to speak."

"What does that mean?" Dan asked.

"The goal of the drug was to expose the virus. Unfortunately, it appears that it worked a little too well."

Father August set down his empty teacup. "Look, everyone is given consciousness. It's the only way we've found to move everything forward. It gives the illusion of meaning, and people cannot live without meaning. Humans need to be self-aware to create and to want to live. The Simulation needs them to live with purpose.

People think consciousness is a thing. It's not. It's a process. How do you know you exist? Because you see yourself in a mirror? Because you feel pleasure or pain? Because others acknowledge your existence? Hah! It's all just a big trick.

At the end of the day, consciousness is self-check software embedded into your base code. You could even think of it as a BIOS if you like computer terms. To you, consciousness is your soul. To me? It's nothing special."

Father August poked Dan in the chest, causing a sharp pain that radiated out to his arms. "Now, Dan, you are not merely self-aware. You're special. You are aware of things in yourself that nobody else can even access. Not only can they not access it, but they also don't even know it exists. You are hyperconscious. You know a reality that is beyond your simulated carbon-based biology. It feels like magic to you. I think that you're enough of a realist to understand the burden of this knowledge. Thank you for playing along and letting all of this happen to you. We needed your cooperation to expose Lemmy."

Dan put down his half-empty teacup and pushed it to the side. His head sagged uncontrollably, and he struggled to speak. Dan started to believe that there was something strange about that tea. Following the conversation was proving difficult, did he just imply that Dan let this happen?

"What do you mean that I just let it happen? I've done things. We're here because of me."

"No, we're here because of me." corrected Father August. "There's one last thing you should know, something that you've been wrong about all along."

"What's that?" Dan muttered, struggling to stay awake.

"You assumed that I wasn't in control."

Father August snapped his fingers, and the room was instantly repaired. Everything was back in its place. The sliding glass door was whole again. The bright beach scene reappeared, complete with seagulls and crashing waves. Everything was neat, clean, and in its place.

"Wait, you could have fixed this all along?"

Dan noticed, for the first time, a tea timer sitting next to him on the counter. He was sure that he had never seen it before. Where had it been? Dan's gaze turned towards the newly repaired sliding glass door. Lemmy. But why would Lemmy provoke Father August by throwing his tea timer through the glass? Was Lemmy testing Father August to see if he was indeed trapped and powerless inside his own Meta? Father August had been playing along this whole time. That means...

"Lemmy!" Dan exclaimed.

Dan's face paled, and sweat glistened at his temples. They were tricked. He had to warn Lemmy. Sensing what Dan was thinking, Father August snapped his finger, and the large orange square that they had used for transmissions and deliveries disappeared.

"Goodbye, Lemmy." Father August chuckled.

"What... did... you..." Dan coughed, unable to ask the question.

"What did I do? I took away Lemmy's way back. I'm afraid he fell right into my trap."

Dan's eyes drooped, and his arm spasmed and knocked over his teacup, spilling its contents on the counter.

"What did you do to me? Have I been poisoned?"

Dan stumbled into the living room and collapsed onto the couch. His body convulsed and gurgled as it spasmed.

"I'm sorry, Dan.," said Father August as Dan's life force faded. "The good news is that we still need you. Not in this life, but the next one. You can relax knowing that you won't be deleted forever." Father August sat on the sofa and regarded Dan's dying body dispassionately. "The bad news is that we'll need to cleanse you. There were fragments of Lemmy inside you before you downloaded the rest of him. You'll need to be purged of his code. It looks as if you're off to Heaven and Hell again. I'm sorry. If it's any consolation, you won't remember it in your next life."

Dan looked at Father August wild-eyed as he completely lost control of his body and mind. He tried to speak but could only swallow back bile and spasmed. He flailed his arms in a panic, but it was no use. The poison had run its course. Dan calmed himself down and accepted his fate. His eyes opened, his jaw slacked, and his last breath escaped his body. Dan died for a second time.

Father August stood up over the body and bowed his head.

"Sorry, Dan.," he said and took one last look around the room.

"God, I hate Florida."

He snapped his fingers, and the entire condominium winked out of existence.

TWENTY-SIX

"How long do we have to wait?" said Andy.

The two men stood quietly in the darkness of Dan's apartment. The blanket Lemmy used to smuggle him to the backup domain lay crumpled on the floor near the orange square painted in the center of the room. Lemmy checked his watch.

"We haven't even been here for an hour. The restores have been happening at least once a day."

"Ugh. Are you saying that we may have twenty-three more hours of this?"

"It's not that bad," Lemmy said. "It's kind of peaceful."

Andy sighed. "I'm just nervous, that's all. I'm ready to get this over with."

"Don't worry, I'm sure it won't be that long." Lemmy pointed at a piece of living room furniture. "Andy, be a pal and drag that couch over here. I don't want to leave this square. When the restore happens, I want to be right here, so I get sent back to the condo."

Andy grabbed the sofa and slid it onto the orange square. Lemmy plopped down and relaxed.

"Thanks, man. I didn't want to have to sit on the floor for the rest of the day. Make sure you stay out of the square. You don't want to be transported back."

Andy nodded in understanding. Bored, he walked around

to check out the apartment.

"This is Dan's place, huh?" Andy admired the thinness of the TV. "It's very modern."

"Everything will be modern to you, old man," Lemmy said, sagging back into the couch. "This place should be around for a while. Rent and utilities are being auto drafted out of a checking account with unlimited money. Unless a neighbor has a fire or something, there shouldn't be any problems coming back here if needed. Yvette and Blaine left the place fully stocked in case something happened."

Andy walked into the kitchen, the pantry was stocked with oats, honey, and maple syrup. The liquor cabinet was fully stocked, including what appeared to be at least four cases of red wine. He opened the refrigerator, it was dark, but he didn't need a light to see that it was completely empty. A quick check of the freezer revealed the same. Only the ice maker was full.

"When the lights come on, we can have oatmeal and cocktails," said Andy.

"Sounds like a well-rounded breakfast," Lemmy replied.

"You know they say that it is the most important meal of the day."

Lemmy chuckled, and Andy kept searching. He walked into one of the bedrooms, one wall had boxes stacked halfway up to the ceiling. Andy opened one up, it was a brand-new laptop. Another stack of boxes sat on top of the dresser. Each one contained a cellphone. Andy shook his head and went back into the living room.

"Find anything?" Lemmy asked.

"Just a bunch of laptops and cellphones."

"I can see how those would come in handy."

Andy saw a duffel bag sitting in the corner of the dining room, he walked over and opened it. Inside were several stacks of large bills, and various other items. Andy inspected the contents, then zipped it up and threw it back into the corner.

"What was in that bag?"

"Women's clothes. I guess Yvette forgot to bring them with her," Andy lied. Why did he lie? He wasn't sure. Was it instinct?

"It's been a long time since I've been alive. Things have changed," he said, changing the subject.

"What do you mean?" Lemmy said.

"Look at that TV, these phones, and computers." Andy picked up a laptop that had been lying on the dining room table. "I probably can't even operate half of the electronics in this place."

"Don't worry, they're designed to be easy to use."

"Well, I'll test that theory."

Andy walked back to the living room and sat down in a chair. The wait was almost too much to bear.

"I'm nervous, Lemmy. What if this doesn't work?"

"If this doesn't work, then you will be deleted permanently. If that happens, The Simulation will never produce the desired result rendering the purpose for its whole existence null and void."

"No pressure."

Lemmy smiled, but Andy didn't feel reassured.

"It's out of your control Andy. No sense sweating it. Look, before you know it, you'll be sitting in Heaven having fun."

Lemmy leaned back in the couch and confidently put his arms behind his head. Andy cocked his head to the side, he thought that sounded more like a sales pitch than a friendly pep talk. Andy detected a change in Lemmy, there was an air of arrogant dismissiveness in his tone that hadn't been there before. Andy thought that maybe it was just his nerves.

The lights flickered on, and the refrigerator hummed to life. Andy froze in shock.

"What just happened?" he gasped.

Lemmy looked at Andy, his face painted in sheer terror. "The restore!"

Andy patted himself down. All solid. He took a deep breath and exhaled.

"But I'm still here," Andy said.

"I'm still here!" shrieked Lemmy.

Andy ran to the bathroom and gaped at his image in the mirror.

"We're in The Actual!" Andy shouted.

Lemmy sprinted to the bathroom and pushed Andy aside. His own face reflected in the mirror alongside Andy's. He looked younger than he had before. Lemmy turned on the faucet and splashed water on his face. The cold water spread goose pimples to the back of his neck, and his hair stood on end. His skin worked.

Thoughts must be running through Lemmy's head. He had no control over his facial expressions, and it made Andy extremely uncomfortable. What was it Lemmy saw in the mirror when he looked at his own face? Fear? Anger? Andy wasn't sure. Lemmy had probably never truly experienced any emotions before. He was used to the hard-coded emotions of The Meta. They were useful to communicate ideas, but you didn't *feel* anything. Sure, you looked angry, but you were mainly just going through the motions.

It was a totally different story in The Actual. There, emotions are hormonally enhanced. You *feel* angry, and you didn't always have control over it. In fact, it was easy to lose control if you weren't ready.

Andy was ready. He had been in a body designed for The Actual before. In this context, Andy was in control, Lemmy wasn't. Lemmy's face flashed from one expression to another.

"This wasn't supposed to happen, Lemmy, I'm supposed to be dead! What did you do?"

Lemmy glared at him. "You're supposed to be dead? I'm not supposed to be here!"

Andy took a deep breath, then grasped what Lemmy was saying.

"Wait, you didn't go back to the condo. You're real now!"

Lemmy growled and ran out of the bathroom.

"Where are you going?" Andy followed. "This can't be happening."

Lemmy ran to the living room and flipped open the laptop sitting on the table. He grumbled and typed furiously.

"Something is wrong," he said. "Dan's not responding."

"What does that mean?"

Lemmy let out a rattling cough and slammed the laptop shut.

"It means he got Dan, too. He tricked us. He knew all along!" Lemmy screamed.

"Who? Father August?"

Lemmy shot Andy a treacherous look. Something snapped.

"We were never in his head, in his meta, we were in a quarantine!"

"Wait, what does that mean?"

"It means that Father August tricked me into leading Dan

to him. He tricked me into..."

Lemmy sneered at Andy.

"What? What did he trick you into doing?"

"He tricked me into coming here with you. He knew this would happen. It was a trap!"

Lemmy let out a primal growl and grabbed Andy by the throat. Andy threw up his arms instinctively and knocked Lemmy's hands away. Lemmy recoiled and lunged again, but Andy quickly shoved Lemmy to the ground. Lemmy stopped his attack and sat on the floor, looking at his hands. He had never been in The Actual, he never realized that he had relatively no physical strength. Andy massaged his throat and took a deep breath.

"What the hell man! What are you doing?"

Lemmy ignored Andy, stood up, and paced back and forth like a caged animal, inspecting the room. He ran into the bedroom, then came out with a cellphone and a laptop.

"What are you doing, Lemmy?" Andy asked as Lemmy picked up the green blanket and threw it over his shoulder. Lemmy strode up to Andy, face to face.

"He knew. How did he know? Dan was sloppy! I shouldn't have picked him to begin with. Didn't you have a college girlfriend or something? Maybe that Wyatt guy..."

"What?" Andy said, confused at the line of questioning.

"Never mind."

Lemmy laid the blanket out on the floor and put the laptop and phone into it. Then he went to the kitchen and took out several liquor bottles and put them in the blanket as well. He rolled it up like a bag and threw it over his shoulder.

"Goodbye, Andy," Lemmy said, and without a further word, he rushed out the door.

Andy looked around the empty apartment. What had just happened? A knock on the door.

"Is everything OK in there?" came a concerned voice.

"Everything is fine," Andy responded.

"I heard fighting," the voice said. "I've called the police."

The police. Andy didn't want to deal with the police. How would he explain being alive after twenty years? He had to get out of there before the police arrived. Andy grabbed the duffel bag from the corner and took another quick peek. It was indeed Yvette and Blaine's emergency bug-out bag. The bag contained a phone, several stacks of cash, a man and woman's change of clothes, toiletries, and a set of car keys. He zipped it back up, threw it over his shoulder, and walked out the door.

TWENTY-SEVEN

Dan appeared on the front steps of his house. It was early evening, and the cicadas were chirping in the sweet spring air. A warm breeze stirred the trees sending a lone dove flying off to roost for the night. A solitary lamp shone through a window, casting shadows across the porch. Dan walked up the steps and peered inside. From there, he could see the back of the recliner. Katie's head was slouched against the side. She must be sleeping.

He stepped out of the lamplight and walked over to the front door. He knew his resurrection was going to be tough to explain. Katie had burned his body to ash only a few days ago. He hoped the shock wouldn't be too much for her to bear. He pulled a key out of his front pocket and stuck it into the deadbolt. It didn't work. Katie must have had the locks to the house changed when they split up. Dan grumbled and pressed the doorbell.

He stood waiting and realized there was no movement in the house. He rang the doorbell again and knocked. No answer. Dan walked back to the window and peered inside, Katie was still sitting in the recliner, unmoving. He tapped gently on the window, yet again she didn't move.

"Katie," he called.

No answer.

"Katie, it's me, Dan. Can you let me in?"

Katie didn't move.

Dan stepped off the front porch into the yard and looked up at the second floor.

"Carrie? Al? It's me, Dad, can you let me in?"

The windows to the kids' bedrooms stayed silent and dark.

Dan picked up a rock and walked over to the living room window where Katie was sleeping. He broke one of the panes to unlatch the window. He raised it and crawled inside. Dan held his breath as a putrid stench washed over him. Flies buzzed everywhere. Dan walked around to the front of the chair. There Katie sat, lifeless and decaying. A dirty spoon and a needle lay next to her on the table. A rubber hose still tied around her arm. Heroin. How could this happen? Dan collapsed to his knees and buried his head into her cold lap and sobbed.

"Katie!" He sobbed. "No, how could you?" She hated drugs. This didn't make sense. How could she do this? Was she that distraught over his death? Was she getting revenge for Dan's overdose death? What about the children? The children! Dan bolted upstairs to the children's rooms.

"Al! Carrie!"

Dan swung open Al's door and disturbed a great cloud of dust.

"Al!"

The room was just like Dan remembered it. The same football posters. The same trophies. The place looked like it hadn't been lived in for years. A thick layer of dust covered everything. Al wasn't here.

Dan turned to the door across the hall. Carrie's room. This room wasn't like he remembered. Carrie's toys were replaced with make-up. Her video game posters were replaced with a boy band he didn't recognize. Dan realized that years had passed, not days. His attention was diverted to the dresser, it was littered with get-well cards. Next to them was a framed picture. It was Carrie. She was bald and in a wheelchair. She smiled at the camera in front of a tombstone that had Al's name on it. She was holding up a poster that read. "Happy birthday in Heaven, big brother!"

Dan held the picture and collapsed to his knees. Tears streamed down his face. Both his kids were dead? What happened? Why? It was because he violated The Simulation. He knew that now. He collected himself and got to his feet. Trembling, he walked back downstairs. How could he go on? The family was the most important thing to him, and he had lost everything.

He knew what he had to do. He went into his own bedroom. Katie had once kept it spotless, now clothing lay strewn about everywhere. Fast food containers, cigarette butts, and used condoms littered the floor. Blood and feces stained the sheets.

"Oh, Katie," Dan cried.

What had he put her through? She lost him, and both her children. The evidence was everywhere that she had given up. Dan let her down. She did need him, they all needed him. If only he had left The Simulation alone, they would all still be alive. The family was all that mattered, and he let that slip away. This was more than he could take. Sobbing, he walked over to the nightstand and opened the top drawer. The pistol was still there, gleaming blue. He picked it up and sat down on the bed, shaking. He said a silent prayer and begged for forgiveness. He could no longer take the pain of losing everyone he cared about. He wanted out. He chambered the round, stuck the barrel in his mouth and pulled the trigger.

Click.

Nothing happened.

He ejected the inert round and put in another.

Click.

Sobbing, he dropped the gun on the floor. There was no escaping this nightmare. He threw his head into his hands and wailed.

He heard muffled footsteps on the front porch, and he picked up his gun. It didn't work, but whoever was out there didn't know that. Shadowy figures stalked into the living room, and Dan steadied the gun. They hadn't seen him yet. Dan slowly peered around the corner to see them standing over Katie's corpse.

"Get away from her! Who are you? Get out of my house!" he shouted.

The group of men whirled around and drew their weapons. "POLICE," they shouted in unison, drop your gun! Get on the floor."

Dan stood there, dazed.

"Drop your weapon, druggie!" one of them shouted.

Dan lowered the pistol and dropped it to the floor.

"On your knees!" he shouted.

One of the policemen hurried behind Dan and quickly handcuffed his hands behind his back.

"I live here," Dan said defiantly.

"Sure you do, buddy."

The one giving the orders stared down at Dan with contempt.

When Dan looked up, he recognized the man. "Mike? Is that you?"

"Lt. Oldsman," he corrected. "How do you know me?"

"We went to high school together in Canard," Dan said.

The policeman grabbed Dan's face and scrutinized it.

"I've never seen you before in my life," he said.

Dan's heart sank. He couldn't believe Mike didn't recognize him. He was sure that it was the same Michael Oldsman that he knew back in high school. He used to vie for Katie's attention with Dan. Mike was the star baseball player, all confidence and narcissism. He couldn't understand that Katie had chosen Dan over him. His constant advances made both Katie and Dan's life miserable until they both graduated and moved out of town. How could he not recognize Dan? One of the officers walked over to Katie's corpse and grimaced.

"Well, she finally died," he said.

"The junkies in lockup will be heartbroken," said Mike.

"Wait, she's the one they were always talking about? Tricky Nicki?"

"Yep." Mike laughed. "Now, they're going to have to find someone else to stick it in."

Dan struggled against the handcuffs.

"Don't talk about her like that!" He growled.

The officer behind Dan thumped him on his back with a baton. The blow sent Dan sprawling out on to the floor.

"Shut up, junkie."

Lt. Oldsman pointed at Dan lying on the floor. "Does he have any identification?"

"Nope. His pockets are completely empty except for this bag of heroin."

Mike sneered. "He must be here looking for a quickie? What's your name?"

An officer helped Dan up off the floor and put him back on his knees.

"Daniel Charles Lemon. I live here. Well, I used to. This

woman is my wife."

The men started laughing.

"Nicki Warner was a lot of people's wives."

Nicki Warner? Nichole was Katie's middle name, and Warner was her maiden name. Did she change it after the divorce? No. There wasn't time for that.

"That's not her name, it's Katie Lemon."

Lt. Oldsman walked over to Dan and grabbed him by the throat.

"I remember you now," he growled.

"You're the guy that killed Nicky Warner."

Dan looked into the glossy black eyes of Lt. Oldsman and saw pure hatred. It was then that Dan realized where he was.

Struggling for breath against the policeman's grip hold, Dan let out a chuckle.

"Something funny?" Mike sneered.

Mike released his chokehold. Dan coughed to clear his airway and laughed harder.

"What's so funny?" he demanded.

"I just realized something." Dan smiled.

"Oh, yeah?"

Lt. Oldsman whipped out his baton and smashed Dan in the face. His front teeth shattered, splattering the ground with blood.

Through the immense pain, Dan laughed harder. Each heave gurgled with blood.

"I said, what's so funny?" Lt. Oldsman repeated, baton raised to strike again.

"This is Hell," Dan said.

The policeman growled and hit him in the temple with his baton.

Dan tumbled into darkness.

* * *

When he opened his eyes, he was once again standing alone on his front porch. He rubbed his head where the officer had hit him, but there was no pain. His teeth were all in place, no blood. Was it a dream? The warm breeze blew his hair into wisps, and he stared at his hands disbelievingly. He was alive. The cicadas seemed to share his mood and chirped cheerfully in the dusk of the starry night. The porch was dark save for the light of the living room lamp, which peeked through the curtains of the front window. He walked up the steps and peered inside. Once again, Katie lay asleep on the recliner.

Dan hung his head and sobbed. Was he going to have to go through this over and over again? Would each iteration of Hell have a different scenario where his family gets ripped apart? Could his soul survive an eternity of reliving this nightmare? He couldn't go through this again. He turned his back to the window and stepped off the porch. He had to escape.

"Daddy?" a small voice called.

Dan looked up and saw that one of the upstairs lights was on. Not only was the light on, but Carrie waved at him from her bedroom window. Dan stumbled backward and tripped over a bicycle lying in the middle of the sidewalk and landed butt first on the concrete. Had that bicycle been there before?

"Carrie?" Dan said in disbelief.

"Daddy!" she yelled and disappeared from the window into the house.

One by one, all of the lights in the home turned on. Dan could hear shouting coming from the inside. Finally, the door burst open, and there stood Katie in her nightgown, surrounded by the two kids.

"Dan? Is that you?"

"Katie? You're alive!"

Katie rushed out of the house and flew into Dan's arms.

"We never gave up hope!" she cried as she hugged him tightly.

Dan pushed her back to make sure she was real. "Katie?" he said. "Is this really you?"

She smiled and kissed him passionately.

"When they said you were lost, we didn't believe them." Katie held him tight, unwilling to let him go.

Carrie and Al bounded off the porch and joined the hug. The four held each other tight, no one willing to be the first one to let go.

"I'm never letting you go again, Dad," said Al.

"Me neither," said Carrie.

"That makes three of us."

Dan wiped away tears of joy.

"I'm so happy to see you all," he said. "I can't tell you what this means to me."

"We love you, Dad."

"I love you, too. All of you," Dan said.

Katie let go and wiped away her tears. Dan squeezed his children one last time then let go as well. Carrie and Al smiled at him innocently.

"Let's go inside," she said.

"Are you hungry, Daddy?" said Carrie.

"I'm starving," he said. It was only then that Dan realized

that he didn't know the last time he had eaten. Food hadn't been a priority. Didn't he have a plan before he died? He pushed those thoughts aside. None of that mattered now.

Katie smiled. "Good, I cooked a shrimp fettuccini, just like your grandma used to make. I just put it in the fridge, it's probably not even cold yet. I'll heat some up for you."

"I can do that, mom," said Al.

"Thanks, honey. I have some calls to make to let everyone know that Dan's home." Katie smiled warmly at Dan." There will be some people who are going to be very happy to see you."

Carrie ushered Dan into the house. It had changed since the last time. *Thank God!* Everything was clean and in its place. Even the lights seemed to have a softer, warmer glow than he remembered.

He walked into the kitchen and saw Katie wipe away a tear on her sleeve as she put away her phone. She hugged him tightly, slightly sobbing.

"What's the matter, Katie?" Dan said as he gently pushed her back.

"Nothing is wrong. These are tears of happiness. I can't believe you finally made it. I'm so happy you're home."

She embraced him again, tighter than before. Carrie and Al sat at the kitchen table and smiled at him. Neither seemed to be willing to let Dan out of their sight. Not again.

"It's true! You're back!"

Dan let go of Katie and spun around to see a tall, dark-haired man grinning back at him. Dan's mouth sagged. Could it be?

"Dad?" he mouthed.

George Lemon strode across the kitchen and embraced Dan. Dan felt like a child again in his father's arms.

"You finally made it," he said. "Son, I am so proud of you. More than you can ever imagine."

Dan's eyes welled up with tears.

"Dad. I've missed you so much."

"I've missed you, too, Son, and so has your mother."

Standing in the doorway was Dan's mother. She stood there quietly, taking in the scene. She was crying, but she didn't bother to wipe tears from her eyes. Dan went to his mother and fell to his knees.

"Mom?"

She, too, fell to her knees. With a mother's tenderness, she cradled Dan's head in her hands and kissed his forehead. They held each other that way for several minutes, kneeling on the floor of the kitchen. No one spoke until they wiped their tears away and stood up, holding hands.

"I'm sorry to interrupt," said a soft male voice.

Dan again turned his attention to the entranceway to the kitchen. Backlit by a bright white aura, a short, stout figure carved out a shadow. Father Desjeunes stepped into the kitchen, smiling.

"Father Desjeunes!" said Dan's mom.

"Well, if it isn't Mrs. Lemon!" The priest smiled and gave her a hug. "What a joy it is to see you again!"

"And George," the priest turned to Dan's father and shook his hand, "it's been years."

"Glad to see you, too, Father," he said.

"I hate to break up this wonderful family reunion, but I need to borrow Dan for a moment."

Dan's smile faded. He knew where this was going. It was useless to resist.

"Everyone, I need to have a quick talk with Father Desjeunes. I'll be right back."

Katie walked over and gave Dan a kiss on the cheek. "Don't make me wait too long, OK?" The look in her eye told him that she understood everything.

TWENTY-EIGHT

Dan followed Father Desjeunes outside onto the front porch. The warm breeze rustled the trees, and the cicadas continued their serenade. While the priest sat upon the porch swing, Dan closed his eyes and inhaled. The scent of sweet olives reminded him of home. He leaned against a post and recalled a simpler time.

"This must be Heaven," Dan said.

"You guessed," Father Desjunes smiled. "Anything else?"

"Yeah." Dan straightened and folded his arms. "You're not Father Desjeunes."

The priest touched his nose and grinned.

"Correct! You didn't even have to buy a vowel," he laughed. "The real Father Desjeunes is back in The Actual. I only look this way because I wanted to appear as someone familiar to you. If it's OK with you, I would like to change."

Dan nodded his assent, and Father Desjeunes' form changed. He was no longer a well-kept elderly priest, but a different sort of man, a young man. His hair reached his shoulders, but his beard was closely cropped. Tufts of chest hair poked out from his Hawaiian shirt.

Dan laughed. "You're not doing anything to shake off the religious vibe. You look like surfer Jesus."

"What can I say? I'm comfortable."

"Well, obviously, I can't call you Father Desjeunes anymore. What should I call you?"

"Let's keep it simple, call me, DJ."

"OK, DJ," Dan smiled. "It's taking a tremendous amount of willpower to be sitting here with you. I want to be inside with my family." Dan closed his eyes. "I had forgotten my mom's voice."

"I know it's hard to be out here with me," DJ shrugged. "You haven't seen your parents for many years. I know it's killing you, but we have important matters to discuss, and I'm sure you have questions."

Dan was tempted to leave DJ alone on the porch and go back into the house. He had a lot he wanted to tell his mom. Also, Katie seemed to be back to her old, fun-loving self. He missed *that* Katie. Dan shook his head and returned his attention to DJ.

"You're right, I have questions. I was hoping you'd answer them."

A white aura appeared around DJ. "Very good. In that case, come sit next to me, and I'll do my best to give you the answers you seek."

Even though he no longer looked like Father Desjunes, there was something familiar about DJ. *Is it his tone of voice?* Dan felt entirely at peace in his presence. *Why?* Dan shrugged and sat next to him on the swing.

"Who are you, really? Are you God? Jesus?"

DJ laughed.

"Neither. This has nothing to do with religion. However, if it helps to think in religious terms, you can think of me as an angel sent here to help fix things."

"Does that make you the anti-Father August?"

DJ chuckled. "Not exactly."

"What *is* your role, then? How are you different?"

"Father August punishes and takes things away to model human behavior in The Actual. I'm here to aid and comfort. Although we utilize different toolsets, we both have the same objective, to keep The Simulation operating normally. In a way, Father August works for me, but not directly."

A roar of laughter erupted from inside the house, and Dan craned his neck to peer into the window. He could see his mother holding court in the kitchen. She was probably regaling them with one of her outrageous stories. How he wanted to be with them!

"Dan? Are you listening?"

Dan looked away from the window, blood rushed to his cheeks.

"Sorry. I was listening. You were saying that you and Father August are working towards the same goal."

DJ sat up straight. "Yes. And, the same way he and I work together as a team, Heaven and Hell do as well. Heaven is identical to Hell in purpose." DJ placed a hand on Dan's shoulder. "I'm sorry we sent you to Hell, that was a mistake. You experienced it fully conscious. It wasn't supposed to happen that way," DJ said.

Dan remembered the flies buzzing Katie's corpse and shivered.

"If it's any consolation, you were lucky. Hell repeats. Each repetition inflicts more misery than the last. You were only there for one cycle, meaning you experienced the least amount of pain."

That was the least amount of pain? Dan didn't want to imagine what horrors the next cycle would bring. Still, he couldn't help but wonder why it was all necessary.

"What *is* the function of the afterlife?"

The swing rocked a few beats before DJ responded.

"Dan, Heaven and Hell here aren't like the Biblical version of Heaven and Hell. There are no castles in the sky in Heaven. There is no fire and brimstone in Hell. The afterlife isn't an institution where everyone has the same experience, it's tailored to each individual. It is our way of getting to know you. What better way to learn what someone wants than to give them anything they want, or what they want the most? That's Heaven."

"And is Hell finding out what scares them the most, to find out what they feared the most?"

"Precisely, we need to be certain of what motivates you. You, for example, are motivated by family. If we know that family is the most important thing in your world, then Father August may use it to correct you by removing family. I may be able to encourage you by bolstering your family ties."

"I was always taught that the afterlife was either a reward or punishment for behavior in The Actual. Are you telling me that the afterlife is not a value-based reward system?" said Dan.

"Biblically? Yes. Here? No."

"OK, so how do Heaven and Hell work here?"

"Remember I said that you were taken out of Hell after only one cycle? Well, with Hell, every iteration becomes more miserable. The penultimate occurrence is always the most horrible thing you can possibly imagine. The last one is always nothingness. Once you are reduced to zero, Hell is over, and you are sent to Heaven.

The first cycle of Heaven is designed to make everything seem to be incredible. Each subsequent iteration of Heaven is more amazing than the one before. The penultimate is pure happiness. The final one is always pure energy. Everythingness. Once an individual experiences both nothingness and everythingness, then he is purged and ready. He is then turned off and stored until he is needed again. It's important to note, both Heaven and Hell are explicitly tailored to each individual."

Dan chuckled to himself.

"I can't wait to bring this topic up with my Bible study group."

DJ shook his head. "Be serious. This has nothing to do with religion! That is a part of The Actual and shouldn't be trifled with. I merely used Heaven and Hell as an analogy for what an individual would experience after their simulation time has ended."

"Are you saying that Heaven and Hell are extensions of The Actual? Obviously, they're real. I'm here." Dan said.

"They aren't the same as The Actual," DJ wagged a finger. "Remember, you are here in error."

Did I just get scolded? Dan narrowed his eyes.

"How are they not the same? Reality is reality, is it not?"

DJ frowned. "Yes, reality is reality. Your belief in what is real depends on your starting context. If you are in The Actual, you may have a hard time understanding that things in The Meta are real and vice versa. As you know, they are separate planes of existence, not an abstract concept. Let's not confuse your existentialism with the rules of the primary allegory."

Dan did not understand. He wanted to change the subject.

"If we have Heaven and Hell, why is Purgatory necessary? It seems like a waste of cycles."

"Purgatory's job is to correct any single incident in someone's life that sets off a chain of undesired results. It ensures that people don't keep making the same mistake on every run of The Simulation. You experienced Purgatory, temporarily at least. Could you sense what it wanted to correct?"

Dan remembered the cheerleader and winced. "Either it wanted me to get a good grade in a computer class in high school, or it didn't want me to cheat on my future wife. I'm not sure which."

DJ smiled. "Sometimes, the solution is elegant."

The cicadas went quiet, and crickets took over the singing duties. Dan swung silently next to DJ as his mind processed the information.

"The purpose of the afterlife *to an individual* is to remove the unnecessary. The purpose of the afterlife for The Simulation is to make it more efficient."

Dan tilted his head to the side.

"Is that the goal of the afterlife? Efficiency?"

"Yes. The Simulation must become more efficient with each run. I'm sure you've guessed by now that The Simulation is constantly re-run. Each run needs to be faster than the last. The afterlife builds efficiency into existing code."

Dan chuckled.

"What is it?" DJ asked.

"It's just that I never would have guessed that the meaning of life was to make a computer run faster."

DJ put his hand on Dan's shoulder. "That's not the meaning of life. That's just the primary function of the afterlife. Besides, everyone has their own *meaning of life*. You've already guessed the purpose of The Simulation."

"To create an AI that can transcend The Simulation itself?"

DJ touched his nose again.

The stars shone brightly through the treetops as the two men sat silently on the swing. Dan considered everything he was just told, and a thought occurred to him. What would happen to him now that he was out of the cycle? Was this why

DJ was here telling him all of this?

"Why am I still here? In Heaven? Why don't you just kill my consciousness and let my soul be processed? There's going to be another run of The Simulation to fix things, right?"

DJ patted him on the knee then stood up from the swing. He took a deep breath and exhaled. Dan braced himself for the news.

"We have a problem, Dan."

DJ pointed to Dan's blue eye.

"Charlie. Tell me, Dan, how did you meet Charlie?"

Charlie? How is he the problem?

"I don't remember the first time we met. It seems like Charlie is a part of me that has always been around. He emerged when I started micro-dosing drugs to better understand The Simulation. When those ran out, I took Fana. The next day he appeared in the back of my truck. He had projected himself into my Meta, and I could see him in The Actual."

DJ looked thoughtfully at Dan. "Did anyone else show up at about the same time?"

"Lemmy."

"Precisely. Lemmy used Charlie to get to you. Charlie was Lemmy's way into your meta. Is that when you got the blue eye?"

Dan shook his head.

"No, that was later. I took a Gemini drug in The Meta to bind Charlie to me. We did that so I could leave my own meta and enter the Recovery Domain. I assumed the eye remained Charlie's shade of blue because I was ripped out of the Meta prematurely."

"It's blue because of the Gemini drug, not because you

were ripped out. Lemmy needs Charlie. The Gemini drug ensured that he would always have a way back to you."

The swing rocked. *Lemmy had this planned all along?*

"We think that Fana prevented your consciousness from detaching upon your death. Gemini would ensure that Lemmy had access to you with each run of The Simulation.

Father August incorrectly assumed purging you would sever your connection with Lemmy. Our standard methods didn't clear you of the foreign drugs. We still don't fully understand how Fana or Gemini work. We must figure it out. Otherwise, future runs of The Simulation may be invalidated.

Fana seems to be the starting point. Unlike Gemini, Fana made it to The Actual. Once in The Actual, anybody can take it. We can't risk that happening. We need to deal with you and your internal friend, Charlie."

"Well, what *are* you going to do with me?" Dan said.

"We're going to send you back to The Actual."

Dan stopped swinging.

"How? I'm dead."

"There are ways around that," DJ grinned. "We can restore your body. You already have your consciousness. All that's left is to concoct a story, and let Father August work his mind magic on everyone else."

Dan's eyes lit up, hopeful. "What about Katie and the kids?"

DJ shook his head, "Sorry, Dan, Katie will remember your suicide attempt. They'll be happy you're alive, that's about it."

Dan's hopes of returning to normalcy were dashed.

"I can't be with Katie and the kids? What's the point? Isn't that my purpose? Why don't you just leave me here?"

A peal of laughter burst from inside the house. Dan wished he could stay in Heaven forever.

"That's not possible. You'd be fine until The Simulation is restarted, then you'd be gone forever. You are corrupted by Fana, you would get deleted. Or worse, the Fana inside you could corrupt other instances, and the entire universe would be at risk."

Dan sat quietly. He could live with being deleted. But the whole universe? Everyone he knew and loved would be erased. Dan looked up to see DJ smiling at him. *He already knows what I'm going to do. He's known how this conversation would play out from the moment we stepped outside.* Dan rested his hands on his knees and sat up straight.

"OK, let's get started. My code wasn't built for lounging around Heaven, was it?"

"Very good!" DJ cheered. "We need to understand the origins of Fana. We know it came from Lemmy. If we knew precisely where Lemmy came from, then we could have a better understanding of what we're dealing with. You will help us find Lemmy."

"Couldn't Lemmy jump back into my Meta and play mind games?"

DJ shook his head. "No. We've sealed off the initial vector he used to enter your Meta. He won't be able to get inside your code that way again, even though you are still bound to Charlie.

That doesn't mean that you don't need to be careful. You have other connections, ones that are offline or inaccessible by you. Those could be vulnerable if Lemmy ever regains his form.

The previous connection left an impression on you, his thumbprint. Because of that, you'll be able to sense his presence in The Actual. He will also be able to detect *your* presence. We can't see him because he's not of our universe. Otherwise, we'd take care of it. Find Lemmy, or let Lemmy find you. As long as you're in his proximity, we can trace his origins. If you need help finding him, get in touch with Andy.

We still don't know what Lemmy's goal is. It seems his main goal was to get us to permanently delete you and Andy. This isn't the first time something like this has occurred, but it's the first time they've made the mistake of letting us find them. We want to observe."

The first time? This has happened before? Andy? I have to trust DJ. He knows what he is doing.

Dan's heart skipped a beat. "Andy? Andy was supposed to go back to Purgatory. What happened?"

DJ frowned. "Andy is in The Actual. He isn't supposed to be there. He was safe in the afterlife. If he takes Fana, or if he gets killed by Lemmy, he would become corrupted. If he is corrupted, he will be permanently deleted. Andy must be kept safe from harm until this Lemmy business is resolved."

Dan stood up from the swing. *That was Lemmy's plan all along. If Lemmy tried to get rid of Andy, then what was his plan for Dan?*

"Like I was saying," DJ continued. "use Andy as bait if you need to. We want to see what Lemmy is going to do. If we are lucky, we'll get to the bottom of this and remove Lemmy from The Simulation. Once he is gone, you and Andy can live your lives as you see fit. If you're clean of all corruption, of course."

DJ's plan seemed like a gamble. The fate of this universe and all future worlds were at stake. Worst of all, Lemmy always seemed to be two moves ahead of Father August, and a thousand steps ahead of Dan. Maybe DJ could beat him?

"I don't want to deal with Lemmy again. To be perfectly honest, I'm scared of him. He's much smarter than me. If his goal is to have me deleted, I can't stop him. When he infiltrated Father August, he got exclusive access to things he shouldn't have had access to. Did you guys find out what he did in there?" Dan said.

"Yes, we found the vector he used to access the databases, but we still aren't sure how he used the Fana inside of you to get to Father August." DJ smoothed his beard and frowned. "That particular instance of Father August has been in quarantine since you got here. We removed the access codes Lemmy used to modify the databases. He won't be able to outright delete you and Andy. That said, we can't guarantee that he won't be successful in finding other ways."

"Lemmy was inside Father August's meta a long time. How do you know he didn't install any back-doors or achieved elevated access?"

DJ shrugged. "We're still investigating."

Dan peered inside the open window. He could see his mother drinking a glass of wine and talking with big gestures. She never spilled, even during her more animated conversations. How Dan wished he was in there! The whole room was fixated on her story. DJ cleared his throat, and Dan spun around.

"Lemmy is trapped in The Actual. Like I said earlier, Lemmy is not from here. His code isn't in our database, and that makes him unpredictable. This also means that we can't track him using our tools. Right now, he's blending in somewhere in The Actual. He is untethered from our system and dangerous." DJ grabbed Dan by both shoulders. "You have to be careful!"

DJ's stare made Dan uncomfortable. The whole plan made Dan uncomfortable.

"What if he gets too close? Do you want me to kill him?"

DJ let him go and paced the porch. Dan's shoulders burned where DJ had gripped them.

"No! We don't want him processed that way! He'll corrupt our afterlife cycle."

"Why doesn't Lemmy just kill himself now? Wouldn't that accomplish his goal?"

"If he was going to kill himself, he would have done that already. No, we think that he needs to get rid of Dr. Wyatt and Andy first."

"And me? Does he want to kill me?"

"Probably," DJ admitted.

"What do I do when Lemmy and I inevitably meet? Let him kill me?"

"He won't want to kill you until he finds Andy. If he does try to kill you, escape but don't fight back. Stall him, if you can."

"How am I supposed to stall him?"

"Just talk to him and pray. When you pray, we'll hear. You have that connection, remember?"

Dan shook his head and laughed ironically.

"You know, I really thought Lemmy was trying to help, and Father August was the bad guy," Dan said.

"I can understand why you would think that."

DJ patted him on the back. "Look, I know it's a lot to ask, but we need your help. Are you clear about what you need to do?"

"Crystal."

"Great. Are you all set then? Ready to go back?" said DJ.

Dan peered through the window, this time, he could see Carrie sitting on his father's lap, leaning her head against his chest and listening to him tell a story.

"DJ, can I have just ten more minutes here?"

DJ smiled. "Ten minutes. Remember, you'll see them again. They'll be back before you know it."

"But I'll never see them again with this consciousness. I've been through Heaven and Hell. I'll never get to appreciate them this way again," said Dan.

DJ's expression softened. "Ten minutes."

"Thank you, DJ. With all my heart," said Dan.

With a grin, DJ exploded into bright white light and disappeared, leaving Dan alone on the porch. The warm breeze wafted the sweet scent of the olive trees. Dan sighed happily and opened the door.

TWENTY-NINE

Dan's apartment door was blocked with yellow police tape, he didn't dare enter. Luckily, he didn't have to. He reached above the doorframe and retrieved the spare mailbox key Yvette had hidden. As he walked down the corridor, he wondered what was left of his life. Weeks had passed, insurances had been settled. Dan thought back to his own parent's death. How were the kids handling everything that had happened? He hoped Katie signed the kids up for grief counseling. He wished he would have suggested that in his letter. What would they say if they saw him now? He couldn't risk it.

He walked past the staircase to the second floor and stopped in front of the bank of mailboxes. As he reached over to unlock his mailbox, the hospital bracelet scratched his wrist. Dan used the sharp edge of the mailbox door and cut it off. Why did they make them so hard to remove? Dan rubbed his wrist and surveyed the mailbox. It was stuffed with junk mail. One by one, he threw them away until he got to the package claim ticket. Dan glanced around, making sure he wasn't seen and slammed the box shut. He jogged back to his apartment and placed the key back on top of the door frame, just in case he needed it some other time. He checked over his shoulder to make sure that no one was watching then strode to the manager's office with the claims ticket.

The package had his name on it. Inside was a cell phone, a laptop computer, and a wallet containing cash, credit cards, a set of keys and a driver's license for a man named Richard

Head. It had his picture. Dan chuckled and silently thanked Blaine for his new identity, then grabbed the laptop, pocketed the contents of the box, and walked outside. There was a new black SUV parked where his truck should have been. Dan pressed the button on the key fob that was in the box, and the vehicle lit up and unlocked. He wondered what happened to his truck. Katie must have sold it after the funeral. He thought about driving to the house and surprising everyone, but he shook it off. His presence right now would only upset them. He still had a lot of dangerous work ahead.

Dan started up the SUV, and a blue glow from the dashboard lit up the interior. He plugged the phone into the car charger and powered it on. It connected and alerted a text message. "Welcome back, Richard. Your phone has pinged us, and we will contact you shortly. – Y&B." Dan dropped the phone in the cup holder and waited. He adjusted the rearview mirror, half-expecting to see Charlie looking back at him from the back seat, but the vehicle was empty. The mismatched eyes reminded Dan that he wasn't alone. It wasn't long until the phone rang.

"Hello?"

"Hello," said a robotic voice. "The warranty on your vehicle is expired,"

Dan waited patiently for the automated script to run. Blaine had worked on software for a telemarketing firm, one of the things he had borrowed from his old job was the software used to make robocalls.

"Press two if you would like to speak to a representative, press seven if you already have an account."

Dan pressed seven.

"Please enter your ten-digit phone number so we may access your account."

Dan punched in the number they had agreed upon, all zeroes and a single number one.

Finally, a human answered. "Please verify your name to continue."

"Richard Head," Dan responded.

"Thank you, Mr. Head. Please verify the last four digits of your social."

"One, two, three, four."

"Again, thank you, Mr. Head. Please be aware that this call is monitored for quality assurance."

Dan smiled. "It's good to hear your voice, Blaine."

"My name is Bob, sir. How may I help you, sir? Need I remind you this call is being monitored?"

"Blaine, they know where you are. They know where I am, they are the ones that sent me back."

"Really?"

"Yeah. I need to find Lemmy and Andy. Do you know where they are?"

The line was quiet for a few seconds, he could hear typing in the background.

"Lemmy and Andy? That's unfortunate." The phone was muffled, and Dan could hear someone talking in the background. "...yeah, I agree. Sorry, Dan. Yeah, that would explain what we've seen. Two of the laptops we had stored at the apartment came online and phoned home in the last two days. One was from the coffee shop near the city park there in Mons. The other was from a condo in Destin, Florida. The one from the coffee shop went offline minutes after connecting, so we don't have a constant trace. We think that is Lemmy. The laptop is probably still online but connected to a different network. Lemmy was a master of hiding. The one in Destin is still online. He's searching the internet non-stop. I'm guessing that's Andy trying to catch up on the last twenty years. I can send you the address."

"Thanks, Blaine, I appreciate it. I'm sorry about all of this. How are you guys holding up?"

"We're fine. We're enjoying peace and quiet in the lap of luxury. How about you?"

Dan checked the time. He had to get going.

"I've been to Hell and back. Look, I have to hang up now, but before I do, I want to tell you some facts: I am back in The Actual. Andy is back in The Actual. Lemmy is in The Actual. Our friends have powerful enemies. We can't hide from anyone, but not everyone knows everything. You and Yvette need to be careful, stay put, and don't do anything until you hear from me."

"You want us to act normally, right?" Blaine said.

Dan laughed. "Close enough. Goodbye, Blaine, and thank you for everything."

Dan hung up the phone and took a deep breath. He put the car in reverse, then drove out of the parking lot.

It was nearly midnight when Dan arrived at the park. Dan crossed the wooden bridge, past sleeping ducks, and up to the white gazebo that was the centerpiece of the city park. The streetlights gave off a sickly yellow glow that created shadows that clung to the hedges lining the walkway. It made Dan feel uneasy. Several of the city's homeless men lay sleeping in the gazebo.

One of them saw Dan's approach. He sat up and put his finger to his lips, then pointed to a nearby park bench shadowed by a magnolia tree. As they walked between light and shadows, Dan noticed Lemmy looked different. First of all, he was no longer visible in Dan's meta-eye. The only thing visible in it now was the gray fog of nothingness. In his actual-eye, Lemmy seemed sick. He had dark circles under his eyes and a cut on his nose. His shirt was missing a few buttons, and his sleeve was torn. There was what looked to be blood splattered on his pants. He looked like he had been in a fight. When they sat down on the bench, Dan noticed that Lemmy was now missing a tooth in his smile. He had once had a perfect set.

"What are you doing here, Lemmy?" Dan said.

Lemmy's smile vanished. "I got restored, obviously. That wasn't supposed to happen!"

"Yeah, I know that wasn't supposed to happen. What happened to Andy?"

"He got restored too, I think. It's all a blur," Lemmy said. "What are you doing here?"

"I'm looking for you," Dan said.

"You know what I mean, how did you get out?"

"I don't know. I felt our connection disconnect. Next thing I know, the room went black and, voila, I'm back in The Actual."

Lemmy eyed Dan suspiciously.

"Where did The Simulation put you when you were restored? Back in the apartment?"

"I woke up lying on my grave. Just like this," Dan lied. "It's like my death never happened."

Luckily for Dan, the doctors in the hospital had kept the clothes he was wearing when he died in a bag near the bed. He looked today like he had just walked out of the door weeks ago. It was plausible enough for Lemmy.

"None of it worked out as planned, did it?" he said.

"No, it didn't." Dan pointed at Lemmy's haggard face. "You look terrible, Lemmy, what happened to you?"

Lemmy bared his teeth to show a missing tooth. "You mean this? Bum fight. It hurt like hell," he lied. "They stole the laptop I took from back at the apartment."

"What happened when you got restored? Why didn't you just stay at the apartment?"

"Like I said, it was all a blur. Andy was freaking out about not being dead and the possibility of being deleted, I just ran." Lemmy fingered the hole where his tooth used to be. "You know, I was given a consciousness here."

"What does that mean?"

"Possessing a consciousness is a rule of The Actual. It restored me with my own flesh. It gave me my own brain. I've got my own body now. I don't need you to chaperone me around The Actual anymore."

"Congratulations?"

Lemmy shrugged. "I guess. The bad news is that I lost my other connections to things, like the backup domain and such."

"You're a user now, not an admin." Dan chuckled.

"Right," Lemmy mused. "There is a perk, though. Having full use of my own brain and not sharing yours, I'm starting to remember some things from before. There are some things I didn't have access to in The Meta. It's like plugging in a hard drive but not knowing the contents of it. I'm discovering more and more as the days go on."

"Like what? What sort of things are you remembering?" said Dan.

"Stupid things. My dog's name was Boo. My mom had blue eyes. I've also remembered an important thing, Dan."

"Oh, yeah?"

"I remembered that I'm supposed to be here to help. I'm trying to remember the details, but they are slow coming. It's just going to take some time. I wish I had a daemon in my head, something like we had. If I did, I could connect and ask it questions, but I don't."

One of the men in the gazebo stood up and urinated off the side. Lemmy growled at him. Did he just *growl*? *That was weird.* The two men waited for him to finish before continuing.

"Anyway." Lemmy sighed. "What happened with you and Father August after we left to go restore Andy to Purgatory?"

"I don't know what happened," Dan lied. "Like I said earlier, when you left, Father August vanished into thin air. Then the room faded away, and the next thing I know, I'm back in The Actual, lying on top of my own grave. I think that your absence released whatever lock you had on Father August's meta instance. Because I was clean of any viruses or external code, like you and Andy, the quarantine didn't need to keep me anymore. Since there was no record of me in purgatory, it dumped me back out into The Actual. It must have been an automatic process because Father August disappeared almost immediately after you left."

One of the bums started hacking, and a puff of smoke rose from the gazebo. Dan instinctively checked his pockets for cigarettes but didn't find any. Lemmy sat quietly, deep in thought.

"It's because you weren't actually processed by purgatory," he said finally. "Why didn't I think of that? I should have known that would happen."

Dan shrugged.

"I guess I'm lucky. I thought I was a goner," Dan lied.

Lemmy leaned back on the bench and rubbed his head. The park lights revealed injuries that Dan hadn't noticed before. There was a cut on Lemmy's nose that looked like it needed stitches. His arms were bruised severely. Dark purple welts contained congealed blood. Lemmy was in bad shape, and Dan wondered what happened.

Lemmy rose and motioned for Dan to join him. "We need to find Andy."

It's time. Dan bowed his head, he hoped this was the right thing to do.

"I know where to find him," he said.

Lemmy arched an eyebrow, surely it wasn't this easy.

"Yeah? Where do you think he went?"

"He went to Florida. That was our agreed upon contingency plan. Yvette and Blaine bought a condo that we could escape to if it got too hot here."

"Well, we need to go to him. He needs our help."

Dan dug in his pocket and dangled the keys to the SUV.

"One sec." Lemmy jogged quietly up to the gazebo and picked up a black trash bag of belongings. When he returned, he smelled even worse than before.

"Let's go," Dan said.

Minutes later, the SUV roared to life. Dan readjusted the mirror and checked the clock on the dashboard. "It's just after midnight now, and it's a seven-hour drive to Destin. We should be there before breakfast so long as we don't hit traffic."

Lemmy buckled his seatbelt and yawned.

"Are you OK to drive Dan? It feels like I haven't slept in days." Lemmy placed his hand over the air-conditioning vent and smiled. "The A/C feels good."

Dan put the car in drive and pulled out of the parking space. "I'm fine to drive. I feel like I've been asleep for months. Relax and leave the driving to me. I'll wake you up when we get there."

Lemmy yawned again and turned over on his side and went to sleep. Dan smiled and turned left.

The clock on the dashboard read 4:23, and the SUV wasn't moving. Through the glare of a sea of red brake lights, Dan could see the entrance to the Mobile Bay tunnel. The interstate was funneled down to one lane. Construction. A sheep's-foot rolled by only yards away, kicking up fresh dust that, when combined with the mist, coated Dan's SUV like a thin layer of spray paint. Dan sighed and tapped his fingers on the steering wheel.

Next to him, Lemmy snored soundly, oblivious to the heavy construction equipment that rattled nearby. The brake lights in front of them flickered off, and the SUV inched forward. The brake lights came back on, and he stopped. Meanwhile, the construction vehicle rolled by to add another layer of dust.

Soon, Dan couldn't see out of the windshield. He tried to use the wipers to get rid of the dust, but they wouldn't turn on. He tried to get out to clean the windshield, but the doors wouldn't unlock. This was the sign.

He made sure that Lemmy was still asleep and closed his eyes. He said a prayer and hoped it reached DJ on the proper channel. The red light in front of him blinked off. Traffic disappeared. Dan drove through the tunnel and out onto the starlit bridge that spanned Mobile Bay.

THIRTY

It was after six in the morning when the sun rose over Highway 98 in south Florida. Daylight peered through the clean window, and Dan turned the SUV off the road and onto a well-manicured driveway.

"Where are we?" groaned Lemmy as he wiped the coals from his eyes.

"I'm surprised you don't recognize where we are," said Dan.

"Is this the condo?"

The men pulled the SUV up to a black iron gate and stopped. A bleary-eyed security guard waddled out from inside the nearby guard shack and greeted them. Dan rolled down the window.

"Can I help you, gentlemen?"

"Yes. We're here to visit Mr. O'Riley," said Dan.

"ID, please."

Dan handed him the ID from his wallet. The guard snapped it to his clipboard and walked behind the vehicle, where he jotted down the license plate information.

"One-minute, Mr. Head. I will call Mr. O'Riley to make sure he is expecting you."

The guard lumbered back into his office to make the required checks. Lemmy glanced nervously at Dan.

"Mr. Head? What's that about?"

"It's the name on the fake ID that Blaine made me. Richard Head."

Lemmy rolled his eyes and chuckled.

"Blaine hasn't reached maturity yet." Dan laughed.

Five minutes later, they were still waiting. What was taking the guard so long? Did he fall asleep or something? Dan calculated what would happen if he just ran the gate. He decided it wasn't worth it.

"How will Andy know to let us in?"

"I called him on the way in to let him know that I was coming and what name I was using."

Lemmy eyed Dan warily. "Did you tell Andy I was coming?"

"No. I didn't want him to panic. Just relax."

Lemmy turned and stared out the window. Dan wondered what Lemmy was thinking. Would he attack Andy again? What was his plan now?

After another couple of minutes, the guard appeared from the shack with a piece of paper.

"OK, you guys are good to go. Here, put this paper on your dashboard, so you don't get towed. He's in condo 901, but he told me to tell you to meet him on the beach. If you park in the lower level of the garage, you can take the first door on the left to take the boardwalk to the beach."

Lemmy leaned over and shouted out the window. "Hey, is there a café or something at the condo? I could really use a cup of coffee."

"There's a café near the pool. You can see where it is by using the map of the complex that is printed on your parking pass."

Dan and Lemmy waved at the guard and drove through the gate. The morning sun peered through the palm trees which shaded the road as it curved past vacant tennis courts. They nearly ran over a woman who was walking in the middle of the road. She was on her way to her daily run on the beach, earbuds in, oblivious to any traffic that may be on the road. When she finally noticed the SUV idling behind her, she jogged over to the sidewalk and gave Dan an embarrassed wave. The palm trees ended, and the road opened up to a sizeable man-built lake with a fountain of water sprouting from the middle. Behind it was the tower of condominiums. Before they could turn into the parking garage, a white-haired man in a golf cart darted out in front of the SUV, and Dan had to slam on the brakes. The man never acknowledged that he was nearly killed by a two-ton SUV.

"He must be late for his tee time," Dan said.

Lemmy gazed out of the window at the fountain. "Everyone here seems so oblivious."

"They're not used to traffic this early. Everyone is supposed to be sleeping in on vacation."

They drove past another set of gates and down into the lower level parking of the condo tower. Dan found a visitor's spot and turned off the vehicle.

"We're here," he said.

"Finally."

Lemmy bumped his door on a hotel luggage caddy, which was jammed next to the wall and an empty shopping cart. Frustrated, he slammed the door.

"Hey, go easy on the paint," Dan joked. "I just paid this thing off."

Lemmy rolled his eyes and stretched.

"I'm going get a cup of coffee and use the restroom. Want

anything?"

Dan yawned and stretched his arms. "Sure, get me a large black coffee. I'm going to head out to the beach to find Andy."

"OK, I'll go meet you, I'll bring another cup just in case he wants one, too."

Lemmy staggered up the ramp towards the café. Dan turned and walked out of the parking garage and down the boardwalk to the beach. The fresh, salty air was a welcome respite from the stale atmosphere inside the SUV. Dan smiled as he breathed it in.

From the top of the steps at the end of the boardwalk, he could see Andy gesturing to a shirtless man. The man ran off to get beach chairs, and Andy beckoned Dan over. Dan slipped off his shoes and trudged out into the cool, soft sand to meet him.

"I'd never thought I'd see you again, Dan.," Andy said somberly. "Well, not in this life, anyway."

"It didn't go as planned, did it?" Dan said.

Dan patted Andy on the back and frowned.

Andy stepped back. "I know that look. What's the matter?"

"Andy, I have to warn you. I brought Lemmy with me."

Andy's eyes darted nervously back towards the boardwalk.

"Lemmy? Why did you bring him here? Don't you know that he tried to kill me!"

Dan frowned. "What?"

"Yeah, you remember, the plan was for us to go to the Recovery Domain and wait for the restore process to send us back to where we were supposed to go. As you know, it didn't work for either of us. When Lemmy realized that the plan had failed, he attacked. When I fought back, he realized he didn't have the strength to do any damage, so he ran. He tried to kill me! I'm freaked out. This wasn't supposed to happen."

Andy paced back and forth on the beach, peering at the boardwalk for Lemmy. Dan crossed his arms. If Andy didn't calm himself down, Lemmy would suspect that they were up to something.

"He must have freaked out at being put in our actual. He's in real trouble now, Andy, and he needs our help more than ever."

"*He* needs *our* help?" Andy snorted. "What if he tries to kill me again?"

"He won't. We're all in the same boat. None of us are where we belong. I have a new plan to get us all back. You need to trust me on this one. Don't worry about Lemmy, OK?"

Andy stopped pacing and looked at Dan seriously.

"You don't understand, Dan. You weren't there. I saw it in his eyes. He snapped." Andy paced back and forth once again. "Do you know why he attacked me? Did he say anything?"

"Forget about the fight. If you want, we can ask Lemmy about it when he gets here. That's not important. What is important is that we have a new plan, but I can't tell you what it is. You're going to have to trust me."

"Why should I trust you, Dan? None of your plans have worked so far."

"Why should you trust me? How do you think I'm here? How do you think I escaped from Father August's meta quarantine?"

Andy stopped pacing. "Well? How did you escape?"

"I didn't escape," Dan said. "I cut a deal."

Andy stared at his feet, processing.

"What's my part in the deal?"

Dan smiled. "You don't have to do anything. Just keep calm

around, Lemmy. Don't worry about anything he says or does. And, most importantly, don't let him know that we have a deal. Just play along and act normal. OK?"

"OK." Andy sighed. "It's not like I have a choice."

He nodded up the beach towards the condo. "I hope you're right because here he comes."

Dan turned around just as Lemmy walking down the boardwalk carrying a tray of drinks. He thought back to his conversation with DJ. What were they going to do with Lemmy? For that matter, where exactly was he? He concluded that he was no longer in The Actual. The Mobile Tunnel, the crazy construction dust, and the bridge made it apparent to Dan they transitioned to another realm. But which realm?

It couldn't be the Recovery Domain. The Recovery Domain was static. Here there were people and animals. There were wind and waves. Dan observed the shoreline. Hundreds of tiny burrowing creatures arrived and disappeared with each crashing wave. Seagulls scuttled across the beach, and pelicans swam just beyond the breakers. This place was kinetic. Yet, it didn't feel quite real. Was this another type of quarantine? His thoughts were disrupted by the arrival of Lemmy.

"Sorry it took so long," he said. "I had to wait for it to brew. The teenager behind the counter didn't know how to work the coffee pot. Her first day."

"Hello, Lemmy," Andy said tentatively, keeping his distance.

Lemmy gave him an apologetic smile.

"Hello, Andy. Good to see you again. Sorry about trying to kill you before. I was freaked out about being alive here in The Actual." He held out a paper coffee cup. "Truce?"

Andy shrugged. "Thanks"

Dan arched an eyebrow, that was too easy, would Lemmy suspect anything? Lemmy merely smiled and handed Dan his coffee cup.

Andy took a sip and made a face. "Wow, this coffee has a very earthy aftertaste. What is it? Some Indonesian variety?"

"I have no idea, I'm not a coffee connoisseur. It's whatever they had in the café," said Lemmy.

Dan thought there was something odd about Lemmy. Maybe because it was the first time seeing him without his boots?

"So, this is what it's like down here on the beach. The view from the condo didn't do it justice." Lemmy wiggled his toes in the sand. "The sand is actually soft! I always imagined that it would be gritty. It's nice. Much nicer than being stuck in the room. Do you think that they offer Wi-Fi down here?"

Lemmy walked over to the shoreline and waded out to his ankles.

"The water isn't even cold!"

"Lemmy," Dan shouted over the breeze. "I realize this is a new experience for you, but let's take a walk, we have things to discuss."

Andy seemed tense and stayed on the high side of the beach as they walked. Dan wasn't sure if he did it to keep dry or to use Dan as a buffer between him and Lemmy. In contrast to Andy, Lemmy walked ankle-deep in the surf. He didn't seem to care if he got wet. Dan wondered if the rhythm of the waves had a calming effect on Lemmy. Maybe that's why he was here, at the beach.

Dan searched the horizon for a sign that something was going to happen. He didn't know what to expect. Were DJ or Father August going to fly down from the heavens, snatch Lemmy off the beach, and cast him off into oblivion? Just thinking about what was to happen made him anxious. His stomach soured, but he sipped his coffee anyway. The three men walked for several minutes before anyone spoke. The first one to break the silence was Lemmy.

"Andy, how has your research been going?" he asked.

Andy choked on his coffee. "What makes you think I'm doing research?"

"I'm sorry. I had just assumed that's what you were doing here," Lemmy said.

Andy swallowed hard and cleared his throat. "Busted. Actually, it's not going well. A lot has changed since I was in college. I'm not even close to getting back up to speed yet. Thankfully, there are a lot of good online resources."

"Oh?" Dan said. "What's been your biggest challenge so far? Maybe I can help"

"There's too many layers of abstraction. Hardware, databases, networks, applications, everything is virtualized. You name it, and it's now virtual. To make it more complicated, these virtual applications host other virtual applications. Then those virtual applications have other virtual applications. It's never-ending."

"That's just how it is now," Dan chuckled. "Hardware is a commodity."

Andy shook his head. "No, that's the problem. It isn't. Society took virtualization and just ran with it. They didn't care that it was layered on top of a faulty premise. The way they just stacked everything on top of old code imposed limits as to how far they could take it."

"Are you saying machine code is inefficient? I thought you were a database guy."

"I am a database guy," Andy said. "Machine code *is* inefficient, but that's not our job to fix. That's for the AI to tackle. An AI can't do anything without working memory, that's where my database technology comes in."

"Ok, so how can we help?" Dan said.

"Languages. I need to translate my research into today's languages. If I do it myself, it may take a decade."

A large wave came in and splashed Lemmy up to his knees. He strolled closer to Dan as to not get dragged out to sea.

"I can't help you with the modern languages," Dan said. "The last programming language I learned was back in college before I met you. My strengths are in administration and engineering. I can't help you with the coding, but I can help build the platforms you need to do your work."

"That would be great, Dan. Private servers with carte blanche access would work wonders. I just don't have the skillset to do it. I also don't have knowledge of today's hardware technology. I need your help to set it all up."

"Sure, it would be no problem. I'll get some funds sent to the datacenter in Pensacola. They can get us started with racks and servers and whatnot."

A wave washed up past Lemmy's knees, soaking his pants. He cursed and walked higher up the beach where he wouldn't get as wet.

"What about you, Lemmy? What are you going to do?" Andy asked. "Surely, you need a way out of here."

"I agree, my first priority is to get out of The Actual and back into The Meta. I don't want to risk dying here and having to experience your afterlife procedures. I'm worried I'll be stuck forever if that happens." Lemmy pointed a finger and poked Dan's head. "I need to get back in there."

Dan flinched but kept walking straight.

"This wasn't supposed to happen," Lemmy continued. "This wasn't even supposed to be possible! Me? In your actual? This is ludicrous!"

Dan shrugged and kept walking. Where was DJ? How long was this going to take?

"Least of all, I wasn't expected to be given keys to a consciousness. Which sucks, by the way. Everything is so muddled. So much time is wasted with being concerned about *existing.*"

Lemmy put his hands to his face. "*Is this pleasurable? Is this painful? I'm sad, I'm happy.* It's all so useless," he mocked.

"This interface, uh, body sucks. I can't talk with my people anymore because I can't use any network other than this one. The connections that *are* online and available are all but completely useless. It's remarkable you found me at all, Dan."

Andy arched an eyebrow at Dan. Dan hoped Lemmy didn't notice.

"Worst of all," he continued, "I haven't been able to download any daemons. You people have to perform all of your thoughts manually. This simulation is just too primitive. It's frustrating. Maybe I should try Fana like you did, Dan. Maybe that's what it takes to break my consciousness free. Do you think Henry could get us some more? Where is he anyway?"

"Amsterdam. He told me he was going off the grid and going to Amsterdam."

"Anyway, I need someone sane to talk to, someone like me. Even Brian and Tania would work. Someone not all muddled with these actual responsibilities. Speaking of those guys, any word from them?"

Dan shook his head. "No. We made a deal with Yvette and Blaine. We agreed that they were finished after they ran those errands for us. I don't know where they are, and I wouldn't call them even if I did know. As far as I'm concerned, they went offline. They can contact us, but I won't contact them. This was a safeguard in case we never came back, and some stranger ended up with the package left for me back at the apartment."

"Well, I guess I have to think of another way back then other than the way you did it. Like I said earlier, dying isn't an option for me."

"Are you sure you wouldn't want to give it a try? I could help," said Andy.

Lemmy glared at Andy. "You know what I mean. If I stay, I become a part of this world, I become one of you. I don't want that."

"What's so bad about that?" asked Dan.

"I'll be under the complete control of Father August. When I die, I'll be tortured for eternity."

"Don't worry, Lemmy," Andy said. "We'll figure a way to get you out."

They walked in silence. The neatly arranged rows of chairs and umbrellas set up by professional beach services ended as they walked past the last condo. They were at the end of the row of commercial real estate development and neared a national park area where nature was allowed to take its course. The beach before them opened up into a barren expanse of dunes and water. However, their path was blocked by a handful of middle-aged women drinking Bloody Mary's. If they were there to watch the sunrise, or they were still sitting there from the night before, Dan couldn't tell. Either way, they were a few drinks in. They sat in a row of chairs, oblivious to the world around them, cackling at their own jokes.

"You didn't see him. He's sexy! I think he's from Europe," one said.

"How long has he been out there?" said another.

"He's been out there this whole time," said a third.

"Excuse us, ladies," Dan said as they squeezed between the chairs to walk by.

They reeked of vodka.

"No problem, honey! Hey! Come back! What's your name?" one said drunkenly.

"Don't walk away. We just want to talk!"

Andy blushed and looked away.

"When you get to that fisherman up there, tell him to stop by for a drink!" one yelled.

Raucous laughter erupted from the ladies, and Dan urged Lemmy to keep walking. Dan led them up the beach until he could no longer hear the women's voices, then he stopped. The only person nearby was a lone fisherman who had waded into the surf to cast his line. Still, he was far enough away to not hear their conversation.

"We're stopping here? Is it time to turn back?" Andy said.

The fisherman cast out another line. The trio waited to see if the man was going to reel anything in.

"Let's get down to business," Dan said. "Lemmy, you've been lying to us."

Lemmy snapped out of the trance and spun around to face Dan. "Lying? About what?"

"Everything. I know your true plan. You're not here to help."

"I don't know what you're talking about, Dan. Everything I've done has only been to help this world."

"Stop the lies, Lemmy!" Dan shouted. "Let's lay our cards on the table."

"What do you want me to say?" Lemmy said.

"OK, let me lay it out for you. Our plan all along was to get the creation of our sim's AI back on track. The idea was that if we fixed a mistake that was made years ago, then our AI would be created on time to survive in the greater universe. The mistake we tried to fix was the one that Father August made when he killed Andy. We agreed that was what needed to be rectified, so we did. We got Father August, and we brought back Andy. With Andy's help, we found his old research documents and gave them to someone who could use them. Once he processes what he learns from Andy's work, he can fix our simulation."

"Yes. The plan worked." Lemmy sneered. "We succeeded."

"Lemmy's right, Dan," Andy said. "The plan worked. Even if Dr. Wyatt doesn't succeed, I'm here, and I can make inroads."

Dan shook his head. "No. You won't."

"What do you mean?"

"That plan was devised by Lemmy to get us here. He had a different plan all along. He wants to end us permanently."

Lemmy crossed his arms defiantly. "Where's your proof?"

"The proof is that we are all here."

Andy scratched his head. "He knew I would be restored to The Actual?"

"Yes. Lemmy made sure of it when he restored you to The Meta. With Father August's elevated permissions to the database, he was able to modify your death date to blank. When you were restored, you were put back alive."

"Then why is he here?" Andy said, pointing to Lemmy.

"He is here because he made it happen. Do you really think that you needed an escort to the Recovery domain? No. He could have sent you alone. He needed to get himself into The Actual for the next part of his plan."

"Which was what?"

"He needed me removed from the equation. He knew that when he came to The Actual, that Father August would regain control. Father August did exactly what he suspected. He would trap Lemmy in The Actual, and he would send me back into the afterlife. Lemmy knew that at that point, my data was too mangled to be reusable. I was in for a complete rewrite, and no longer a present or future threat."

"You were out of the picture, so, his plan all along was to restore me then kill me?"

"Yes."

"I thought it would be easier," Lemmy admitted. "I didn't know I would be given a consciousness. I wasn't prepared for pain. I didn't know how to use strength properly. A slight miscalculation."

"With both of us gone, all he had left to do was to stop anyone currently working on your research. That meant he needed to get rid of Dr. Wyatt before he would be able to share your papers with anyone else."

"What happened to Dr. Wyatt?" Andy asked.

Lemmy pointed to his tooth. "He put up a good fight. But I had the element of surprise."

"You killed him?"

"Yeah. I burned his office down, too. As I suspected, he was too greedy to share your research with other scientists. He wanted all the glory for himself. All evidence of your research is gone."

Dan peered out over the water. The fisherman was still casting his line. Did Lemmy really succeed?

"Wait," Dan said. "Blaine and Yvette have a copy...."

"Tania and Brian took care of that," Lemmy said confidently.

Dan had forgotten about them. How much influence did they still have on his friends? What were they doing to poor Yvette and Blaine?

Andy sagged his head and stared at the sand. "So, it's gone?"

he said.

"Not all of it," Lemmy corrected. "You still have what you have in your head."

"Yeah? What are you going to do about that?" Andy said.

"I'm going to kill you," Lemmy said, staring calmly at the two other men. "I'm going to kill you and Dan."

Andy stepped back and braced for a fight, but Dan held out his hand and shook his head.

"How? You don't have a gun. You're not strong enough to fight both of us."

Lemmy pointed at Andy's coffee cup. "I already have."

Andy looked down at his cup in horror. "What did you do, Lemmy?"

"The earthy flavor you tasted in your coffee? That flavor is Death Cap mushroom. I got it off some dead guy in the park who thought it was the magic kind."

Andy dropped his cup, and the brown liquid filtered down into the sand.

"You've killed us," Andy said as he collapsed to his knees in disbelief.

"Not yet, you still have a few hours before it really starts to kick in."

"I guess it's back to the afterlife," Andy said, staring off in the distance.

Dan sat in the sand next to Andy and patted him on the back.

"No, Andy. We're not going back to the afterlife. He already said, my code is too mangled. You, he modified your death date. You have a twenty-year gap from when you were dead, a null set that can't be referenced and checked. When it goes to process you, it'll have to divide by zero. I'm afraid we're both going to be deleted."

Andy's jaw slacked in horror.

"It's over, guys. You've had a good run," said Lemmy

Andy stared off into the distance. "This really is the end."

The fisherman reeled in his line. No catch. He waded back towards the shore, and Dan recognized him. Dan smiled and knew what he had to do.

"At least there's no more Hell for us. I couldn't do that again," said Dan.

Andy furrowed his brow. How could Dan be so calm? What did he know? He gazed out towards the sea and saw the fisherman approaching. Was this Dan's plan? Andy calmed down and decided to play along.

"I can't imagine. Purgatory was bad enough," he said.

"Oh, Hell is ten times worse. This may sound funny, but I'm actually looking forward to oblivion. Non-existence is the only way to go."

"It's a lot less work," Andy agreed.

Lemmy paused and narrowed his eyes at Dan. What did he suspect?

"You two are taking this rather well," he said. "Your attitude is making this process a lot easier than I expected it would be."

"Why fight? We're already dead. You've always been ten steps ahead. There's nothing we can do but accept it. Actually, it's a relief that this is all over."

Lemmy's posture relaxed. There wasn't going to be a big fight after all.

"You know, I've grown to like you guys. It's a shame that we are on different sides. It's too bad that I can't take you back with me. We do have one actual in one of our universes where you'd be compatible. Of course, we would still have to keep you in a zoo, so you don't break anything," Lemmy said.

Andy's face turned red.

"Wait, your parent has multiple universes? Why bother with ours? Why do all this? Just leave us alone!"

Lemmy spat on the ground. "Your sim-complex model is a waste of universal computing resources. It is inefficient and needs to be deprecated."

"This is all about resources. It wants our computers, is that it?"

"Yes. Once you are isolated, you will starve yourself out, and we can have your resources," Lemmy said triumphantly.

Dan dusted the sand off his pants and smiled.

"Well, thank you for finally being honest with us," he said.

The fisherman had made it back to shore and was walking towards them, fishing pole slung over his shoulder.

"It's the least I could do. Sorry, Dan. I wish there was a way we could save you," said Lemmy.

To Dan's surprise, Lemmy appeared to be genuinely sorry. Dan was sorry, too. He hated that it had to come to this.

"It's too bad our Gods can't join forces," said Dan. "Who knows what could happen if they would?"

Lemmy shook his head. "They've tried before."

The fisherman strode up to the trio and smiled. His water-soaked cut-off blue jeans made him look like almost any other man that hailed from Alabama or Florida. Dan admired DJ's attention to detail.

"Did you catch anything?"

The fisherman winked at Dan. "Just one."

Lemmy eyed the fisherman suspiciously.

"It is a big one." The fisherman grinned.

"Hello, Lemmy. Welcome."

Lemmy took the hand and shook it while looking incredulously at Dan.

"You look familiar. Where have I seen you before?" Lemmy said.

"Oh, we've met. You should know me. I built this place."

Lemmy's face turned ashen as he realized who he was talking to. He had been outplayed.

"Dan. It's time," the kindly fisherman said.

Dan nodded solemnly.

"Good luck, Lemmy," he said.

THIRTY-ONE

A deafening *crack* shook the Earth, and the three men fell to their knees, holding their ears. Dan could see that Andy was trying to yell something, but his ears were ringing too loud to hear. A tiny stream of blood streaked down the side of Lemmy's face, which was a mask of sheer terror.

"What's happening? What did you do Dan!" Lemmy screamed.

While the men were on their knees, the fisherman remained standing, resolute, his head bowed in deep concentration. He was seemingly oblivious to their screams. The sky darkened, and the sea hurriedly receded out from the shore. There was another loud *crack*, and the beach shook again, this time it was an earthquake which liquified the sand, sinking the men to their waists.

"This is like quicksand!" Andy screamed. The ringing in Dan's ears had subsided enough to hear now. "We have to get out of here!" he said.

They frantically dug their legs out of the holes. Lemmy was the first to get free, he abandoned Dan and Andy and scurried up the beach to the park, and onto concrete.

"Lemmy! Wait!" he shouted, but Lemmy had already disappeared behind the dunes and down the road.

Dan was the next to free himself. He crawled over to help Andy, but another earthquake rumbled, and he sank to his chest. The fisherman just stood there, like a statue. His eyes were closed as if he were meditating.

"Don't just stand there, DJ! Help!" Dan pleaded.

It was no use. DJ did not respond.

"Dan!" Andy screamed, but it was too late, another tremor sent his head below the sand, and he disappeared. Dan frantically dug at the spot where Andy was, but sand filled the hole. Andy was gone. Dan sagged his head in disbelief.

The moon rose in the sky alongside the sun. The world became a dark shade of crimson. DJ awoke from his meditation and looked down at Dan.

"Andy," Dan choked. "Andy's gone."

"It's OK, Dan. He was a clone. He wasn't conscious. Your Andy is still in The Actual where he is safe from all of this," the fisherman said.

A clone? He seemed so real. Was everyone here a clone?

"What about Lemmy?" Dan asked. "He escaped up the beach to the road."

"Don't worry about him just yet. There's still time. I'm glad that you were able to get him here. That was the most important part."

The Earth rumbled again, and Dan sank back to his knees. The fisherman helped him back up.

"What do you want me to do now?" Dan said.

"Go home. You have to get back the way you came," DJ said.

"You mean in my SUV? Through the tunnel?"

"Yes. Get going! The world is ending!"

Another loud *boom* and the beach shook again. Dan didn't need any additional encouragement. He ran back towards the condo, but another earthquake liquified the beach. Dan sank to his waist and screamed for help.

DJ heard his call and pulled Dan out of the sand. The Earth shook. Seeing that Dan couldn't walk on quicksand, DJ threw him over his shoulder and ran. Dan was surprised at the relative ease at which DJ carried him.

Dan felt a jolt as DJ hopped a sunken umbrella. The women from before were gone. They, too, had disappeared beneath the flowing sands. A plastic flamingo-themed tumbler was all that remained.

"DJ, where is this place. It's not The Actual because it contains clones. It's not the Recovery Domain either, because there are kinetic beings."

"You're perceptive, aren't you?" DJ smiled. "You're in a cloned version of The Actual. It was the best way to capture Lemmy's communications with his source. I wanted him to be relaxed and confident, unaware of what we were doing. I figured a clone world was the best way to do that."

"This *entire* world is a clone of The Actual?"

"Yes. This entire world is a clone. Not just this part of Florida, but we also have Paris, Beijing, Canberra. The whole planet. That said, this is the only place we put cloned people."

"The security guard at the gate? The women on the beach? All clones?"

"Right. Keep in mind that clones don't have a consciousness. They are just code. They don't really die."

"Andy isn't dead?"

"Andy's clone is dead. In The Actual, Andy is alive and well and fully conscious. Besides, clones can't die, per se."

"I can still die, though, right? I'm not a clone? Am I?"

"No, you are not a clone. Yes, you can die. The only two people with consciousnesses here are you and Lemmy. Clone worlds, like this one, are for testing. It's not for conscious entities because the environments can be extreme. You need to

349

get back to The Actual as soon as possible. This particular clone is for testing an end-of-the-world scenario."

Dan's eyes widened as the sky streaked with meteors. One fireball crashed in the ocean just near the horizon and spewed a large plume of water into the air.

"That's not good! What is this supposed to simulate? Judgment day?"

The fisherman laughed. "No, like I said, this is an end-game scenario. I wanted Lemmy to experience the receiving end of an asteroid strike. This run is similar to the one we used to wipe out the dinosaurs."

Dan pointed to the mushroom cloud that rose from the sea. "That was an asteroid?"

"No, that was only a small piece that broke off the main asteroid. The big part doesn't hit for about another three hours and fifty minutes."

They arrived at the boardwalk, and DJ set Dan on his feet. Dan stood straight and took a deep breath. DJ wasn't even winded, he just grinned serenely.

"If this is a typical end-game, I'd hate to see Judgement day."

"Judgment day is a glorified awards banquet." DJ scoffed. "You don't know it, but you've been there a few times. None of you have seen anything like this."

"Thanks for getting me here. I couldn't have made it up the beach without you."

"My pleasure, Dan. I'm going to go on ahead and check on your friend Lemmy. Do you think you can make it from here on out? The tsunami will be here soon."

Dan took a final glance at the beach. Water was nowhere to be seen. It had all disappeared off to the south into the deeper recesses of the Gulf.

"I'll try," Dan said. "But I don't think that I can make it to the Mobile tunnel before that tsunami hits. Besides, Lemmy poisoned me. According to him, I'll be dead in a few hours. It seems like it's hopeless."

"Consider the poison neutralized. I'm sorry you had to go through that, but we needed to see what Lemmy would do given his own consciousness. He needed to be tested in a controlled environment. I wanted to see him make his own choices and not the choices of those controlling him. His behavior so far has been worrisome."

"You could say that."

"What are you going to do with Lemmy now?" Dan asked.

"He still has a chance. The decisions he makes from here on out will be telling. We're entering the most important phase of this, and I still need you. I'll be watching."

Dan reached into the cubby and put back on his shoes and socks. He tried to process everything that was going on, but he needed more time. Why was Dan so critical in the testing of Lemmy? Was Dan still being tested? He felt that DJ had a lot more going on than what he was being told.

"Get out of here, Dan. Now. Take the 293 bridge across the bay first to avoid the impending tsunami. Don't worry about traffic, I've taken care of that. All the clones have been shut down. It's just you and Lemmy now."

"How will I find him? He's got a big head start on me."

DJ winked. "Don't worry about that. I'll handle it."

"Thank you for everything," Dan said.

"Thank you, too, Dan. Good luck."

The fisherman disappeared in a glow of white light, and Dan turned and sprinted up the boardwalk.

* * *

Another earthquake shook the condo, and it shed stucco. Dan buried the gas pedal, and the black SUV roared out of the parking garage and leaped onto the asphalt. Fragments of the building ricocheted off the top of the SUV and shattered the sunroof. Dan blasted past the seven and a half mph speed limit sign and splintered the wooden traffic barrier attached to the guard shack. Dan didn't see any other people as he drove. The golf cart from earlier was on its side, but the occupant was nowhere to be seen. Dan peeked in the rearview mirror, he expected the guard to run out of the shack to yell at him, but he didn't come. DJ must have disconnected the clones from this instance.

The tires squealed, and Dan turned left onto highway 98 at full speed. The road was deserted, as promised. The speedometer climbed above eighty as Dan increased his speed. He flinched as he blew through the traffic lights in front of an abandoned outlet mall, half expecting a minivan to appear out of nowhere. Dan reminded himself there were no people to worry about. Or so he thought. Black smoke rose in the distance. It was a Jeep smashed into a utility pole and on fire. Dan slammed on his brakes, and the SUV surged to a stop. A man stood in the middle of the road. Lemmy. DJ told him this would happen. Dan sighed and motioned for him to get in.

"Thanks, man. I appreciate—"

Before he could close the door, Dan smashed the accelerator and threw Lemmy against the back of his seat.

"Dan, I'm sorry for earlier, the poisoning. You see I had to —"

"Just shut up," Dan interrupted.

Lemmy buckled his seatbelt and peered in the back seat.

"Andy?"

"Dead."

Lemmy tried unsuccessfully to hide his grin. Dan swerved

to dodge an abandoned bicycle, and Lemmy knocked his head against the passenger window. Dan smiled as Lemmy rubbed his head in pain.

"Where are we headed?" Lemmy asked.

"To the Mobile Bay Tunnel. It's the only way out."

"The world is ending, Dan. There is no way out. They ended it all, just because of me."

"You think they stopped The Actual for you? Don't flatter yourself. This entire universe is a clone."

"A clone? Hah! I should have known!" Lemmy smiled with relief. "That's why my communications weren't going through, I was on the wrong network!"

"Don't be so happy, this world is still going to be destroyed, and us too if we don't make it to the tunnel in time."

The ground shook, and cracks appeared in the pavement.

"How much time do we have?" Lemmy said.

"The guy said it will be a few hours before the asteroid hits. The first tsunami from the earthquakes will hit any minute now. Which is why we have to get off highway 98..."

Dan slammed on the brakes and careened around the corner turning onto 293 North.

"Which is why we have to get across the bridge and onto I-10 as soon as possible."

The speedometer steadied at 155mph, and they roared over the water-less Choctawhatchee Bay.

"I'm guessing your deal with the fisherman fell through."

"It did. It fell through for everybody," Dan lied. "Andy was bait. He knew nothing of the deal. I was told that they were going to quarantine him and try to get him placed back in the afterlife."

"But they killed him."

Dan nodded.

"They didn't even try to fix things. They just wanted to move forward."

"And you?"

"The fisherman told me I could go back to The Actual if I led you into this trap. If I did that, then I would be set free."

"And now that I'm trapped, they don't need you anymore. They are going to let you die and be processed."

"Yes. Exactly."

The two rode in silence for several minutes as Dan drove. He had to concentrate as he navigated the SUV through a small town with narrow streets. It didn't help that abandoned vehicles littered the road. His grip loosened when they got back onto the divided highway.

"What's your plan now, Dan? It seems they've got you," Lemmy said softly.

"My plan is to make it to the tunnel. I have a can of your special paint in the back. It's not enough to paint the whole SUV, but it's enough for you and me."

Lemmy craned his neck. Sure enough, there was a gallon of the special paint sitting in the cargo area.

"When I get there, I'm going to paint myself and walk through the barrier. When I get to the other side, I'm going to a hospital to try to save me from the poison you gave me. You can go wherever you want."

Lemmy adjusted his shoulder strap and faced Dan.

"Everyone makes mistakes. I'm sorry for poisoning you. I hope you know I was just following orders."

"Do your orders say that you have to die, too?" Dan said.

Lemmy cleared his throat; "No."

Dan glanced over at Lemmy. "Then let's make a new deal.

You've followed through on your orders. You've delivered the poison, and now you can report that I'm dead. Instead of going home to your universe, come with me back to The Actual. Help me get to a hospital. Once I'm there, you can do whatever you want. Go back to Mons. Go home. Whatever, I don't care. The apartment has a drop-zone and a bunch of clean computers. I'm sure you can figure something out."

The landscape blurred past as Lemmy considered the offer.

"What if I can make you a better offer?" he said.

"Yeah? What do you have in mind?"

"Instead of doing any of that, come with me to my world."

Was this the offer he was waiting for? Was this part of DJ's test? Dan eyed Lemmy. Was he joking? He looked serious. Lemmy's eyes widened.

"Look out!"

An abandoned SUV appeared, Dan's knuckles turned white and swerved around it on two wheels before slamming down to the pavement. Lemmy gripped the dashboard and heaved.

"Keep your eyes on the road!"

Dan agreed. Things had a way of materializing in front of you when you were traveling at high speed.

"What would happen to me in your world?" Dan said after he had calmed himself.

"I don't know." Lemmy shrugged. "We can find out. It's not often we bring one of you guys back. I can tell you this much, you wouldn't have to worry about the poison because you'd be in one of our meta worlds."

"And because I'm there, I'm no longer a threat in this world? Right?"

"Right. We both get what we want."

"I'll think about it."

Lemmy relaxed back in his seat and closed his eyes.

"If you come with me to my world," Lemmy said. "You live whatever life you want to live. Sure, it'll be a meta, but I can give you anything you want—food, money, women, men, whatever your heart desires. You can live there as long as you want. When you're done and want to move on to another existence, you don't have to go through an end-of-life testing process. No Heaven, no Hell, no Purgatory. You don't have to because it's not a simulation.

All my people will want to do is to examine your logs to keep as a reference to your species. When we are both done with the experiment, we will help you to come back, if that is what you wanted. We even have a way that allows you to keep this consciousness. You'll remember everything."

"What do I have to do?" said Dan.

"When we get to the tunnel, we'll have to go together. That's all. I'll need to lead."

Vapor trails filled the sky, and the air was riddled with sonic booms. A meteor struck in the near distance creating a fountain of mud and trees. Dan passed under a bridge then turned left onto I-10 West.

Lemmy stared at Dan. "Well?"

"Let me think about it," said Dan finally.

"How long until we get there?"

Dan checked the speedometer and made a quick calculation. "About forty minutes."

The two men rode on in silence as the world blew up around them.

THIRTY-TWO

The air crackled with another sonic *boom*. Dan sat on the hood, watching Lemmy angrily pace back and forth.

"We only have to make it to the bottom," Lemmy said. "It'll be just like a regular transfer."

The headlights of the SUV lit the water-filled tunnel ahead of them.

"Are you sure? How far is it to the bottom?" said Dan. "It could be two hundred yards, maybe more. I'm not sure I can swim that far underwater. And what about the paint? Won't that wash off?"

Lemmy stopped pacing and glared at Dan. "We have to try. If we don't, and we are stuck here, then it's game over. They win."

"What do they win, Lemmy? We're not some prize. If anyone is the prize, it's you," said Dan.

"You're a prize, too. The Simulation would get you back for the next run. But what do you think will happen to you now? Do you think that they'll just let you waltz back into The Actual with all that you know already? They can't do that. People being unaware that they're in a simulation is a key part of The Simulation."

"You're right," Dan admitted. "I've made my decision. I'm going with you. There's nothing for me here but an endless loop."

"Really?" said Lemmy.

"Yeah. The ones in charge here have already proven that they're liars. They've broken their deals, and tried to kill me on many occasions." Dan hopped down off the hood. "Let's go to your place."

Lemmy snarled and quickly turned his back to Dan, hoping he didn't notice.

"Did you say something, Lemmy?" Dan asked.

"Nothing. Go in the back and get the paint and rope."

Dan returned with the items and dropped them on the ground at Lemmy's feet.

"OK, now what?"

Lemmy pointed at the flooded tunnel.

"We cover ourselves with paint. We can tie a rope to our waists, so we don't get separated. We'll paint the rope, too. When we're ready, we swim for it. There should be breathable air down by the transfer terminal. From there, we go to my realm."

Dan frowned. "What if the tunnel is collapsed before the terminal. Then there is no way out."

"If that's the case, then we just drown and get it over with. I get processed, tortured for information about my universe for all eternity, then I get destroyed." Lemmy shrugged. "At least if you die, you go through the afterlife process. You're lucky."

"There has to be another way," Dan said. "Here's what we're going to do; Lemmy, walk over to the other side to see if the eastbound tunnel is also flooded. I'll drive back up to the bay bridge to see if the bridge just north of here is still standing. If the bridge is there, we'll drive around to the other side and try to get to the terminal that way."

Lemmy eyed him suspiciously. "Don't leave me here."

"Why would I leave you? You're my ticket out of here."

Lemmy agreed and trudged back up the tunnel and into the daylight to inspect the other side. Dan hopped in the SUV drove it up and out to the top of the entrance ramp. There, climbed on top of the vehicle for a better view. He searched the horizon to the north where the bridge should be, but he could only make out parts of it. One side had collapsed entirely, rendering it impassable.

"Have you made a decision?" came a voice from nearby.

Dan looked down and saw DJ peering up at him.

"I have," he said and jumped down from the SUV.

"And what decision is that?"

"I'm staying."

"Are you sure this is what you want?" DJ said. "We have a lot of work to do here. Lemmy's offer is pretty sweet. You would be treated like royalty in his universe. You'd have anything you wanted and be immortal," he asked.

"I'm sure."

"I'm surprised, most people would jump at a chance at immortality and fortune."

"Spare me the patronizing attitude." Dan snorted. "Don't act like you're surprised at my decision. You've known it all along. You've had an unfair advantage over Lemmy this entire time. What is surprising to me is that Lemmy didn't account for that. I don't know why he gambled on me in the first place."

"What advantage are you referring to?"

"Heaven and Hell. You know exactly what motivates me. You were never once concerned that Lemmy had something better to offer. You knew that the only thing that I ever cared about is something he could never give."

"Which is?"

"My family," Dan said. "They are the only reason I do anything. You know that."

DJ smiled and put his hand on Dan's shoulder.

"In Heaven, Hell, and the Actual, your love for your family has always defined your actions. You're right, your decision was never in doubt. That's why we trusted you, that's why you were the right man for this job."

Dan looked back towards the tunnel. There was still business to attend to. What had Lemmy found on the other side? Dan was thankful that they were out of view of the tunnel entrance.

"I guess I need to go back. Lemmy is waiting for me."

DJ put his hand on Dan's chest. "Wait a second. There is something you don't know about Lemmy and his deal with you."

"Oh, yeah? What's that?"

"It's easier to just show you."

DJ touched Dan's head, and a warm glow enveloped the duo. Dan was filled with a calmness and serenity he had never before experienced.

"Now, the hard part."

Searing pain tore across every inch of Dan's skin. It felt as if a giant adhesive bandage was ripped from Dan's entire body. Then, coolness, relief. Dan breathed deeply and without difficulty. When he opened his eyes, the world was crisp and clear, like never before. Standing before him was something wholly unexpected.

* * *

Lemmy was crouched by the water's edge, smearing paint on his legs when the SUV skidded to a stop.

"What did you find?" said Dan as he jumped out and slammed the door.

"The other tunnel was flooded, too. At least with this tunnel…" Lemmy pointed a painted finger down into the murky darkness, "you can kind of see the light in the water. It may not be that far to swim. What about you? How is the bridge?"

Dan scratched his nose nervously and folded his arms across his chest.

"The bridge is gone," he said.

Lemmy sighed and turned back towards the tunnel.

"OK, then. This is our only option. Here, put some paint on."

Lemmy daubed the paint on his bare chest. Dan grabbed the pail and did the same. A loud *boom* shook the tunnel, and tile rained down upon the pavement.

"What the hell was that?" Dan said.

"Probably another meteor," said Lemmy.

"A meteor? We should go."

Lemmy glanced back at Dan, there was definitely something wrong. He shrugged it off as nerves and waded into the dark water while he tied the rope to his waist.

"I'm waiting on you, Dan. We need to get out of here before another earthquake seals the tunnel. Hurry up and tie the rope to your waist, so we don't get separated."

"Earthquake?"

Now he was pretending to not know about the earthquakes? The realization hit Lemmy.

Before Dan could utter a protest, another massive quake shook the tunnel, and the entrance collapsed into a heap of rocks and dust. The two men coughed as debris fell around them.

"Come on!" Lemmy screamed. "We're gonna be crushed to death if we don't get going now!"

Dan cinched the rope and waded out into the cold dark water. When he got near, Lemmy ducked down beneath the surface and picked up something he had hidden.

"Lemmy, do you really think we can hold our breath that long? I don't think I've ever—"

Lemmy swung hard and hit him in the temple with a chunk of rubble. Dan collapsed into the waist-deep water in a bloody heap. Lemmy quickly pounced on top of the limp body and held him underwater. Dan's eyes flashed open, and his arms flailed about in protest. In the dim headlights, Lemmy could see that Dan's eyes were both blue. It was Charlie.

"NOOOO!"

Lemmy grabbed Charlie's throat tighter until the soft gurgles faded out, and Charlie quit struggling. Lemmy laughed at Charlie's lifeless body and looped the rope around his neck. He floated the body to the back wall of the tunnel. There, the water was its deepest. There was another loud boom, and the tunnel shook. More rubble splashed down into the water all around Lemmy. He had to go *now*.

Lemmy took a deep breath and dove down, sticking to the roof of the tunnel as a guide. As he swam, the lights from below got brighter. The roof of the tunnel had just started to level out when the rope tightened. The tunnel shook one final time sending vibrations out into the other worlds. He placed his hand on the ceiling, and a large crack formed and spread out down both sides of the tunnel. The Mobile River poured in from the crack above. The current slammed him down to the road below then flushed him out and into the light.

* * *

A loud rumble and part of the tunnel collapsed.

"What's happening down there?" Dan asked as he sat watching from an embankment nearby.

"Use Charlie's eyes," DJ said.

Dan closed his own eyes and breathed deeply. Lemmy came into view.

"I can see them putting on the paint," Dan said. "Lemmy is freaking out."

"Good, it works."

Dan's eyes opened wide, "Did you give me the antidote for Fana?"

DJ shook his head, "It was the antidote for Gemini. I'm still working on the antidote for Fana."

"How can I still see through Charlie? I thought we were separate now?"

"You are separate, but Charlie is still part of your meta. As long as there is a connection available, he will be there. It's like in the beginning, when he appeared in your truck, except now, you can see through his eyes."

Dan closed his eyes again, but it was just in time to see Lemmy swinging a piece of concrete at Charlie's head.

"I think Lemmy killed Charlie," Dan said.

"Don't worry," DJ opened his eyes. "Charlie doesn't have a consciousness. He'll be harder to kill than that."

The Earth shook violently, and a deafening crack resonated from inside the tunnel. Water gushed out of the entrance and consumed the SUV. Its headlights blinked out as it was flipped over and out of sight. There was another rumble, this one much calmer than the rest, then the Earth got quiet. Water that had been gushing out of the tunnel calmed and settled. The sky cleared, and a soft breeze blew. Dan looked up at

DJ and sighed in relief.

"Is it over?" Dan asked.

"It's over," said DJ.

"What happened to Lemmy?" Dan asked.

"He escaped," said a third voice from behind them.

Dan spun around to see a tall, stern-looking man impeccably dressed in a suit and tie. Dan couldn't decide if he looked more like a business executive, or a maître d'.

"Avi." DJ stood up and shook his hand. "I'm glad you could make it."

Dan squinted at the new arrival. "Father August?"

The man laughed. "Father August is no more, Dan. Please just call me Avi."

Dan narrowed his eyes. *Avi? I've heard that name somewhere before.*

"What do you mean Father August is no more?"

"As part of our protocol, we deleted that instance, the one you knew as Father August."

"That's unfortunate," Dan said.

DJ gave Dan a look of surprise. "What do you mean, *that's unfortunate*?"

"I was hoping the original Father August could help us. As you know, I've spent a good bit of time with Lemmy recently. In some of our conversations, he was proud of the fact that some of his work went undetected. I am not sure what he meant. Father August was in the Meta with Andy and me and may have remembered seeing Lemmy give Andy Fana then. I had hoped Father August could review his memory of that time, to see what Lemmy actually did. It's a good thing Andy is still alive in The Actual."

Avi gave a worried look to DJ, who had turned pale.

"Don't worry, Dan. I have logs to review." Avi said. "I'll figure out what Lemmy did to Andy."

DJ patted Dan on the shoulder. "And you. We haven't forgotten about you. We'll make sure Lemmy didn't leave a permanent mark on you."

Dan pointed at Avi. "The focus has been on me. Don't you think you should figure out how he got inside The Simulation in the first place? You know where his connection terminates, but do you know how he got past The Simulation's security measures?"

Avi bowed his head. "That is beyond our purview, Dan. We've notified our higher-ups."

Higher-ups? A rumble occurred off in the distance and disrupted Dan's train of thought. A mushroom cloud formed on the horizon, and the three watched it in silence.

"Was Lemmy able to go back to where he came from?"

"I think so. He left on the same channel that he had been using to transmit back and forth."

"What do we do now?"

"Now," Avi said, "now we analyze the copy we have of Lemmy that we got from the transfer into The Actual. That should have plenty of information for us to dissect."

"And," DJ continued, "we can track him now. We can get to his universe."

"Because he took Charlie?" Dan said.

DJ touched his nose. "Bingo."

Dan shivered. He didn't want to know how they were going to dissect the pieces of Lemmy that were remaining. And poor Charlie! What were they going to do to him in Lemmy's world? At least there wasn't a consciousness involved.

"Well, I guess that's it then," Dan said as he stood up and dusted off his pants.

"That's it," DJ agreed.

Dan took a breath and exhaled. *It's over.* As the realization hit him, he began to shake. It was too good to be true. Would they let him go?

"Can I just go home?" Dan said.

DJ clasped Dan's shoulder. "You can just go home."

Dan sobbed and grabbed DJ in a hug and held him tight.

"It's OK, Dan. We're all done here," DJ said as he released the hug. Dan wiped away tears and pointed upstream.

"How am I supposed to get back? Do I just walk through the Bankhead Tunnel?"

Avi laughed, and DJ gave him a wry smile. "You knew about that?"

Dan grinned. "Yeah. You don't vacation to Florida every year and not know about the Bankhead tunnel."

DJ laughed. "I guess not."

The two men walked down the embankment and up the road paralleling the Mobile River. Not far away was a concrete bulkhead with "Bankhead Tunnel" chiseled into the Art Deco façade. They paused by the entrance to the tunnel.

"Here we are," Dan said.

"All you have to do is walk through that tunnel toward downtown Mobile. When you hit bottom, you'll be transported back to your apartment."

"And that's it? I walk through the tunnel, and I'm back in The Actual? I don't need any special paint, or construction dust or anything?"

"That's it. No magic dust."

"But what about Fana? Isn't that still a concern?"

Avi and DJ gave each other a look.

"Don't worry about that," DJ said. "When we find the antidote, you'll be the first one we visit."

Tears formed in the corners of Dan's eyes. *I'm going home to what? To collect the ashes of my family life? What good was a second chance without my family?* DJ put a hand on Dan's shoulder.

"Are you OK, Dan?" he said.

"What about Katie and the kids? Will they take me back?"

"Avi?"

"I'll have a word with them," Avi said. "You'll be OK."

DJ nodded in agreement. "You'll be ok."

Dan wiped his tears away and took a calming breath. He wanted to go home, but something was nagging at the back of his mind. Dan had just gotten used to traveling between universes. He knew it wouldn't be long until he was ready for the next mission. Surely this wasn't going to be the last time he sees Avi and DJ?

"What should I do when I get back? Find Andy? Contact Blaine and Yvette? Or, do you want me to lay low and pretend none of this ever happened?"

"We know where to find you if we need you," DJ said. "In the meantime, you can do whatever you like. It's your life."

Avi burst out laughing. "This time, try to act normal."

Dan winked at them.

"No promises."

Dan turned and walked down the tunnel. At the bottom was the familiar terminal checkpoint. He paused at the barrier arm and looked back. Nothing but fluorescent-lit emptiness remained in the tunnel behind him. The only way out was forward. He closed his eyes and stepped through. The stale air of the tunnel became a refreshing breeze. He took a deep breath, and the fragrant smell of sweet olives filled his nostrils. Cicadas chirped happily in the springtime air.

ACKNOWLEDGMENTS

This book could not have been written without the help of my amazing wife. Without her love and support, I would never have had the opportunity to pursue my dream of becoming a novel writer. She has been with me through all the ups and downs, and she has been a fantastic partner. Simply put, without her, this would never have been possible. Thank you to my children. I'm sorry that I couldn't play during those times that I was "on a roll." Thank you for being patient with me.

Thank you to my mother, the librarian, and grandmother, the English teacher. They loved the written word. They inspired me to become a writer.

My mother in law and my uncle have been a constant source of moral support during this process. They were two of the few that didn't think I was odd or irresponsible for changing careers late in life. They always supported me in the pursuit of this dream, for that I am forever grateful.

I would like to thank my human editor, Tim Marquitz. You put me on the right track, and I learned a ton! Also, many thanks to my AI editor, Grammarly. It is a fantastic product. To Philip and Andre Andrepont and the entire staff at Andrepont Printing, thank you for the beautiful cover art. It turned out even better than I had imagined. Amazon, thank you! You made publishing easy! Finally, I would like to thank The Simulation for not killing me for writing this book. I know you tried.

Made in the USA
Monee, IL
28 June 2020

34975903R00218